Praise for Jinny Alexander

This is a light-hearted cosy that will delight fans of M C Beaton's Agatha Raisin. […] Highly recommend it to those looking for a frothy, enjoyable read that is low on violence and high on feel-good entertainment!

MAIRI CHONG,
The Dr. Cathy Moreland Mysteries

Well-written and intriguing, this mystery revolving around members of a weight-loss group is one that will keep you turning the pages until the very end.

KELLY YOUNG,
The Travel Writer Cozy Mystery Series

Jinny Alexander's outstanding cosy mystery *A Diet Of Death* is a real treat. (And not the kind with calories!)

J. IVANEL JOHNSON,
The JUST (e)STATE Cozy Mysteries

The whole book was a warm, comforting read for anyone who loves mysteries. Highly suggested for fans of *The Thursday Murder Club*.

ALISON WEATHERBY,
The Secrets Act

This tale is a homage to those much loved classic detective authors, and is perfect for escaping the worries and stresses of the world.

LOUISE MORRISH,
Operation Moonlight

Jinny Alexander embeds her murder mystery with the satisfying atmosphere of rural Ireland. […] Cozy mystery readers who enjoy stories of friendships and murder possibilities will find *A Diet of Death* unusually strong in its atmosphere, which does equal justice to both the murder mystery component and the entwined lives of a small village […]

MIDWEST BOOK REVIEW

A DIET OF DEATH

The First Jess O'Malley Mystery

JINNY ALEXANDER

ISBN Paperback: 978-1-916814-00-4

ISBN ebook: 978-1-916814-01-1

Cover Design: Wicked Good Book Covers

Map of Ballyfortnum: Jinny Alexander and Dewi Hargreaves

2nd Edition

First Published by Creative James Media, 2022

www.OverSpilledInk.com

Visit www.jinnyalexander.com

This book is dedicated to my husband.
The Marcus to my Jess.

A note to my American-English readers

I'm so glad you're here! I'm a British author, living in the Republic of Ireland, and all my books are set in Ireland or the UK. As such, I use British English in my writing so you'll notice a few extra letters – **U**s after **O**s, for instance, and **L**s that come in pairs. I make up for these extras by using fewer **Z**s…

I hope you'll enjoy my natural English voice and immerse yourselves fully into my UK and Irish settings and characters, but if you're still not convinced, I recommend a nice cup of tea.

Over here, a nice cup of tea fixes *almost* everything.

Love, Jinny xx

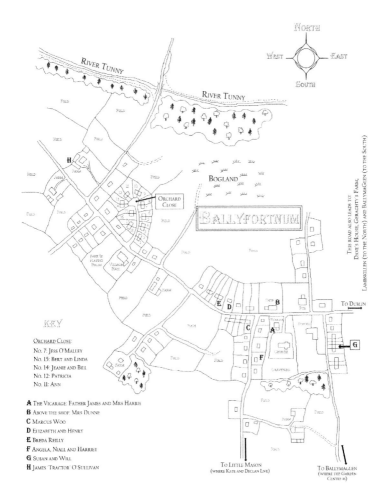

NORTH
WEST EAST
SOUTH

RIVER TUNNY

RIVER TUNNY

FIELD

FIELD

FIELD

FIELD

FIELD

FIELD

H FARM

BOGLAND

ORCHARD CLOSE

FIELD

BALLYFORTNUM

THIS ROAD ALSO LEADS TO:
DAVE'S HOUSE, GERAGHTY'S FARM,
LAMBERKILLEN (TO THE NORTH) AND BALLYMAGLEN (TO THE SOUTH)

PARK &
PLAYING FIELDS

VILLAGE HALL

FIELD

FIELD

FIELD

E **D**

B

C **A**

TO DUBLIN

G

F CHURCH

GRAVEYARD

FARM

KEY

ORCHARD CLOSE:
No. 7: Jess O'Malley
No. 15: Bert and Linda
No. 14: Jeanie and Bill
No. 12: Patricia
No. 11: Ann

A The Vicarage: Father James and Mrs Harris
B Above the shop: Mrs Dunne
C Marcus Woo
D Elizabeth and Henry
E Breda Reilly
F Angela, Niall and Harriet
G Susan and Will
H James 'Tractor' O'Sullivan

TO LITTLE MASON
(WHERE KATE AND DECLAN LIVE)

TO BALLYMAGLEN
(WHERE THE GARDEN CENTRE IS)

Chapter One

No one appeared to be eating the food. Jess helped herself to a sandwich and took the proffered glass of warm white wine.

Kate, the far side of the coffin, caught her eye. She looked down at Jess's glass and nodded.

Taking the hint, Jess stuffed the sandwich into her mouth and picked up a second glass of wine. Skirting around a huddle of Bert's red-eyed relations, she made her way across the room to Kate. "Here." She pushed the glass into her friend's hand.

"Another one," Kate said. She took a huge swig from the glass and patted her mouth with the back of her hand.

"I could only carry the two," Jess said.

"Not the wine—him." Kate nodded at the coffin. "He's another of mine. That's three in as many months. I'll be skint at this rate; no one left to attend classes."

Jess knew Kate well enough to guess at an unspoken thought—"the buggers"—tagged on to the end of the sentence. Trust Kate to be thinking of Bert's death only in relation to how it may affect her. She nudged Kate gently to hush her before she said anything untoward in earshot of Bert's grieving relatives. Jess looked down at Bert, his face waxy and pale against the bright sheen of satin.

"I'll miss him." She took a step towards him and touched his cold hand. "He pruned my roses for me, you know?" She said it more to herself than to Kate, who was only interested in gardens when there was a cool glass of wine and a comfortable patio set on offer. One hand still resting on the coffin, Jess turned back to Kate. "Poor Linda. I'd better go and see if she needs anything done." Leaving Kate to her wine, she threaded her way through the crowded room to find her newly-widowed neighbour.

Most of the village had turned out for Bert's wake, well-liked and well-known as he had been. It took Jess some moments to cross the room, murmuring polite variations of "hello" and "yes, very sad, so sad" to assorted neighbours as she made her way towards the kitchen at the front of the house. There, she found Linda being fussed over by both of her daughters and Jeanie from Number 14. Linda, quite bewildered, was being gently pushed into a kitchen chair by her eldest. Jeanie, a little wobbly herself, seemed shrunken under the weight of the borrowed teapot she was dithering with. Father James had rallied the church china and sundries, knowing that the turnout would be significant, but he had overlooked that the teapot was almost as large as many of the elderly ladies who would be busying themselves about Linda's kitchen.

"Come here, let me take that." Jess rescued Jeanie from the teapot. "You sit down there with Linda; keep her off her feet for a while?"

"Eh, I'm grand ..." Jess cut off Jeanie's objection by nodding subtly towards the exhausted Linda, slumped at the kitchen table. "Ah, sure, why not—thanks, love." Jeanie sank into the empty chair without further protest.

Pouring first for Linda, Jeanie, and Linda's daughters, Jess then swept back out of the kitchen with the teapot and thrust it into the hands of one of the younger neighbours.

"Would you mind?" she asked apologetically. "I'm just going to ..." Jess nodded towards the kitchen. She wasn't really sure what it was that she was going to do, suddenly overwhelmed at the thought of making polite, sympathetic small talk with so many of her neighbours for the second time in a month. Third since Christmas, as Kate had said. Tears threatening, Jess ducked back into the kitchen.

From Bert and Linda's kitchen, Jess could see straight across Orchard Close and into her own front garden. Unlike the layout of this house, Jess's kitchen was at the back, with a wide, sunny dining space and French doors opening out onto her patio. She'd sneak away soon; get away from all these people. Perhaps she should usher some of 'these people' away first; Linda looked like she was crumpling under the strain of the two days since Bert had died. Poor Bert. Poor Linda.

Jess wiped away the spill of fresh tears and busied herself with washing the sinkful of used teacups. She'd get the first lot cleared, and then she'd get the other lot cleared: the washing up and then the people. Give Linda time to rest before the funeral tomorrow, when they would have to go through all this tea-and-sandwiches rigmarole for a second time.

The pile of dirty dishes and most of the well-wishers cleared away, Jess left Linda and her immediate family to sit beside Bert for one last night. Hopefully they'd take turns, get a bit of rest in between—you could never tell with these rural Irish wakes. As she pushed open her own front door, Fletcher leapt at her as if she had been gone forever, tail wagging and tongue slobbering.

"Down, Fletch, get down!" Jess rubbed his head affectionately as she pushed him off. "You're right, though, let's go for a walk; I think I need it as much as you do." If she kept busy, maybe she wouldn't have to give headspace to the thought that had been niggling at her ever since Kate's earlier comment. A walk would clear her head and help her sleep, with any luck. She changed into her walking boots and wrapped a scarf around her neck, grabbed a tennis ball from under the hall table and clipped on Fletcher's lead.

"Come on then, boyo, we'll have a quick run round the park." She hoped Fletcher would not notice the half-truth—Fletch might run, but Jess most certainly would not.

"Fetch, Fletch!" Jess bent to unclip the leash with one hand, whilst throwing the ball with her other.

Fletcher, temporarily obedient, shot across the playing field after it. He ran straight and true towards the place the ball had landed, then continued past it without stopping. Fletch had noticed what Jess hadn't seen in time—another person using the park. At the far end, spotlit in the gathering darkness by one of the park lights, a man Jess couldn't identify from this distance was walking a small white dog. Fletch, delighted, was on his way to greet them.

Jess started after him. "Fletch!" she yelled. "Fletch! Fletch! Fletcher! Come here!" She knew it was futile, but it would make a better impression if the stranger saw—or heard—her trying. Ruing her earlier confidence that she would not be running, she jogged along the path towards them. After only a few yards she stopped, doubled-over and breathless. Once her breathing steadied, she straightened and hurried on, but only at a brisk walk.

As she neared, she called again.

Fletcher took no notice. He was already bouncing around the man and his dog, alternating ducking down onto his front legs in the 'play with me, play with me' pose with jumping up at the man, giving joyous little yelps. The small, white dog was growling at the Labrador as Jess approached. Fletch, undeterred, carried on.

Panting a little, Jess grabbed his collar and hauled him off. "Sorry. So sorry, I thought we had the park to ourselves, I wouldn't have let him off." She glanced guiltily at the sign on the fence behind where they now stood—a list of park rules and dog-related etiquette about keeping dogs on leads and so on.

"Westie?" she asked, hoping to deflect the attention from her own badly-behaved companion as she surreptitiously clipped his lead back on.

"Yes, hello, no worries, I sometimes let this guy off, too, you know?" the man said. "I won't tell if you don't. Marcus. Marcus Woo." He held out his hand. "You're Jessica O'Malley, aren't you?"

Now Jess had Fletcher safely back on his lead, she looked properly at the stranger and realised that she had seen him only a few hours before. He, too, had been at Bert's wake.

"You're Marcus? I thought …" she tailed off as she shook his proffered hand. Typical that she finally got to meet the local Garda at the exact moment she was breaking the park rules. She blushed at the thought. "Yes, I'm Jess. I live over there." She nodded to the cul-de-sac of neat semis on the opposite side of the road to the park. "Although I guess you already know that, too? I saw you at the wake, but I didn't know who you were."

They stood in silence for a moment, as Jess remembered the sight of Bert lying pale and peaceful against the dark mahogany of his coffin.

"Poor Bert," they both said at once, breaking the silence.

"Poor Bert," Marcus Woo said again. He bent to pat the Westie's head. "This is Snowflake." He smiled wryly, lightening the mood. "Not my choice of name."

"Snowflake?" Jess hid her amusement by bending to pet the little dog, but her voice quivered, and her shoulders shook just a little as she murmured, "Hello, Snowflake."

Snowflake, appeased by Fletcher's capture and restraint, was now happily sniffing at him, growls forgotten and tail wagging. Jess watched the dogs play, enjoying their happiness, and felt the tension in her shoulders ease for the first time all day.

Chapter Two

The day of the funeral dawned much like any other February morning in Ballyfortnum. By nine-thirty the sky had lightened to a marginally paler shade of grey than it had been through the night. Jess dropped her black high heels onto the living room carpet and leaned over the sofa to yank open the curtains.

As she opened them, Kate pulled up outside the house, her car wipers sweeping too fast against the thin drizzle.

Jess raised a hand in greeting as Kate emerged from the car, elegant and refined in a black skirt suit which showed off her legs and expensive, red-soled shoes. Jess smoothed down her own black dress and pulled her unruly hair back into a hasty chignon, then closed the living room door on Fletcher, containing him momentarily so Kate could let herself in without the dog escaping.

The front door slammed; the living room door opened, and Kate tottered through, on into the kitchen.

"You ready then?" Kate said. Without waiting for an answer, she sat at the table and rifled in her bag for lipstick and mirror. "I've hit my target—finally made a size eight." She glanced up at Jess, before returning her attention to touching up her make-up.

Jess grunted non-committedly, her back turned to Kate as she filled the kettle. A fleeting image of Bert proudly announcing a similar thing—he'd hit his target but would never make anything close to a size eight—just a couple of weeks ago was replaced by the memory of him lying in his coffin. She sighed, exasperated at Kate's selfishness, but said nothing. Kate had hardly known Bert—only as Jess's long-time neighbour—until he'd joined her slimming group last autumn.

Jess was happy for her friend, of course she was, but, seriously, another dress size down and Kate was looking ... well, skinny. Really skinny. Kate had now gone down three dress sizes in the last twelve months, and had looked particularly gaunt since Christmas. True, this weight loss was a great show of willpower from Kate—she was much better than Jess at sticking at things. Especially things like giving up cake. Jess had given a fair bit of thought to this over the past months as Kate had shrunk and shrunk and then shrunk some more. She was, by now, certain this niggling concern was not jealousy, but a genuine worry that Kate's rapid weight loss was, well, quite unhealthy.

Jess, unquestionably overweight but not dramatically so, was unwilling to do anything more about her own weight than walk Fletcher a bit farther than she used to. She didn't like exercise; she did like food. Real food. Not that artificial, chemical crap that Kate ate. She really couldn't share Kate's enthusiasm for the slimming group, especially after what her sister had been through, with her own 'issues'. She certainly wasn't going to get excited about Kate having lost yet another few pounds. Jess pushed the thoughts aside as the kettle reached its boil. After all, they had a funeral to get through today, and Kate's drastic weight loss hardly seemed the most pressing of subjects to be thinking about right now.

"Well done, that's great," she said to Kate, trying to inject some conviction into her belated response. "Anyway, I'll be ready in a minute—we've just time for a cuppa and then we'll head?" She stirred instant coffee into two china mugs and set one down in front of Kate.

Kate rooted in her handbag again and extracted a small, plastic tube. She dispensed three white sweetener tablets into the coffee and stirred it some more.

Jess bit her tongue. She retrieved her shoes from the living room and busied herself with hopping around the table, trying to pull them on without having to bend down.

Fletcher, excited by his mistress putting on shoes, misread the signs and bounced around the kitchen, anticipating a walk. Jess wobbled, clutching at the edge of the counter to regain her balance as she glared at the excited dog.

"Shove off, Fletch." Jess pushed him away before he could cover her new black tights with dog hair. "You don't really think these are clothes for walking you in, do you?" She took a gulp of her coffee and shrugged into her coat. "C'mon then, let's get this day over with."

Together, Jess and Kate (without Fletch, relegated to watching them yearningly from the back of the sofa) left the house and walked to Kate's car. A dearth of neighbours' cars along Orchard Close suggested Kate's insistence that she collect Jess to ensure she was not late to the church had been futile.

"It's okay," Jess said, glancing at the clock on the dashboard, "we've heaps of time."

In the centre of the village, Kate double-parked, barely leaving room for a bicycle to pass along Ballyfortnum's main street. "Not like anyone will need to get through till we come out again." She justified her actions, zapped the car doors locked, and sauntered towards the church. The car park, unsurprisingly, was packed. The road through the village was clogged with cars parked higgledy-piggledy; some with two wheels on the kerb; some fully on the pavement, and others jutting at odd angles into the road. Kate had a point. No one would be getting through until the funeral was over. It reminded Jess of when her nieces had upended a box of toy cars across the floor, leaving them scattered everywhere. Kate's own bad parking would not make the slightest difference.

Kate, elegant and comfortable in heels, led the way over the road and up the driveway of Ballyfortnum Church—the Catholic Church of Our Lady, Mary, Blessed Virgin and Sacred Mother of Jesus Christ—to give it its full title. Mostly it was known as either 'the church' or simply 'Mary's'.

"I reckon the sign-writer was paid by the letter," Jess whispered to her friend as they approached the steps. Kate rolled her eyes but didn't slow down. Struggling to keep up, Jess teetered in Kate's wake, wobbling slightly as they paused in the porch to assess the crowded church.

"Up there." Kate gestured towards the front, and strutted onward up the aisle as if she were the most important person there. She stopped abruptly when she reached a row about four rows from the altar, on the left-hand side, where Jess's neighbour Jeanie sat with her husband, Bill, and a few other Orchard Close residents.

Jess smiled apologetically at them as she and Kate squeezed in. It would be a squash, but the neighbours wouldn't mind. It was either that, or they'd have to stand at the back, and then they'd be stuck for ages in the receiving line. Jess wanted to be able to get to Linda's house well before the after-funeral crowd, to get the urn switched on and the sandwiches unwrapped. She jostled herself more comfortably into the pew, fleetingly grateful that Kate, at least, didn't take up much room.

The service was long, and the receiving line longer. Despite being so near the front, it still took them a full fifteen minutes to reach Linda and her family once the service was over. A hug, a kiss, a shake of the hand of a lesser-known relation, then Jess reached Linda and wrapped her in a gentle hug.

"It'll be over soon, love, you'll be okay. I'm going back to yours now to get that kettle ready," she whispered. She gave Linda another peck and wobbled towards the side door.

At Linda's house, Jess once again found herself wrestling the enormous teapot. She wound her way through the packed living room, uttering sympathetic small talk to friends, neighbours, strangers, and an assortment of 'regular funeral-goers'. The local politician, Barnabas Bannon, was one such culprit. He made sure to attend every funeral within a twenty-five-mile radius of his home. *If only he did as much for the living ...* it was an uncompassionate thought, and Jess had to make a conscious effort not to 'accidentally' pour tea into his lap.

Kate appeared to be networking. Perhaps that was unfair, Jess conceded—Kate now genuinely considered most of her Get Slim members to be amongst her 'closest' friends. And most of them, it appeared, had attended the funeral. *We are gathered here today...* Jess's thoughts uncharitably echoed the words of the priest earlier that morning. *...to mourn the loss of 'one of our own' and watch our fellow members discreetly to see who takes more than one of the limp ham sandwiches being offered around.*

Among the slimming group members, a low murmur vibrated around the room like the humming of an overworked fridge. As Jess circulated with the teapot she picked up a distinct refrain: "Should have joined us sooner," "If only he'd lost the weight," "Shame he left it so late," and "If only we'd had the group years ago." Collectively, the slimming group members refused sandwiches, crisps, or cake with a wave of their hand and an aside to whoever was standing next to them about "the amount of sins in that."

Jess kept her thoughts to herself. Later, once the congregation had dispersed, the washing up done, and the crockery re-boxed for return to Father James in the morning, she kissed Linda goodbye and crossed the street to her own home. She let Fletch out for a pee with a "Sorry, mate, too knackered to walk you now," and poured herself a glass of wine. Her black shoes lay capsized where they had fallen as she kicked them off. Curling her aching legs underneath her on the sofa, she leaned her head on the cushions and sighed.

Fletcher padded over and jumped up beside her, nuzzling his head onto her lap and closing his eyes. Only then did Jess finally say what she had been thinking.

"It's like Kate said yesterday, Fletch." She rubbed his ears. "That's the third one this year. Something's not right." Too tired to explore the thought further, she flipped on the TV, skipped through the channels, and settled on an old episode of Jonathan Creek.

Chapter Three

Kate was a Dublin girl, but had moved down to the Midlands about eight years ago, with her husband, Declan—Decko, she usually called him. Jess had met Kate a few years back when they worked together in an office in town. They had got chatting over coffee breaks out the back, where Jess drank black coffee while Kate chain-smoked cigarettes. She would light one from the other, claiming she really needed them and no way she was giving them up. They had used the coffee breaks to plan their mutual break-out from the job with excitement and determination, urging each other on. Kate and her husband lived a few villages over from Ballyfortnum, in Little Mason—a tiny hamlet barely big enough to sneeze on. Her relative proximity to Jess's home had enabled the friendship to continue easily after they left the shared workplace.

Kate had set up the Get Slim classes in Ballyfortnum back in October, or thereabouts. Jess couldn't remember exactly. Not long before Christmas but not really close to it, either. Since then, Kate had been spending more and more time around the village, keen to share tales of her new enterprise with Jess. Jess sat unfocused through many a story that Kate began with, "I can't tell you who, obviously, client confidentiality and all that, but I've got to tell you ..." Usually, by the time Kate got to the point of the story,

Jess's mind would be well and truly drifting; *Kate barely even knows these people. They're* my *neighbours,* my *friends, not Kate's. Just because she knows how much they weigh in any given week, seriously, that does not mean they are friends.*

So, although the first death Kate had referred to at Bert's wake had happened to a member of her group, the group had been only a couple of months old at that point. Poor Dave had only just joined, so it wasn't as if Kate actually *knew* him, was it? Jess didn't really know him either, except to wave to in passing. She certainly couldn't recall ever actually speaking to the poor bloke other than a polite, "Hello, how're you?" in the village shop from time to time. She knew who he was all right—he sat outside the pub in the village most afternoons—but until he had died, she hadn't a clue as to what he did to be able to afford to spend so much time drinking.

It was early January when Dave had died. Jess remembered being out with Fletcher the morning after. She had been wrapped in her red bobble hat and thick, warm mittens. Her breath had made clouds in the air. She knew this, because she'd been puffing out little clouds, just for the fun of it, then been somewhat embarrassed to notice Elizabeth and Breda walking towards her. Jess often met the two women while she was out walking Fletcher.

Fletcher, always delighted to see Elizabeth's little King Charles spaniel, had been all waggy-tail and sniffy.

Breda's whippety mix, less friendly towards Fletcher, danced on the end of her lead, yapping in annoyance as Breda held her out of reach of the two boy dogs.

Jess and Elizabeth had exchanged the normal pleasantries while they smiled indulgently at their dogs, enjoying seeing each one's obvious delight in meeting their friend.

"Cold, isn't it?" Elizabeth had probably said. She usually started with some comment about the day's weather. Their conversations mainly consisted of that kind of banal talk you get when people meet regularly but don't really know each other well. Neighbourly talk; that was all.

Except on that day, it hadn't been all they'd talked about. Elizabeth had asked Jess if she'd been out anywhere else that morning, through the village, out for milk, anything like that.

"No, why?" Jess asked, slightly confused by the departure from their normal small talk.

"They're out looking for Dave Green," Elizabeth had continued. "He didn't show up for work and he's not at home."

"What does he even do for work?" Jess asked.

"He's a labourer, for Geraghty's, mostly, but you know these farm lads, they help out where needed," Elizabeth explained. The Geraghty farm was a mile or two out the far side of Ballyfortnum.

"Been with them a good few years, so he has." Breda's dog had finally quieted enough to allow Breda to join the conversation. "There every morning; five o'clock without fail, help with the cows and home to bed for a nap by nine-thirty. Every day, so he was."

Jess was amazed to hear Dave had been able for such an early start given that his afternoons in the pub notoriously stretched into late nights and frequent lock-ins. She'd been equally amazed when Kate had said he'd turned up at the Get Slim group sometime into its second month. He'd not really struck her as the weight-conscious type, she'd said to Kate, back in the winter when Kate still oozed with the gleeful enthusiasm of one whose new venture was an instant success.

Kate had been defensive. "You don't have to be overweight to be health conscious," she'd said. "People come along for all reasons. Sometimes their doctors recommend they come, you know. Especially if they are unhealthy in other areas—" She broke off and looked at her shoes. "Not that I'm saying that's why he comes to the group. I can't divulge that kind of information. Client confidentiality."

Jess had hidden her smile behind her coffee cup. Kate took herself so seriously—talking as if she were a doctor, a lawyer, or even a priest She was so protective of her new clients, yet innately too pleased with herself in her new role as the village slimming consultant to not want to talk about it.

The conversation with Breda and Elizabeth had tailed off as the dogs tired of each other's smells and strained at their respective leads, eager to move on.

"I expect he'll turn up in a ditch somewhere," Jess had said, laughing, as the three dog-walkers said their goodbyes and parted company.

It hadn't been so funny when she had heard that was exactly where Dave had turned up later that morning. She'd popped into the little village shop to pick up milk and found Mrs Dunne with her elbows planted onto the counter, regaled in gossip with Susan from down the lane opposite the school. Seeing as how Mrs Dunne was clearly not going to serve anyone until the story was told, Jess resigned herself to listening in, as Susan shuffled her body angle to eagerly encompass both Jess and Mrs Dunne in the saga.

"Well now." Susan had begun the story again, for Jess's benefit. "What my Will said was this ..." Mrs Dunne leaned more heavily onto her forearms, and Jess shifted her own weight slightly to rest one of her legs. "See now, when Dave didn't show up for work, Old Man Geraghty had to milk the cows himself, didn't he? But once that were done, well then, he thought to ring around the neighbours, like. He were wondering if Dave'd been called out to one of them for an emergency, weren't he?" Susan knew all this, she had said, because her Will had been out with them. All the local farmers knew Dave quite well, it transpired, as she continued the tale.

"Good with livestock, he were, and he used to see our eldest, too, Helen, that is, for a while," she said.

Jess hid a laugh behind her hand, trying not to snigger at the incongruous link.

"So a search was got together, all the farmers, and some of the others, like my Will. And anyways, so they was out looking for him, checking around near his house, and the way home, and all."

Susan went on, in her roundabout way, to say they had found him in a drainage ditch, around lunchtime. Just lying by the roadside with his bike on top of him. The ditch was deep and overgrown, which went some way to explain why he hadn't been seen by anyone just passing by. Susan had not known specifically— "*pacifically,*" she'd said—where he'd been found, but had gestured vaguely in the direction of Geraghty's, towards the Dublin road. He'd been lying in a couple of inches of stagnant, icy water, stiff with both rigor mortis and cold.

"Poor Will," Susan said. "He's still in shock. They're in the pub, the lot of them, having a drink. And to think, I were only out there on the road myself, coming home from town, weren't I? I might have passed him lying there, God rest his soul." She shuddered and crossed herself.

"That poor lad, God rest him. They deserve a wee drink," Mrs Dunne said. "God Bless them all—Will I take for that, love?"

Jess, somewhat stunned by the news, handed her the money for the milk, and walked away without waiting for her change. The bell on the door jangled as Mrs Dunne called after her, but Jess waved a dismissal and left.

Chapter Four

Dave's death had been attributed to natural causes. The postmortem had kicked up nothing conclusive, according to the papers and local gossip, at least. There was no evidence to convince the Gardai he had not simply fallen into the ditch, drunk on his way home from the pub the night before.

After only a few days' delay, many of the villagers stood huddled and shivering in the graveyard of Mary's to pay their respects as his coffin was lowered into the icy ground. Dave wasn't as well-known at Jess's end of the village as Bert had been, but the farming community had turned out in force, scrubbing the earth from their faces, and stuffing their bodies into the unfamiliar constraints of 'good clothes'. The church had been full enough, Linda had told Jess over tea and shortbread later during that cold January day; he'd had a decent send-off, poor bloke. Jess hadn't gone, although Kate had asked her to go along with her. She hardly knew him, and she didn't hold with this rural nonsense of attending every funeral in a fifty-mile radius just because you'd once said hello in the street or knew the deceased's mother's uncle's neighbour. Handy enough when she'd had a proper job, to be able to say she had to attend a neighbour's funeral anytime she fancied a lie-in or a day off, but now she wasn't working, she needed no such excuses.

Jess had stopped work almost two years ago, to care for her father in the final stages of his illness, and afterwards, had somehow forgotten to return to work. She'd have to one day, but for now, there was no need—not financially, anyway—and she was quite content to be kicking around the village recovering, taking time out to breathe, to reassess what she really wanted to be doing with herself.

George O'Malley had lived in Orchard Close since not long after Jess and her siblings had left home. Ready to retire, her parents had left the bustle of the commuter belt and moved further out, looking for peace and quiet to live out their retirement. George longed for a garden; a country outlook reminiscent of his years in the English countryside in the early years of their marriage, and birdsong instead of traffic noise. Doreen, his wife of over thirty years, had also been ready to move to a quieter place. She had talked about rediscovering her lost interests now her time was her own after raising her three children. Except, for Doreen, it turned out that the quiet, rural village in the Irish Midlands wasn't what she'd wanted after all, but the expat life in Spain with a younger man.

"He makes me feel young again," Doreen explained to Jess as she learned to Skype, in a too-small bikini, from a *Costa-del*-poolside.

George, stunned and bereft, continued to potter alone in his village garden and became a much-loved member of the aging community in Orchard Close. The neighbours took him under their wings, delivered meals to his doorstep, and gained much in return from his new-found gardening knowledge and practical goodwill. After the initial shock of Doreen's departure, George had steadily rallied, although the shadow of sadness that had added new lines to his face never quite faded.

Jess visited often, enjoying the rural space and calm surroundings. She slipped easily into the affections of George's neighbours, who told her many a time how much they enjoyed seeing her young face around, and wasn't she great to mind her father so well. Jess quietly accepted the compliments and didn't tell them that she came down to Ballyfortnum for herself as much as for her father.

When Doreen had first upped and left, Jess came as often as her job and social life would allow. Back then when she still lived in Dublin, however, with the man her dad only ever called Whatsisname, and working a full-time office job with overtime and wine-bar evenings, she had little free time for hoiking out into the sticks at weekends. Gradually, she'd found more reasons to come out to the village, and fewer reasons to stay in the city living the party life she was beginning to find exhausting.

Whatsisname—Owen—came out to the country with her once or twice, but he was uncomfortable and fidgety away from the city. He couldn't relax without a 24-hour shop within walking distance. He craved a bakery to stroll to for fresh croissants on weekend mornings. He wanted a plethora of sandwich bars, offering baguettes with several choices of fillings for lunch.

Jess soon realised that as much as Owen felt out of his comfort zone in Ballyfortnum, she found herself yearning for the quieter life and friendly neighbourhood. She whiled away many hours gazing through her office window, trying to block out the white noise of office gossip, phones ringing, printers whirring, and the non-stop sounds of the city outside on the streets below. Her mind filled with thoughts of the countryside, and she became increasingly distracted by the longing to be free of the constraints of the city.

When her office opened a branch in the Midlands town of Lambskillen—only fifteen miles from Ballyfortnum—she'd leapt at the chance to transfer and eagerly volunteered to relocate.

After splitting from Owen, in a break that left her only feeling sad about how un-sad she seemed to feel about their parting, Jess moved into a poky studio flat in Lambskillen and began her new position in the Midlands office. That poky flat was sandwiched between the disused canal and the railway, and she had tried to become used to the rattle of the train fourteen times a day and the disheartening view across the road into windows and lives that echoed her own. With little to do in the small dead-end town, and Ballyfortnum closer now, she would drive out to visit her father most weekends. She spent hours keeping him company in the garden while he weeded, tidied, planted, and pruned, stopping often to chat to the neighbours in the quiet cul-de-sac. In the evenings, she'd hook her arm into the crook of her father's arm and the two of them would stroll to the park, or up to the village centre, or around the country lanes leading out to the west of the village, with George's little Scottie, Buster, running at their heels. George had got Buster from a Scottie Rescue a year or so after Doreen had left—he'd been called Bill then, but with a neighbour called Bill already, Jess had persuaded him to change the dog's name, loosely following their childhood tradition of naming the family pets after their storybook heroes.

"I know it's not exactly right," she'd urged, "but Enid Blyton's Buster was almost a detective ... he helped the Find-Outers with many a case."

"Buster doesn't really follow the rule," George protested half-heartedly.

"But *Dad...*" Jess had regressed to childhood pleading. "He's a *Scottie*. It's the only possible name to suit him *and* follow the tradition."

George had acquiesced, and Buster joined the ranks of Marple and Poirot, a long-buried pair of tabby cats, and Watson, Jupiter, and Nancy, dogs that Jess and her brother, Eric, had fought over naming for their favourite teen detectives, Jupiter preceding Nancy by six years and the toss of a coin won by Jess's older brother. (Watson, longest-gone, was named by George before Jess was born, but held a special place in Jess's heart as her most loved childhood companion aside from Eric.) Jess and Eric had even named a pair of goldfish Cagney and Lacey, carrying them home from the fair one summer in triumph and dripping plastic bags.

Sadly, for those golden-hued ladies, rivalry amongst storybook detectives was rife in the house Jess grew up in, and this unfortunate pair succumbed to the stealth of Poirot late one evening when a door had accidentally been left open. It didn't need much sleuthing to determine that the spilled bowl and soaked carpet were significant clues as to the culprit. The squeal of a scolded cat caught with a small orange tail still half-hanging from its jaws was the final, indisputable clue to the murderer on that particular occasion.

Even now, lurking somewhere around the fields and hedgerows backing onto the houses in Orchard Close, was her father's most recent feline acquisition; a straggly half-stray he'd named Maigret, who had outlived her father only by virtue of having a few of its nine lives still to spare. Jess rarely saw the scrawny tomcat, although he often howled a fervent plea to the female neighbourhood cats outside her window at night. George had threatened to trap him and take him to be neutered but had never been successful.

Jess still vowed to catch the errant cat herself, but it was something she never quite got around to thinking about until he disturbed her sleep. And at those times, although it became the most pressing thing on her mind, she would do nothing more than stagger sleepily over to the window and yell a stream of abuse down at him or pull a pillow over her head and go back to sleep.

Fletcher, curled up on her feet, would rarely open an eye or cock an ear. He was well-used by now to the frantic wails of that bad-mannered tomcat. Fletcher was of little benefit as a guard dog, but he was a useful bed-warmer and companion in the house that, although jointly owned by her siblings, Jess and Fletcher now lived in alone.

Chapter Five

The black SUV was still parked in Linda's driveway when Jess pulled her curtains open the next morning. Fletcher rested his front feet on the window sill and pressed his nose to the glass, straining to understand the cause of his mistress's groan. On the plus side, the day after Bert's funeral had dawned a little brighter, a little clearer, and with the tiniest hint of blue peering around the restless clouds. Jess had slept late. She grabbed her warm towelling robe from the back of the door and stuffed her feet into her slippers. Half-asleep still, she stumbled down to the kitchen, flung open one of the French doors for Fletch, and filled the kettle. Shivering against the cool air, she yanked the door shut again and drew her robe tighter around herself.

Coffee drunk, and breakfast debris piled haphazardly into the sink, Jess dressed in a thick, warm jumper and jeans. Coatless and still in her slippers, she dashed over the road to tap lightly on Linda's door. Linda, tired-looking but welcoming, ushered Jess inside.

"How're you doing?" Jess asked. "I thought you might need a hand with tidying up after everyone?" Yet, as she entered the kitchen she noticed that someone had already done all the clearing up. Linda's kitchen was as spotless and gleaming as if fairy-tale elves had been working at it long into the night.

"I was keeping busy," Linda admitted, "but we can have a cuppa. Sit yourself down there, lovey." She gestured towards the kitchen table. Jess tried to protest, offering to make the tea for them both, but Linda, wanting to bustle, passed over an old Quality Street tin, saying, "It's grand, love, sit down there and have some shortbread."

As she prized off the lid, Jess could almost forget for a minute that anything had changed; it was easy to believe Bert might still walk into the kitchen at any moment.

Helping herself to a piece of the crumbly biscuit, Jess asked, "Sophia still here then?" It was an unnecessary question, since she knew the SUV in the drive belonged to Linda's younger daughter, but the house, aside from the busyness in the kitchen, was quiet and still.

"Aye. Sean's taken the boys back up to Dublin. Soph said she'd stay on a few days, help out, keep me company." Linda nodded towards the ceiling. "She's still in bed—I took her a cup of tea up an hour ago."

Jess didn't offer any comment on the kind of help Sophia might be, helping herself instead to another slice of Linda's homemade shortbread.

Jess and Linda's tea-drinking and low chatter must have spurred Sophia into surfacing, and as Linda was pouring Jess a second cup, the kitchen door swung open and Sophia entered, freshly-showered and immaculate as always.

"Jess." She greeted her mother's neighbour with a cool detachment. "Mum, have you given some more thought about coming back with me? You really should. You'll only fret and worry here by yourself with nothing to do all day. Come and stay with us in town for a while." Sophia turned to refill the kettle. "And I do wish you would get a coffee machine. It's quite tedious. Why don't I get you one for your birthday?"

Linda rubbed her forehead, smoothing wrinkles with a crumpled hand, and sighed. "I'm grand here, love." She got up, pushing her chair back and reaching to take the kettle from Sophia. "Sit down, lovey, let me do that for you." She turned back to Jess and said, "It'll be some time before I stop putting out a cup for Bert. I keep expecting him to come blowing in, brandishing the paper and a pint of milk."

Jess gave a sad smile. "It's only been a few days; it'll get easier. I'm going up to the shop now anyway—I only came to say I'll get you some milk. Do you need anything else?"

Linda shook her head, flashing Jess a brief, tired smile. "Just a pint of milk, thanks, love."

Jess got up, nodded goodbye to Sophia, and bent to kiss Linda on the cheek. "No, stay there, I'll see myself out."

Ten minutes later, Fletcher bouncing along beside her, Jess was on her way to the village shop, deep in thought. She pulled her phone from her pocket and called Kate.

"Kate, hi, how're you?" she said, panting a little from the exertion of walking and talking at the same time. "Listen, just thinking, you know how you said about the three of them... them who... well, you know... who died... all being from your group, right?" She paused while Kate answered. "Well, yeah, I was thinking, it is a bit strange, isn't it?"

Jess stood outside the shop, still talking to Kate, until someone tapped her on the arm and whispered, "'scuse me, pet," at which Jess guiltily moved out of the shop doorway, shut off her phone, and looked up to see whose path she'd been blocking.

Susan smiled apologetically, holding the door open so Jess could enter the little shop in front of her.

As Jess crossed the shop to the fridge, Susan took the poster she was clutching straight to the counter. Mrs Dunne took it from her and pinned it haphazardly to the wooden panelling on the front of the counter, below eye level for all but the smallest children of the village.

"What's that about?" Jess bent to look at the poster, noticing its familiar logo and colouring. "Get Slim?" Her brow furrowed. "There's a poster on the door already for it," she said, gesturing with a toss of her head.

"This one's for my group, int it, pet?" Susan said. "Over in town."

"Your group?"

"Sure, ha'nt I been at it far longer than that friend o' yours? I've three groups on the go, ha'nt I? Two in town an' one over in Ballymaglen." She nodded in the general direction of the next village. "Shoulda had the one 'ere, shouldn' I, till your one came all swanning in with her high and mighty Dublin accent and took it from under me, dint she?" Susan huffed, as Mrs Dunne reached around her for Jess's proffered money.

"You're a Get Slim consultant, too?" Jess was surprised. Susan, though tidy and well-dressed, was what Jess would call 'frumpy' if she had thought about it. Susan's ruddy, weathered face and greying curls topped off a slightly dumpy body, that Jess would not have thought a suitable advert for a slimming adviser.

"Been one for over seven years, ha'nt I?" Susan answered. "I've a great busy group and had Slimmer of the Country three of them years, too. Good at my job, I am, an' I don't hold with no newcomer blow-ins taking my clients." Susan, usually mild-mannered and gentle, thumped a hand onto the counter, causing Mrs Dunne to flinch away.

Heat rushed to Jess's face. "I'm sorry," she said, feeling somehow guilty for her association with Kate. "I didn't know that."

"Ah, sure, an' why would you?" Susan calmed herself and smiled. "How's Linda coping today?"

Jess gestured with a bottle of milk to reinforce her answer. "I was just in with her now; I'll pop this in on my way home. Sophia is staying for a few days."

All three women rolled their eyes.

"Poor love," Susan said, and the other two nodded their agreement.

"Yes, poor Linda—first Bert and now having to cope with Sophia too." Jess rooted in her pockets for her shopping bag. Outside, Fletcher barked in excitement, frantic and insistent. Jess gave up on the bag, gathered her purchases in her arms, and scurried from the shop.

Chapter Six

The drainpipe creaked in protest as Fletcher strained away from it to reach the object of his attention. His new friend, the little white Westie, and its owner, Marcus Woo, strolled across the road towards the shop; the Westie trotting along demurely at his master's heels.

Jess tumbled her shopping into a heap on the ground to unhook the lead before Fletcher brought the shop's gutters crashing down around them.

Fletcher, frantic to greet his friend, knocked her off balance as she scrabbled to gather the scattered groceries. On her knees, she scooped everything up and tried to stuff it into the shopping bag she pulled from her pocket, while Fletched tugged at her arm.

"Here." Marcus reached out and took Fletcher's lead from Jess, freeing up her hands to organise her shopping. "Sorry," he added, as the two dogs danced around each other as if they hadn't seen each other in months. "Bad timing." He smiled as he wrapped the two leads around his hands, shortening the leashes and holding the dogs apart at arm's length.

"Are you going home?" he asked. "We're just off for a walk. We were going to head to the park, but perhaps it would be easier if we went the other way?" He looked down at the two dogs, still trying to circle his legs and each other in their desire to play, then back at Jess.

"It's fine," Jess said. "He needs to learn to walk sensibly in company. If you don't mind his idiocy, then of course you're welcome to walk with us." Her shopping now contained, she took Fletch's lead from Marcus. "Thank you."

Marcus fell into step beside Jess, Snowflake trotting neatly at Marcus's heels and Fletcher doing his best to weave between them.

"How's Linda coping?" Marcus echoed Mrs Dunne's concern for Jess's newly-widowed neighbour.

"Bearing up," Jess grimaced as she answered, "but it's hard enough, losing someone. And her daughter is staying, which probably doesn't make it easier." Before Marcus had a chance to question that statement, Jess spoke aloud the thing that had been niggling at her over the last couple of days.

"Marcus," she said, "—can I call you Marcus?" She didn't wait for him to answer. "Do you think it's a bit weird how they all belonged to the Get Slim group? Bert and Dave and Angela, I mean? All the ones who've died recently?' She swung around to study the policeman's reaction, crumpling her face in concern. Fletcher twisted across her to sniff something on the verge. She stumbled over him and turned from Marcus to focus on where she was going.

"Were they?" Marcus said. "I hadn't known that."

Jess explained that Kate had mentioned it at Bert's wake; how until that point she also hadn't given it a thought, but now Kate had said it, she couldn't shake it from her mind—that there might be a connection, somehow.

Marcus said little, although he proved to be a good listener, making non-committal agreeing noises whenever Jess paused for breath.

"I'm sure it's nothing," he eventually said. "Didn't they all die naturally, if suddenly? I heard nothing odd about any of them. It happens, especially in the winter, you know?"

Jess nodded slowly, feeling a weight slide from her that she hadn't known she was carrying, as Marcus allayed her concerns—her worry, her suspicion? She wasn't sure exactly what it was, but she knew she felt happier for having shared her thoughts. They parted ways at the entrance to the park, Fletcher disappointed and dragging back towards Snowflake as she pulled him along Orchard Close to deliver Linda her milk.

Later, as she busied herself about her own kitchen, she tried to recall anything Kate had said about any of the three deceased neighbours. Not much, she conceded, what with her pretensions of client privacy and all that, but Jess was sure she recalled Kate telling her Dave had surprised the group by achieving Slimmer of the Week after only his second meeting.

Jess had laughed at the thought. "Not bad for a skinny bloke," she remembered saying, and Kate, as usual, had become defensive of her 'clients' and told Jess that Dave had, in fact, done very well, and surpassed his target, vowing even to try to cut his drinking by a pint a week initially, working up to one pint less every day.

Kate had gone quite pink as she had defended her decision, Jess recalled. They'd changed the subject fast enough, but it had amused Jess that someone as skinny as Dave could have had much of a weight-loss target to start with. Surely his target would have been insignificant enough that *anyone* could have managed to smash it?

Although Jess attended neither Dave's wake nor his funeral, his death was the subject of village gossip for many weeks after. Despite the apparent lack of evidence, speculation as to how he had died was rife in the village. Jess hadn't paid much attention at the time, but she presumed that, as a sudden death, there would've been an inquest. She would ask Marcus, if she could make it come across casually. She would look out for an opportunity to talk to him again just as soon as possible. There hadn't been much of a wait before Dave's funeral, though, she remembered—if he was found dead on the Wednesday and buried by the Saturday, surely then there couldn't have been any real concerns as to how he'd died? Most of the village thought he'd simply fallen, drunk, into the ditch, on his way home that night. Some gossip had wondered if it had been a hit and run, but she'd never heard any more about it. Dave's death had narked Kate, Jess remembered—he had been her rising star and she had taken personal smug satisfaction in attributing his success to her own expertise in slimming advice. Kate had sulked about his death for days.

Then there was Angela. Overweight and middle-aged, Angela had fitted Jess's idea of a typical slimming group client more easily than Dave had. Angela had lived just a short way down the Little Mason Road out of the village—the road between the church and the little row of traditional workers' houses where Marcus lived. Angela's detached bungalow backed onto the church grounds—a nice, quiet outlook if you didn't mind dead neighbours, Angela's daughter used to joke. With Angela gone, her husband, Niall, was alone with their daughter, Harriet, and a university-age son. Jess saw them out and about sometimes, all still raw from the shock and grief.

Chapter Seven

Angela was the second of Kate's group members to be buried since Christmas. Angela died in early February—only a couple of weeks before Bert's death—and once again, Jess had heard most of the news in the shop one frosty Saturday morning as Fletcher sat outside, thawing the ice with his warm doggy breath while he waited for his mistress.

"Did you hear?" Mrs Dunne had asked. "Angela has passed!"

"Passed what?" Jess picked up a bunch of carrots and put them in her basket.

"No—passed. Passed on. Gone over."

Jess dropped the loaf of bread she had just selected and swung around to face Mrs Dunne. "You what?"

"Angela has left us, love." Mrs Dunne's eyes sparkled with what could have been either sadness or drama. "Deceased."

Jess stared at Mrs Dunne; her mouth open but no words forming. She stood frozen next to the bread display. "Dead?" she eventually managed to say, in little more than a whisper. "Dead? How? When? What happened?" She'd only seen her a few days before; they'd chatted for a few moments outside the shop about nothing in particular—how the kids were getting on; wasn't it grand that Harriet had settled so well into the local art college; her older one still loving his university course, that kind of thing.

"Well ..." Mrs Dunne shoved some newspapers aside and leaned onto her thick forearms. "... looks like it may've been something she ate; they'll have to do some of them test yokes. Rushed her off to hospital last night, so they did, but it did no good, God bless her. She was too far gone."

"Have you seen Niall?" Jess had asked. "And where are the children? Have they come home? Do they know? How do you know? Who told you?" The questions came thick and fast but Jess didn't pause long enough for Mrs Dunne to offer any answers, until at last she stopped for breath, picked the bread up, put it down again, then picked it back up and put it on the counter with the rest of her shopping.

"Gerry," Mrs Dunne said. "He called with a parcel, didn't he? And Niall's sister was there. She told him." Gerry was the postman. What he and Mrs Dunne didn't know between them was not worth knowing.

Jess paid for her goods and packed them haphazardly into her shopping bag. "I'd better call up in a bit, see if they need anything." She left in a daze, without saying goodbye to Mrs Dunne, and almost tripped over Fletcher as he leapt up at her as she came out of the shop door.

Before she even got halfway home, Kate had rung with the same news.

"How the heck do you know everything that happens in Ballyfortnum before half of Ballyfortnum does?" Jess had asked. Apparently, the Get Slim group's Facebook page had announced the tragedy a few minutes ago—another of the group lived next door to Angela and posted the information, triggering a thread of punctuation-lacking *rip*s, sad-faced emojis, and speculations that Jess read through with a mix of interest and disgust once she got home. She usually ignored the notifications from that page and really didn't understand why it was even an open page anyway. Who needed constant reminders of how much weight they should lose and how many sinful foods they were eating on any given day? Not Jess, that's for sure.

She noticed the thread below that one was the weekly recipe suggestion—a seafood salad with far too much lettuce for anyone to truly enjoy. Jess remembered her parents excitedly whipping up prawn cocktails in Babycham glasses a million years ago back in what must have been the later part of the '80s. This Get Slim seafood salad was only a rearranged prawn cocktail without the help of mayonnaise to make it at least somewhat palatable. She shut off Facebook and wondered if it would prove to be the Get Slim seafood salad that had been Angela's demise.

At the thought, Jess shuddered, remembering how, on the Wednesday of that week, she had bumped into Breda in the refrigerator aisle of one of the supermarkets in Lambskillen. They chatted for a while in front of the fish section, each clasping a warming bag of prawns while discussing the merits of various shellfish. Breda had never had mussels before, she'd said, peering dubiously into the fridge.

"Nor any shellfish, sure I haven't," she'd told Jess, brimming over with the enthusiasm of one discovering new tastes. She gestured back towards the fridge. "Nor octopus ... sounds suckery—however would you cook it?"

There was a whole section of seafood recipes in the newest Get Slim magazine that she was going to try out, Breda said, managing to sound both wary and excited. Adding a jar of tartare sauce to her basket, Breda moved on.

Jess returned her own lukewarm bag of prawns to the fridge, and selected instead a bag of battered onion rings from the freezer below, tossed them into her trolley, and wheeled off into the wine aisle. She waved at Breda across the car park as they loaded their shopping into their respective car boots.

Three days later, as she'd considered the news Mrs Dunne had shared, she wondered if Angela had been trying out the same recipe. Food poisoning, Mrs Dunne had reckoned. Dodgy prawns? Jess shuddered as she relived the moment she'd decided to choose unhealthy—but delicious—battered onion rings instead of the nakedness of wrinkled prawns, put off by the thought of accidentally purchasing something healthy that Kate might construe as a sign to try to persuade Jess to join Get Slim.

In fairness, Kate did stop badgering Jess to join up after the first few weeks. Although Jess suspected that this was more to do with Kate's in-gratiation into the community as care for Jess's health and well-being. She probably thought the villagers would be less inclined to be Kate's new besties if Jess was there to hold onto the community status in which she was already established: "Good neighbour, friend to all, general village helpmate," as Kate had laughingly called her on more than one occasion.

Jess loved being a part of the village community. Everyone had rallied around her dad when he was sick, and they had taken Jess under their collective wing after he had died. Jess was grateful for that, and more than happy to give something back, now she was untethered by work and had more free time than she knew what to do with.

When she wasn't out with Fletcher, or drifting in and out of neighbours' houses, running errands in exchange for company, cups of tea, or home-made baking, Jess was gradually redecorating what she still thought of as her father's house. The decor she had inherited in the neat semi was dated and old-mannish, and she had decided to liven it up ready for either selling, if or when her siblings agreed that was what they must do, or for her own comfort while she was living here in guardianship.

A few days after Angela's death, Jess had got up early, determined to paint the hall. It was an easy enough task—it only needed a fresh coat of the brighter-colour paint she'd already bought a couple of months back and then never got around to doing.

When Kate rapped on the front door and let herself in later in the afternoon, she found Jess balanced precariously on a ladder, wielding a paintbrush, singing along to the radio, turned up loud to spur her on.

"Not stopping; I'm on my way to work," Kate announced, squeezing past the ladder. In the kitchen, Kate filled the kettle, discrediting her words.

Jess came down the ladder and followed Kate into the kitchen. "Go on then," she said, brandishing the paintbrush towards Kate. "What's up?"

Kate assumed a sad expression and pulled a pack of tissues from her handbag. She extracted the last tissue from the pack with her manicured, pink-painted nails and dabbed at her eyes without smudging her make-up. "It's going to be very difficult," she said, crushing the empty tissue packet into a ball and tossing it towards the bin. "Everyone will be so dis-traught. I'll have to make an announcement." She sniffed emphatically.

Jess sighed and wrapped the paintbrush in cling film, stooped to retrieve the tissue wrapper, dropped it into the bin, then spooned coffee into two mugs. Kate reached into her bag again for her sweeteners.

Jess sat the steaming mugs on the table and plonked herself on a chair opposite Kate.

"They all already know, you dope," she told her friend. "You won't have to announce anything. The funeral was *yesterday*." It had been raw and emotional, the church packed.

"I'll have to say something," Kate had insisted. "It's my job as their consultant to be supportive in difficult times. And we'll have to do some kind of a memorial thing. She was an inspiring member of the group and an example to them all."

Jess blew on her coffee to disguise her sigh. Kate could be very dramatic sometimes.

"We didn't do a memorial for Dave and I feel terrible about it." Kate dabbed more frantically as a sob broke free and her eyes filled with genuine tears. "I should have done something …" Kate's voice broke and Jess shoved the box of tissues towards her. "I should have done something to remember him … and …" Kate sniffed loudly, blew her nose, and crumpled the tissue into her fist, her knuckles pale as she struggled to regain composure.

Tears prickled Jess's eyes as she recalled holding the sobbing weight of Harriet in her arms, trying to offer comfort at the graveside the previous afternoon. She snatched the tissues back across the table to extract a wad of her own.

Kate's emotional outburst was back under control. "… and Angela was already a Silver member, and on target to make Gold in the next few weeks. I had nominated her for Slimmer of the Year last year."

Jess had no idea what that meant, and chose not to question just then how anyone could be Slimmer of the Year if the group had only been running for a few months.

"I wonder if they would give a posthumous award ... I could nominate her again this year," Kate had said, draining her cup and getting up to leave. Jess stood up with her.

"I'm coming out now, too," she said. "I must pop up to Niall and see what I can do for them." She shut a protesting Fletcher into the living room, grabbed her coat, and followed Kate out the front door.

Chapter Eight

Barely three weeks since Angela's funeral, and only a week since Bert's funeral, Kate stood once again on Jess's patio, cigarette in hand, while Jess shivered at the kitchen table.

"Hurry up, would ya," Jess said. "It's freezing." She looked at Kate's skinny frame, wondering if it were at all possible that her friend had lost even more weight. "I could close the door to an inch and you'd still fit through it," she muttered.

"I know, right, I've lost loads," Kate said, spinning in a slow circle to show off her figure.

Jess winced. "That's not what I meant … I mean … don't you think …?" She tailed off, leaving the thoughts unsaid. Instead, she shoved the untouched plate of Linda's latest offering—chocolate chip cookies—aside and pulled on her boots. Rising, she grabbed Kate's bag off the table, picked up Fletch's lead, and stepped outside. "C'mon," she said, "I'll walk with you."

Kate's Get Slim group was due to start in half an hour. Jess held out the bag for Kate to take, opened the gate, and stepped back, gesturing for Kate to exit first. Aside from her own differing viewpoint—liking to eat, not liking to exercise, that sort of thing—Jess was increasingly worried about her friend's drastic weight loss. A very skinny—bony, even—size eight and still shrinking did not suit Kate at all. She looked so fragile, as if she might snap in a light breeze. Ice cracked in a puddle underfoot as if to emphasize the thought. Jess stopped short as she rounded the corner of the house.

"Oh yeah, your car!" The strain of the last week must be getting to her. "Sorry," she said to Kate, "I'm narky and bad-tempered, what with Bert, and their bitch of a daughter, and the crap weather and all that. I'll walk Fletch over and meet you there, help you unload."

Kate beeped her horn as she passed them a moment later, and was waiting in the car park with the boot open by the time Jess had crossed the road.

Jess hooked Fletch's lead around the bench outside the hall, promising to walk around the park with him as soon as they were done, and grabbed a box of 'nutritious & healthy' Get Slim bars from Kate's boot to carry inside.

"Take a couple with you," Kate said, nodding at the bars.

Jess couldn't tell her that she found the bars truly disgusting. Nutritious and healthy, maybe, but if 'artificial' and 'cardboard' were ever branded as flavours, these would be the prototype samples of the taste. Kate was always banging on about how delicious they were: "New flavour!" she'd gushed as she opened a box of mocha bars last week, dumping a handful into Jess's bag. Unbidden, the thought sprung into Jess's mind that if you really wanted to poison someone, you could inject the most noxious or bitter drug into these and they'd still taste better for it. *Poison*, she thought, remembering Angela, and shoved the word back into the corners of her mind to withdraw later.

Leaving Kate in the hall to meet her clients, Jess strolled across the car park and into the sports field to give Fletcher his promised walk. Kate wasn't the only one getting skinny around here these days; the car park was already half-full, as group members arrived for the meeting. In fact, Jess sometimes thought she may be the only one in the area who didn't agree with all this Get Slim nonsense. Despite the cold, the track around the park buzzed with the panting of group members anxious to sweat off a few more vital pounds before the evening's weigh-in.

As Jess moseyed around the perimeter of the park, three separate joggers and a pair of power-walking neighbours overtook her, their breath wafting into ghostlike clouds as they passed by.

Others walked around in the opposite direction to Jess, most of whom only managed a breathless grunt in response to Jess's friendly greeting as they crossed paths. If the number of cars in the car park and people in the park were anything to go by, then half the village seemed to have enrolled in Kate's slimming group. Although it was only set up a few months ago, as always in rural villages, word had spread as fast as the collective weight of the parishioners diminished.

The flurry of activity in the floodlit park ascertained that it wasn't just talk either—there was a sudden spate of exercise running through the village like ... well, like the runners themselves. Even Ann and Patricia from Orchard Close had taken up jogging. They puffed along past Jess's kitchen window every morning, just as she herself was still only stumbling, bleary and pyjama'd, around her kitchen, groping groggily for that first cup of coffee.

"Who in their right mind would want to go out *jogging* in these dark wintery mornings?" she would grumble to Fletcher before padding back to bed for another half hour under the warm covers. Even Father James had taken to wearing Lycra—a worrying sight in itself—and Jess was certain that every single time she popped out to the shops or down to the post office, there he was, pedalling as if chased by bears. Red-faced and sweating, legs whirling like the blades on the new turbines on the mountains in the distance. Not befitting for a man of the cloth at all, if you asked her. Besides, the red-faced look was most incongruous against his freckled Irish complexion and greying ginger hair. And then, of course, even poor eighty-year-old Bert had joined up, counting sinful food along with the rest of them.

Poor Bert. Jess shook her head, trying to dispel the memory of last week's ambulance and the echoes of gossip murmuring that he'd lost far too much weight far too fast. She left the park and its plethora of Get Slimmers and headed for home. She'd pop in to Linda; have a cuppa with her before cosying up for the night in her PJs and slippers.

As she rounded the bend in the close, she stopped in her tracks, her mouth falling open into the start of a scream before realising the flickering blue light was just the glow of a television pulsating through the curtains of Number 5.

Jess tapped on Linda's door to announce her arrival, then swung it open and called out a cheerful hello as she stepped inside. Fletcher wagged his tail against Linda's hall table, causing a framed photo of Bert to wobble. Jess tugged Fletcher away from the table, straightened the photo, and closed the front door with her foot.

Linda, in neat slacks and mule slippers with a small heel, appeared in the kitchen doorway as Jess slipped off Fletcher's lead.

"Hello, you two," Linda said with a smile, as she stooped to fondle Fletcher's ears. Fletch, in return, slobbered over her trousers.

Jess followed the pair of them into the kitchen, where Sophia sat at the table, a glass of wine and a half-full bottle in front of her. Fletcher, undiscriminating with the recipients of his drool, transferred his attention to Sophia, who pushed him away as he licked her arm.

"Sit." Linda gestured Jess towards a chair. Fletcher, obedient at the most obscure moments, assumed the instruction was aimed at him and immediately returned to Linda's side, where he plonked himself into a smart sitting position in front of her.

Sophia, noting the look of shock on Jess's face, softened, laughed, and pushed the wine bottle towards Jess. "Have a drink," she offered. "Mum, grab Jess a glass, won't you?"

Linda selected two fresh glasses from a high cupboard, and poured first for Jess, then for herself. She topped up Sophia's glass to empty the bottle and Jess's shoulders relaxed as some of the stress slipped from her day.

"*Sláinte.*" She lifted her glass towards Linda, then Sophia, took a swig and curled her legs up beneath her on the hard kitchen chair. She took another sip and let out a long sigh. "I can't imagine how tired you two must be," she said, "but I'm completely wrecked. It's been a long week, hasn't it? How long are you staying?" She directed the last question to Sophia.

"I've to be back next week. Work. They really need me back. I can just imagine how much I'll have to deal with by now. It will be pure chaos. I have to say I'll be glad to be back in civilisation though," Sophia said. "Are you sure you won't come too, Mum?"

Linda slumped into her seat and yawned. Jess knew that this had been their main topic of conversation ever since the funeral.

"I'll keep a good eye on her," she said, suddenly feeling sorry for Sophia. She reached out and patted her hand. "She will be okay, really she will, but she really does want to stay in her own home, near to his things, their friends, you know? Don't you?" Jess glanced at her elderly friend, then back at Sophia. "She'll be all right here, it's her home."

Linda's eyes filled with tears.

Sophia stared down at the table, turning the wine glass in her hands, swirling the liquid in small sploshes up the sides of the glass.

Linda took a deep breath and reached for Sophia's hands. "Jess is right, love, I really couldn't face living back in Dublin. I like it here. I will tell you if I change my mind, I promise." She got up and went to the counter, taking the old Quality Street tin from under the fruit bowl. "Now, who wants a piece of Bakewell tart?" she asked, searching out plates and pulling a knife from the block next to the oven.

"It's nice to see you girls tucking in. Bert hadn't eaten my cakes for so long—he always said it would be my cooking that killed him but as it turned out it was dieting that finished him off, not over-eating my baking." Her face crumpled and she began to sob.

Jess, nearest, pulled the older woman into a hug before turning her into her daughter's waiting arms.

"Oh, Mum," said Sophia, and the two women stood in the middle of the kitchen in a long embrace, until Linda's sobs had subsided.

Jess busied herself with cutting each of them a generous slice of the pie. As the two drew apart, Jess laughed softly. "I know that was my cue to tiptoe out quietly," she said, "but I wasn't going to leave without sampling this Bakewell."

Chapter Nine

As Jess let herself in through her own front door, a thought niggled at her. Linda's comment about how it would be overeating that finished Bert off, rather than losing weight, had triggered a worrying idea. Despite Linda's love of baking, Bert had never been able to eat much of it. He was on small rations of sugary foods not for weight reasons, but due to his diabetes. And by losing weight so rapidly, Bert had put his health at risk.

Linda had explained it to Jess a while back. She'd been worried by his rapid weight loss since joining Get Slim. Bert himself had been so proud of his achievements, as happy that Kate and the others in the group were spurring him on as Linda was unhappy.

Linda quoted a medical leaflet as she'd sat with Jess, over tea and a large slice of freshly-baked coffee cake: *The goal is to lose body fat ... not muscle. The slower you lose weight, the greater the percentage of body fat loss. The faster you lose ... the more muscle you lose ... this ... makes diabetes control harder ... slow steady weight loss ... best.*

Bert had been hovering around, in and out of the garden, but disinclined to stay to listen. "Don't nag, dear, there's life in me yet," he had admonished, swigging down his tea and disappearing back out to his roses.

"Slimmer of the Week, he was again," Linda had said, pouring out another cup for each of them. "Right proud, he is—third time since he joined up, but it's no good for him—he's lost eight pounds in three weeks and I'm worried it's too fast. The doc's always telling him to lose a bit, but not this much this quick." A frown had deepened the lines on her face as she'd crumpled her napkin into a tight ball, before unfolding it and smoothing it out on the tabletop.

Had Kate been negligent? Jess hadn't allowed the thought to fully surface before, but now she was unable to suppress it any longer. She bit down on her bottom lip, and stood, unmoving, in her hallway for a moment before she kicked off her shoes and stooped to rub Fletcher behind his ears.

"What do you think, boyo?" she asked the dog.

He looked up at her with hopeful eyes, wagging his tail back and forth across the floor with an energy that sent her shoes skidding into the skirting board.

"Is Kate really so hell-bent on *Targets!* and *Success!* and 'aren't you doing well, here's a nice certificate' that she overlooked Bert's diabetes?"

Fletch's only answer was to tug gently at his lead, still fastened around his neck, and to reach up and lick Jess's face.

Jess didn't bother to switch on the television or pick up her book as she slumped onto the sofa and tucked her legs under her.

Fletch jumped up beside her and rested his head in her lap.

Jess leaned her head against the cushions and closed her eyes, recalling how the ambulance had disturbed her on that Sunday evening just over a week ago. She'd been snuggled in bed, duvet pulled to her chin, reading one of the many detective novels that had adorned the shelves on the landing ever since her parents bought this house for their retirement. The books were much-loved remnants of Jess's childhood, and as much a part of her upbringing as her siblings were. Many old favourites were dog-eared, creased at the spines, prone to shed pages as soon as their old covers were opened, but Jess and her brother still loved to read them. They would stroke the spines as gently as they may caress a pet cat, perusing the titles and recalling the stories, before committing to their selection and curling up somewhere to lose themselves in mystery for a while.

Even now, whenever her brother came to visit, he wouldn't be in the house for long before going to the shelves to select an afternoon read. His children already loved these old books just as much as Jess and Eric, and when they came to stay Jess took great delight in sitting in front of the bookshelf, her two young nieces cross-legged beside her, as they peered through the titles to select bedtime reading. Bryony, the elder of his daughters, was already able to read the easier Secret Seven books by herself, but it didn't stop her demanding her aunt to read aloud. They were steadily working through the Enid Blyton mystery series from where Jess's dad's old Scottie, Buster, had found his name, but Jess was longing to revisit another old favourite, Nancy Drew, when the girls were a little older.

Jess's thoughts shifted back to that dreadful Sunday night. She had been caught up in an ancient Agatha Christie and at first didn't react as the blue lights threw ghostlike flashes of colour across her front garden and onto her bedroom walls. Engrossed in the book, it took her several moments to realise that the lights were real and not a figment conjured by her imagination.

Confused, but not yet concerned, she tossed back the covers and padded to the window, still clutching the book, but on seeing the ambulance parked across Bert and Linda's drive, the Poirot tumbled from her hand. She left it lying where it fell on the bed, not even stopping to bookmark her page and close it properly.

Jess shrugged into jeans, pulled a jumper over her pyjama top, and ran downstairs and out the door, slamming it shut in an indignant Fletcher's face.

Many neighbours were already out of their houses: a small, worried gathering in Bert and Linda's front garden, all hastily dressed in an assortment of dressing gowns, slippers, wellies and coats.

As Jess approached, the door to Number 15 swung open.

Bill exited first, shooing the neighbours aside to clear the path for the paramedics to wheel out a trolley. In the near-darkness, Jess could not tell which of her neighbours was the blanketed shape on the trolley, but then Linda emerged with another blanket around her shoulders and Jeanie's arm around her waist. The paramedics guided the trolley, then Linda, into the ambulance.

There were a few moments of tense silence, the crowd's worried faces lit by the pulsing blue light, then one of the paramedics jumped from the ambulance and slammed the door closed, leaving his colleague in the back with the still figure on the trolley and his pale-faced passenger.

The male paramedic swung himself into the driver's seat, where he switched off the blue strobing lights before slowly driving away through the silent, watchful neighbours.

"Oh no." The sound was hardly audible, and Jess didn't know who had said it, until Jeanie took her hand and Jess realised she'd uttered the words herself.

Jeanie squeezed Jess's hand and led her towards number 14. "Come on," Jeanie said. "I'll get Bill to make us a nice cup of tea. We've all had a nasty shock."

"Drop of whiskey in it too, dear. Go in and sit yourselves down," Bill said, holding the door open for them.

Jess and Jeanie sank into the pair of matching armchairs and Bill shuffled into their kitchen.

"Now where do we keep the tea, Jeanie, dear?"

Jeanie pulled herself up from the sofa almost before she'd had time to sink fully into it, and made tea for the three of them. The three neighbours sat there long into the night, talking little, until Bill had walked Jess back across the street to her door, where she'd allowed Fletcher to curl up on her lap and lick away the flow of tears that came once she was alone in her house.

Jess smiled as she recalled Bill's valiant but short-lived attempts to make tea and comfort the two women, but the smile was tinged with sadness and faded as fast as it had formed, as she turned her worries over in her mind.

Chapter Ten

J ess swung Fletcher's lead in circles in front of her as she walked down the farm track. Fletch, far ahead of her, chased imaginary rabbits and bounded through the puddles. Much as she liked to chat with the neighbours, this was where she walked when she wanted to be alone. The track nestled in a deep rut between two hedgerows, which, later in the year, would be buzzing with insects along its mile or so length. By May, it would flaunt a vibrant patchwork of purple vetch, the bright pinks of campion and cranesbill, blue speedwell, and the yellows of cowslips and the statuesque flag irises that grew in the wet edges of the ditches.

Now, in early March, its palette was as many shades of brown as any woodshed could hold. The trees were still winter-bare, only the first early promise of green speckling a very few of the twiggy tips of branches. The track was sodden from the endless winter, with deep puddles left from the heavy tractor tyres, and Fletcher was already filthy.

Today, Jess sloshed through the muck without noticing how it splashed up over her wellies and speckled her jeans. Most days, when the lane was wet, she kicked through the puddles in childlike pleasure, confident that her expensive Canadian boots would keep her feet both dry and warm. A relation from Canada had visited some years back, and Jess had instantly coveted the thick, padded boots she'd brought with her to wear for "your quaint little Irish walks." A few weeks after the cousin returned home to Canada, she'd parcelled up a new, robin-breast-red pair of the same style of boots and shipped them to Jess via George O'Malley's Ballyfortnum address, much to Jess's delight. They'd lasted years, until Fletcher destroyed them as a teething puppy and Jess had needed to fork out for the current replacements.

Today, though, her mind was elsewhere, her eyes cast downward to the ground, and it wasn't until she rounded the bend and smacked into someone that she realised two things. First, she was not alone on her lane for once, and second, Fletcher had been barking idiotically for a while.

Startled, she looked up, straight into Marcus's deep-brown eyes.

He, too, stumbled backwards, caught off balance. He must've been bent forward to pet Fletcher, Jess realised, as he put a hand down to stop himself falling.

Fletcher, excited by the game, took the opportunity to jump up at Marcus, and any attempt to retain balance was lost.

Snowflake greeted Fletcher like a long-lost friend as Marcus sank to his knees, squelching into the soft, wet earth while the two dogs leapt around him, throwing dirty splashes across his coat like a mud-coloured Jackson Pollock.

Jess's cheeks warmed with embarrassment. She held her hand out to pull him up, her apology hampered by an unfortunate stuttering while the appropriate words tried to form in her brain.

Marcus, getting to his feet, shoved the two dogs away and laughed. He had a deep laugh that wrinkled his eyes, and instantly Jess felt more at ease. "I've been in worse," he said. "In my job, I've lain for hours in a ditch or two."

"You'd better come back to mine to clean up a bit," Jess said, relieved now that it was the friendly local Garda she'd knocked flying and not anyone unsavoury or bad-tempered. "Have a cup of tea and clean the worst off, and then I'll run you home?"

"It's no bother," he assured her. "I'll be grand, really." He tried to brush the mud off, but it was too wet, making it smear further across his hands.

Jess was insistent. "Orchard Close is nearer. Come on. Linda dropped me in some shortbread—there's an incentive. Besides, I wanted to ask you about something anyway."

"You didn't need to knock me over to ask me something." Marcus grinned again, and Jess couldn't help but think how nice he was. "What's up?"

Jess directed Marcus to the bathroom to clean himself up as best he could while she made a pot of tea. He emerged some minutes later, cleaner, but with damp patches on the knees where he'd sponged away the mud.

"I'm sorry I've nothing to offer you to change into," Jess said. "I finally got rid of all my dad's clothes." She paused, choking back a sudden pang of sadness as an image of her dad's baggy jumpers came into her mind. "I kept one old jumper for a long time."

Marcus caught her melancholy and patted her arm. "Your dad was a fine man."

Jess hadn't realised they had known each other and said so.

"I used to see him at Bowls," Marcus said. "I used to drive out every week to play, long before I moved here—that's how I knew I liked the village.

Many a Monday evening he beat me good and proper. He and Bert made quite a team."

They sat in silence at Jess's kitchen table, remembering both men. Tears sprang to Jess's eyes. She ducked her head and wiped away the tears with her sleeve.

"What is it that's worrying you?" Marcus asked, his voice soft and caring.

Jess got up again, and reached for the tin of biscuits Linda had pressed into her hands that morning. She busied herself with finding plates, keeping her back to Marcus as she voiced her concerns.

"It's like I started to say the other day," she eventually said. "It just seems, well ... odd."

"Odd?" Marcus prompted, raising an eyebrow.

"Odd ... I mean ... all of them in the slimming group, all of them from this small village. All of them dying kind of unexpectedly, I mean ... I know Bert was getting on a bit, but eighty isn't so old these days, is it? And Dave was young enough ... and poor Angela—she wasn't much older than *me*." Jess clenched her fingers around a piece of shortbread until it crumbled onto the plate, such was her indignation at the thought of someone dying in only their earliest forties. "I know Dave drank, and all that, but ..."

She spun around to look at the policeman, then coloured at her outburst and let her gaze slide downwards to where Fletcher and Snowflake, exhausted from their run, lay sprawled at Marcus's feet. Fletcher's head rested on Marcus's shoe, and Snowflake's head nestled on Fletcher's front paws.

Marcus followed her gaze. He flashed a quick smile, the skin around his dark eyes crinkling into well-worn furrows. "Picture of innocence, aren't they?" A serious expression replaced his smile. "I did a bit of checking, after you said it before. The tests on Dave were inconclusive; it was listed as natural causes in the end, although no one could be a hundred per cent certain he wasn't knocked into the ditch. There was no evidence of him having been hit, but it is possible, of course, that someone knocked his bike off the road. They may not even have noticed doing it, in the dark, on that corner. An unfortunate accident, it was recorded as."

"But what if someone did hit him?" Jess persisted. "What if it was even someone from round here? Be most likely to be a local too, at night."

"He'd alcohol in him," Marcus said. "I'm not supposed to discuss it. You know that, but anyone around here would know that without being told. Chances are he just stumbled, knocked himself out, couldn't get up. Fell asleep on his bike, even." He helped himself to another biscuit.

"Marcus," Jess said. "What if ... I mean ... what ... I mean ... Kate ..."

"Go on."

A sudden flash of loyalty towards her friend stopped Jess saying what she had meant to say, and instead, she continued with, "What if someone's got a grudge, you know, against the group, for some reason?"

"How do you mean?"

"Did you know that Susan runs Get Slim groups in Ballymaglen and Lambskillen? She's really mad that she didn't get offered this group too."

Chapter Eleven

A Lycra-clad figure splashed dirty puddle-water over Jess as she rounded the bend. The cyclist swerved to avoid ploughing into Jess, who swore loudly as she leapt backwards into the hedge. The bike wobbled as its rider braked, skidding on the wet road; the cyclist dug a heel into the ground and whirled the bike around so he was facing Jess. She swore again as she realised she'd sworn at Father James.

"Shite, Father, sorry. I mean, erm, sorry ..."

He laughed, brushing her apologies aside with a wave of the hand that wasn't straightening the bike. "No, no, Jess, it's me who should be sorry, I nearly ran you down. You're soaked too. I'm so sorry ..." The priest dismounted, and Jess could see that he, too, was sodden, although whether from the rain or from sweat she couldn't be sure. He held out his hand to her and she stepped out of the hedge and back onto the slick wet tarmac.

"I didn't see—"

"I didn't hear—" They both said at the same time.

"You're soaking," Father James said again, dripping water from his dishevelled hair.

"I don't think I'm as drenched as you are. Where are you off to in this weather?" Father James and his bicycle had become a familiar sight around the village since the Get Slim group had started. Kate had been ridiculously over-impressed to have bagged such an important figure of the community. "One of mine, you know—the village priest *and* the school principal *and* Barnabas Bannon too," she was fond of mentioning. Often. Kate was of that upbringing where professions such as teaching were regarded as untouchable, admirable, and worthy of worship, and where the clergy were akin to, well, God himself.

Jess hadn't time for such adorations herself, believing that a profession counted for nothing if the holder of the position was either unpleasant or no good at the job. Jess was particularly unimpressed by the principal of the Ballyfortnum school. It was widely speculated that she had achieved her position only because her father had been principal many years before her, and she was 'one of our own' according to the school Board of Management. That she was bad-tempered and disliked by children and parents alike seemed irrelevant. She was also frumpy and dumpy and, in Jess's view, an entirely suitable candidate for a slimming group.

Jess was no less enamoured by the senator, Barnabas Bannon, who showed up at anything he could, if it gave him hands to shake and votes to garner, so it was no surprise he'd signed up. Jess also wouldn't be surprised if he'd expected free membership, given his perceived stature in the community.

Father James, however, Jess did like.

Father James, young for the priesthood—mid-forties, Jess would guess—had arrived in the parish a few years ago to take over from the decrepit octogenarian predecessor. Kate, of course, knew exactly how old he was, but couldn't share such confidential information as that: "Client confidentiality, you know, but he's not yet fifty ..." she'd say, whenever the subject came up, as it often did. That the priest was young, friendly, and not unattractive had been a topic of great discussion when he had first arrived in the parish. The older parishioners deemed it unsuitable to be lumbered with a young, vibrant priest, and found his jolly manner inappropriate somehow. "Wet behind the ears," they complained to each other. "Doesn't take it seriously." Or, "Ah, sure what could he know, a young whipper-snapper like that?" The younger villagers held the opposing position: "A breath of fresh air," being their usual cliché of choice.

It was widely known among the villagers that Father James was keen on keeping fit even before the group launched, but Kate, of course, was quick to attribute his regular exercise and muscular physique to his association with Get Slim. Jess, however, felt certain his membership was more about the tea and gossip and a show of support and solidarity to his parishioners.

Now, the priest fell into step beside Jess, retracing the way he had already come. "It's too wet to cycle anyway," he said, falling into easy conversation as they walked towards the village. "How are you keeping? It's not been an easy time for you lately, has it?"

It was his job to notice, Jess supposed, and she'd caught him glancing over at her once or twice as she'd bustled around helping Linda to organise things after Bert's death. Father James had presided over Jess's father's funeral too, and although Jess was not a regular churchgoer, she had appreciated the priest's kind and gentle concern and attention as she juggled grief with practical necessities and ceremony.

It was true, of course; it hadn't been an easy time for her. Bert's death had brought all the memories of her dad's death rolling back over her like a cloud of thick fog, threatening to engulf her. The months after George's death had sent Jess spiralling into a dark melancholy. Fortunately, her neighbours had become aware that hidden behind the closed curtains of Number 7 Orchard Close, Jess was suffering. For a while, she barely left the house, except to walk Fletch or head to the shop, offering only short perfunctory greetings and barely looking up as she passed people while out walking.

Fletcher and the neighbours ... Fletch and all those long, long walks, and the kindness of her neighbours: those were the things that saw Jess gradually regaining her naturally buoyant character and getting on with things. George had been her rock in so many ways, and without him, she felt lost and untethered. After her mother left him, Jess and George had become closer, sharing many companionable weekends together.

Of the three of Doreen and George's children, Jess had come to need her father most, and he her. Her brother had moved away down towards Waterford, to build his life with his lovely wife and their two adorable daughters. Although he phoned George now and then, he was too far away, too busy, too married, to come up to Ballyfortnum as often as any of them would have liked.

Their sister, Alice ... well, Alice was Alice. They'd all done what they could, of course, but eventually, her constant relapses had worn them all down. Even Jess's patience had worn thin. Jess still made sure they got together once a month or so, but the differences between the sisters were so great that the meetings were more of a chore than a pleasure. Alice didn't like to come out to the country, and Jess, more comfortable out of the city, was tired of being the one to compromise all the time. Alice's years of self-destruction had worn Jess down and broken her heart.

Jess preferred the sister she remembered from childhood to this un-recognisable woman she had become; she preferred to think of her sister as that lanky, pig-tailed girl that Jess had aspired to catch up with ... an Alice still revered and adored by her baby sister, who had struggled to keep up with the older girl. Alice, five years older, swatting her away like a bothersome fly. Jess, always buzzing after her; small and irritating. Always smaller ...

Until Alice stopped eating. And then, as a teenager, Jess had caught up. By her late teens, Jess had overtaken Alice, and Alice was shrinking away. True, she seemed to have it all under control in the last year or so, but too many years of numerous relapses had put huge stress on all the family—their brother, Eric, away to university in England, a year in Nigeria, and then down south with Belinda and the girls once he'd returned to Ireland; Doreen, away to Spain as soon as her youngest had left home and she was able to shirk off her parental responsibility. Jess—even Jess—had had enough. Wasn't the big sister supposed to be the responsible one? How had it fallen on Jess, the youngest, to be the grown-up? She kicked out at a stone lying in the road and was surprised to hear someone speak.

"Penny for them?" Father James interrupted her reverie, breaking her thoughts into tiny fragments that mingled with the drizzle and drifted away. They had arrived in the village already, and whether they'd walked the last ten minutes in total silence or whether Father James had been talking as they walked, Jess had no recollection.

"Sorry." She offered a sad smile. "I was thinking of Alice."

The priest looked at her with kindness in his eyes and laid a gentle hand on her arm. "Come on over to the house for a cup of tea," he said. "You look like you could use some company for a while. There's scones too; the ladies left some after their meeting this morning." He knew as well as the rest of her neighbours that fresh baking was an offer Jess was unlikely to refuse.

She didn't need asking twice, and a few minutes later she sat at the long refectory table in the Parish House kitchen with a large plate of scones and the related paraphernalia placed down in front of her by Father James's housekeeper.

Mrs Harris had been housekeeper to the vicarage for as long as anyone in the village could remember, and pre-dated Father James by what Mrs Dunne often said seemed like centuries.

Jess helped herself to a large, crumbly scone. She was slathering it with butter and homemade jam by the time a dried-off Father James pulled out the chair opposite, his Lycra cycling gear changed for his more customary jeans, shirt, and clerical collar.

Fletcher lay contentedly under the table at Jess's feet, having already devoured a sausage endowed on him by the housekeeper.

"Don't tell Father—it was meant for his tea," Mrs Harris had warned him with firm words, and a conspiratorial wink aimed at Jess.

Jess picked up the large teapot, topped up her own cup, and filled a cup for Father James. "Thank you," she said, feeling better already. "It must be the rain ... sorry. It's just sometimes ..."

Father James reached across the table and patted her hand. "I know," he said, taking a scone for himself. "After your dad, then Bert; you'd become very close, it's brought it all back. No harm in being sad about the loss of two of the most important people in your life, is there?"

After George died, while Jess came to terms with his loss, she had spent more and more time with Linda and Bert, sitting on their patio, watching Bert potter around in his garden, imparting his green-fingered wisdom to her as she nibbled on whatever delights Linda put in front of her that day. Missing the quiet companionship on a Sunday where she used to curl up on the sofa and spar with her father over which old black-and-white detective film to watch together, she'd instead come to spend many Sunday afternoons in a cosy armchair in Number 15. She'd spend hours chatting with Bert, the two of them bent over the Sunday papers, while Linda bustled in the kitchen.

On good days, they could even complete the crossword without Jess having to resort to Googling for answers while Bert scratched his head with his pen and admitted defeat. She missed them both, her father and Bert, and although the pain of losing her father was no longer constant, the ache in her chest was stronger today, as it had been during the past week or so since the busyness of Bert's funeral had calmed into the emptiness of the subsequent days. *Why did they have to die? Why now; why Bert?*

In the vicarage kitchen, Jess swirled her tea with her spoon, watching the ripples slosh gentle waves towards the rim of the teacup. "Father James, I know you're one of the group, and all that, but ..." Her words tailed off as he laughed at her.

"Which group? I'm in more groups than anyone should be in."

Jess let out the beginnings of an involuntary laugh, but it was cut short as the cloud over her day returned. She followed the train of her thoughts and continued to speak. "Kate's group. The slimming one."

"Oh, that one." He chuckled again. "I only go along for the tea. And to show support, of course. It's been a good social opportunity for some of the parishioners," he said. "Some of them don't get out much, don't really see anyone, get lonely, you know? It's good to see them out and about, having focus."

"So, you think it's good for the village?" Jess asked.

He studied her thoughtfully, his buttery knife poised in his hand and crumbs spilling onto the table. "Well, I must admit, some of them are awfully competitive now. It was more supportive and encouraging in the beginning, but—why do you ask? Are you thinking of joining up?" He passed her another scone and reached for the jam.

"No, no way." Jess looked up into his kind, green-grey eyes, then at her plate. "It's just that ... that ... they're all, well, dying."

Chapter Twelve

"Mm," said Father James, "it is getting a little risky, this slimming business. What with the dangers of cyclists running down pedestrians whilst keeping fit, and elderly people having heart attacks, I can see why you're worried." He winked at her as he got up to make a fresh pot of tea.

Fletcher got to his own four feet, wagging his tail and turning expectant eyes towards Father James as he walked past the fridge.

"Ah, Jess." Father James softened his expression into a more serious one. "People die, love, you know that."

"But it's not just cyclists running people down," Jess said. "What about cyclists being knocked down, too? What about Dave?"

"Ah sure, that was just an accident. Didn't he just fall down and not get up again?"

"Drunk, you mean?" Jess asked. "Yeah, but …"

"I wouldn't say that; we can't be speaking ill of the dead, God rest his soul, but it was an accident."

"But what if it wasn't? What if someone knocked him over?" It was a relief, voicing her concerns aloud, first to Marcus Woo, and now to Father James, but neither of them seemed inclined to take her very seriously. "And

Angela? Aren't you at all concerned that three of the group have died suddenly? Unexpectedly?"

"Ah, Jess." Father James stood at the kitchen sink, the freshly filled teapot heavy in his hand, and looked at her sympathetically. "Bert wasn't well, his heart gave out ... it was his time. God has plans, you know?"

"He wasn't really sick though." Jess was persistent. "I mean, I know he was diabetic, and all that, but his heart was okay. He was okay, I know he was. He walked with me sometimes, he was always busy in the garden, he was *okay*. Linda minded him. He was fine until he started all that diet nonsense." She stared back at Father James's steady gaze, unblinking, until he looked away and sighed.

He placed the hot teapot down on the table and pushed it towards her. "Jess, you know I'm here to talk to you, anytime you feel down. It's been hard for you, I know. But Bert wasn't a young man. Perhaps he just lost a little too much too fast? Maybe added a little strain on his body? Everyone misses him. He was well-loved; you know that. He was a very special man, and we all miss him, but it was his time."

"And Dave? And Angela? They were both so young. Angela has *children*. Was it her time too? What plan would God have for her that was more important than seeing her children grow up?" Jess raised her voice in indignation, stirring her sugarless tea until it slopped onto the table. She rubbed the spill with her sleeve and wiped her eyes with the back of her hand. "It's not fair. And it's strange."

For a while, the only sound in the kitchen was the ticking of the large clock and Fletcher's peaceful breathing. Jess and Father James sipped their tea, each deep in quiet thought.

"Tell me about the group." Jess broke the silence. "Tell me what happens when you meet up. Tell me what Kate is like as a—what does she call herself—a consultant?"

Father James sighed again. "Ah Jess, I'm not one for gossip. Why don't you come along on Tuesday and see for yourself? It's not always the same crowd, you know? Some come every week, some only now and then. We weigh in, drink a cup of tea, that sort of thing. I usually just pop in briefly to make encouraging noises, that's about it, really. Now, tell me, how's Linda getting along? I must call in to her this week." He drained his cup and stood up. "I'd best be getting on, I've to be out again later, house calls, sermons to prepare. You're welcome to sit as long as you like; finish that pot." He glanced out of the window.

Jess followed his gaze. "It's not getting any drier out there. I'd better get home. Thank you for the tea. And the scones, of course." They shared a conspiratorial smile, in guilty acknowledgement of how nice the scones were, and just how few were left on the plate.

"I'd offer you some to take away," he said, "but since we seem to have only left one, I'll be having that with my coffee this evening. There is a limit to what a priest is willing to give to his favourite parishioner, you know." He lifted the plate from the table and held it behind his back, as if to hide it from her.

"Ah fair enough." Jess pretended to brush a tear from her eye, but couldn't hold the fake sadness for long. "I guess you deserve it. Anyway, Linda will be bound to have something to share later. I'm lucky I'm not the size of a small house ... perhaps I should come to the group after all. Don't tell Kate I said that." Jess pushed back her chair, scraping it along the worn wooden floorboards, and got up. "I'd best get moving. I'm going to bring Linda down to the library this afternoon."

Linda had mentioned how hard it would be for her to visit the library without Bert. She loved her three-weekly trips to the cosy library in the nearby small town of Ballymaglen, but this would be the first time she would go without Bert, and the thought of returning his last selection of borrowed books had brought a fresh pool of tears to her eyes. It would be the smallest of things, Jess knew, that would trigger the saddest memories.

She remembered opening a Poirot novel not long after her own father had died, to find a scrap of paper marking a page. It bore her father's neat handwriting listing carrots, tea bags, and toilet paper. She'd kept the scrap for a long time, until she realised that her father's memory would remain in the pages of all the detective novels on the bookcase, whether she kept his shopping list or not.

She smiled wistfully at the memory of climbing onto his lap as a young child, as he read her the pages of a Jupiter Jones story. He'd balked at reading from her Nancy Drew collection, not wanting to read a 'girly' book. George O'Malley had been a little old-fashioned in many ways, but his youngest daughter had certainly inherited his own love of those old mysteries ... in her blood, they'd say, laughing together.

Those books her dad had introduced her to instigated so many of Jess's childhood memories; the hours of games with Eric, where they would go off 'snooping', spying on unsuspecting neighbours from the high-up branches of trees they climbed, or using their dad's old bird-watching binoculars to gaze into gardens and living rooms.

Thinking of the old mysteries she'd loved so much, Jess said her good-byes to Father James, pulled on her coat, and walked back towards Orchard

Close with fresh resolve. Were the deaths of Kate's Get Slim group a mystery to solve? Was there a connection? Jess pulled her hood up against the rain, tucked her hair under the fabric, and strode down the church drive.

Fletcher wagged his tail and trotted beside her, sensing her energy and walking in a sensible, non-pulling way for once. Jess would get home, grab a quick lunch, then collect Linda as arranged, and while she was waiting for Linda to select her new books, she would see if she could locate any newspaper reports about Dave's death.

Chapter Thirteen

T he library was cool and quiet; its air of musty stillness disturbed only
by the hum of a couple of computers at the desks in the corner by
the long picture window.

Linda, left to browse in the large print and Irish romance sections, would
be a while.

The librarian provided the access codes for the papers from the week of
Dave's death, and Jess selected an empty computer station away from those
already. She leaned back in the battered, vinyl chair and closed her eyes for
a moment, waiting for the computer to whir into life. Unsure as to what
exactly she was looking for, Jess was certain she was, at least, looking for
something.

For a few moments, she became distracted by the other trivia of that
week back in January—sales adverts for the shops in town and the dai-
ly headlines. These told everything an outsider needed to know about
small-town Ireland. Some of the front-page grabbers included an article about a burst frozen pipe necessitating the installation of temporary
standpipes in one of the housing estates; an extension plan for the local
swimming pool, and a good-news story about a dog reunited with its owner
after being missing for six months.

She scrolled through the pages until she found the births, marriages, and death notices. Beginning with the day after Dave's body was found, Jess trawled each file from that date until a fortnight after his death, but aside from noticing a colleague from her old workplace welcomed a new baby boy that week, there was nothing of interest in the columns. Weird how fast she'd lost touch with her old work colleagues, except for Kate, of course ... She suspected Kate kept in touch with a few of them still, for drinks on a Friday night; that sort of thing.

Jess gave the computer a wry smile as she realised she would become as much of a hermit as Dave at this rate, no one caring enough to list her death in the local papers. She sighed and leaned back into the chair again, before jolting upright with a start as she felt a hand on her shoulder.

"Sorry, I didn't mean to startle you." Elizabeth was standing behind her, a pile of books balanced in her free arm. "How are you? We haven't seen you out with Fletcher lately."

Jess smiled. "No, we've missed you too," she agreed. "Fletch has missed seeing his friends. We must have been out at different times the last few days, trying to dodge the rain. And not very successfully, to be honest." She laughed and Elizabeth nodded in sympathy. "How are you?"

"I'm grand, nothing much to report. Henry's been busy in the garden."

Henry was Elizabeth's husband, a quiet, jocular man, who Jess didn't know particularly well, but who always had a quick smile and a kind word for Fletcher whenever they passed him by. Whether he was cutting the grass, or sweeping leaves from the driveway, or washing one of the cars when Jess walked past, he would stop what he was doing, tip an imaginary cap to her, and say the same thing: "Who's a mighty handsome dog then?" before carrying on with whatever task was doing.

Elizabeth peered over Jess's shoulder at the computer screen. "Research?" she asked before turning her attention to the pile of books she clutched. "I've a book here you might like." Elizabeth pulled a new mystery novel out of the middle of her pile, showing it to Jess. "Have you read this one?"

It was well-known around the village that Jess O'Malley, like her father, was a mystery-novel fanatic. Most of the neighbours had known her father well and he had been forever talking about his children and their interests. George's own past career as a forensic scientist in Dublin, and across the UK before that, had been a favourite topic of conversation amongst his friends, and his love of mystery and work-related stories were renowned in the pub and amongst his bowling friends. That his younger daughter had continued the interest in crime, although not his career path, was no great surprise to anyone who had known them and seen the close bond between them.

"I'll reserve it, get hold of it once you've returned it." Jess smiled. "Meanwhile, I've a mystery of my own to solve." She gestured at the computer screen. "I'm trying to find out more about Dave's accident. There's not much to find in the papers though. Not even a death notice. I guess he had no family?"

Elizabeth put her books in a neat stack on the table and bent to squint at the screen. "No," she agreed, "he had no family here, poor lad. His mother's in a home somewhere I think." She pointed to a name in the obituary column. "I knew that man though. He died the day before Dave. I was at his removal that day, while poor Dave was lying dead in the ditch."

"What time did you get home?" Jess asked, suddenly wondering whether Elizabeth could have seen anything suspicious as she drove home that night. "Did you pass anyone; notice anything? Do you think he was already there when you drove by?"

Elizabeth shuddered. "I try not to think of it. I think we would have noticed him, wouldn't we? I keep thinking maybe we could have done something, saved him, stopped it, maybe we passed him ... what if he was there, when we passed, and we could've done something?" She sank onto the chair at the computer station next to Jess, who reached out and put her hand on Elizabeth's arm.

"No one seems to really know what happened, though. No one really knows what time he died, or when he fell, or how long ..." Seeing Elizabeth's face creased in fresh worry, Jess didn't finish the sentence. As she noticed her friend's expression, the most pressing question in her mind was to find out what time Dave had died—or, more importantly, what time he had fallen into the ditch. And, had he really just fallen, in his drunken state, or slipped on the icy road—tipped off his bike in the dark—or had a passing car knocked him into the ditch? Her mouth fell open as she realised with a cold shiver that Elizabeth could even have been the one to knock him down.

"We?" she asked Elizabeth. "You said you were with someone when you drove home that night? You and Henry, do you mean?"

"Yes. Henry was driving. He always does, when we go out together."

Jess repeated her earlier question, "What time did you come home that night?"

"Oh, it must have been around seven, I should think. Must have been about then, because I wanted to have time to change before slimming group. And I would have got down there before quarter to eight—any later than that and we wouldn't bother to go. Any later than quarter to and there's not time for weighing *and* a cup of tea and a chat with the others.

That was the night we got the stew recipe; I remember because it was cold and icy, and Kate was talking about warming recipes for winter nights. I've a copy of the recipe, I'll drop it round to you, you could make it up for yourself, put portions in the freezer for convenience?"

Jess nodded, although she wasn't a big fan of stew, nor did she like being reminded that she lived off meals-for-one these days. Still, Elizabeth's eyes were kind, and Jess knew she meant well. Of course Elizabeth hadn't killed Dave; she wouldn't harm a fly … would she? She turned back to the screen and typed Dave's name and 'ditch death' into the search bar.

Elizabeth gathered up her pile of library books. "You take care of yourself now, dear," she said. "Don't be fussing yourself over this now, sure, wasn't it just an unfortunate accident, God bless him?" Elizabeth carried her books to the check-out counter.

Jess turned her focus back to her search results to see a small news article displayed on the screen.

It had little more detail than Jess already knew: *An as yet unnamed body of a young man, thought to be local, has been found in a ditch just outside Ballyfortnum village. Anyone who may be able to offer information should please contact the Gardai at Lambskillen Garda station.* It gave the phone number of the station, but that was all. The article was from the day after the body was found, but further searches produced no more information, save for a mention in the local village notes section a few days after to express *regret on the passing of Dave Green, Ballyfortnum village, may he rest in peace; funeral details below.*

"Contact the Gardai," Jess read aloud to herself, "… contact the police." Marcus. She'd ask Marcus about it. She closed the windows on the computer, shut down the machine, and went in search of Linda, who she found sitting on a stained brown leather sofa in the Hobbies section, a book on roses open in her lap, and tears in her eyes.

Jess perched on the arm of the sofa and put her arm around Linda. "C'mon, love, let's get home?" She gave Linda a squeeze, and glanced at the picture on the open page. "They are beautiful, aren't they, but not a patch on Bert's."

The two smiled sadly at each other, then Jess lifted the book from Linda's lap, closed it, and set it on the little glass-topped table. She held out her hand to Linda, helping her up.

"Let's get home," she said again; not a question this time. She picked up Linda's books, and together they walked to the counter to check them out.

Chapter Fourteen

It was a Get Slim evening in Ballyfortnum. Kate, as had become usual, called in on her way to set up the class. She was hanging out of Jess's patio doors with her cigarette dropping ash onto the paving slabs.

Jess leaned against the kitchen counter; her hands wrapped around a steaming cup of coffee. She lifted it to her face and inhaled, enjoying the aroma of the strong, black liquid that was still too hot to drink.

Kate stretched out her leg, skinny in black leggings, and ground the stub of her cigarette out under the sole of her Louboutin. She pulled her leg back inside and slid the door shut. "Of *course* I knew about his diabetes." She glared at Jess. "I am a professional. We have standards. Guidelines. There is a checklist that every new member has to go through including a *rigorous* health questionnaire." She yanked open the clasp of her handbag and twisted the top off her sweeteners with a vigour that sent Jess cringing backwards into the counter. "Sometimes I think you *want* me to fail at this! I love this group. This is my *vocation*."

Jess bit back a laugh at the force with which Kate spat out her defence.

"I'm really good at this job," Kate continued. "My members respect me and count on me." She sat, stirred in the tablets, and tipped the container back into her open bag.

"Defensive, much?" Jess said. "I only said I wondered if you'd known. I know he wasn't always willing to admit to his condition, didn't want people knowing his personal business." She sat opposite Kate. "Kate," she said, holding her friend's gaze, "doesn't it worry you that three of them are dead?"

"Yes." Coffee sloshed over the edge of Kate's mug as she stirred. "Yes, of course it concerns me. Three of my clients have passed away in a really short time, and my numbers are down, and if this gets out, then people will stop coming. I haven't had any new members sign up since Bert died. Of course I'm worried."

Jess sighed. There really was no point in spelling out to Kate that it was not her client numbers that were Jess's biggest concern. Sometimes her friend could be so exasperating. She tried another tack. "Was there anything ... well ... odd? I mean, did they have anything in common, except the group and living round here? Any connecting interests, shared recipes, fabulous dieting tips? Anything like that?"

Kate shrugged. "Anything in common? Don't think so, nothing I'd noticed. They were all doing well. Bert had lost loads." She glanced at Jess again. "Yeah, maybe a little more than he should've, given his condition, but that wasn't my fault, I told him he was well on target, but he kept going over it, losing more. He'd been Slimmer of the Week a few times. He was doing so well. Proud of him, we were, in the group. He was a star."

She took a swig of her coffee. "Come to think of it, so was Angela. She was nominated for Slimmer of the Year last year, too. The group was right proud of her, too."

Jess remembered something Kate had mentioned a while back, about Dave. Hadn't she also said he'd been given some accolade or another, not long after he'd joined up?

"Doesn't everyone get Slimmer of the Week at some point?" she asked.

"God, no." Kate was indignant. "They have to earn it. I don't award it to just anyone. That would undermine the whole concept. They have to deserve it."

"Do you still have a good turnout every week?" Jess asked.

Kate picked the teaspoon off the table and stirred the dregs of her coffee. She stared into the mug as the rhythmic clonking of spoon against china reverberated into the quiet room while Jess waited for Kate's answer.

"Yeah, it's going really well," she said to the table after a pause. In the early days, when the group had started, Kate was full of enthusiasm, counting numbers, gleefully sharing every new member joining up: "four more last night," "another six today," "two more of your neighbours—can't say who ... client confidentiality—but you definitely know these two."

She reported back after every meeting for the first couple of months. Lately though, she was quieter, less inclined to gloat over numbers, and Jess suspected the group had gone the same way as anything new in this village. People were always interested—nosey—in the beginning. They couldn't resist trying out whatever was new, afraid to miss out on something to gossip about, but many would never stick at anything for longer than the first few sessions. Jess could guess the names of a handful of committed members, but was equally willing to bet on those who'd shown up to the earliest sessions, brimming with intentions and enthusiasm but fallen by the wayside as soon as they'd opened the first box of Christmas biscuits. Plus, of course, those who'd literally fallen by the wayside—Dave—and those who would not hurry back once a few of their friends gave it up. Jess suspected the group was not as viable or buoyant as Kate had hoped it would be, but she also knew her friend would not admit defeat in a hurry.

Fletcher whined and scratched at the door as Kate looked up at the clock on the kitchen wall.

"How does he know?" she asked Jess. "How does he always know when it's time to go over to the hall and set up?" She called the Labrador to her and caressed his silky ears.

Jess stood and unhooked her coat from the back of a chair. She picked up Fletcher's lead from where it lay on the door mat, discarded carelessly after their last walk. "He knows it's walk time, once you have to go." She beamed at her dog like a mother with a newborn child. "He's very smart, for a daft dog." She patted his flank and clipped the lead to his collar. "C'mon then. I'm hoping to bump into Marcus tonight."

Kate looked up in surprise. "Marcus? The Garda? What for? You kept that quiet. Bit old for you, isn't he?"

Heat crawled up Jess's neck, tingeing her cheeks as it spread across her face. "Not at all," she protested. "It's nothing like that. I want to pick his brains about something, is all."

"Yeah right. It's about time you met someone." Kate stood too, and shrugged into her coat.

Jess and Fletcher walked Kate to her car, shoving the driver door shut for her once she'd settled into the seat. By the time Kate had reversed out of Jess's driveway, Fletcher was already sniffing the hedge at Number 3.

Kate tooted her horn as she passed, and crossed from the entrance of Orchard Close to the village hall car park without stopping.

By the time Jess reached the end of Orchard Close, Kate already unpacking boxes from the boot, her car skewed across the doorway of the hall. Jess waved at her across the car park, but rather than helping, entered the playing field by the road gate, squinting across the dark football pitch in the hope of spotting Marcus.

Fletch's pricked-up ears and excited wagging told her that he was also looking out for his own new friend. With better eyesight—or perhaps a better sense of smell—than his mistress, he yapped in excitement, tugged on his lead, and dragged Jess towards the furthest corner of the park.

Peering into the greyness spilling beyond the bright patches under the lights, she saw only the blurriest of figures moving around the path, and was unable to make out who Fletcher pulled her to meet.

Chapter Fifteen

Fletcher yanked at Jess's arm, and they set off at a faster pace than Jess was ready for, towards the darker end of the park, away from the streetlights of the road and the car park. The lights around the park were dimmer than those on the road, and every now and then a bulb was out, leaving most of the track in charcoal-darkness. The first indistinct figures emerged from the night into a pool of washy light. Breda and Elizabeth; dressed in jogging bottoms and doing what Jess could only presume to be an attempt at power-walking.

They stopped as Jess approached, Breda puffing a little, Elizabeth not so much. Both looked pleased for the excuse of stopping for a breather.

Elizabeth stooped to make a fuss of Fletcher.

Breda bent just to pant, hands resting on her thighs, as she caught her breath.

"We're just getting in a few laps before weigh-in," Elizabeth explained before turning her attention back to Fletcher to tell him that their dogs were not allowed to attend class and were shut up at home dreaming of cats and bones.

"We've done three already," said Breda, still puffing.

"How's it going?" Jess nodded in the direction of the lit-up village hall, asking more from politeness than real interest. She couldn't contemplate anyone choosing to do three circuits of the park for fun—she only walked here when it was too dark to walk anywhere more interesting, like the flower-filled farm tracks or the lonely stretches of bogland where she would lose herself among the bleak landscape to a backdrop of birdsong and heather.

Elizabeth straightened, giving Fletcher's flank one last pat as she did so. She smiled in the dim light of the park. "Very well," she said, the pink tinge to her face apparent even in the dimness. "I've lost three pounds this week. I'm delighted. The walking is paying off ... and the eating more sensibly." She grimaced. "I do miss my morning biscuits, though."

Breda looked guilty under the park light. "I had two Custard Creams with my morning coffee. It's bloody hard work, this slimming." Even in the near-dark, an obvious frown creased Breda's features. Elizabeth was a lot trimmer these days, but Breda most certainly was not.

"Better go and face it," Breda said. "See who's doing well this week." There was an edge of bitterness in her voice.

Jess grimaced in sympathy.

The two women turned away to continue towards the hall—or perhaps to walk another lap. Jess hoped for Breda's sake that this was indeed their final lap and that a cup of tea and a sit-down was within her grasp.

"Nothing wrong with a couple of Custard Creams," she said to their departing backs. "In fact, I had a Jaffa Cake or three myself this morning. I shouldn't, I know, but ... you know ... a Jaffa Cake is a Jaffa Cake, and when a Jaffa Cake calls you ..."

Breda paused and grinned over her shoulder at Jess.

Jess waved, smiling back. "See you later. Come on Fletch." She walked on, away from the hall and its weighing scales and diet magazines and disgusting, cardboard-flavour Get Slim bars.

Elizabeth and Breda continued in the opposite direction, towards the hall, one of them with more spring in her step than the other.

Fletcher, no longer distracted by Breda and Elizabeth, yanked on his lead again, sniffing at all the delightful park smells as he pulled Jess onwards.

A dog yapped somewhere ahead of them, hidden by the gloom.

The owner of the dog was not Marcus, but a man Jess didn't recognize, walking a rather handsome Dalmatian. The two dogs stopped to greet each other as if they were old friends, sniffing and fawning and wagging.

"Hello," said the stranger. "Just walking the dog while the wife gets weighed." He flapped a hand in the direction of the hall. "Nonsense, if you ask me. I'd far rather she stayed a little curvier and a lot less fussy about how many roast potatoes I'm allowed with my Sunday roast."

Jess laughed. "I know! Who has the discipline to cut down on roast potatoes? Not me for sure. It's always nice to meet an ally."

"Have you ever tried that diet gravy muck? Vile watery liquid, I'll tell you for nothing. I'll waste away while she gets this slimming nonsense out of her system."

"Don't hold with it much myself either," Jess agreed. "A girl's got to eat, and where's the fun in crap-tasting food?"

The Dalmatian owner looked at her appraisingly. "Aye," he said, "you're a sensible lass all right." He rubbed Fletcher's head. "Bye now." He raised his hand in farewell and pulled his spotted dog away.

As they parted ways, the man still whittering about gravy, Jess chuckled into her scarf; her thoughts turned to imagining ways that she could engineer a meeting with Marcus. She could call him, she supposed, but she still wasn't entirely sure what she wanted to ask him. Besides, she suspected that whatever it was she wanted to know, he wouldn't want to volunteer. An accidental meeting would be preferable, so she could strike up a casual conversation and slip in a few questions innocently. She'd better walk down the village again in the morning ... What with him living almost opposite the shop, she'd have more chance of seeing him, or at least she could ask Mrs Dunne if she knew what times he came and went. Mrs Dunne *would* know. She knew everything about everyone, and never minded a bit of idle gossip.

Jess and Fletcher finished the circuit of the park, crossed the road into Orchard Close and towards home. As they walked along the quiet cul-de-sac, she considered what it was she really needed to discover, relaying her mental checklist to Fletcher. "Food. What poisoned Angela, Fletch? Did Dave eat anything dodgy too, do you reckon? Was there a postmortem thingy I wonder? There'd have to be, wouldn't there, what with him dying suddenly? Suspiciously, eh Fletch?"

Fletch cocked his leg against a lamp post and didn't bother to look at her.

"They do postmortems for sudden death, don't they? What about Bert? Was it really just a heart attack? Why Bert, Fletch, why Bert?"

When her voice quietened with sadness, Fletcher looked up at his mistress, nuzzling his wet nose into her hand as they strolled up the path to the blue front door of Number 7.

Jess unlocked the door, kicked off her boots, hung Fletcher's lead on the door handle, and strode straight to the kitchen to open a bottle of wine.

Wine glass in one hand, the open bottle in the other, she slumped onto the sofa and flicked on the television. Jess skimmed through the channels, sipping her wine, catching a few minutes here and there of quiz shows, which she lingered on long enough to note she'd seen them before, or news, which she skipped away from.

Finding little to snag her interest, her thoughts drifted to her dad, her sister, and the happier days of her childhood when her parents had been together, when Alice had still eaten with the rest of the family, and when the most they ever worried about was which book to read next. She refilled her glass and settled on an old favourite, a Miss Marple—*The 3.05 to Paddington*—which was only a few minutes in. When the first advert break came on, she picked up her phone to call her brother, but instead of pulling up his number, she composed a text to Marcus.

Hi Marcus, sorry, it's me, Jess. I don't want to bother you but I'm still worried there's something weird going on with the Slimming Group. Can I ask you something? As soon as she hit SEND, she wished she hadn't. He would think she was unhinged. She shoved the phone down the side of the sofa cushion, but the damage was done. She covered her face with her hands and sighed.

Alerted by the sound, Fletcher climbed into her lap.

Jess stretched down to pluck the wine bottle off the floor, almost tipping off the sofa as she held her glass, tried not to dislodge the dog, and grabbed at the neck of the bottle. Righting herself, she poured herself a generous glassful, balanced the bottle on the arm of the sofa, and fumbled between the sofa cushions to retrieve her phone. She wouldn't let the embarrassment of one unfortunate not-even-drunk text worry her tonight. She turned it off and tossed it onto the other sofa, out of reach and temptation.

With another deep sigh, Jess dragged her attention back to the mystery unfolding on the television screen. She had seen it many times before, but still enjoyed spotting the subtlest of clues that Miss Marple would piece together with ease. "We need Miss Marple, Fletch. We need Miss Marple here in Ballyfortnum."

Chapter Sixteen

J ess needed a distraction. She was overreacting, worrying too much about a connection she was probably imagining. She groped for her phone, silencing the alarm with a groan, and pulled herself out of bed. She would paint the kitchen today. She'd wanted to do it for ages, even before her dad died. A cheery, sunny yellow, to brighten it up and catch the morning sun. That would do. She would get herself up and at it, turn the radio up loud, and blow away some cobwebs.

Her stomach flipped as she reached for her phone, suddenly remembering her late-night text to Marcus. Her face burned at the thought, and instead of checking her phone for messages, she stumbled into the bathroom and turned on the shower.

Wet hair soaking a damp patch through the back of her T-shirt, she took her coffee outside to the patio. The warmth of the morning sun was a pleasant change after the run of grey they'd had through most of March so far. With the patio chairs still damp from overnight rain, she stood instead, teetering on the edge of the patio slabs. She turned her face to the welcome glow of the sun, closed her eyes, and inhaled the morning. Perhaps spring was finally on its way. It was definitely a good day to update the kitchen.

She opened her eyes and looked around the neglected garden. Who would help her with it now Bert was gone too? New shoots poked through the mulch with pointed determination and a promise of the green that would soon fill the garden. Crocuses? Snowdrops? She had absolutely no idea. Without her dad or Bert around to tell her, she must make it her mission to find out for herself. She straightened, stretching her back and enjoying the pull of muscles as she tightened her stomach. She put her coffee on the table and spread her arms wide, flexing her fingers, clasping at the new day and her new resolve. "Time to take charge, Jess. Time to take charge."

Fletcher cocked his head to the side, grinning a doggy grin as Jess picked up his tennis ball and tossed it away down the garden for him to chase.

"Right, Fletch, let's do this thing." She pulled the slobbery ball from his mouth and threw it again. "You'll have to wait for your walk; I'm going to buy paint." She threw the ball a few more times before gathering up her keys, her coat, and her purse, and heading out to her car. She shifted the car into gear and shunted out of the driveway, while Fletcher gazed after her from his vantage point on the back of the sofa in the bay window.

It wasn't until she was in the car and at the junction signalling to pull out of Orchard Close that she realised she hadn't picked up her phone, never mind checked it for messages.

"If he didn't already think I've lost the plot, he will now I've not even replied to his reply," Jess told her reflection in the rear-view mirror, ignoring the voice in her head reminding her that she didn't know if he had answered her yet anyway. "Ah well." She shifted into second gear and pulled out into the main street, driving out through the village and onwards to Lambskillen.

In the paint shop, Jess was browsing through swatches of fancy wallpapers and contemplating whether she should try her hand at hanging paper instead of just slapping paint onto the walls when someone spoke her name.

"Jess?"

She spun around to face Angela's husband Niall, and their teenage daughter.

"Niall, Harriet, hello. Great to see you." She hadn't seen much of them since Angela's funeral, only popping round a couple of times in the immediate aftermath. After that, not wanting to intrude, and then side-tracked by Bert's death, she'd left them to their grief. She hadn't seen them at Bert's wake, and suspected if they had attended his funeral they'd have lingered towards the back of the crowded church. They'd have wanted a hasty exit after the service rather than having to deal with talking to another crowd of mourners offering endless sympathy. All that small talk that was meant to give comfort, but didn't even scratch the surface. "How are you both? How are you bearing up?"

Harriet's polite smile didn't lighten her eyes. The shadows of sorrow were still evident, and the girl was thinner than Jess remembered her being the last time she had seen her. Jess had known Harriet since the girl was about nine or ten, and had babysat her from time to time.

Harriet had always been a tall, lanky child, but now, just on the brink of blossoming into adulthood, she was pale and drawn. She still had braces on her teeth.

Jess ached with the realisation Angela would never get to see her daughter's straightened smile.

"We decided to finish painting the sunroom," Harriet said. "It's the room she loved most, and we decided we should finish it for her—she'd just started it before …"

Jess smiled. "That's a nice idea. What colour had she chosen?"

They made small talk for a few moments more, and then Harriet noticed the swatches Jess was rifling through. "Ooh," she said, with a hint of enthusiasm creeping into her voice, "That one is beautiful—are you getting that?" Harriet moved nearer to Jess and leafed through the next few pages of the sample book.

"She's still planning on being an interior designer," Niall told Jess, smiling at Harriet with undisguised affection. "Aren't you, love?"

Harriet flipped through the wallpaper samples, murmuring approval now and then.

Jess could see a glimpse of the child she had been just a few months ago, when she was making plans for college and her mother was alive and the future was mapped out ahead of her. A sudden rush of anger bubbled in Jess's throat and she ducked her head over the sample book to hide the welling tears. How could it ever be fair that this poor girl had her mother ripped away from her? Jess's earlier resolve to put aside her worries evaporated.

She turned to Niall, moved a little further away from Harriet, ensuring the girl wouldn't hear. "Niall … do you wonder about the fact that Angela and Dave and Bert all died so close together?"

Niall jerked his chin upwards, to meet Jess's eyes. He opened his mouth to speak, then closed it again without words forming. "Well," he said finally, "I can't say I'd thought about it, to be honest. Why?"

It was Jess's turn to open her mouth, close it again, and then begin again. "I don't know. It's just …" She shrugged, pausing to search his eyes, looking for permission to go on.

He nodded; a tiny movement of his head that she would have missed had she not been watching him.

"It's just a niggling feeling I can't quite shift. I'm sorry. I know it's still so painful for you." She turned her gaze from Niall and stepped closer to Harriet to peer over the teenager's shoulder as she flipped through the wallpaper samples. "Did you find anything nice? I want to cheer up my kitchen. I was going to just paint it in a nice sunny yellow, but now I'm wondering if I'm brave enough to try wallpaper … just for the back wall where the table goes? What do you think?"

They turned a few more pages, browsing together. Some of the samples flaunted traditional florals or stripes; some were more unusual, featuring animals, shells, abstract patterns, and …

"Prawns?" Jess said, raising her eyebrows. "Who would think to put prawns on wallpaper, for goodness sake?"

"Not me anyway." Harriet shuddered, a dark cloud crossing her face. "Mam made seafood the day she … it was the last …"

"Oh, Harriet!" Jess clamped a hand over her mouth. "Harriet, I'm so sorry! My big mouth … I'm so sorry." A prickle of embarrassment crept up her neck, but Harriet giggled. It was only a brief burst of uncontained laughter, over as fast as it had come, but left a wan smile on her face.

"It's okay," she said. "It is pretty funny to have prawns on wallpaper, but I reckon Mam would've loved it. She was going through a seafood phase since joining that Get Slim club. There were a bunch of recipes in the magazine thing, and they were all at it. You'd think no one had ever heard of eating seafood before that. I came home one night and there were a load of the women, all sat in the kitchen, talking about prawns as if they were the newest invention in sweets. Mad, they were, all of them. They were talking about new recipes and stuff, but they were all giggling like kids. Worse than my friends, they were. It was one of them women that brought the bag of stuff around that she cooked—" Harriet swung her face back to the book. She traced her fingers over the pattern and her eyes filled with tears.

Jess put her hand on Harriet's back and rubbed in gentle circles. "Oh, sweetheart," she said, "it's so difficult, and my heart is broken for you. I miss my dad every day, still, but it will get easier. It will. I promise you." She pulled the girl into her arms and hugged her tightly. Over Harriet's blonde head, she caught Niall's eye and mouthed, "Sorry."

"Tell you what," she said into Harriet's hair, "you can come and help me do my kitchen if you like? Practice for your course. We can learn how to hang wallpaper together, and if it goes wrong—wonky or wrinkly—I'll have someone to blame."

Harriet sniffed. "If it goes well," she said, with only a small tremor left in her voice, "you can give me *all* the credit. You can pay me, even." She gave Jess a watery smile and wiped her eyes on the back of her hand. "Text me when you've chosen what you want, and I'll come and splatter glue all over your kitchen for you."

Niall held up the two cans of paint he had been holding throughout their meeting. "Okay you two, that's enough about wallpaper. If I stand here much longer holding these, my arms will give out. Let's get home and get cracking. See you around Jess."

Jess gave Harriet another quick hug, and they were gone, leaving Jess to make her selection and wonder about who had given Angela the bag of seafood that had killed her.

Chapter Seventeen

J ess surveyed the rolls of wallpaper and assorted decorating paraphernalia that lay across her kitchen floor where she had dumped it. Now
the shopping part was over, she regretted her hasty decision to buy the
wallpaper. A quick coat of paint would have been easy, but this ... she had
never even helped her dad to tackle wallpaper before and had no clue where
to begin.

With the kettle, Jess. She switched it on, then ran upstairs to retrieve
her phone. She would text Harriet—perhaps the girl really would like to
help, and they could work it out together, this papering lark. Perhaps the
enthusiasm of a seventeen-year-old art student would carry them through
the project, overriding the lack of experience and DIY skills that may let
them down.

Her phone beeped into life, bearing a barrage of notifications and reminding her that she had yet to see if Marcus had answered her text from
the night before, but the first three messages were all from Kate. The last
of the three to be sent—the first Jess had opened—said, *oh bugger it, I'm
sure you are there really, I'm on the way.* Jess didn't bother to read the other
two but scrolled on down. She was certain whatever drama Kate was about
to drop on her would be regaled in great detail at the kitchen table very

soon, so there was no point reading the messages first. She'd missed a call from Alice too—*You have one new voicemail*. She ignored that one as well. If she stopped to call Alice it would dampen her mood for the rest of the day. Alice could wait. The fifth notification was a text from Marcus—*Sure Jess, what's up?*—and suddenly, with that short answer and question, she felt it all rushing back—Dave, dead. Angela, dead. Bert, dead. And her dad, too. If the three latest deaths were connected somehow, it would be a good idea for someone to find that connection and stop it from happening to anyone else. Too many people in Jess's life had died lately, and she didn't think she could handle any more funerals for a long time. True, she hadn't really known Dave, but nonetheless, he was still a neighbour and his sudden death had shocked the community.

Sure, she'd only met Marcus very recently, but he was fast becoming a friend—she already liked his easy company and calm manner—and in his position, he had to take an interest in local affairs, didn't he? She'd pick his brains after all and not feel bad about it. What's a policeman for if not to allay neighbourhood fears? And crime—is that what this might be? A crime?

Despite the increasing feeling that something weird was going on, she hadn't considered there might actually be a *crime*. She gazed at Marcus's text, running her thumb across the screen every time it faded, to keep it from closing. She was sure there was a link between the deaths. And she thought something dodgy was going on, so ... then ... wasn't she also concluding that someone was *causing* the deaths? Ballyfortnum was usually such a sleepy village; surely there couldn't be a killer in their midst ... could there? Jess spun the phone around in her hands, while she considered what to say to Marcus. She walked slowly back down the stairs, jiggling the phone from hand to hand.

She poured herself a cup of coffee, decided what to say, and stirred the granules for far longer than necessary while tapping out, *Are you any good at hanging wallpaper?*

As she hit SEND, Fletcher barked and ran to the front door, feet scrabbling on the wooden laminate of the hall floor.

The latch of the door clicked and Kate shouted, "Get down, you brat. Get down!"

Jess groaned and padded towards the hall. "Hiya, what's up? Get down Fletch, come here." Fletch, too delighted to see Kate, took no notice. Jess grabbed his collar and hauled him off, pushing his rear end down to make him sit.

Kate, always a pushover for Fletcher's sorrowful chocolate eyes, acquiesced to his woeful expression and squatted down to rub his ears. "All right, Fletch, all right. Anyone would think you hadn't seen me in ages." She pushed him off and stood up. "Kettle on?" she asked, heading for the kitchen. "Wow." She stopped just inside the kitchen doorway. "What are you at? Looks like you went a bit mad. Do you even know how to do wallpaper?"

Jess bristled. A lie slipped easily from her mouth that she instantly wished she could retrieve. "Yeah, 'course! Done it loads of times, with my dad, loads of times. Dead easy it is." Oh shite. Now she'd really have to make a good job of it. She shoved the scattered brushes and paint trays and wallpaper paste along to the end of the table and pushed the paint cans and paper rolls against the wall with her foot. "Coffee?" she asked, already spooning granules into a mug. "So, go on, what's up?"

"Me and Decko ... Hang on a sec." She rooted in her bag and extracted the familiar white tube of sweeteners and her packet of cigarettes, then scrabbled around some more until she found her lighter. She set them on the table in a neat row. "You know we've been ... we haven't been getting on so well lately, since I chucked in the job and started up my own business?"

Jess turned away and stirred Kate's coffee so she could hide her smile. It amused her to hear Kate call a couple of slimming classes a week a 'business' but she knew Kate aspired to gain more groups and build her franchise.

"And then this morning he told me I'm not doing enough, and I should go back to my other job, and you know how shite that was and how much we hated it, and he says it's a waste of my time and he doesn't take it seriously at all, the gobshite." Kate pushed open the French doors and lit a cigarette.

Jess crossed the kitchen and stepped outside, holding Kate's coffee out to her. "Hmm," she said, shuffling her feet on the cool patio slabs, "it's not as warm as it looks, hang on." She went back inside, stuffed her feet into her slippers, and grabbed the kitchen towel before stepping out again. "Here, sit down." She wiped the dampness off a couple of the patio chairs, gestured to one, and sat on the other.

"I expect he's just concerned," she said. "I'm sure he does take it serious-ly. He knows how much you hated working in the office." Jess didn't really believe that. Declan, in her unvoiced opinions, was an idiot. He was a city boy who hadn't taken well to living in the sticks, as he referred to the tiny hamlet of Little Mason where he and Kate lived.

Declan commuted to Dublin on the early train every morning and expected his dinner on the table when he arrived home in the evenings, now Kate wasn't "working." Jess had only met Declan a handful of times, on rare occasions when she had called at Kate's house on a weekend, or if she'd still been sat at Kate's kitchen table drinking coffee and solving the world's problems in an evening when he'd arrived home. But lately, Jess had little reason to go to Kate's. Now Kate had the group, she was in

Ballyfortnum every week, making it far more likely for Kate to be in Jess's kitchen drinking Jess's coffee than the other way around.

Kate rolled her eyes and lit a new cigarette from the burning stub of the first, tossed the spent one to the paving slabs and ground the ball of her boot into it as if she were killing a wasp that had already stung her.

"He never took it seriously," she said without taking the cigarette from her mouth. "Never." Her gritted teeth clamping the cigarette made the word come out with a viciousness Jess had not heard from Kate in a long time. Not since she'd confided in Jess about an office affair that had ended abruptly some years back. In fact, that was how they had become friends—Kate had been out the back of the office building, a cup of cold coffee in one hand and a burning but unsmoked cigarette hanging between the fingers of her other hand. A fragile column of burned ash had dangled threateningly over Kate's leg as she slumped on the stoop in the bright sunshine. Jess had noticed the ash, and that it would surely fall, before she noticed how Kate's makeup streaked dirty pathways down her face, and that under the black lines, her face was as grey as the cigarette ash.

Until that day, she only vaguely knew Kate as a colleague who worked somewhere in the same building. They sometimes chatted over work, or on breaks and at company socials, but they hadn't got to know each other beyond small talk and office gossip. On that day, though, as Kate sat crying, Jess sank onto the step beside her and put one arm around her shoulders. With her other hand, she reached for the cigarette, plucked it from Kate's quivering hand, and tossed it away into the car park. It arced through the air and the ash crumbled free. The butt rolled slowly into a clump of weeds and lay there, exhausted.

Sniffling noisily, the confession spilled out. Kate had been seeing some bloke from packaging, and he had just ended it. Kate was both indignant and bereft. Kate, it transpired, was also married.

Jess offered comfort, a fresh cup of coffee, and a shoulder to cry on.

After a week or so of stomping around the office with her eyes flashing danger signals at anyone who came near her, and snapping at anyone who got in her way, Kate had seemingly attacked her marriage with fresh determination, and put the affair behind her. Declan, Jess suspected, once she'd met him, and heard a lot more about him, had not been exactly faithful to their relationship either. But, for the few years since Jess and Kate first became friends, she had been under the impression that things were, well, okay at least, if not exactly rosy.

Chapter Eighteen

J ess regarded the array of discarded cigarette butts that Kate had strewn across the patio and swore. Drama or no drama, she could at least pick up her rubbish.

After copious amounts of coffee and a disgusting Get Slim bar—"Here, I brought you some more; chocolate without sins, have one,"—Kate had left. Although it was a while since she'd gone, heading into town for some retail therapy—more shoes, probably—Jess was still sitting at her kitchen table in the shaft of sunlight that poured through the French doors, gazing at nothing specific.

The sunbeams threw smeary patterns across the kitchen, casting strange shadow-shapes from where the windows needed a clean. Jess idly traced her fingertips around a shadow that fell onto the table in front of her. Was Declan so against Kate's Get Slim fixation that he might want to scupper it for her? Jess shook her head. No, it couldn't be possible. How in the world could he know when Dave would be biking along that stretch of road, and hadn't Harriet said it was one of the Get Slim women who had delivered the rogue bag of prawns to Angela? She really was letting her imagination overreact now ... The beep of her phone nudged her out of her reverie and she hit OPEN without first checking who the message was from.

Marcus. *Wallpaper?? No expert but happy to help - when?*

Dammit. Now she'd have to answer him. What to say? *When suits?*

She immediately followed it with another: *An excuse, really. I want your professional advice.* Better to be upfront.

Although, that didn't solve the wallpaper problem. She added a third text, *But also, have wallpaper to hang in kitchen and no idea how to.* To this last, she added a smiley face for good measure. "Blimey Jess," she told her phone as the screen shut off, "he'll think you're deranged." *Or fancy him.* She blushed at the thought, and waved her hand back and forth to fan the heat that rose over her face. Aside from anything else, it would be most inappropriate—he was a good ten years older than her, and the local policeman to boot. She'd better make a start on this decorating before she went off the whole idea of it.

She shoved her phone to the far end of the table and climbed onto the chair to lift down the kitchen clock. Stepping from one chair to the next, she also unhooked the bright Monet print, and the calendar, noting that she hadn't yet turned from February to March even though it was almost St Patrick's Day. Jess flipped the page and dropped the calendar onto the table before jumping down from the chair. She shoved a few odds and ends off the counter into random cupboards and drawers, and went upstairs to change into scruffy jeans and an old T-shirt.

Five minutes later she banged on Jeanie's front door, hoping to borrow the step ladder from Bill's garden shed. A quick cup of tea and a Bourbon Cream biscuit with Jeanie while Bill dragged the ladder around to Jess's own front door, and then she was back home with the ladder unfolded and a paintbrush in her hand. The yellow she had chosen was the colour of the first golden crocuses blooming in the garden; the same yellow of the runny egg yolks she remembered dipping bread soldiers into as a child.

She had chosen it for the bright, warm memories of her childhood and for the cheery glow with which it would bathe her kitchen on even the dullest days.

As the old sage green gave way to the new golden yellow, the radio sang out the songs of her teenage years. With the spring sunshine streaming in through the patio doors, she began to sing along. Tunelessly, loudly, but happily. She jumped down from the ladder, paintbrush brandished like a wand, singing along to the Spice Girls ... and realised someone was standing in the kitchen doorway, having let themselves in through the front door and down the hallway without so much of a whimper from Fletcher.

"Marcus!" She put a hand to her mouth, hoping to shove her erratic singing back into her throat, and brushed her hair out of her eyes.

"I knocked," he said. "Several times, in fact. I could hear that you were here, although I eventually guessed you couldn't hear me. You've paint on your face." He gestured to where she had just pushed her hair back. "I yelled from the front door, too. Thought your guard dog here might bark, but he just licked me nearly to death instead. Good thing I'm not here to rob you." He ruffled Fletch's ears and the dog rolled over onto his back, offering up his belly for Marcus to rub.

"Bloody useless he is at guarding." Jess turned away from him, reaching for the kettle and filling it with one hand, paintbrush still clutched in the other, ducking her head to hide her blush. "I can't believe you caught me singing and causing such a racket," she said to the kettle as she snapped the lid down. She straightened and faced him, her face still hot, but unable to stop her smile.

"Singing? Is that what it was?" Marcus spread his arms and shrugged. "I came to help, at your request, but it looks like you have it all under control."

"Sit." She pointed to a chair with the paintbrush. "Coffee? Or tea, of course. Let me just finish this patch while the kettle boils, and then I'll get you something. Hold on." She climbed back up the ladder, the brush dripping with freshly-laden paint, but instead of sitting as she'd instructed him, Marcus rooted in the cupboard for mugs. The kettle burbled and wobbled while Marcus took milk from the fridge and a spoon from a drawer as if he burst into strange kitchens all the time. He probably did, with his job, come to think of it.

"I suppose you're used to catching people in odd situations and calming them down with cups of tea?" Jess finished the wall she was working on and dumped the brush down onto the paint can lid. She washed her hands and rubbed them dry on her jeans, gestured at him again to sit, and took the coffee jar from the cupboard.

"Coffee?" She waved the jar at him. "Or tea?"

He pointed to the box of teabags behind her. "Tea, thanks. Milk, no sugar. So … nice colour. Cheery." He gestured vaguely at the walls. "Where's the wallpaper going then?"

Jess laughed. "On the wall."

Marcus's eyes crinkled in what was becoming a familiar expression. "Stupid question. Except, it looks to me like you are putting paint on the walls. Are you going to cover the paint with the wallpaper? Is this why you need help? Do you need someone to explain that you don't stick wallpaper on with yellow paint—you use wallpaper paste, you know? Like this here." He reached across the table and patted the bucket of paste.

"Blimey. You're not a policeman for nothing, are you? That kind of observation is just what I needed you for." Jess smiled, but the light-hearted moment passed as she explained why she had really wanted to talk to him. "Really, though, thanks for coming. I really do want to ask you something properly police-y." She put a mug of tea down in front of him, pushed the carton of milk in his direction, and sat.

"Marcus," she asked, "what happens when someone dies suddenly? I mean, like, do they have to have a postmortem and stuff? How can I find out if someone had to have one? Can I find that stuff out? Will they tell just anyone, I mean, or only family?"

Chapter Nineteen

M arcus gazed at Jess for a moment, his dark eyes serious. "Jess ..."

She held his gaze. "What if I'm right, Marcus? What if there is something strange going on?"

He sighed and stared into his tea. "People die, Jess. I see it all the time. Natural causes, accidental death, the circle of life." He spoke in what Jess suspected may be the voice he used for breaking bad news to distraught relatives.

"Marcus," she said again. "What if I'm right?"

"Okay, I'll hear you out. Go on. Shall we paint while you talk?" He pushed up his sleeves and took a fresh brush out of the packet on the table. "Which wall next?"

Marcus demonstrated a careful painting hand around the kitchen units while Jess tackled the wall with the doorway into the living room.

As she streaked yellow over green, she let her thoughts spill out in a stuttering ramble.

Marcus listened without interruption.

By the time each had finished their allocated wall and they sat at the table once more, with a packet of chocolate digestives open between them, Jess had shared all her worries about the connection between the deaths. She raised an eyebrow at Marcus, helped herself to another biscuit, and relaxed against the back of her chair, waiting.

Marcus studied her thoughtfully, his chin propped on one hand and his brow wrinkled. "Okay. I'll look at the files," he conceded. "I won't be able to tell you what's in them, but I will take a look. I doubt they'll show anything untoward, but if it puts your mind at rest, I'll check it out. You can't keep accusing everyone around here of killing people though. Be careful, or you'll be upsetting your friends." His gentle tone softened the stern gaze. "Don't let your imagination run away with you."

A brief flutter rose in Jess's chest as she met his eyes. She looked away and took a sip of her tea. "Okay," she said, not wanting to push him any further. "Thank you. I do appreciate it. You're right though, it's probably nothing."

Marcus's phone buzzed in his pocket. He eased it out, glanced at it, and stood. "I need to go. Sorry; work. I'll help you finish—" He gestured to the wallpaper and the empty wall. "—Another day. I'm off on Friday, if you like?"

After Marcus left, Jess washed the paint brushes in the sink, musing over the things she'd said to him: *Kate ... Susan ... Declan ... someone else ... who would gain from the deaths? Why would anyone want them dead? Who could possibly want Bert dead?* That was the question that reverberated most often in her mind. She squeezed watery paint out of the bristles with a force that dug her fingernails into the flesh of her hand as she tried to quench her thoughts. "I'm being silly. Overreacting," she told Fletcher, who was nuzzling at her leg in hopeful anticipation. "Okay, I agree; it's time for a walk." She lay the brushes on the draining board and dried her hands on her jeans.

"Hello, Jess!"

In the driveway outside Elizabeth and Henry's house, Henry stood at the back of his car, evidently about to retrieve something from the open boot. Next to Henry's newish car stood Elizabeth's older run-around, gleaming from a recent wash, but scratched and marked from years of use.

The front door to their large, detached house was also open, and as Jess lifted a hand in greeting, their little King Charles spaniel bounded from the house. He scooted between the two cars in the driveway and ran out of the gate, where he launched himself eagerly at Jess—or at Fletcher, to be more exact.

Jess stooped to intercept the dog before it reached the road. She pulled Fletcher onto Henry and Elizabeth's herringbone driveway to encourage the excited spaniel to follow them back towards its owner.

Henry had started towards them and spoke sternly to his own dog before greeting Fletcher with his customary, "Who's a mighty handsome dog then?" and a pat on the head. He straightened, tipped an imaginary cap to Jess and thanked her for "catching the little rascal." He belied his efforts at reprimanding the spaniel by scooping it up in his arms and rubbing its belly, whilst crooning, "Oh Stanley, you bad boy," in a voice which implied not a hint of real crossness.

"How're you then, my dear?" Henry asked.

Alerted by the voices, Elizabeth appeared in the doorway of the house and called a cheery hello. With apparent relief, Henry didn't wait for Jess to respond, but dipped his head towards her in acknowledgement of handing her over to his wife. He turned his attention back to the car boot, leaving Jess and Elizabeth to exchange pleasantries. The upper half of Henry disappeared into the boot, to re-emerge with a tray full of colourful pansies.

The flowers triggered something in Jess's mind and she paused in the conversation with Elizabeth, trying to recall the thought.

Pansies ... that was it ... as she drove into Lambskillen the other day, she had noticed fresh flowers at the roadside to mark the spot where Dave's body was found. She always gave those roadside shrines a second glance, mystified that people would want to mark the site of tragedy rather than adorn the graves of their loved ones. But that wasn't it ... no, it was that she'd wondered *who* had arranged flowers beneath that little wooden cross on the roadside in Ballyfortnum, to remember Dave, when he had no relations in the vicinity.

"Who does that?" Jess turned her gaze away from the direction Henry had carried the plants and put the question to Elizabeth. "Sorts the flowers for those roadside things, I mean? Like where Dave was found? It's not like he had any family around here."

Elizabeth shrugged. "Different people, different reasons. I laid a bouquet there myself just after ... you know ..." She shuddered and Jess remembered the guilt Elizabeth had voiced in the library when she had wondered whether Dave had been lying in the ditch alive and helpless as she and Henry had driven by. "Lots of the villagers did. Could be anyone really ... someone he worked with, that girl he used to date—Susan's girl, Helen—or just someone who doesn't like to see a marker with no flowers below it. There's plenty who would think it disrespectful to leave a memorial cross standing without flowers."

Jess decided to walk a little further, onwards to the site to see if there was any clue as to who may have laid this newest bunch of bright flowers. She said goodbye to Elizabeth, and called a cheerful farewell to Henry, still out of sight in the back garden somewhere.

Fletch rubbed his nose to the spaniel's, and wagged his tail as Jess gave his lead a soft tug to tell him it was time to move on.

A small dent in the bumper of Elizabeth's car reflected the morning sun, momentarily dazzling Jess as she started down the driveway.

Jess and Fletcher plodded through the village, enjoying the bright weather and dry ground underfoot. As she walked, the same questions played on a loop: How had Elizabeth dented her bumper? Had she been in her own car on the night Dave had died or had they been in Henry's? Not for the first time, Jess forced herself to shake the idea of lovely, gentle Elizabeth as a potential killer from her mind and focus on enjoying the walk.

The low sun warmed Jess's face. The fresh scents of spring filled the air today, and alongside the road, lambs and ewes called to one another in the fields. New shoots peeping from the verges promised that the daffodils would provide roadside colour for several more weeks yet, and primroses brightened the grassy banks beneath the hedges. While the hedgerows themselves were still barren and wintery, the larger trees showed the first hints of green as their leaf buds cracked open. Jess inhaled and the tension in her shoulders dissipated. She always loved this time of year, when winter was past and the days were lengthening. Soon the village would be fully alive in the bright glow of all its spring glory. Over the next few weeks, the gardens would burst into the riot of colour that helped ensure Ballyfortnum maintained a high placing on the National Tidy Villages leaderboard every summer. It really was a lovely village, with many keen gardeners and a team of hardworking volunteers always willing to prune, rake, pick up stray rubbish, or paint fences.

Or, thought Jess, jolted back out of her reverie, keep roadside memorials tidy. She stopped in front of the wooden cross. A polished, brass plaque displayed Dave's name and the date of his death. Someone had repaired the fence, but the hedgerow and verge were still gappy and sparse where they had been crushed by Dave's fall and the consequent recovery efforts.

A bunch of chrysanthemums lay crumpled and wilting in a cellophane wrapper at the foot of the cross. Jess poked it with the toe of her boot, then, feeling somewhat ashamed of her irreverent actions, she bent to straighten the bouquet and smooth out the cellophane. There was no sign of any card, and Jess guessed the flowers were a generic supermarket offering—three-ninety-nine a bunch, if even that much. "It's the thought that counts, eh Fletch," she muttered more to herself than to the dog. Too busy sniffing at something in the hedge, he took no notice. "Although, if you ask me, laying a cheap plastic-wrapped bunch of imported flowers doesn't count for much except rubbish to pile up in the ditch."

With sudden visions of a queue of field mice, hedgehogs and rabbits marching out of a Beatrix Potter book and into the inevitable suffocation of the plastic, Jess pinned Fletcher's leash beneath her foot to free both her hands, and squatted beside the cross. Carefully removing the wilting flowers from the cellophane, she arranged them more aesthetically beneath the memorial. She stood, and folded the cellophane into a small parcel which she tucked into her coat pocket. She nodded down at the cross, murmuring a barely audible, "Rest well Dave," then blushed at the realisation she was talking to a dead man she didn't know at a cross his body wasn't buried at.

"C'mon Fletch." She scooped up his lead, turned on her heel and set off towards home.

Chapter Twenty

Jess kicked off her boots and left them discarded outside the French doors. She crossed the kitchen to flick on the kettle, shrugging out of her coat at the same time. The cellophane wrap crinkled in the pocket. She removed it and smoothed it out on the table, her fingernail picking at the sticker she hadn't noticed earlier. It advertised the same supermarket she'd met Breda buying prawns in just before Angela's death. The same discount supermarket half the village shopped in. The same supermarket she herself shopped in at least once a fortnight. This gave her no clue as to who could have left the flowers, or why they might have done so. She crumpled the cello wrap in her hand and stuffed it into the bin, taking satisfaction in the smack of the lid closing on it.

"Dammit," she said to her fresh, yellow walls. "Dammit." The rolls of wallpaper in the corner reminded her of her promise to Harriet and she fired off a quick text to Niall to see if the girl might be free after school on Friday, or at the weekend. It would do Harriet good to spend a couple of hours singing along to cheesy pop songs … Jess would make up some popcorn and find a good film for them to curl up with after tackling the wallpaper.

When Harriet was younger and Jess still lived in her poky apartment in Lambskillen, Harriet would come to Jess's on occasion, to be babysat, instead of Jess going to Niall and Angela's house for the evening. They'd drop Harriet off on their way to some restaurant, or theatre event in town, and collect her on their way home, carrying her to their car and strapping her in to inevitably nod off to sleep for the drive. It would be fun for them to rekindle one of those long-ago fun evenings ... they'd watch some naff Disney film, with sing-along lyrics scrolling across the screen. Jess pulled up the search engine on her phone and typed *How to hang wallpaper* in preparation for the task ahead.

An incoming text from Kate interrupted her reading. *You still there?*

Jess sighed and ignored the text, not in the mood for whatever Kate's newest drama might be, but the phone beeped again.

We've split up. Can I come over?

"Again?" Jess said aloud to the message. "Seriously? What's happened now?" She rolled her eyes and groaned, unwilling to face Kate's latest drama. Nonetheless, her good nature overrode the urge to collapse on the sofa and flip on the television, so instead, she answered with a brief *sure* that she knew would suffice as an invitation for Kate to turn up.

A moment later, feeling guilty for her initial lack of sympathy, suspecting things with Declan must have escalated since that morning, Jess sent a follow-up; *Bring wine and pjs? I'll make up a bed.* It would be fun to have a girly night in—possibly two in one week if Harriet fancied staying over at the weekend, although an evening with Harriet's company would have to be alcohol-free, obviously, although she was certain the teenager already drank plenty with her new college friends. She grabbed a couple of bottles of white out of the back of the cupboard and shoved them into the fridge in preparation for a long night of listening to Kate's woes.

Within the hour, Kate stood jiffling on the doorstep, blotchy-eyed and clutching a bottle of wine in each hand, trying to nudge the door open with her knee.

Jess waved from the living room window. "Hang on, I'm coming," she called, going to Kate's aid and opening the door to relieve her of the bottles before standing aside to let her in.

Fletcher leapt upon Kate as if he hadn't seen her for years, and for once, Kate didn't shove him off. She dropped to her knees and flung her arms around him, cuddling the soppy dog to her. "Oh Fletch," she sobbed. "I needed that hug."

Jess laughed sympathetically and shoved the door shut with her foot. "Come here." She held out her arms to Kate and folded her into a hug, the dog wriggling away from between them in protest. "I'll put pizza in, shall I? There's salad, too ..." she added as an afterthought, thinking of Kate's slimming.

"Bugger that." Kate peered at her through streaky mascara. "Bung in a huge pile of chips. I know you've a freezer full of them ..."

Jess nodded, but Kate wasn't finished. "... and onion rings? Have you got any of those? I haven't had an onion ring in months ... and garlic bread?" She raised an over-plucked eyebrow in hope.

Jess didn't bother to pretend her freezer wasn't full of the kind of junk food Kate had reeled off. She ate quite healthily most of the time, but in winter, when the neighbourhood's home-grown vegetable supply was running low, she liked to have some backup, emergency comfort food in stock too.

"Go on through." She gestured Kate to head to the kitchen, waved her onto a chair, and opened a bottle of the white wine she'd put to chill earlier. And a bottle of red from the counter, too. "Here you go." She passed Kate the white and set the red down at the opposite side of the table, scooped two wine glasses out of the cupboard, frowned at them, put them back, and switched them for shorter, fatter, tumblers. "I reckon we're gonna get drunk," she said, "so we may as well be prepared with stable-bottomed glasses."

Kate managed a weak smile. "My bottom will be anything but stable after we're done tonight. But I'm having the night off."

They glugged wine into their respective glasses, each taking a satisfying swig before Jess spoke again.

"Go on then; spill. What's happened since you left earlier?"

Over pizza and the first bottle each, Kate relayed how Declan had once again suggested that Kate's Get Slim business was not a real business, not bringing in enough income, and a total waste of her time and energy. "He said he's fed up with me arsing around in Ballyfortnum and banging on about my job all the time." She tore off a sheet of kitchen roll to wipe her eyes, and took another swig of wine.

Jess practised her diplomacy skills and remained quiet, except for the sloshing sound of wine topping up almost-empty glasses. Kate ranted for an hour or so, but by the time she'd opened the second bottle of white, she was slurring and giggling between the bursts of rage and tears.

Late into the evening, they stood out on the patio, blankets huddled around their shoulders. Kate eventually managed to light her cigarette after a few drunken false starts, inhaled, and blew a long stream of smoke into the frosty air.

"You know," she spat out, "he even accused me of having an affair! Said I'd been far too upset about Dave and was obviously far too involved with the group and asked what was I hiding and was it Dave or someone else and was I really even running this bloody group or just off shagging a fancy man when I said I was working?" She broke off and scowled. "He actually said 'fancy man'! I mean who even says that anyway? I think that was the exact moment I realised I didn't even love him anyway. Bloody stupid git. Fancy man!" At this, Kate let out a burst of laughter that gave way to fresh sobs.

Jess, too drunk to offer comfort, could only repeat, "Fancy man!"

Kate exploded into fresh giggles, her tears still flowing, but now tears formed more from hilarity than despair.

"Who needs men anyway? Bloody more trouble than they're bloody worth. Bloody, bloody men. I'm better off without him. Bloody git." She lit a new cigarette and tossed the spent one onto the stones. She ground it under her foot as if it were Declan himself she was grinding to dust, then jerked her attention back to Jess. "You get by fine without one."

Jess's head was swimming and she was too busy trying to work out why she had more patio chairs than normal and why the fence was moving, so she said nothing.

Kate filled the silence with another question. "What's with you and that policeman bloke anyway?" She pointed an accusatory cigarette at Jess, who cringed away from the hot red glow and fell backwards, landing awkwardly on one of the chairs. Kate sat down next to her and they dissolved into fresh giggles.

Jess tipped her head backwards and gazed at the clear star-filled sky.

"Look," she said, pointing. "Look at all that. We are nothing. We are stars. Declan is nothing. He's a dead star."

The two of them gazed profoundly at the sky for what seemed like hours until Kate scrambled to her feet and pushed the chair back with a shove that tipped it over.

"Bloody freezing. Going in," she declared, and tripped up the step back into the kitchen, smacking her shoulder into the door frame. She stepped back and tried again, this time entering the kitchen successfully.

Late the next morning, Fletcher woke Jess with a persistent licking of her face. "Mate," his doggy expression said. "I really do need to go outside. Please wake up."

Jess groaned and sat up. Fletcher tipped his head to one side and gave her a quizzical look. He whimpered, and it was only as she watched him standing hopefully by the door that she realised she was on the sofa and not in her bed upstairs. She stretched her cramped legs and groaned again.

"Fletch," she moaned, her voice croaky and raw, "get me a glass of water, won't you?"

Fletch, unsurprisingly, did not.

Jess swung her protesting legs onto the floor and forced herself upright. The blast of cold air as she opened the door to let him out cleared her head a little. She picked up the fallen chair and sat for a moment. The cool metal against her thighs alerted her to the fact she was still fully dressed in yesterday's clothes. She grimaced. "It's been a long time since I drank that much," she mumbled, heading back inside in search of revitalisation. She drank straight from the kitchen tap and rummaged in the cupboards for Paracetamol and a loaf of bread. The smell of coffee brought Kate staggering down, also looking rather worse for the wear. Jess pushed a piece of toast towards her.

"Peanut butter and Marmite," she said. "Best hangover cure I ever had. It helps, honestly. I feel better already."

Kate dubiously nibbled the edge of the toast.

"Kate," Jess went on, "you said ... you said Dec said ... were you—are you having another affair?"

Chapter Twenty-One

Later that day, after Kate had gone home and Jess's head felt less like it was stuffed with cotton wool, she collected Linda and drove them into town. Jess had promised to bring Linda to collect a prescription, and despite a slight uncertainty as to whether she should be driving after her vast alcohol consumption the night before, she didn't want to let her neighbour down. As they drove past the site of Dave's demise, Jess asked Linda the same question she had posed to Elizabeth earlier in the week—did she know who might have left the flowers? Linda, like Elizabeth, was vague, adding only that she'd laid none there herself, what with not really knowing Dave, and it being too icy to venture out.

"I really don't like to drive in the dark, love," Linda said, "or in ice." She chuckled and added, "Or snow, fog, or rain. And if it's too sunny, that's a problem too. It's not easy to see if the sun is in your eyes, is it love?"

Jess laughed. Linda didn't like to drive even on dull, dry days. She reached across the handbrake and patted Linda's arm. "I don't like driving in the dark or in ice, either," she said, "and I am certainly glad I wasn't out on the road that night—I'd hate to be worrying that maybe I had passed him by … or that I'd knocked him down."

"Mm," Linda agreed. "We'd come by earlier in the day, after paying our respects at a removal in town." She named the same man whose wake Elizabeth had attended on the evening Dave had died. "But we were back before it was fully dark, and the roads weren't frozen at that time. That's why we went early; to avoid being out on bad roads: the forecast had promised a big freeze overnight. We were tucked up in front of a roaring fire by the time the five o'clock news came on."

The throb of relief under Jess's ribs surprised her—she hadn't even considered Bert or Linda may have been responsible for Dave's death, but now that Linda offered up an unrequested alibi, Jess realised any one of the villagers could have been the culprit. She pushed away the brief flash of surprise that Linda could remember that day so clearly. After all, everyone would have recollected their actions that night as soon as the news got out someone had died.

In stark contrast to that cold January night, today offered a beautiful bright spring afternoon—unseasonably warm for mid-March—and the sun bounced off the lake as they passed by. Jess never tired of the view of the lake, however many times she drove past. The air was still, and the water reflected the tree line in mirrored perfection.

Linda sighed.

Concerned, Jess glanced across at her passenger, but Linda was smiling. "It's beautiful, isn't it?" Jess said, her eyes darting between the road ahead and the glorious view.

In town, they wandered around the shops for a while, meandering through the alleys where the charity shops nestled.

Jess spotted a branded 'Get Slim' hoodie tucked onto a rack labelled 'SIZE 18'. "I hope they managed to trade it for a smaller size."

Linda muttered something that may have been agreement or may have indicated she was too busy rooting through a pile of books to be listening.

"One of Kate's clients, I suppose," Jess said.

Linda didn't respond.

Or one of Susan's.

Behind the counter was a poster advertising Susan's town-based group. Tuesday nights, same as Kate's group—and the same evening of the week that Dave had ended up in the ditch. Which meant that Susan would have certainly been one of the locals out on the road that night. In fact, hadn't Susan said as much herself, in the shop the day they found Dave? She'd said she was driving home from town that night Dave died, said she'd probably even passed him lying there. Jess filed the thought in her mind along with the other information she was storing relating to the deaths. Was Susan still angry that Dave and Helen had split up? She remembered Susan saying how upset Helen had been and how the girl just moped around crying all the time ... ages ago now, though, way back before Christmas.

Linda and Jess pushed open the door to the pharmacy on Green Street, the bell above the door jangling to announce their presence.

A familiar voice called out a greeting.

"Hello." Breda stood behind the counter, shuffling a sheaf of prescriptions. "Linda, Jess, how are you? I haven't seen you for a few days? Not been around the village much; Daisy has been missing her walks while I've been doing a spot of overtime."

Jess stepped closer to the counter. "I didn't realise you worked here. Have you been here long? All this time I knew Elizabeth was a nurse, and here you are, living next door to her, and a pharmacist, and I never had a clue." She laughed. "You must spend hours talking about patients and cures together."

"I usually work in a different branch," Breda explained, "but one of the girls here got married, so I'm covering. What can I get you?"

Linda shoved her prescription back into her handbag and coloured. She turned to face the nearest shelf display and grabbed a bottle of shampoo. "Shampoo. Just picking up some shampoo." She waved the bottle towards Breda. "And perhaps a nice conditioner, too, if there's one you could suggest for my hair?"

Jess ducked behind a display of candles to hide her smile. People were so funny about others knowing their business in some areas, yet only too happy to gossip about it at other times. Many a time she'd bump into one of the older neighbours who would regale her with tales of their piles or their weak bladder, yet here in a pharmacy, where the staff would be used to hearing about all kinds of medical complaints all day long, they could suddenly become so shy. Of course, she had no idea what Linda's prescription was for, but guessed that her friend would not be collecting it from this pharmacy.

Small talk and pleasantries behind them, and shampoo bottles stashed into Linda's Bag for Life, Jess and Linda decided to get a coffee in the new little coffee shop that had opened a month or so ago. Jess liked to support new businesses—it was so hard for newcomers to get established in this town when so many locals resisted change. Oftentimes they closed again within a few months of opening.

As Jess had silently predicted, once they had gathered their breath, drunk their coffee, and had a homemade cherry scone each, Linda steered Jess towards the pharmacy at the opposite end of town.

In the typical fashion of an Irish small town, before they got back to the car, they had bumped into several more neighbours or other acquaintances, and Linda was quite exhausted from a fresh wave of condolences, sympathy, and "How are you bearing up?" from people she hadn't seen since Bert's funeral. The worst was in the little wool shop, where the owner had not yet heard the news and Linda's wool-buying became half an hour of sympathizing before the wool was packaged and paid for.

By the time they drove back past the lake, the sun was setting. Across the far side of the water, the trees stood silhouetted and still, the sky streaked like fire above and behind them. The clocks would spring forward soon, and the days would stretch on forever. Jess hoped that with the brighter days and longer evenings, Linda would find her feet again and things would get happier in Orchard Close.

"Why don't we do a gardening course, Linda?" she said, surprising herself with the sudden thought. "What with Bert and Dad gone, we don't want our gardens to let down the Close." Besides, she thought, warming to the unbidden idea, it would do them both good to have something other than death to focus on.

Chapter Twenty-Two

"I could bloody kill 'er, so I bloody could." Susan swept out of the village shop on Friday morning, her rugged face even redder than normal.

Jess stepped aside, holding the door to allow the angry woman to exit.

"Jess," Susan acknowledged, but didn't stop to expand on her annoyance.

Jess let the door swing shut behind Susan's departing back, and continued into the shop. "Hello," she called across the shop to Mrs Dunne, raising her eyebrows quizzically. "What's up with her?" she asked, as she grabbed a carton of milk from the fridge.

Always happy to gossip, Mrs Dunne shoved a few things aside and placed her elbows firmly down on the counter to lean forward conspiratorially. "Ah now, aren't there another few of her group from town upped and changed over to join your wee friend's group down here in Ballyfortnum? Stands to reason it's going to be easier for them, doesn't it? Can't really blame them for not wanting to cart all the way over to town if there's a group right here on the doorstep, can we, eh? Poor Sue isn't happy about it though, can't blame her neither really, eh? Can't be holding with all that nonsense myself, but she does have a point, doesn't she? What with her being from round here and your wee friend a foreigner, like?"

Mrs Dunne paused for breath as Jess tried not to bristle at the implication that Dublin was a foreign place, and never mind Kate now lived in a neighbouring village, too. It was hard enough for outsiders to be accepted into rural communities and Jess was still somewhat confused as to how easily she herself had been welcomed in, in comparison to other "foreigners."

Mrs Dunne was speaking again. "I know she's your friend, and no offense, like, but your one has rocked the boat a bit round here, what with taking business from one of our own and bringing her high and mighty ways down into the village. Never set foot in our wee shop to buy so much as a pint of milk, but doesn't she like to swan in here with her posters and her leaflets and her, 'Won't you recommend the group to your customers for me please, it's a grand thing for the community,' eh?" Mrs Dunne put on a passable attempt at what she would call an uppity Dublin accent, and Jess laughed.

"It is strange, though," she agreed, "that they would give the Ballyfortnum group to Kate when Susan lives right here in the village and is already an established consultant. Mad, really. You'd think they would realise that someone local would know more people and get more clients in ..." She tailed off in thought as she sifted through the packets of bread, checking to find the one with the longest use-by date. "... unless, of course, they thought that an outsider would be more professional—I mean like someone who doesn't know everyone already, and maybe people would worry less about sharing their true weight and all that personal stuff?"

Jess was thinking out loud—who could ever fathom how anyone's business minds really worked? And it wasn't as if the UK-based head offices of

Get Slim would have the faintest idea of the politics of rural village life in Ireland anyway. "I dunno, Mrs Dunne, I really don't," she concluded, and paid for the milk and bread. "She did look annoyed, though. And what with half the village dying recently, it may've been a poor choice of words to say she'd want to kill anyone, don't you think?"

Jess left Mrs Dunne propped up against her shop counter, turning Susan's outburst over in her mind. Would Susan really be angry enough to jeopardize Kate's group? Surely not? She pushed open the door to the shop again and stuck her head through the gap.

"Mrs Dunne," she called into the gloomy interior, "has Susan had much to say about Kate's slimmers dying? Dave, Angela? Do people die in her group? Actually … is there much gossip about it from anyone? Does *anyone* think there's anything weird about three people from the village dying so close together and two of them so young?" She stepped back inside the shop and the door swung closed behind her. "Did anyone ever talk about how come all of them went to the slimming group here in Ballyfortnum?"

On the counter, the shop telephone trilled into life. Mrs Dunne waved an apologetic hand, and Jess left the shop after all.

Henry, Jess noted as she walked homeward bound through the village, had been busy. The borders along his and Elizabeth's long sweeping driveway glowed with fresh colour from the newly-planted pansies, and together with the later daffodils and early tulips, the garden was a delightful riot of cheerfulness. By contrast, next door, Breda's concrete driveway was bordered by neat shades of green, reminiscent of a walk in a manicured forest with its low-growing conifers, mossy stone edges, and dark wooden gates.

Daisy, Breda's yappy whippet-mix, barked as they approached. The little dog galloped back and forwards behind the gates, sending Fletch into a tugging frenzy at the end of his lead.

"Sh, Daisy, sh." Jess spoke firmly but without consequence to the noisy dog. A movement from the house caught her eye.

Breda raised a hand in greeting as she twitched back the net curtain of her front room to see what the fuss was about.

Jess waved back and tugged Fletcher away, Daisy's barking abating as they rounded the bend out of sight. Enjoying the spring blooms of the village, thinking of the riot of colour in Henry and Elizabeth's garden, and the soft greens of Breda's, Jess remembered her suggestion to Linda to join a gardening course. She pulled out her phone, switched on her mobile data, and tried to Google local courses as she walked along.

Weaving erratically back and forth across her path, Fletcher made it too difficult to continue, so instead, she called Kate to see how she was bearing up in her newfound singleness.

Declan, apparently, had wasted no time in shooting off to Dublin. Kate hadn't even asked him where he was staying, but the speed and lack of protest he'd offered up when Kate had told him to leave led her to suspect he had easily found a place to stay. Jess kept quiet, aside from an odd non-committal, "mm-hm," but from what she knew of Declan, it would not surprise her at all to hear he was already shacked up with someone else. Kate, meanwhile, continued to vehemently deny seeing anyone else.

Jess couldn't help but wonder if she protested a little too much. She felt her cheeks redden as she remembered Kate's drunken grilling about Jess's own love life on Wednesday night. It really had been far too long since Jess had anyone 'significant' in her life, Kate had said more than once during that evening.

Kate picked up the refrain once more. "You can't lock yourself away in a dead-end street full of old ones for the rest of your life."

Jess moved the phone a little further from her ear. "I quite like it, actually." She refused to rise to what was becoming a common chorus from many of her friends and some of her neighbours. "The old ones are easier—no pressure to look good, or to go out clubbing, or to watch my weight." She laughed, enjoying the sun and the walk too much to let everyone's persistent concerns about her single status annoy her.

Kate, more conscious of her looks than Jess, seemed to be rallying nicely from the trauma of kicking Declan out, and had already taken herself off into town to get her hair and nails freshly done to be sure she didn't look "like someone whose husband just left me" before the group met on Tuesday.

Really, thought Jess, only half-listening to Kate as she walked, whoever cared what anyone's eyebrows looked like, and really, who needed the hassle of plucking them out only to draw them back on every morning? Kate may've let herself fall apart for a time, letting Jess see her tearstained and dishevelled on Wednesday night, but by the time Jess next saw her she would undoubtedly have her makeup back in place and her usual cool, elegant appearance firmly re-established.

As she disconnected from Kate's call, Jess noticed a message had come in while they'd been talking. Marcus. Jess vaguely recalled Kate having quizzed her specifically about Marcus that drunken night, but the details were blurry, and she couldn't remember what either of them had actually said. She opened the text to find Marcus reminding her of his promise to help with the wallpapering at the weekend: *Can come today? Or Sat? Free both, which suits best? M*. She'd already explained she'd promised Harriet could help, and Marcus had offered to show them both the tricks of the trade if there was a day that suited them all. She paused in a gateway to reply.

Sure, Saturday'd be great. Thank you. Any news on the inquests? She deleted the last question, deciding it would be better to ask in person, and sent the rest of the message. She'd have to make sure he arrived before Harriet, so she could quiz him about Angela without upsetting the motherless child. She fired off a PS to the first text: *2ish?*, then texted Harriet, suggesting 3 o'clock on Saturday would be great.

Chapter Twenty-Three

O n Saturday afternoon, Marcus leaned back in his seat in Jess's kitchen, legs stretched out under the table and a mug of tea steaming in his hands.

"Harriet'll be along in a bit," Jess said, neglecting to add she had suggested that the girl come a little after she'd arranged with Marcus, to allow her time to talk to him about the postmortems. "We won't start till she gets here—I promised her we'd learn together. I hope you're a good teacher; I've never done it before." She smiled at Marcus across the table. "I begged some goodies off Linda to bribe you with—look." Jess pulled the lid off a cake tin and revealed a plump, sugar-dusted Victoria sponge. "Want a slice now?"

They agreed on "just a small slice while we wait" and once Jess had settled a plate in front of each of them, she broached the subject she'd been itching to tackle.

"Any news on the inquests?"

Marcus looked up sharply. "Jess ..."

"You said you'd try to find out," she reminded him. "I heard Susan say she wanted to kill Kate yesterday. What if she's already killed the others? Didn't she already tell me she was out on the road the night Dave died?"

Marcus watched her in silence for a moment, then shook his head. "You're being dramatic. People say they'll kill people all the time. I'd kill for another slice of this delicious cake," he added, nodding at his plate, his deep brown eyes peering up at her from under his lashes.

Jess laughed. "Spill the beans and I'll cut another slice."

"Jess, you do know I'm not really supposed to tell you anything official, don't you?"

"Right," she agreed. "But I can ask questions and you can answer. Was Angela poisoned?"

Marcus swallowed a mouthful of the cake. "That's no secret anyway," he said. "It always did look like food poisoning, and the last thing she ate was seafood."

"But people don't usually actually die of seafood poisoning, do they? I've been reading up on it. I mean—it can make you pretty ill, but most people recover well enough."

"Hmm ... Fishy isn't it?" Marcus said with a straight face and Jess giggled.

"And," Jess went on, "Harriet told me that one of the others in the group had brought the prawns round to her mum. She couldn't remember who, but it's a dodgy thing to keep out of the fridge. I nearly bought some myself that week, but they got warm in my hands while I was talking to Breda and I put them back—" She stopped and clasped a hand to her open mouth. "Oh help. I hope I didn't make them bad for someone else, warming them up like that. I'd never thought of that. Do you think that could happen?"

"Anyway," Marcus continued, evading Jess's last question, "while it was almost certainly the prawns that made Angela so ill, and ultimately killed her, there is nothing to suggest it was anything but an unfortunate accident—a particularly bad and unusual reaction. There is simply no way someone could have anticipated such an extreme reaction unless they knew someone was allergic."

"Which Angela obviously was not," Jess added. "Harriet said her mum had cooked loads of seafood lately. Harriet was quite fed up with it, she said. The smell alone had put the rest of the family off seafood for life, she reckoned." She got up to let Fletcher and Snowflake in through the French doors, exhausted from chasing each other around the garden. "C'mon you two, come in and lie down quietly. Could you give someone dodgy prawns to make them ill, though?" she asked, turning her attention back to Marcus. "What if the death was not deliberate, but the intention *was* to make her sick? Is that possible?"

Marcus thought for a moment. "I suppose so," he eventually conceded, "but surely there are easier ways to make someone sick?"

"Like what?" asked Jess. "I wouldn't have a clue."

"No." He shook his head slowly. "I wouldn't either—my job is to catch criminals, not to be one."

"What about Dave then? Any info on what time he died or anything like that? Or whether he died when he fell in the ditch or after ... or if he died from the cold or the fall or the ditch water?" Jess shuddered. The idea of slowly drowning in freezing ditch water was not pleasant, and even though she hadn't known Dave well, probing into the way he died perturbed her. She brushed the unease away, reminding herself if he had not fallen in that ditch drunkenly and unaided, then it would be a good thing to find out just what had happened to him that cold January night.

"Again," Marcus replied, "nothing conclusive. Time of death is estimated to be anytime between six pm and midnight. They'd usually be more precise, but the freezing temperatures would have cooled the body more quickly than is ideal. His bike was partly underneath him, a bit battered, but it would be, going off the road like that and having him land on top. He didn't drown, probably hypothermia got him, although he'd hit his head too. Bruising consistent with falling off a bike. That's a summary anyone could access from the records, give or take."

"Would bruising be the same if you fell or if you were knocked off, I wonder ..." Jess swirled her half-drunk mug of tea and gazed into it as if the ripples would give her the answers.

"There might be something if a car made contact with the body," Marcus said, "but if a car hit the bike—"

"Did they check the bike for signs of impact?" Jess asked.

"Nothing conclusive," Marcus said again. "It was an old-enough bike, scratched and dirty. Some scuff marks of paint that could've come from anything really. It's almost as daft riding a bike drunk as driving a car," he added, almost to himself, as Fletcher and Snowflake leapt up from where they had settled just moments beforehand under the table. Tumbling over and under each other, they ran, barking, towards the door.

The doorbell rang, somewhat unnecessarily, given that Jess was already following the dogs to the hallway to see what the commotion was about. A minute later she returned to the kitchen, followed by Harriet, the two dogs twining around their legs and doing their best to trip them up.

"Cake first, or wallpaper lesson first?" Jess asked the teenager, who had dumped her backpack in the kitchen doorway and was already sitting in the middle of the kitchen floor with two excited dogs lovingly savaging her.

Harriet's eyes sparkled with pleasure as she petted the dogs, enjoying a moment to forget she had lost her mother less than two months before.

Tears prickled as Jess watched Harriet, looking for all the world like the happy, young child she had used to look after sometimes, instead of the bereft teenager she had become. She turned away before Harriet noticed her tears, and wiped her eyes on a tea towel.

Once she had regained her composure, she turned and said with forced brightness, "Let's get this thing done then, shall we?" She cleared the cups and plates out of the way, so they could spread the wallpaper onto the kitchen table for pasting, and told Harriet to start unwrapping the first roll.

For a sticky couple of hours, they worked in companionable silence, forgetting the sadness rippling through the village and the mystery of the deaths, as Marcus instructed Jess and Harriet in the art of hanging wallpaper.

"Wow! We've done a great job. It looks brilliant!" Ignoring the few bumps, and one slightly crooked piece around the wall cupboard, Jess nudged Harriet in the ribs, and whispered, "Knew we could do it. Girl power!" She winked at Harriet, then threw a wide smile at Marcus.

"It's amazing!" Harriet spun in a circle in the kitchen, arms outstretched to encompass their achievements. "We're awesome!" She high-fived Jess and collapsed in exaggerated exhaustion onto the floor. She lay flat on her back and gave a loud, fake yawn, but the dogs, thinking this was a new game for them to play, bounced over to her, pawing and licking her until she sat up, giggling. Harriet peeled a stray torn piece of wallpaper off Snowflake's back, then leapt up again and wrapped her arms around Marcus.

"Thank you," she said, hugging him with the exuberance of an excited child, "that was the best fun." She released Marcus from her embrace and turned to give Jess the same appreciation, the huge sploshes of wallpaper paste on their clothes squelching between them.

Marcus grinned. "And to think I'd got away with not being covered in the stuff, until you covered me with it," he admonished with a smile. "Good job, girls, you'll get the hang of it yet. No pun intended."

Jess finished cleaning the brushes and the table, and once again turned her attention to cutting slices of Victoria Sponge—generous slabs this time—and making fresh tea for them all.

"Yes, thank you, Marcus," she added her thanks to Harriet's. "It really was good of you to help, especially when you're so busy catching criminals and busting crime." She raised her mug in salute.

"A pleasure," he answered, raising his mug back at her, then clinking it against Harriet's.

"The three musketeers, wallpapering together to save the world." Harriet added her contribution to the toast. "I think we did pretty good. Obviously, though, I did the good bits."

"Obviously," Jess and Marcus said in unison, smiling at each other across Harriet's head with a conspiratorial smirk.

Once they'd eaten the cake, Harriet disappeared upstairs to the bathroom to clean herself up. Jess felt a sudden pang of self-consciousness. The half-memory of Kate quizzing her about Marcus on Wednesday night came unbidden and she wondered whether there was any truth in Kate's comments. No, she decided, Marcus was too old, too nice; just a friendly neighbour watching out for her like so many of the others around the village did since her dad had died. Nonetheless, the thought made her awkward, and although she had more questions to ask Marcus about the deaths, she was conscious, too, that Harriet could reappear at any moment.

Instead, she offered a half-hearted, "Will you stay for dinner?" which Marcus gallantly refused on the grounds of leaving Jess and Harriet to their evening of Disney films.

Chapter Twenty-Four

Harriet lay curled up on the sofa under the window with Fletcher draped on top of her.

Jess sprawled across the other sofa, her back against the sofa's arm and her legs stretched over the cushions. Lyrics scrolled across the television screen while implausibly-shaped and impractically-dressed princesses danced with impossibly good-looking princes, and dodged monsters, witches, and countless other evils. "It's all a bit stereotypical," Jess said through a mouthful of popcorn. "Not exactly PC these days, is it?"

"I could be a Disney princess now," Harriet said, stroking Fletch's ears absent-mindedly.

"Why's that?" Jess regretted the question as soon as she said it, already sensing the answer.

"None of them have mothers anymore." Harriet was matter of fact; solemn as she gazed towards the screen.

Jess held the bowl of popcorn towards the girl. "You could get to marry a gorgeous prince though?"

"D'ya reckon Dad'll marry again and I'll end up with a wicked stepmother?"

Jess smiled sadly, blinking away the threatening tears. "Not just yet, I shouldn't think." A thought struck her, and she took advantage of the moment of solemnity. "Harriet, love, your mum had loads of friends, but can you think of anyone who didn't like her—anyone she'd fallen out with, ever?"

Harriet was quiet for a moment, fondling Fletcher's soft fur as she considered Jess's question. Eventually, she replied, not with an answer but with another question. "Why?"

Jess shrugged. "Nothing really ... just ... well ..." She stuffed another handful of popcorn in her mouth, wishing she hadn't said anything. She hadn't planned to interrogate the poor girl. But ...

While Jess's mouth was full, Harriet filled the silence. "Not really, I don't think. I mean, there was a bit of an argument once with one of my friend's mams lately. I was at hers for a party and there was a bit of drink. Mam was raging about that. We had a huge fight about it, wish I'd been nicer ... I know she was just looking out for me ..." She jabbed at the arm of the sofa with her fingers, sniffed, and wiped her face with her sleeve.

"Ah, love, I fought with my dad all the time. It's what we do. You can't change it, and your mum often said you were better than most teenagers! She understood, you know. She loved you heaps."

Harriet tugged a tissue from her pocket, dabbed at her eyes, and waved the remote control at the TV to select the next film. "Her and Dad had a row with our neighbour ages back, over a tree or something stupid, but he's moved. They still bring it up sometimes ... I doubt he even knows she's ... she's ... you know?"

Jess had noticed Harriet still couldn't use the words to say her mother had died. She remembered that feeling well. It felt so final to say the words. Even now, she found it hard to say her dad was dead and usually used similar vague non-sequiturs when talking about it. Harriet's forehead crumpled with concentration now, as she tugged at Fletch's ear. Despite her initial assertion about her mum having no enemies, she recalled more run-ins with people as she considered the question.

"Susan was bummed that Mam swapped from her Get Slim class in town to the one here with that friend of yours. She got right narky with Mam about that. And some of those others in the group could be right bitches. Worse than the girls at school, they were. Mam used to say they were all sweet and light and pretending to be delighted when someone lost a few pounds but behind backs they were ecstatic if anyone put on a few pounds or slipped up." Harriet looked up from the popcorn. "Bunch of bloody drama queens if you ask me."

Jess chuckled. "You sounded just like her then. She used to say that about you and your friends. I bet my mum did too, about me."

"Do you ever see your mam, Jess?"

"Nah, my mum's too tied up with her new bloke and pretending she's not old enough to have children my age." Jess hadn't spoken to her mum in ages. "I suppose I should tell her about Bert actually, now that I think of it. She'd probably want to know ... or maybe she wouldn't care. She's kind of moved on from life in Ballyfortnum."

"Don't you miss her?"

Jess was silent for a moment as another Disney heroine sashayed onto the television, this time with less stereotype and more Tim Burton darkness. "No," she said. "I really don't, but that's probably because I know she is still there, albeit a million miles away and not really interested in what we're up to anymore. I should call her tomorrow; see how life is in *Costa del* ex-pats. I do miss my dad though. All the time. I should phone my brother more, too ..."

Onscreen, Disney's Alice became small enough to slip inside a rabbit hole.

"And Alice," she added as an afterthought, feeling a slight pull of guilt at having not spoken to her sister in a while. In fact, she hadn't even returned the missed call last week. She rummaged down the cushion where her phone had fallen and fired out a quick *How're you doing, any news?* text to both of her siblings. She tossed her phone onto the cushion by her feet, but it bounced off and landed on the floor with a thud. Jess turned her attention back to the Disney Alice, shoving thoughts of her sister to the back of her mind.

It wasn't until the Red Queen came into the story that either Jess or Harriet spoke again, but as the large-headed, red-headed Helena Bonham Carter appeared, Harriet stifled a snort and glanced guiltily at Jess.

"What?"

"Nothing."

"No, go on, what?"

"Well," Harriet said, "it's just that, don't you think your friend Kate looks a bit like her, with her eyebrows, and her skinny figure making her head look all huge and all that loads of makeup? 'Specially since she's dyed her hair that weird red." Harriet giggled into a handful of popcorn before stuffing it into her mouth.

Jess launched for the remote control and hit the rewind button, pausing with the Red Queen pouting her stupid thin lips at them. She laughed. Harriet was right, there was a resemblance all right. Although, come to think of it, Jess's sister Alice had had that same lollipop head that comes so often with anorexia for a while, and it hadn't been funny at all. Shite. Was Kate really losing so much weight that she was getting as bad as Alice had been?

"Harriet," she said seriously, the queen still frozen on the screen, "do you think Kate is too skinny?" Harriet only vaguely knew Kate, so would be able to see her much more objectively than Jess.

Kate's weight had played on Jess's mind for a while, true, but had Kate really got as bad as Alice without Jess noticing or doing anything about it? And did Jess really want the ordeal of being the one to have to deal with it? Once was enough.

"You're frowning," Harriet said. "You've gone all wrinkly. You look about three hundred years old when you do that. But yeah, she is a bit, you know. Even I know she's not a great role model if she thinks it's good to be that thin. Opposite of Susan though—she's not exactly got a figure to aspire to either." Harriet smirked, one side of her mouth pulled into a half smile. "Glad I'm not fussed about my weight, though some of my friends are already dieting ... I like eating, I do. Like you."

She grabbed the bowl of popcorn back from Jess and scooped another handful into her mouth to prove the point. "At least Mam was sensible about it; she always ate healthily but never stopped us having treats too. She only joined Get Slim to make sure she could still wear her favourite dresses for longer. She liked the social life of it, too, she used to say, getting out without having to go too far, lazy cow." Harriet was quiet again. "Oh, Jess, I miss her so much." Tears pooled in her eyes then spilled over; silent tears giving way to loud, racking sobs. A scattering of popcorn fell across the carpet as she groped in her pockets for another tissue.

Fletcher, always helpful in times of crisis, bounded to the rescue and hoovered up the spillage.

Jess scooted onto the sofa beside Harriet and wrapped her arms around her until the crying subsided. "I know, love, I know." She kissed the top of Harriet's head and mouthed an inaudible whisper into the girl's hair: "That's why I want to find out if it was really an accident."

Chapter Twenty-Five

It had been ages since she'd been up to Dublin, but the evening with Harriet had convinced Jess that she should try to spend a bit more time with her family while she had the chance. Alice and Eric had both replied to Jess's text with a generic *Fine, how're you?* kind of answer, but after Harriet had gone home, Jess followed up by suggesting she and her siblings get together soon.

Early the following Saturday, Jess left Fletcher with Linda, who was delighted to have his canine company for the day. By a little after nine, Jess had tucked her little car into the station car park and was daydreaming in carriage C of the Sligo to Dublin train. She loved travelling by train. The clacking of the wheels on the track and the rhythmic swaying provided a great place to think, dream, or simply doze.

As the train rattled towards Dublin, Jess's thoughts turned to Alice. How would it be seeing her after so long? Different scenarios rolled in and out of her mind as the countryside rolled in and out of the train window. How would she be? Would she eat anything? Would she still be well? The last time Jess had seen her was just before Christmas, and Alice had seemed ... well, *better*, at least. She was still thin, but not desperately so, and had eaten as well as Jess could ever remember. It was the worry of not knowing how long it might last that Jess found hardest, and this was the main reason why she didn't see Alice very often these days. All those years of constant strain had taken a toll. Jess, exhausted by it all, had gradually retreated into her little sanctuary in the house in Ballyfortnum, and the sisters had drifted apart.

Still, today, Alice had suggested meeting for lunch, so that had to be a good sign. For as long as Jess could remember, they had never met anywhere for lunch. Or for dinner, afternoon tea, or morning coffee. Anywhere that served food had become somewhere for Alice to avoid. More recently, once the worst was over and Alice was on the road to recovery, Jess realised that for about four years of their life, she had not seen Alice ingest anything at all. Yes, she decided, it was definitely a good sign that Alice had suggested lunch.

The train jerked onwards.

Jess's thoughts drifted to Kate. When had she last seen Kate eat? Coffee, yes. Cigarettes, yes. Actual food—apart from the drunken binge the day after Declan left—Jess really couldn't remember. Maybe she could ask Alice for advice ...

Down on the canal, a lonely boat bobbed on its moorings and a family of ducks drifted in haphazard zigzags. Trees blurred together as the train picked up speed and left the canal behind.

Asking Alice for advice ... that would be a real improvement ... A sudden stab of longing pierced her chest as she wondered if, at last, she might get her older sister back. It had been *forever* since Alice had acted like the older sibling.

Jess's eyes brimmed with tears. She scrubbed them away with the back of her hand, hoping none of the other passengers had noticed. She scrabbled in her coat pocket for a tissue, blew her nose, and told herself firmly to think of something else. She would not waste energy getting her hopes up about Alice, not when she could use this time to think about what she knew so far about the deaths in Ballyfortnum. She stuffed the tissue up her sleeve and rummaged in her bag for a notebook and pen.

By the time the attendant manoeuvred the tea trolley through the carriage twenty minutes later—"Two-fifty please, love, d'ya want milk and sugar?"—Jess had doodled abstract swirls over most of a page and scrawled three names linked to a central idea by a merging arrow: *Dave. Angela. Bert. Get Slim.* She doodled some more, realised she'd left no room to add any more writing, and turned to a fresh page.

Again, *Dave, Angela, Bert.* This time, she wrote the names neatly across the top of the page and circled each one emphatically. A vertical line drawn downwards from Angela's name met the angled lines coming down from Dave's and Bert's, all merging to meet above the words *GET SLIM* written in bold capitals and circled twice. She knew there was a link. There just had to be.

She drew another arrow, leading away from the Get Slim circle, to a new name: *Kate.* Jess gave Kate's name its own circled outline. Next, she added other links, each one spidering off the Get Slim circle: *Ballyfortnum* (which she linked back to each of the three names along the top of the page.); *New group, Nov/Dec?*; *When did they join?* She underlined this last heading three times in the hope it would remind her to find out. *Members?—Who?* she added, again underlined. Already, the diagram was messy and confusing. She could redo it with colour—if she had anything worth redoing once she got home.

She took a swig of the tea, frowning at the cardboard cup as if it could help her somehow. Under *Members*, she listed those she could think of in tiny, neat letters. It wasn't a long list, but it was a start. It occurred to her that maybe Dave hadn't even been the first member to die. There must be lots of members that Jess didn't know, like those who lived outside of Ballyfortnum. She'd have to ask Kate. Thinking about mystery slimmers who came from other areas, Jess added *Susan's Group* as a new branch of her diagram and drew a couple of new arrows coming from it, inviting additions later if she could only decide what to add that might be relevant.

Draining the last mouthful of tea, she added two large questions under the rest of the mind map—*WHY?* and *HOW?*—and then looked up in surprise as the train drew to a halt in Connolly Station. Around her, fellow passengers were already standing, grappling for their belongings. She hurriedly scrawled one last note—*ask everyone*—before shoving the notebook into her bag and rising from her seat, ready to alight the train.

After mooching around the shops for an hour or so, Jess found the little café where Alice had suggested they meet. A weird feeling fluttered in her midriff and her hands shook as she pushed open the café door. *Please let her be okay, please let her be okay, please let her be okay.* Jess repeated the mantra silently as she scanned the room for her sister.

Chapter Twenty-Six

At first, Jess couldn't see Alice. She swept her gaze all around the café, before swinging back to a serene figure seated alone at the table in the corner. *Alice?* For the first time in years, as Jess approached her sister in that Dublin café, noting a cup of half-drunk coffee in front of her and a book open in her hands, Alice appeared relaxed.

As Jess neared, trembling with disbelief, Alice glanced up and smiled.

Alice rose to greet Jess, who crossed the room in three long strides. Alice looked like the Alice Jess remembered from *before*. From her childhood. Like the Alice who Jess had wanted to be as an aspirational six-year-old—the Alice she had followed like an eager puppy and longed to emulate.

For the first time in nearly four months, Jess stood face-to-face with her older sister. She flung her arms around Alice. Then she burst into tears. The flood of sudden tears surprised them both, but Alice wrapped her arms around Jess and held her close for the few moments it took for her to regain her composure.

"What's wrong?" Alice guided Jess onto a chair. "Hold on a sec." She went to the counter to pull a wodge of napkins from the dispenser. "Here."

She shoved them across the table to Jess. "Now, do you want coffee? Or tea?"

By the time the coffee was on the table, Jess had taken several deep breaths in the poky toilet cubicle at the rear of the café, washed her face in the tiny, cracked basin, and re-emerged still slightly blotchy, but with her composure at least somewhat regained.

Alice had not come down to Ballyfortnum for Bert's funeral, and Jess hadn't wanted to bother her with how bereft she'd felt in the few weeks that had passed since Bert's death. Indeed, she admitted to her sister now, she hadn't really realised just how bad she'd been feeling, or how much she'd missed her family since Bert had died.

"Yes." Alice reached across the table and put her thin hand on Jess's. "I guess it triggered all the memories of Dad's death for you." She squeezed Jess's fingers and smiled sadly.

"I miss them both so much." Jess scrunched up a napkin and gave another tearful sniff. "Bert had filled the gap a little, but now the gap just seems so much bigger." She blew her nose on one of the napkins and offered Alice a weak smile.

All those years while Alice was ill, Jess had been the strong one, the one who liaised with the hospitals, the doctors, and the family. Jess had juggled her work and her relationship with her then-boyfriend with trying to hold the threads of her family together and stop her sister from her hellbent path to self-destruction. It had drained her. And through all that time, she had never once told Alice how angry she was with her and towards her illness, or been honest with her sister about how it had made her feel.

Now, as Alice slipped into the role of 'the eldest one' that she had neglected for so long, Jess felt like a small child again. The child who, from quite a young age, had stepped into the role of minder, mentor, and even mother, and some of that suppressed anger broke free.

"Why, Alice? Why did you put me through all that? All those years when I thought you would die ... and you wouldn't eat, and we could see you disappearing, and you never loved us enough to stop it ..." Jess would never understand. Wiping away fresh tears with the remnants of a shredded napkin, she took a deep breath, sighed, and straightened her shoulders. When she spoke again, she was calm, quieter, and firm.

"I am so angry with what you did to us, Alice. Are you really better? I really would like my sister back now please."

Alice placed her hand on Jess's again and squeezed. "You know there are no promises." She stared at Jess's tear-streaked face. "I feel okay now. I think it's for real this time. I still see someone about it, but I think it will be okay. I've been better for months. You know at Christmas I had made so much progress, and I think—no, I know—I've just kept on getting better." Alice's gaze dropped to their entwined hands. She gave Jess another squeeze before releasing her grip and wrapping her hands around her empty coffee cup. "I am sorry, you know. I am really sorry, Jess."

Alice ordered a salad for lunch, in contrast with Jess's large tuna melt with a side of crisps and salad garnish, but she ate it. She ate it all, without playing with it or pushing it around her plate or hiding any of it in her bag—all those years of practice meant Jess still watched to be sure. While they ate, they talked about the village news, and the neighbours Alice hadn't seen since their dad died. Even on the couple of occasions when she had come to Ballyfortnum, Alice barely left the house. If any of the neighbours had popped round with goodies or gossip, Alice would keep out of the way, curled on the little chair on the landing pretending to read, or hidden away in the bedroom she'd claimed as her own during the worst of her illness, when her parents coaxed her home for care between hospital stays.

Back then, Alice couldn't face the well-meaning neighbours, all seemingly determined to offer food and observations about her weight; her appetite— "Aren't you wasting away, come on now, eat one of these lovely scones I just baked this morning"—and various other intrusions. Their mother had become increasingly frustrated at her behaviour. In recent years Jess had come to suspect this had been a major contributor to Doreen leaving. Over time, Alice had cut herself off from the neighbourhood as well as the family, throwing their mother into despair.

"I've been very rude to them all, haven't I?" she acknowledged as she stirred her spoon in her empty cup. "I will come and visit soon," she said, vowing to her sister that she would try to make peace with the neighbours who had looked after her dad and Jess so well.

Jess ordered fresh drinks for them both, then told her sister about the more recent events in the village. She had texted Alice when Angela had died, but at the time, Alice had only answered with a brief *sorry to hear that,* and didn't mention it again. Now, briefly recapping Angela's death, Bert's death, and that of Dave, who Alice didn't know at all, Jess brought Alice up to speed with her worries that the three deaths were linked somehow.

"...and, Alice, here's the thing ... they all went to the same group—" she stopped abruptly and looked away. Was it a good idea to mention the group was for slimming? Was that a step too far in terms of Alice's progress?

Alice, however, urged her on, intrigued by the unfolding drama.

"You always did tell a good story. It's like those mysteries you and Eric are always reading," she said, with a glimmer of excitement as she recalled their long-ago childhood games. "Remember when you two stole my new scarf so you could disguise yourself before you followed that old woman? What was her name? You know, the one with the really tall hedge? You followed her to the shop and back because you thought she was trying to steal our cat?"

Jess sniggered into her cup. "We thought we were so subtle. I still can't believe she recognised us!"

Alice chuckled.

Jess couldn't remember the last time she and Alice had sat together and laughed, and a warm happiness spread through her that even the deaths couldn't cool.

"Go on," Alice urged. "Why do you think they are connected? What is the group for?"

Jess was silent for a long moment, and when she did name the group, Alice's reaction was one of quiet sadness. "I didn't like to do my slimming in public," Alice said softly. "Maybe it would have been better if I had."

It was Jess's turn to reach a hand across the table and lay it gently on her sister's. "Alice?" Jess looked at her sister hesitantly. "Can I ask you something else? Only, really, I don't think there's anyone else I can ask, or I wouldn't, but ..."

"You're rambling. Out with it. I can handle it."

The worries about Kate came tumbling out in a jumble of half sentences and incoherent fits and starts. By the time Jess stopped for breath, she had shredded two more napkins and peeled apart four sachets of sugar. Suddenly self-conscious, she swept the spilled sugar into a neat pile and scooped it onto her plate. "Oops. So, do you think I should be worried about her? Should I do something? I don't know if I can go through it again, to be honest."

Alice offered a sad smile. "I dunno. She probably won't want to talk about it. You know how it is."

Jess glared at her sister. "No. I'm not going to just sit by and watch her destroy herself. Not this time." The flash of anger faded and she softened her voice. "Not this time, Alice. I can't let her do what you did. I'll have to talk to her."

By the time Alice waved Jess off at the station barrier, she had promised to come down to stay for a night, in a fortnight's time, not only to pay her belated respects to Linda over Bert's death, but also to "have a chat with Kate, if you like?"

Jess stepped lightly onto the train, as if a load had been lifted from her. For the first time in her adult life, she was looking forward to seeing her sister again, instead of the lingering dread their meetings usually left her with.

The train was busy, but Jess grabbed a window seat, settled back against the velour seat, and pulled her book out of her bag. Before the train even pulled out of Connolly Station, Jess was flying through the pages of the fun, historical mystery novel that mimicked Sherlock Holmes in a most amusing way.

It wasn't until the voice repeated its greeting for the third time that Jess realised that someone was talking to her. She tore her attention away from the pages of her book to discover they had just left Maynooth station and Father James was standing in the aisle, talking to her.

Chapter Twenty-Seven

The young, head-phoned, studenty-type man sitting in the seat next to Jess graciously deferred to the priest and gave up his seat. Father James slid into the vacated space and dumped his cardboard cup on the table, sloshing a little of his tea as he did so. He shook his hand to cool it, dabbed at the spillage with a crumpled paper napkin, and shuffled until he was comfortable in the seat before turning his attention to Jess.

"I've been to see Alice. We had lunch." She smiled at Father James and he smiled back, genuine delight lightening his eyes and crinkling the skin around them. Jess knew he would understand how much it meant that Alice had had lunch.

"What about you?" Jess asked. "Been to the college?" Maynooth University housed Ireland's priest training college, in a beautiful old brick building that stood proudly at the end of the town. Jess had been in once to look around and remembered how stunning and serene the wood-panelled chapel was.

"Just meetings." He waved a hand in dismissal and picked up his cup again. "So, how is she? She sounds well?"

They made small talk, mostly about Alice, as the train rattled on towards the midlands and the little station in Ballymaglen where Jess and Father James would alight the train.

"She's coming down soon. She promised to talk to Kate. Did I tell you I'm worried about how much weight she's losing? Kate, I mean, not Alice, not anymore, and now she's split up with Declan, too ... Kate, obviously, again, not Alice."

"Ah." Father James nodded. "That would explain it. I thought she seemed artificially bright on Tuesday, as if she was trying too hard to be cheerful for the group. I'll have a quiet word with her next time; see if there's anything I can do."

"Alice said that sometimes, when she was at her sickest, she got very irrational. I remember, of course—she was miserable and grumpy and hideous all the time—but to hear her say it herself ..." Jess paused, weighing up what to say next. She didn't want to think Kate could be driven to murder, but hearing Alice admit she had behaved erratically while she was so ill, and had thought many dark thoughts, had left an uncomfortable niggle in Jess's mind. "She said she often felt violent towards people, although of course she never had the strength to act on those thoughts. She wouldn't have, anyway ... You don't think ... Kate ... maybe ..." She didn't finish the question, but instead looked helplessly at Father James, her hands out in front of her, palms upwards, passing her thought to him to deal with.

"Oh, Jess, you really are worried about this aren't you?" Father James was sympathetic. "I can't imagine there's anything suspicious about the unfortunate passing of Dave, or of Angela or Bert, but it is true that it's unusual for two young people in the parish to pass away so close together. Bert, of course, was older, and not in the best of health ... but those other two, God rest their souls ... I always wear a hi-vis vest if I am out late on my bike, and of course, I have good lights. Dave's bike was older, and a bit battered from cycling around the farms. Even if he was hit by a car, it's likely he wasn't well-lit, and somebody simply didn't see him? Of course, if that were the case, they would have stopped, or come forward after. Sure, wasn't it most likely just a tragic combination of too much to drink and icy roads?"

Jess stroked the edges of her book, idly flicking the pages as silence hung between them for a moment. "Hmm. One accident, yes, of course. No one really thought much about it, after—once he was buried. I mean, people still gossiped about it and speculated a bit, but no one really seemed to *know*. And, without family around, I guess no one bothered to pursue it ... but *two* accidents? Angela too? That's a bit weird, I reckon. And Bert may not have been a picture of glowing health, but he really *wasn't* sick ..." Jess had insisted the point so many times lately, she suddenly doubted her own convictions. "... unless he was, and I didn't know? Maybe they didn't tell me, you know, because of Dad? I'll ask Linda when I collect Fletcher." She said the last words more to herself than to Father James, who was now in deep thought himself, picking at the cardboard sleeve on his cup and gazing intently at nothing.

"Okay then," he eventually said, as the train halted at Lambskillen to let the townsfolk off, "let's say, for a moment, you might be right ... but then the question is why would anyone want them dead?"

"That's the problem. I've come up with a few different ideas, but none of them really seem to be good enough reasons to actually kill someone ..." Jess tailed off, staring out at the racing countryside between Lambskillen and Ballymaglen.

The sun was low in the sky now, and the lake, still as glass, glowed in shades of orange, the trees on the little island silhouetted sentinels watching the train speed by.

"Are there ever good reasons to want someone dead?" Father James countered. He sighed, gesturing at the shimmering water. "Beautiful, isn't it?"

Ahead of them, to the west, the sunset threw the distant hills into dark relief whilst the glowing orange of the evening sky turned the lake to fire.

The train slowed.

Jess gathered her book, notebook and pens and stuffed them into her bag.

Father James stood, stepping backwards into the aisle to let Jess go ahead of him.

They alighted the train and walked companionably along the platform towards the exit gate.

Mrs Harris was waiting for Father James, parked in the disabled space at a haphazard angle, both indicators blinking rapidly as if that would justify her illegal occupation of the space.

"I do wish she wouldn't ..." Father James mumbled to Jess as she stood under a street light to search in her bag for her keys. "I do keep telling her, but she just says it's only for a moment. Have a good evening, Jess, love. Give my best to Linda and tell her I will call in to see her after mass tomorrow if she still isn't feeling up to coming along."

Jess hadn't realised Linda hadn't been attending mass. Too much of a reminder of Bert's funeral, she supposed, making a mental note to offer to bring her next Sunday if necessary. She triumphantly retrieved her keys from the depths of her bag as another familiar figure exited the station.

"Hello, Jess."

"Breda! Hello. I didn't see you on the train. Have you been in Dublin today, too?"

Breda frowned. "No, I only got on in town—I had to work today. My car is still playing up; wouldn't start again this morning. Henry dropped me down to the station this morning. Been up to the city yourself, have you?"

"Yeah, I went to see my sister." Jess paused, then nodded. "It was lovely. Really lovely. It's been a while since I saw her. D'you need a lift home then?"

Breda's relief shone from her in a broad smile. "Oh yes, thank you. I was going to walk up to find a taxi. A lift would be wonderful."

Jess pressed her key fob and her car doors unlocked with a click.

Breda settled herself into the passenger seat and placed her bag primly on her lap.

"What's up with your car then? Not that I've any clue about cars myself—I won't have any idea what you tell me!"

Breda laughed. "I'm like that myself. I have absolutely no idea, but it's not been right since before Christmas. Poor battery connection, dodgy alternator, spark plugs-something-or-other, the mechanic said—they keep trying to fix it, but to no avail. I suppose I'll have to get myself another one soon. It's just an expense I could do without right now."

As they pulled out of the station and turned towards home, Jess remembered her scribbles in her notebook on the way into Dublin that morning—*ask the neighbours*—and decided she may as well start with Breda while she had her captive in the car.

"Breda," she began, not sure how best to start her interrogation. "Have you ... Are you ... Does it worry you that three of the Get Slim group have died recently?" She didn't give Breda time to answer, but ploughed on. "I mean, you're in the group—do you not worry there's something weird going on? I think I'd be getting a bit nervous if I were in the group." Realising how ridiculous she sounded, she laughed. "I'm sorry, I do get a bit over dramatic, don't I? Must be all those mystery books I read."

"I—"

"But—"

Breda began to speak, but Jess continued at the same time so Breda fell silent again.

Jess blurted out the question she really wanted the answer to. "Where were you the day Dave died? Do you remember? I saw you and Elizabeth out walking the next day, remember? It was you two who told me he was missing." She paused for breath, flipped on the indicator, checked her mirror and swung out onto the main road.

Breda took advantage of Jess's focus on the traffic to answer some of the barrage of questions. "Yes, of course. I was at work all day. The car wouldn't start that day either. I had to leave it at home; it made me late. And then there should've been Group in the evening—Slimming Group, that is. Except then I didn't get to that either—worked late, again, short notice ... I really must get the car fixed ..."

"So, you didn't use your car that day at all then," Jess confirmed, more to herself than for Breda's benefit. Jess's shoulders relaxed, and she realised how tense she'd been while waiting for Breda's answer. Was it really a good idea to start quizzing all the neighbours about their movements on the days people had died? What if one of them really was a murderer? She probably should be a bit more careful and only ask questions when she wasn't alone with anyone.

She dropped Breda at her gate and waved as the older lady walked up her driveway and let herself into her dark house. Jess waited until the light came on in Breda's hallway, then in her living room, before giving a little beep of the car horn and driving off.

Chapter Twenty-Eight

As had become usual on Tuesdays since Declan had left her, Kate had been loitering in Jess's kitchen since about three o'clock in the afternoon. Jess was considering maybe she should get a job after all, or at least chase up the gardening course idea. It wasn't exactly that she had anything better to do with her days than hang out in her kitchen doing absolutely nothing, but she felt a bit out of sorts at Kate's presumption that she was always available for endless coffee.

She shivered. "Pull that door shut, won't you? I'm chilly."

"I'll just finish this." Kate waved her cigarette at Jess.

Yes, thought Jess, *and then you'll light another one off that one and I'll still be bloody freezing in my own kitchen while you huff the stink of your smoke into it, because even though you are holding the cigarette outside, you pretty much bring it inside to smoke the damn thing, since you won't step all the way out there yourself. Because, you know, it's bloody cold out there ...* "All right," she said aloud, "let's walk up to the bog. Fletch hasn't had a good walk in days, what with all the rain lately."

It was the first clear day since Thursday, and Jess and Fletcher had done little more than mooch around the park for very half-hearted walks, during the last few days.

"I think I have cabin fever," Jess conceded. "It's making me bloody bad-tempered. And fat." She bit her lip, wishing she could take back the words.

Too late—Kate jumped straight in. "You could always join up, you know. There are great member offers right now, and God knows I could use a new member or several. D'ya feel like helping me with leafleting again this weekend?"

Jess did not. The last lot of leafleting they'd done had involved Kate sitting in the driving seat smoking and giving unnecessary instructions while Jess leapt in and out of the passenger seat like a drunken Jack-in-the-box. And—she shuddered at the memory—she had almost got her hand bitten off by one particularly over-enthusiastic dog as she'd stuffed a leaflet into a too-small letterbox.

"I dunno; I think I'm busy ..."

"With what? You said it's not until Saturday evening Alice is coming, and what else do you ever do at weekends these days?"

Jess clenched her hands and bit back a retort. It might be true that she enjoyed her quiet life and rarely did much at the weekends, but the insinuation she had become old, boring, and reclusive stung. She glared at Kate, but Kate had turned away to take the next drag on her cigarette, so Jess's anger fell only on Kate's elegantly-styled hair.

Even with her back to Jess, Kate continued talking. "... and no, I can't go for a walk now, not in these shoes ..." She gestured to her high black shoes. "... and my work gear. It'd get ruined. Don't want my hair getting messed up either; it cost me a fortune to get it done." She'd had her nails done again too, earlier in the day.

Jess had a fascinated awe of anyone who could function with nails as long as Kate's newly-acquired false ones. They were beautifully finished in a shimmery pink, and almost the first thing Kate had talked about when she'd arrived on Jess's doorstep an hour or so ago.

Dammit, Jess thought. *Of course she won't bloody walk in those bloody high bloody shoes and that bloody tight bloody skirt.* Stupid of her to have forgotten. It wasn't as if Kate ever wore trainers or sensible flat shoes anymore. Well, except that night she'd come round after Declan went off, when she was like the old Kate Jess used to have more of a laugh with. She patted Fletch sympathetically, hoping he could correctly interpret her 'sorry, mate, she's a pain in the backside, we'll walk soon' look.

"So," Kate went on, undeterred by Jess's silent fuming, "how about Saturday afternoon, we can target the village again with flyers, I haven't redone this area since I first set the group up. It won't take long. Couple of hours?"

"I'll give you an hour," Jess said, inwardly cursing her inability to think of a decent excuse or simply say no. "But only if you shut that bloody door before I freeze to death."

Kate took a final drag, tossed the stub into the border, and closed the door.

"So," Jess said, as Kate plonked her skinny frame onto a kitchen chair, "will you have one of Linda's buns? They're delicious." She didn't wait for an answer before presenting Kate with a beautifully iced cupcake. "Don't they look gorgeous? She should bake for a living instead of just feeding all the neighbours for free all the time." Jess broke a large chunk off her own cake while Kate toyed with the decorations on hers and nibbled non-committedly on a sugar flower. "Kate." Jess swallowed down her own mouthful of cake, studying her friend thoughtfully. "What exactly *have* you eaten today?"

It was Kate's turn to glare. "Just because you don't care about your figure," she said icily, "does not mean that I don't care about mine. I am sticking to a well-regulated diet, as you full-well know. I am eating plenty. I just don't eat the crap you do."

Kate's dieting obsession concerned Jess too much for her to rise to the dig at her own figure, or get into an argument about which of them really ate crap. "Kate. I am seriously worried about you. You are skin and bones. You are going to make yourself ill if you don't put on a bit of weight. You are not a good role model to your group. You are eating next to nothing." Jess stood, taking her own empty plate to the sink. She slammed the plate down onto the counter beside the sink with such force that it cracked. "Shit. Dammit!" She swung round to glower at Kate. "Do you really want to end up like Alice?"

Kate shoved aside her uneaten cake and stood up. "I am perfectly in control of my diet, thank you very much. I follow the Get Slim guidelines very carefully and I am a much better role model than that Susan one, I'll have you know. My members who used to go into town to her group say that they feel more encouraged by having a consultant who clearly practices what she preaches. I am meeting my targets every week, and as you well know, I still attend my other group for my own weigh-ins—it's not professional to weigh in at my own group. Some people do get quite discouraged when others are doing well.

"So, I thank you for your concern but I have to go now; time to get set up." She stuffed her cigarettes and sweeteners into her handbag and bent to pet Fletcher. "We'll bring you on Saturday," she promised him, "when we do the leaflets." With that, Kate gave Jess a smoke-scented peck on the cheek and swept out of the house.

"Well," Jess said to Fletcher, "that went well." She shoved her feet into her walking boots and helped herself to Kate's untouched cake. "Now we really must go for a walk, boyo; walk off this extra cake." Jess crammed the last half in her mouth, freeing up her hands to tie her bootlaces.

As soon as they stepped out the door, the cheery spring flowers in the front gardens of Orchard Close brightened Jess's mood. Daffodils, tulips, and hyacinths brought a burst of colour to the day, and as Fletcher brushed by, the heady scent of the hyacinths wafted in the air.

Fletcher stopped to sniff a particularly pungent lamp post in front of Number 2, where a plethora of tulips bobbed sunset-coloured heads at Jess.

She smiled back at them, her bad temper subsiding further. However annoyed and worried she was about Kate, the leaflet drop might be a useful activity. She would get to call on every house in Ballyfortnum, and maybe she would see something or someone she had missed while racking her brains about who could possibly have a big enough grudge against Dave, Angela, and Bert to want them dead.

Her phone vibrated in her coat pocket. When she pulled the phone free, her little notebook came with it, falling to the ground. She picked it up and checked the phone. Kate. She must've got the room set up quickly. Jess imagined her sitting elegantly in the meeting room waiting for her clients, tapping away on her phone with those manicured nails.

I'll pick you up at 2 then? Fletch can come, I'll make room in the car x

Kate clearly hadn't held onto her annoyance. Jess, who most definitely *was* still a little annoyed, stood in a gateway and started to type that she would give her an hour and then walk Fletch back from the village after that. As she typed, she remembered Alice and deleted the half-written message to compose a new one.

OK. You can pop in after and say hi to Alice. But you'll have to bugger off after a cuppa so I can catch up with her properly. That should give Alice time to check out whether she thought Jess's concern about Kate's weight was valid, whilst still making it clear to Kate that she wanted Alice to herself for the rest of the evening. Hopefully.

"Otherwise," she said to Fletch, tousling his head, "if she doesn't look like she's leaving, we'll have to literally push her out the door if she stays too long, won't we?"

Fletcher panted at her in what she took to be agreement.

Tucking the phone into her jeans pocket, she glanced at the notebook she was still holding. She would have to look through it when they got home, see if she could add anything before Saturday, anything to look out for. "Proper sleuthing, Fletch; that's what we'll do on Saturday. Proper sleuthing."

Chapter Twenty-Nine

Saturday dawned dry and bright, April mere days away now, and the weather offered the promise of a warm spring. Throughout the morning, Jess erratically tidied the house; picking things up, putting them down again, moving them to the same places she'd just moved them from.

"Jess, love, it's only Alice coming." Linda's voice still echoed in her ears after a brief visit earlier to drop in a bunch of freshly-picked spring flowers from Bert's garden, and a plate of fruit-laden scones. "They are low fat, and have no extra sugar—that fruit is lovely and sweet—you can tell her, so she will have no excuse not to eat one."

Linda had got it just right, Jess thought, as her neighbour gave her a firm hug and told her not to worry.

"It's not that I'm worried, as such," Jess had said. "It just feels different somehow this time—like my sister is coming to see me, not just that sick, shrunken ... *imposter* who's been around for the last few years. I'm excited, mostly. And a bit scared too, I guess ... What if I'm wrong? What if she's not really better and I was wrong? I'm only tidying to keep busy, really—but you know that." Jess laughed as she acknowledged her feelings to her neighbour.

"Bring her over to say hello, won't you? Or if you'd rather, text me and I'll pop over here later. It will be lovely to see her, especially if she's well."

Jess had given Linda another quick hug and turned the vacuum cleaner back on, waving a farewell as Linda had let herself back out through the front door.

Now, almost done, Jess squirted cleaning fluid down the toilet, lit an incense stick on the landing, threw open a couple of windows, and collapsed in a heap onto the sofa.

Fletcher jumped onto her lap and gazed up at her adoringly.

"Aw, thanks Fletch, I think I've done a pretty good job too, to be honest. Go on and make me a cup of tea, won't you?"

Fletcher yawned, as if he were the one who had done all the hard work, and closed his eyes.

Jess rested her head against the cushions and closed her eyes in solidarity. "Five minutes, boyo, then I'm going to have to get some lunch before Kate arrives. I'm buggered if I'm going running around all those houses without eating first, whatever Kate chooses to do."

Some thirty minutes later, Jess stirred a pan of soup on the stove top, flicking idly through the pages of her notebook as she waited for the soup to warm, mentally planning the route she and Kate would take through the village. Hopefully, a good few of the villagers would be home, and happy to chat for a few minutes on a sunny spring day ... half of them would most likely be in their gardens, now the Tidy Village contest was looming.

April usually brought a flurry of outdoor activity around Ballyfortnum, just as soon as the contest officially launched. As a previous winner, the stakes were high. Come springtime each year, even reluctant gardeners often found themselves swept up by the pressure of their more enthusiastic neighbours. Jess scribbled a doodle in her notebook—the word *gardens*, sprouting swirls and shoots and childlike five-petalled flowers.

Stirring a dash of cream into her soup to cool it, she had a flash of inspiration—the gardens themselves would not tell her much, but what about the cars? On a Saturday, everyone would have their cars parked in their driveways, or on the road in front of the smaller cottages, taking a rest from the weekly commute. Of course, some would be out and about, running errands in town, or off on a day trip, but most of the village would probably be at home.

Going door to door with Kate would give Jess a perfect opportunity to check every car for bumps and scratches … hadn't Marcus mentioned how battered Dave's bike was? And marked with paint scratches? Someone must've knocked him into that ditch—surely if he was just drunk, he'd have got back up and carried on home to sleep it off? She stretched across the kitchen to grab her phone from the counter and fired out a text.

You know you said Dave's bike had paint stains on it? What colour was the paint? Almost as soon as she had laid the phone back down and picked up her spoon, an answer beeped into her inbox. Abandoning the soup once more, she opened the message.

Red bike, black and blue paint scratches. Brown rust. Black oil. Mud coloured mud. And yes, I'm fine, thank you for asking.

Jess laughed out loud. Sarcasm by text. *Sorry! How are you, Marcus? I hope you are well and enjoying this perfectly pleasant Saturday.* She finished her soup, dumped the bowl in the sink and took one of Linda's scones out of the tin. The phone beeped again, and she snatched it up, still smiling.

Alice. *C U later. Can't wait xx* That sounded promising. Even Alice's texts were cheerier now. She really did seem so much better.

Me too. You driving or coming by train? As Jess answered her sister, Fletcher barked and ran to the door.

A moment later, Kate greeted him in the hall, having let herself in.

"Be ready in a min, come on through," Jess called, rinsing her lunch things and leaving them on the drainer to dry. "How're you?" she asked as Kate came into the kitchen.

Kate was casually dressed but still managed to look like she had just stepped off a catwalk, even in jeans, trainers, and a ponytail. Jess felt scruffy beside her in her sloppy sweatshirt and old jeans. "Hold on while I just run up and change, won't you? And, I need to meet Alice's train at five, or if we aren't back in time, you can run me out to meet it?" Even as she was saying it, Jess realised this could be a better plan anyway. Alice and Kate could talk in the front on the drive home while Jess kept Fletch under control in the back seat. That would give Alice a good, natural opportunity to quiz Kate on how she was and what she was up to; the kind of small talk anyone would make when giving someone a lift somewhere. She pulled off her tatty sweater and swapped it for a cleaner, form-fitting jumper. She pulled a comb through her hair and re-tied it into a neat chignon.

"That'll do," she told herself in the mirror, before running back down the stairs. "We'll just walk round the close first, will we?" Jess suggested, pulling Fletcher's lead from the hook in the hall. "Do you think it's warm enough to not bring a coat, or would that be asking for it to lash, d'you reckon?"

"Coat, deffo. Let's go." Kate grabbed a handful of leaflets out of her car and handed a wodge of them to Jess.

"You go one way; I'll go the other?" Jess had thought this through already and gestured for Kate to go in the direction towards the park. Jess walked that way most days, so could easily check out the cars at the open end of Orchard Close another day. Today, she would scrutinize the cars belonging to some of her closest neighbours, but those whose houses she never walked past unless she was visiting one of them. Most of the residents of the close were retired, with just one car per household, neatly parked in the driveway in front of each neat semi like an advert for suburban bliss. Jess soon fell into a routine where she would walk along the left-hand side of each car as she approached the letterbox, pop the leaflet through the door, and check out the other side of the car on the way back down the short driveways. This way she would be able to look at all four sides of each car—except for Jeanie and Bill's, which one of them had parked so close to their garage door that she couldn't get around the front of it. Still, she hardly suspected them of murder anyway—hadn't they been so kind to her the night Bert died, and been just as distraught over his death as she was?

Most of the cars were new-ish, clean-ish, and well-maintained. Jess's own little car was, without doubt, the dirtiest in the close. She'd clean it tomorrow if it were still sunny, she silently promised the neighbours, embarrassment warming her face. As she shoved a leaflet through the final house at her end of the close, she concluded that, out of all her neighbours' cars, the only one with a dent or a scratch was her joined-on neighbour at Number 8. That damage, she knew, was from last summer when he hit a pheasant and decided it wasn't worth the hassle or expense of getting the small dent in the wing knocked out.

Kate was already waiting back at Jess's house, leaning against her car, cigarette in her hand. Jess opened the back door of the car and Fletcher, always excited to have a road trip, jumped in.

Kate turned right as they exited Orchard Close, her plan being to start at the least populated end of the village, then move systematically towards the village centre, and then onwards, all the way up to the main road. There were only a handful of houses in the parish to the north and west of Orchard Close. Most of the houses in that direction, close as they may be, fell into the confines of the neighbouring parish, and Kate and Jess had agreed to stick strictly to the parish of Ballyfortnum for today's goal. The houses here stood far apart from each other, mostly well set back in large parcels of land, and several of them the older style of farmhouse. Consequently, they almost all had driveways long enough to warrant mounting a letterbox on the gate pillars rather than in the front doors of the houses themselves. They wouldn't be talking to many of the villagers up this way, then.

Jess made another mental note to walk Fletcher in this direction another day, if they discovered nothing of interest at this stage of the outing. In fact, they only spoke to one person out of the dozen or so houses they delivered leaflets to in this direction. The forty-ish-year-old farmer, known locally as Tractor O'Sullivan, was mending a fence just inside the driveway of his farm.

Before Jess could undo her seatbelt, Kate had leapt out of the driver seat, calling, "I've got this one! It's good networking if I talk to them myself," as she pushed the door shut.

"Networking my arse," Jess muttered to Fletcher. Everyone in the village knew this particular farmer as something of a playboy. He was youngish, single, wealthy, and one of the parish's largest landowners. And always on the pull, hence his nickname.

"Something of a catch," the older women of the village often said to Jess, before adding the inevitable, "if only he hadn't such a reputation." He wasn't bad looking, either, if you liked the rugged, ruddy-faced types.

Kate was swinging both her hair and her hips as she sashayed back to the car after a good five minutes of 'networking'.

Fletcher tried to jump over the seat back, his tail wagging as if Kate had been gone for weeks.

"If you take that long with them all, we'll be out till Christmas comes around again. Get down, Fletch. Sit!"

Kate was indignant. "He said he'll come along, now the evenings are lighter and he's not so rushed. It pays off to be nice, you know. And he's loaded."

Jess turned to look out of her window, so Kate wouldn't see her smile. "I wouldn't have noticed. Or did you just mean money-wise?" she said, trying to maintain her composure, but unable to contain a smothered snort of laughter.

"Both, by all accounts." Kate sniggered, and as they drove back past Orchard Close they were both giggling uncontrollably. Kate pulled into the entrance of the park and they sat chuckling stupidly for several more minutes until Kate felt able to drive on.

"Kate," Jess said, also calm again now, "while we're out, let's check out everyone's car, see if any have any sign of a knock ... you know, in case someone local did hit Dave?" Jess hoped she managed to sound as if she'd only just thought of the idea, knowing Kate would be happier to play along if she didn't think Jess had pre-planned the whole thing.

Chapter Thirty

In the village centre, Jess's prediction proved to be true. Many of the neighbours were outside, giving their lawns a first cut of the season, tidying hedges before nesting season officially began, washing cars, or planting out brightly-coloured bedding plants. The buzz of activity made the village cheerful and welcoming and not at all the kind of place where a murderer may be hiding.

Kate parked at the church so they could both walk, making the most of the sunny weather. As they got out of the car, Jess realised she was quite enjoying herself. She opened the back door to allow Fletcher to jump out, and the three of them stood beside the car and turned their faces to the sun to bask in its warmth for a moment before walking down the driveway towards the road.

"I'll take this side, you take that." Kate gestured across the road towards the pub, indicating that she would stay on the church side of the main street.

Jess had a better plan. "No, let's stay together so we can chat as we go—we'll walk together but take alternate houses. Then we can also both skim our eyes over each car too ... two pairs of eyes and all that?"

Fletcher tugged on his lead.

"And," Jess added, nodding down at him, "that way if there's a mad dog loose in anyone's garden it will be easier—you can do those ones and I can keep this boy out of the way." She wouldn't get her fingers bitten off, either, if she made Kate tackle the dog-inhabited houses.

Jess linked her arm through Kate's, determined to be a better friend than she had been lately, and together, they turned left out of the church driveway, posting a leaflet into the vicarage post box as they passed by.

"Ah sure, he came along last week, and the housekeeper's been to every meeting since the first one, but they can have a leaflet anyway." Kate dismissed the foreboding stone house with an airy wave, and they turned left again beyond the vicarage onto the Little Mason road leading to the south, out of Ballyfortnum between the church and Marcus's house. Only a dozen or so houses stood along here, spread over about a quarter of a mile, before giving way to open fields, another O'Sullivan farm—one of Tractor's brothers—and a pretty patch of woodland. Beyond the farm, the lane became little more than a winding track until it reached the edges of Little Mason. The third house on the left was Niall and Angela's house—well, Niall and the children's now, Jess remembered with a thud in her chest.

Kate started towards the gateway, but Jess pulled her back, persuading her that no, it would not be appropriate to put a Get Slim leaflet through their door. Acquiescent, Kate skipped the low apricot-coloured bungalow and moved on. Most of the other inhabitants of this lane Jess knew only by sight. Two were local farm labourers, she thought, but most of the others commuted into Lambskillen for work. A couple of the houses had a plethora of brightly-coloured plastic toys scattered around untidy gardens, and one had two small children playing noisily behind its closed gates.

Jess approached with a leaflet, and they bounded to the gate to greet her, stretching their arms eagerly through the iron bars to pet Fletcher.

"Woah, steady on," Jess cautioned. "Fletch is friendly, but some dogs aren't so nice! Is your mum home?" She looked past them for any sign of an adult, wanting an excuse to continue through the gate so she could check out their car. A tatty blue estate car was parked at a haphazard angle at the front of the house.

"I'll take it." A grubby child held out her hand.

"No, me!"

"I said it first!"

By now, the children were swinging on the gate and Fletcher had tangled himself around Jess's legs in his excitement at being worshipped by these two small creatures. Jess gave up trying to get past and handed a leaflet to each child.

"One each. Give them to your mum?"

Kate glared at her. "Those leaflets cost me money, you know. Go easy on them." Jess did not retort that Kate had left one at the vicarage where she already had two regular clients; had wanted to leave one in at Angela's house, and had stuffed one through the empty, half-derelict house on the far side of Orchard Close earlier on.

"You never know," Kate had justified against Jess's objections. "The builders might be interested in coming along."

"Don't be daft," Jess said. "Better to send two happy kids back with two leaflets than to have them go bawling and screaming and their parents hating you for making that happen." She frowned at Kate, who smiled back and nodded. "I couldn't see the car properly either," Jess went on, "but it looked so wrecked you wouldn't know whether a bump was old, new, or a new dent on top of an older one. Any luck with yours?"

Kate shrugged. "Nothing obvious."

They crossed over and walked back towards the village on the opposite side of the lane to Angela's house.

As Jess turned from shoving a leaflet into the house opposite, she noticed Harriet in the garden and gave the girl a wave.

Harriet ambled over, dropping to her knees on the pavement to hug an ecstatic Fletcher. "I saw you go by just now. What're you up to?" she asked without getting up.

Jess flapped a handful of leaflets towards her. "Nothing much. Just helping Kate with some marketing."

Harriet stood up. "Jess, I know you said before maybe someone had … well … someone might have killed Mam … on purpose, like. Well, seems like it wasn't just food poisoning—she had a heart attack, too. I heard Dad on the phone to Auntie Margie. It happens, he said, sometimes, if someone is really ill, and their organs can't handle it, like, but …" She tailed off and held Jess's gaze for a moment, willing her to understand as her eyes teared up.

Jess stroked Harriet's arm. "I know, love," she finished for her. "It might be significant somehow …"

"Probably not," Harriet said, "but, just, I—I dunno … Mam was pretty tough you know, I don't reckon her heart would give up that easy …"

Poor Harriet. Jess gently patted the girl's shoulder. A flutter of guilt threatened to surface, but Jess pushed it away. It might be painful to talk about it, but if there was something suspicious going on, surely it would be better to uncover it and get some justice for losing her mum? "D'ya want to help us with these?" Jess waved the leaflets again.

"Nah, I have a ton of homework, I just came to say that. And to say hi, obvs." Harriet gave Jess a quick hug and Fletcher a much longer one, then crossed back over the road and disappeared into her house.

"Come on, you're slacking." Kate was almost back at the junction, where the Little Mason road joined Ballyfortnum's main street, and shuffled impatiently on the pavement next to Marcus's garden. He lived in an old worker's cottage on the corner; one end of a row of tiny, terraced bungalows. Most had bulky, ugly extensions stretching out into the gardens behind them, but Marcus's only boasted a neat kitchen extension, a dormer window, and a well-built conservatory. A thick beech hedge concealed most of his garden, but as Jess and Kate drew level with the house, the hedge gave way to a neat, wooden fence.

Fletcher's ears pricked up and his tail wagged, tentatively at first, then in frantic enthusiasm. He scrabbled at the bottom of the fence, then leapt against it to look over the top. Yelps, yaps, and an echoing scrabble of paws from the other side of the fence suggested that Snowflake was making a valiant, but unsuccessful attempt to greet his doggy friend.

Marcus stepped out of his conservatory, in jeans and bare feet, to investigate the racket. "Oh, it's you. Hello Fletcher, hello Jess, Kate. Does he want to come in and say hello properly then, before he has the fence down?" Marcus's smile softened his words, and he stepped near enough to reach over and pat Fletcher on the head. "If you shut up for a minute, you can come in and play, hang on."

He disappeared back into the house only to emerge a minute later with his feet jammed into unlaced trainers. "Come in, Jess; let him off for a run-around. Snowflake will be delighted—he's not had a walk today, I'm not long awake after a night shift." He was unshaven and dishevelled, and Jess's cheeks flushed with heat.

"Did he wake you? I'm so sorry, I didn't think you might be sleeping."

Marcus shook his head and yawned. "No, I was awake, just making breakfast. Or lunch ... or afternoon tea. Depends on how you look at it.

Want to come in for a cup of tea?" Jess glanced back at Kate and raised her eyebrows questioningly.

Kate held her hands out in mock annoyance. "You're a bloody useless leafleter," she complained, "but don't let me stop you." Hidden by the fence, she nudged Jess in the ribs and whispered loudly, "Go on, you know you want to."

"Kate!" she hissed, and pressed her foot down hard onto Kate's. "I'm helping Kate with getting these leaflets out, I can't stop now … a promise is a promise and all that." She smiled her most artificially angelic smile at Kate, hidden from Marcus by the angle of her head.

"Why don't you leave Fletch here to play then? Collect him when you come back past? Where are you headed next?"

Jess agreed, grateful to be relieved of her over-excited, pulling dog. "We'll just do these." She gestured to the rest of Marcus's row. "And those …" She pointed at the group of houses opposite."… and get him once those few are done? If you're sure."

Jess, Kate, and the very excited Labrador walked together to the front gate, Fletch dancing and leaping and twisting around their legs in his desire to get to his friend.

Jess lifted the latch, unclipped the lead, and Fletcher bounded into the garden without looking back. Jess closed the gate behind him, called her thanks to Marcus, and grabbed Kate's arm to drag her away before she embarrassed Jess any further.

Marcus waved them off and disappeared into his house to his afternoon breakfast.

As soon as the door had shut behind him, Jess swung around to glare at Kate. "Would you ever stop it?" she said. "I do *not* fancy him. He's way too old and, besides, he might even be gay—his dog is called Snowflake, remember? And he's definitely got some secrets in his past ..."

"Like what?"

"Ah, I don't know, probably nothing. He told me when I first met him that Snowflake was not his choice of name for the dog, and even though we've become friends, he never says anything much about himself, really. He's a good-looking older man who lives alone, with a small dog with a silly name. I bet there's a man in his life."

"Stereotyping, much?" Kate dug her fingers into Jess's side and they both laughed. "But you do admit he's good-looking now, at least. And he's not that much older than us—ten years, give or take." She cast a sly look at her friend.

It was true, thought Jess. She knew very little about the policeman who had quickly become her good friend and easy confidante. She must try to talk less about her own problems and ask him more about himself the next time they got together.

"Now, come on, let's get these leaflets done while the sun is still shining. We've got to meet Alice at five, remember, so let's get a move on." They reached the end of the terrace and crossed the road. "I'll go over to Breda's neighbour—Mrs Gregg, isn't it? You run up to Breda, or are you skipping her and Elizabeth?"

Chapter Thirty-One

J ess strolled up the pathway to the semi-detached house that made the other half of Breda's. She didn't know Mrs Gregg or her elderly husband except to say hello if she passed them in the street or met them in the shop. They had lived in the village forever, born and bred in Ballyfortnum by all accounts, and Mrs Gregg was now confined to a wheelchair by some ailment that may have simply been old age and arthritic knees. Their car was shiny, new, and adapted for her needs, according to the sticker on its rear window. It gleamed in the sun and there wasn't a scratch on it. Jess bet that if she sat inside the car, it would still smell of showroom and new upholstery.

The Greggs had been the first in the area to get that year's new car, and they'd taken delivery of it in the first week of January. It would be extremely unlikely they could have bashed it and managed to get it patched up to look like new without anyone hearing about it, Jess decided, as she bullied a leaflet through the horrible hairy brush-lined letterbox.

Kate met her at the end of Breda's drive.

"Yeah, yeah, I know, she already comes to the group, but I need them to keep the momentum up. Some aren't coming as often as they used to. Besides, I shouldn't really be telling you who is already a member anyway, so we will do every single house from now on, no exceptions, for reasons of maintaining confidentiality."

Jess snorted. "Kate. I already know that Breda and Elizabeth are members, and you know I know, and they know that I know, because they have both told me themselves, and they know that you know that I know and you make me die laughing sometimes with how serious you take this. Okay? Now, how was Breda's car?"

Kate was more relaxed than Jess had seen her in weeks, and grudgingly joined Jess's laughter, acknowledging that, of course, Jess knew half the village had joined the group. "But," she added in a warning tone, "I am still not telling you about anyone you don't know about already, and you know I can't tell you anything about their weight loss or any personal stuff."

Jess stopped and swivelled on her foot to face Kate. "Kate, you are completely mad. I really don't care how much anyone in the village weighs, or what they eat for breakfast, or how many chocolates or double whiskies they may have in any given day. Seriously, I don't care!" Her laughter faded as her face crumpled into a frown. "Unless—unless, of course, someone has poisoned them. Then I care." *Or*, she added silently, *if they are starving themselves to death and they are my friend*. She didn't want to spoil the fun they were having, so she kept this thought to herself. Let Alice bring it up later, she decided, looking at her phone to check the time.

"Breda's car?" she prompted, although she remembered Breda had not been driving home the evening Dave died—she'd told Jess her car hadn't started on that day, so she was already in the clear.

"Not a scratch. Not that I could see anyway," Kate assured her.

Jess swung open Elizabeth's gate and jogged to the front door, glad not to have Fletcher in tow as Elizabeth's spaniel—Stanley—leapt joyously around her. She rapped on the knocker and posted a leaflet through the letterbox. As she turned, she remembered the dent she'd seen in Elizabeth's car the other day. She'd have to ask Elizabeth about it. Henry's silver car gleamed in the sun, parked in the driveway beside Elizabeth's older, black car. It was well-cared for, with the look of a car that gets polished every Sunday afternoon, and hadn't a scratch on it. Jess was still squinting at his bumpers when Henry appeared from around the side of the house, clutching a pair of gardening gloves and rubbing his back.

"Just me, Henry, how're you? I'm not stopping; just helping Kate deliver leaflets. I only knocked in case you wondered why Stanley was barking his head off. Say hello to Elizabeth for me?" Jess stepped away from Henry's car and waved, retreating down the drive guiltily. At the gate, she stopped and swung around. "Oh, Henry, what happened to Elizabeth's car? Did she have a knock? She never said anything, is she okay?"

Henry tilted his head and frowned. Jess pointed towards the dented bumper.

"There. I just noticed the dent," Jess lied. "Is it new?"

"Oh, that? I've no idea. It's from a while ago, back in the winter. Neither of us know how it happened, didn't notice anything at the time. Could've been anything, a knock in a car park probably."

"Glad no one was hurt then. Gotta go; I'm meeting my sister at the station soon and we've still half the village to do with these leaflets. See you!" She waggled her fingers at Henry and manoeuvred carefully out of the gate, squeezing through the smallest possible gap to avoid letting Stanley escape.

It only took a few minutes to deliver leaflets to the few houses between Elizabeth's and the shop.

Kate offered to do the little lane beside the pub—"... then we'll move the car along a bit and do the school road next?"—while Jess ran back to Marcus's house to collect Fletcher.

"He could stay, if you've more to do—are you sure you don't want a cuppa?" Marcus asked.

Jess, thirsty from the walking and the sun, and more than a little curious to see inside Marcus's house, thought about it for a long moment.

"I really can't," she said with regret. "We still have to do the other side of the church and out to the main road, and be finished in time to collect my sister from Ballymaglen. She's already on the train by now. Another time? Fletcher could do with more playdates." Jess felt her face colour yet again. Did she do nothing but blush in Marcus's company? After all the digs Kate kept making, now she had used the word 'playdate'. And, as if that wasn't a stupid enough word to use at the best of times, would he think she wanted a date herself? She cringed inwardly and hoped he hadn't noticed.

"Sure," Marcus said, smiling and holding out Fletcher's lead to her. Her fingers brushed his as she took the lead, and she stepped back quickly. "Anytime. Have fun with your sister."

By the time Kate and Jess had completed the leafleting, it was twenty to five, and they were hot and exhausted. Kate ducked into the shop for bottles of water, which they gulped down in inelegant slurps and glugs. Kate was uncharacteristically appreciative, and Jess was suddenly glad she had agreed to help. Kate had been difficult lately, and Jess had often found herself irritated in her company, but today had reminded her why they had become friends.

"It was fun," she told Kate, as they headed a little too fast along the main road towards Ballymaglen to meet the train. "Plus, we got three new dents and a few more alibis."

On the school road where Susan lived, they had spotted a car with a large dent in its passenger-side wing. No one had come to the door, but Jess knew a young couple lived there, with two or three children attending the school. She'd have to get Susan gossiping again to try to find out if she knew how her neighbour's car had got dented, and where the couple had been that cold night in January.

No one had been home at Susan's house, either, a few doors before the dented-car house. This, Jess thought, was quite a relief, given the woman's annoyance with Kate and her rival Get Slim group. It also meant Jess was unable to ascertain whether Susan's own car showed any newish dents to its bodywork, and, considering Susan had already admitted to being in the right place at the right time, Jess made a mental note to check on Susan's car as soon as possible.

In a muddy yard further along the main street, a little beyond Dave's house, they'd spotted a battered farmer's jeep. Dave's little cottage still stood empty, but a half-filled skip stood outside, and the house showed signs of renovation. Getting ready to sell, Jess guessed. The farmer who owned the dented jeep also owned the house where Dave had lived and was amongst those who searched for Dave the morning after he died. Dave probably worked for this farmer too; she wasn't sure. Kate hadn't said much, but from her secretiveness, Jess inferred this farmer was also "one of hers," giving him yet another link to Dave.

"But," Kate had protested, "aren't farmers always banging into things—sheep, fences, big deep ruts? That's the point of them having these big old jeeps, isn't it?"

The third of the new dents was further out again, at almost the last house in the parish just before they joined the main Dublin road. The postmistress from Ballymaglen lived here and had been pottering around in her garden when Jess had dropped off the leaflet.

"Oh, yes." Sheelagh Flannery glanced at it dismissively. "I go to this—oh wait, no, that's Ballyfortnum, sure, I go into the other one, down in the town."

Chapter Thirty-Two

The train pulled away from Ballymaglen station just as Kate drove into the car park.

"Just in time," Jess sighed. Kate had driven the ten-minute journey between Ballyfortnum and Ballymaglen station with Jess loudly and persistently worrying they would be late and Alice would have to wait around.

"Told you it would be fine," Kate called after Jess as she jumped out of the car.

Jess jogged towards the station building, leaving Kate shunting the car back and forwards to turn it around in the crowded car park.

Before she reached the station lobby, Alice appeared from the small pedestrian gate beside the station house, walking confidently towards her. Alice's hair hung in a long, glossy sheen that swung around her shoulders. Dressed casually in jeans and a light blazer, she could have stepped from the pages of a catalogue. Her arm hooked the handle of a terracotta leather holdall, but as Jess approached, Alice let the bag fall to the ground. She stood, bag at her feet, with her arms outstretched, and as soon as Jess was in reach, she pulled her into a tight hug.

Jess hadn't realised she had been so tense until she relaxed into her sister's embrace. It was going to be fine. Alice was going to be fine.

Alice acknowledged Jess's relief. "It feels so good to be here this time." She gave Jess a quick kiss on the cheek, scooped up her bag, and let Jess lead her to the waiting car.

"Kate's car." Jess pointed to where Kate was waiting, two wheels on the kerb. "I was helping her with some stuff, and we got a bit late, so we came straight here. Fletch is in the car, too; you'd better get in the front or he'll lick you to death. Besides, then you can talk to Kate?" She raised her eyebrows. "Remember what I said?"

"Sure." Alice slid into the front seat while Jess flung the bag into the boot. She grimaced at the cardboard boxes full of Get Slim bars, hoping that Kate wouldn't foist any more of the hideous things on her.

Bag stashed, Jess pulled open the back door, deftly catching hold of Fletcher's collar as he lunged for freedom. She shoved him back onto the seat, thwarting his escape, and scrambled into the car beside him.

Alice and Kate were already deep in the "Haven't seen you in ages, how are you?" kind of conversation people have with the friends of their siblings or people they have known for a long time but don't know very well.

"I heard your bloke has buggered off back to Dublin." Alice gave Kate a sympathetic look. "Better off without him, from what I hear."

Jess had forgotten Alice used to work with Declan and their paths occasionally crossed at corporate events and networking meetings.

"Have you seen him?" Kate sounded both curious and disinterested at the same time. "He was a git. I don't know why I stuck with him so long. Is he seeing someone up there then?"

"Mmhm, dunno really, he's usually in a group. Bit of a lad, I'd say. How're you anyway? I mean, really? Jess said she's been worried about you?"

Jess shrank into the seat.

Kate threw her a quizzical look in the rear-view mirror.

Jess looked away. Trust Alice to be so direct.

"Jess thinks you are losing too much weight."

"Alice!" Jess protested, as Kate's eyes blazed with anger.

"I know, I know, you don't want to hear it, everything's fine, you're great, yeah, yeah. There is nothing you can teach me about denial, Kate. Nothing." Alice's voice rose a little but kept its firmness. "Now, I've come down here this weekend to catch up with Jess and to try to finally be the big sister I haven't been for the last God-knows-how-long, but part of that is stopping her worrying about you. You know what I put my family through and if Jess thinks you are headed down that same road, then ..." Alice ran out of steam and shifted her gaze from Kate to the countryside rushing past the passenger window.

"I ..." Jess didn't know where to start. "... erm ... It's true though; I am worried, sorry." She shrugged apologetically as she looked into the mirror to meet Kate's eyes for a second before Kate returned her attention to the road.

Kate didn't speak as they left Ballymaglen and re-joined the main road. For five miles or so she held the silence, although whether fuming or contemplative, Jess couldn't decide.

Fletcher, standing on the seat behind Kate, panted hot doggy breath onto her neck, and eventually, the uncomfortable silence was broken by Kate trying not to laugh at him.

"Okay, Fletch, you win. I suppose I should be pleased that you care. But really, I'm fine. I just haven't been hungry, with all the stuff that's been going on."

As they left the main road and approached the outskirts of Ballyfortnum, Alice changed the subject, enthusing at how pretty everything looked at this time of year and wondering aloud why she didn't spend more time in the countryside.

Jess shoved her knees against the back of Alice's seat, making her sister squirm.

"You hate the country. You love Dublin. You hated living here. You had a flippin' breakdown when Mum dragged you back here, and you legged it off to the city as soon as you could and never looked back. That's why you don't spend more time here, Alice."

"Oh, yeah. I suppose ... but it does look lovely." Alice leaned back in the seat and gave a contented sigh. "I think I might like it more now. I know it sounds naff, but I do feel like a different person recently somehow. I think finally finding a decent counsellor really helped. I like myself more now." She shrugged again, but glanced meaningfully at Kate. Kate acknowledged the look with a silent nod before returning her focus to driving.

Jess couldn't help but agree—the village really did look lovely. Between the houses nearer the main road and the more built-up edge of the village, the open bog lands blazed with golden yellow, and the heady scent of coconut wafted through the wound-down windows. The gorse made everything seem summery, even though it was only the tail end of March.

In the village centre, a new lime-coloured fuzz of fresh leaves clothed many of the trees, and outside the shop, church, and pub, hanging baskets cradled an abundance of pink and purple pansies. Several gardens, like Elizabeth's, shone with newly-planted bedding plants or established spring bulbs. Not for the first time, Jess felt lucky to call Ballyfortnum home.

"Did Jess tell you about her policeman?" Kate gestured towards Marcus's cottage as they passed.

This time it was Kate's seat Jess prodded. "He's *not* my policeman. I told you that a million times."

Kate shot Alice a conspiratorial look. "Protests too much?" she asked, with a wry smile.

By the time they swung into Orchard Close, the light-heartedness of the earlier part of the day had returned and any temporary frostiness between Alice and Kate long dissipated.

Jess decided to ask Kate to stay for the evening after all. "It would be nice," she said, and surprised herself by meaning it.

Chapter Thirty-Three

After picking at a slice of pizza and a serving of salad, Kate drained her second glass of wine and left them to it. (Alice, Jess had noticed, had eaten three slices and a good heap of salad.) Two glasses, Jess suggested, were too many to drive on, especially without eating much, but Kate had brushed aside her concerns.

"I'll be grand. Sure, aren't I used to a bit of drink? But, yeah, I guess I should head off now before I have any more."

"Be careful, won't you," Jess cautioned, not sure if she should let Kate drive, but unwilling to lose her evening alone with Alice by inviting Kate to stay.

"I'll be grand, honest. I won't let your Marcus catch me." Kate and Alice erupted into a fresh burst of giggles, but Jess glared at her friend and pushed her out of the door. Alice, having followed them into the hall, wrapped an arm around Jess's waist, and the sisters waved from the doorway until Kate had driven out of sight.

Back inside, Jess and Alice each claimed a sofa. They sprawled out with a second bottle of wine open on the coffee table between them and settled into the first real girly evening they had enjoyed together since becoming adults. Jess curled her feet beneath her and sank back into the cushions, her face aching from the smile she couldn't restrain; comfortable around Alice for the first time in years. She had always been on edge before, constantly studying Alice for signs of illness or discomfort, alternating concern with annoyance. Now, it was as if they had been friends all their lives, instead of slightly estranged sisters in a role-reversed relationship where the elder was irresponsible and needy and the younger one strained under the burden of care.

Jess opened another bottle, already giddy with the wine she'd already drunk. "It's so lovely Alice, it's all so lovely." Happiness spilled from her with the slops of wine she splashed onto the carpet as she jiffled against the cushions to shift her legs. "It's so lovely to be the little sister finally. Finally, Alice, it's so nice don't ya think?" Her good humour was infectious, and Alice's world-weary look softened.

She, too, collapsed into childlike giggles, and for the rest of the evening, they laughed stupidly at nothing and everything, the television flickering a backdrop of a film they didn't watch.

Planning for the weekend, Jess had deliberately understocked, mindful of past dangers of Alice drinking too much and eating too little. So, once they had drained the second bottle, she made them hot chocolate, adding a sprinkling of fluffy pink marshmallows onto the top of hers.

Alice declined the marshmallows with a shake of her head, but sipped at the chocolate, albeit slowly and with much abstract stirring. She let half the cup go cold and eventually abandoned it, but Jess could not imagine another time since before Alice was about fifteen when she had even sniffed at a cup of hot chocolate.

Not long after midnight, Jess huddled under her duvet with Fletcher snoring softly on her feet, and Alice ensconced in her old bedroom across the landing. Like children left alone in the house while their parents are out, Jess thought, with a pang of sadness as she remembered afresh that their father would never be in the house again. Come to think of it, their mother wasn't likely to set foot in the house again either—it was years since she'd come over to Ireland, never mind visiting the house she'd left her husband in, bereft and lonely. Jess put down her book and clicked off the light, comforted in the knowledge that for once, there was someone else with her in the house at night.

She snuggled into the duvet, twisting her legs around Fletcher, and closed her eyes.

Outside, the stray tomcat yowled.

Jess groaned, threw back the covers, and stumbled to the window to yell at him. The cat looked up, its eyes bright in the light of the orange street lamps, and then it was gone, under the hedge and into the shadows. "We really must catch him, Fletch," she said into the night.

Fletcher opened one eye, cocked one ear, found nothing to alarm him, and went back to sleep.

Sunday morning was lazy. Jess opened a pack of readymade pancakes and chopped fresh fruit into a bowl. She shoved open the French doors and pulled the cord of her dressing gown tighter against the chill that greeted her.

"Hmm, still too early to sit outside, I think." Alice stepped around her sister to pull the door shut again. She ignored both Jess's scowl and the pile of pancakes on the counter. Instead, she rooted in the fridge for Greek yoghurt, spooned a dollop over a generous helping of fruit, and padded to the sofa.

Jess, unable to fully resist the pancakes, rationed herself to just two, hid them under a mound of fruit, and followed her sister to the living room.

"Let's go and see Linda?" Alice suggested, once she had helped Jess clear away the breakfast things.

Linda, unsurprisingly, was delighted to see them. She welcomed Jess with their customary peck on the cheek and enveloped Alice in a warm hug. "Come in, come in." She ushered the sisters towards the kitchen and placed a freshly filled teapot in front of them. "I've been baking," she said as the smell of fresh baking wafted through the house.

After her lighter-than-anticipated breakfast, Jess's stomach rumbled in appreciation.

Alice took a piece of proffered shortbread without fuss or drama, and then a tiny second piece afterwards.

Jess sighed, her whole body relinquishing the last vestiges of tension with a sudden certainty her sister really was well on the road to recovery. For the first time since Bert's death, hope and contentment washed over Jess. Alice appeared to be genuinely contrite as she apologized to Linda for not having come for the funeral a month earlier, and as she made her excuses, she was uncharacteristically honest about her own problems.

"You know I've had some health problems," she explained to a sympathetic and understanding Linda, "and I just couldn't face so many people together in one place, or for Jess to think she had to look after me when I know she wanted to look after you ... I am sorry, I did want to come. I just ... wasn't quite ready for it."

"None of us were ready for it, love." Linda patted Alice's arm, softening the words into sympathy rather than accusation. She poured fresh tea into each of their china mugs. "You are right that your Jess was an angel, though. She is a blessing to us, but it would do her good to get up to Dublin a bit more often; get away from us old fogies now and then." Linda smiled at Jess, a hint of the old sparkle glinting in her tired, grey eyes.

"Yeah, I'll try to drag her up to the city now and then, but hopefully we'll also see a bit more of each other here—I'll come down more often, for sure." Alice poked Jess with her foot. "I think I could get to like coming out here a bit more, especially after staying away for so long, you know ..." She tailed off into thoughtful silence while Linda and Jess chattered idly about the garden and how nice it was to see Bert's legacy brightening the pretty borders in the front garden of Number 15.

"Oh, that reminds me, I found a course for us. Wednesday mornings in Ballymaglen, at the garden centre. There's a course starting next week, straight after the clocks change." Jess pulled a crumpled leaflet from the pocket of her jeans and thrust it at Linda. "Are you up for it? It's for the next ten weeks. What do you think?" Jess wandered through into Linda's sitting room and gazed wistfully at the back garden. "Let's try to learn at least enough to do them proud, huh?"

A flurry of blue tits clustered on Linda's laden bird table, and the stray tomcat strolled nonchalantly across the lawn.

"I'll just pop down some food for him." Jess hadn't noticed Linda come to stand beside her, so lost was she in remembering Bert, and how much time and love he had put into keeping her little garden neat and tidy after her dad had died, and how afraid she was that the weeds would take over and ruin it. Linda's words jolted Jess from her reverie, but the older woman had already retreated into the kitchen to rummage for something to give the cat.

She reappeared holding a pretty china bowl filled with tuna. As soon as Linda opened the back door, the stray approached cautiously, careful not to stay too close, but happy to dart forward, snatch mouthfuls of fish from the bowl and retreat to devour its prize a few feet away, safely beyond Linda's reach.

"Wow," said Jess, stunned to see the unfriendly cat almost domesticated.

"He's nearly tame now," Linda said. "For the first couple of weeks, he wouldn't come to the dish until I came back inside and closed the door. I've been feeding him since ... you know, since ... Bert. Like a mission." She chuckled. "I am determined to tame him. I'm getting there, look." Linda stepped back to stand just outside the patio doors, beside Jess, and the cat remained at the dish, watchful, wary, but undeterred by their presence.

"Wow. Good for you. He'll be great company if you can calm him."

"Hideous, loud, squealing company." Alice joined them, stopping short of the open door to avoid frightening the cat. "If he's what was making all that noise last night?"

"Dad called him Maigret. He used to put a bowl out now and then, but I admit that I hardly ever think of it." Jess turned from Alice to Linda. "Wouldn't you rather have a kitten? Or even a little dog?"

"No," said Linda. "This Maigret and I understand each other. He's lonely and appreciates good food. He'll be in the house curled up on that chair in the sunshine within a month. Perhaps now I know his name it will be easier—I've been trying a few different names and he's not seemed impressed." She faced the sisters with a determined smile and Jess could see that maybe this scrawny, noisy, feral cat was exactly the project Linda needed to help her come to terms with Bert's death. "We'll do our gardening course, and I can ask about planting catnip. This Maigret of ours has been digging in Bert's borders and we can't have that. Now, will you girls stay and have a proper dinner with me?"

When Jess had left the protesting Fletcher at home, telling him they would only be half an hour, and he could manage to stay home alone for that short time, she had not anticipated that, three hours later, she and Alice would still be sitting in Linda's sun-filled living room. Each of them was ensconced in a cosy armchair with their feet curled beneath them. The aroma of Sunday roast lingered in the air and the soft whooshing of the dishwasher lulled them into inertia. Jess had the Sunday paper spread open on her lap and called crossword clues to Linda whenever she got stuck for a solution.

Alice gazed through the window at the wide acres of blue sky, interrupted only by picture-book clouds and the odd bird. The risk of Alice missing the last train back to Dublin was all that stopped them from dozing off.

"Mmm." Alice swung her legs reluctantly onto the carpet. "We really should go and get sorted for catching that train. But this has been the best family Sunday I can remember in years."

Chapter Thirty-Four

T hey arrived at the station with only minutes to spare.

Jess hugged Alice goodbye on the platform, tears spilling. Alice squeezed her tightly, mirroring the sparkling dampness in her own eyes. "Thank you," she whispered into her sister's hair. "Thank you for all those years, Jess. I'll make it up to you."

Jess waved until the train was out of sight, a strange mix of excitement, happiness, and the tiniest twinge of sadness flickering in her chest. They had wasted so many years, but now, quite unexpectedly, the future of her dysfunctional family seemed brighter. She sat in her car and texted first Alice—*It really was great xxx*—and then their brother—*OMG, had the best time with Alice! She seems so well! You should come too next time; real family catch-up? Love to girls xx*—before driving back to Ballyfortnum with the radio at full volume, and a smile aching her face.

Slowing to pass through the village, she was still singing along to the oldies hour: "Blimey, Fletch." She glanced at him in the rearview mirror. "When did *that* become an oldie?"

Fletcher ignored her and drooled down the window instead. He had spotted Snowflake on the pavement by the church.

Marcus raised a hand in greeting.

Jess waved back, then realised with a start that she had barely thought about her 'mystery' whilst Alice had been with her. Seeing Marcus reminded her what Harriet had said, and she jammed on her brakes and backed up a few yards along the road to pull level with him. She wound down her window.

"Hiya, how's things? I didn't thank you properly for taking Fletcher off my hands yesterday. Thanks, it really was a great help."

"Anytime." Marcus reached in through the open back window to receive Fletcher's appreciative lick. "How was your sister?"

"She was great. We had such a nice day. Linda made us a fab dinner. I just want to go home and flop on the sofa and snooze it off now, but this poor boy still needs a walk ... I'd best get on before he climbs through that window to join you." She wasn't sure how to casually drop Angela's heart failure into the conversation, so she left it unsaid. They parted with a promise that Jess would take up yesterday's offer of "come in for a cup of tea" soon, and she made a silent promise to herself to broach the subject of the deaths when she cashed in the offer.

Once home, Jess gave Fletcher a too-short walk to the farm-track junction and back—"Sorry, boyo, I really am too stuffed and too tired to go any further today,"—and spent the rest of the evening exactly as she had told Marcus; on the sofa, snoozing.

Monday dawned bright and clear. Jess, after a lazy evening, an early night, and a good sleep, matched the morning and woke with determination to get something useful done. Over breakfast, she jotted notes into her little book, hoping for inspiration or revelations to come as she doodled. On a fresh page, she wrote a bullet-point list in tiny, neat writing.

1. Walk Fletch—proper good walk today.

2. Book gardening course (starts Wed)

3. Text Kate re group ... what did she say about them????

She chewed the end of the pen, staring across the garden without seeing any of the bright spring flowers or fresh green of the lawn. Kate had said something about them all—the three of them—but what was it? Jess wracked her brain, trying to drag the memory to the surface, but it refused to rise. She drew a wobbly circle around the question, dropped the pen onto the table, and swore quietly. There was definitely some important link that Kate had mentioned. What the heck was it?

"Okay, Fletch, if I walk you first, will you help me remember?" Often, walking helped her remember the things she had forgotten. The trick, of course, was managing to keep remembering those things until she got home again. "Here's the deal," she told the dog, "I'll just book that course, then I'll take you on a lovely long walk." She rooted in a pile of leaflets for the information, then realised it was probably still scrunched into the pocket of her jeans.

Upstairs, she pulled the crumpled jeans from the wash basket and extracted the flyer, lucky she'd found it before it went through the washing machine. She reprimanded herself with a guilty glance at her reflection in the bathroom mirror before running back down the stairs and dialling the number for the garden centre to book the course.

Five minutes later, she grabbed the lead from its hook and snapped it onto Fletch's collar. "That's that done, let's go! We'll just run over and tell Linda, then I promise it's walk time."

Fletch wagged his tail in approval, and the two of them set off energetically across the road.

The first two chores on her list already tackled, Jess relaxed into the walk. The hedgerows had greened and the spring air offered a mix of damp earth and fresh shoots layered with the scent of peaty smoke wafting from village chimneys. She had intended to stroll down the farm track to the bog, where Fletcher could have a good off-lead run, but the track was blocked by a tractor, upsetting the solitude the bog usually offered. "Dammit. We'll keep going then, I guess. Come on."

Fletcher resisted Jess's tugging of his lead, pulling towards the track and the tractor.

"I know, I know, I wanted to go that way too." Jess pulled him away, and he rewarded her with a baleful doggy glare. "We'll go up to the village then, hm?" She'd have turned the other way out of Orchard Close and gone to the river if she had thought for a moment that someone else might have the audacity to use her farm track—even if that someone was the farmer who owned the land.

The bog lane behind them, the village ahead, the road curved into a blind bend. Jess didn't hear the approaching car until it was almost upon them, hurtling along the country road far too fast. She leapt into the hedge, dragging Fletcher with her.

The driver beeped an angry reprimand and raced away.

Jess's earlier bright mood had already faded, and this washed away its last remnants. She swore loudly after the car as it vanished around the corner.

Fletcher's ears pricked at his mistress's annoyance. He had learned long ago that an angry Jess would walk him a lot farther, stomping along until she was calm again. He tugged at the lead as if to urge her on.

Jess kicked a loose stone across the road with enough force to send it bouncing up onto the opposite verge, and decided rather than continue through the village, they'd turn down Angela's road. It had been ages since she'd walked that far ... maybe they would even do the whole loop—along the Little Mason road until it forked, then take the right-hand turn to bring them back around the back of the park and into the entrance of Orchard Close from the opposite direction ... a good five-mile walk. It would do them both good after yesterday's laziness.

Full of these good intentions, Jess took the right turn just beyond Marcus's cottage. His car was absent from its usual parking spot on the edge of the road in front of the house, and the little Westie barked mournfully inside the conservatory as they passed. "We should offer to mind him when Marcus works," Jess told her excited Labrador as he whined a sympathetic message to his friend.

Half a mile or so up the road, Fletcher whimpered once again, straining hard on the lead to get ahead.

As they neared Charles O'Sullivan's farm, a woman's high-pitched shouts carried on the breeze. Jess quickened her step. As they rounded the bend, she realised the cause of the commotion. Someone was calling in vain as a whippety-shaped dog ran in delightful circles around a herd of cows.

She broke into a jog. Charles O'Sullivan, bad-tempered at the best of times, would have no patience with an errant dog terrorising his herd. Elizabeth stood hopelessly at a field gate, with a frantic Breda fussing beside her. Stanley, obediently sitting at Elizabeth's feet, watched the drama with only the mildest interest.

As Jess approached, Stanley barked once, greeting Fletcher, before resuming his half-sleepy, half-curious viewing, with the manner of a bored cinema-goer awaiting the interesting part.

Breda called, cajoled, and shouted for Daisy in alternate unsuccessful measures. In the field, beyond an electric fence Breda wouldn't cross, the whippet was having the time of its life.

"She slipped her collar," Elizabeth explained, as Jess stopped beside her. "Won't come back, she's having far too much fun … good thing they're cows and not sheep."

"If they were sheep," Jess said, "I'd go in after her, but I'm not going into a field of stampeding cows. Fletch, call her back, won't you?" Fletch, always willing to help—or possibly over-excited by the drama—barked obligingly.

The whippet, hearing him, left the cows with one last 'thanks for playing, but now my friend is here' look, and bounded towards Fletcher at a speed worthy of her greyhound ancestry.

"Wow, nice one, Fletch." Jess ruffled his head as Breda grabbed Daisy by the scruff of her neck, hauling her back under the wire to the safe side of the fence.

Tears streaked Breda's cheeks and her face was an unflattering shade of red. Once the whippet was back on its lead, reprimanded, a stream of fresh tears spilled free.

Jess, noting Breda's trembling voice and gently shaking shoulders, touched her lightly on the back. "No harm done, look, the cows are grazing again—they've already forgotten. It's okay." She gestured to the now-calm herd, heads down, tails swishing at flies, as if nothing had happened to add any excitement to their day.

Breda tried to speak, but her words were garbled and her voice tremulous.

"It's okay," Jess repeated, "But maybe you should get home and sit down with a cup of tea and something sweet?"

"Yes dear, let's go back; I'll make us all a nice cup of tea," Elizabeth suggested. "That was rather too much excitement, I think."

Breda walked one side of Elizabeth, and Jess held Fletch on the other side of Elizabeth, keeping space between him and the female dog. Leashed and back under control, Daisy had reverted to her usual snippy self, and had already forgotten how delighted she had been to see Fletcher moments earlier.

The three women and the three dogs walked back towards the village, spread across the width of the quiet country road.

"Well," said Jess, "it's certainly proving to not be the day I had intended. All this drama."

Closing Elizabeth's front gates behind the three dogs, they assessed the situation.

"We can't leave the three of them out here together," Elizabeth said, after a long pause. "They will almost certainly fight. One could come inside, perhaps ... or one could stay out here?"

"No, don't worry." Breda's voice still held a slight tremor. "I'll just pop Daisy home."

"Tell you what," Jess offered. "Why don't I do that for you; you two take Fletcher inside with you, so he doesn't follow me? Is your door unlocked?"

Breda, without protest, handed Jess her key, and they swapped charge of their canine companions. Fletcher accompanied Breda happily towards Elizabeth's front door, while Daisy trotted obediently beside Jess as she turned back towards the gate she'd just latched.

"Oh, you don't need to go up and down the drives," Elizabeth called. "There's a little gate just at the side of the house that joins our gardens. You can go through there."

With the whippet safely returned to the confines of its own home, and left in the hallway with firm instructions to behave, Jess relocked Breda's door, and called one last, "Be good, Daisy," through the letterbox. She swung her legs over the low fence between the two front gardens, eschewing the side gate she'd come through, and squeezed between the garage door and Elizabeth's car.

As she peered at the dent she'd noticed in the front bumper, her breath caught in her throat with a soft gasp. There was, unmistakably, a tiny smear of red paint in the scratch at the centre of the dent. At last, something to write in her notebook ... but what could it mean? She already knew Elizabeth had an alibi for the night Dave had died. Was the pleasant, friendly ex-nurse lying about where she had been? Jess shook her head, and rapped on Elizabeth's front door.

"Come on in," Elizabeth called from deep inside the house.

Jess pushed open the door and kicked off her boots in the hall.

"We're through here! There's tea just about brewed."

Jess had never been this far into Elizabeth's house. The kitchen was large, bright and comfortable, overlooking the back garden. The garden itself was no surprise—Jess knew Henry tended it well. Aside from several neat flower borders, a tidy vegetable patch contained orderly strips of emerging vegetable seedlings. Towards the back fence, a greenhouse reflected each ray of the March sun, and a freshly-painted garden shed threw shadows onto a stretch of manicured lawn. Beyond the garden, the view gave way to open fields and, in the further distance, the bluish-purple of faraway mountains.

"You've a beautiful view."

"We love it," Elizabeth agreed.

"I never tire of it," Breda said. "It's one reason I stayed in the house after Fergus left ..." She sounded wistful as she mentioned the man Jess presumed to be her estranged husband. Jess had heard he'd left years ago, for another woman, but it was such old news, she had never heard any real details.

Elizabeth carried a tray towards the table, laden with pretty china mugs, a dainty sugar bowl, and a steaming teapot. "Won't you just get the milk out, Jess love?" she asked, nodding towards the fridge. "Jug on the shelf in the door."

Nestled amongst a half-empty bottle of orange juice, a carton of prune juice, and a couple of bottles of more expensive wine than Jess would ever buy, sat a pretty china jug of milk. As she moved it, she knocked over a tiny bottle of the brown-glassed, safety-capped type that usually contains medicines or vitamin supplements. She tucked it back into its place, noting the new label stuck over the original, boasting the word 'digitalis' scrawled in thick black pen.

Chapter Thirty-Five

The light drizzle of Wednesday morning glistened on the array of blooms lining the outside aisles of Ballymaglen garden centre. Jess inhaled the wet earthiness with a contented sigh. Finally, she was doing something other than sitting around in Orchard Close or traipsing up and down the lanes around Ballyfortnum. As the gardening tutor—"Seamus, but call me Shay, everyone does,"—demonstrated how to pot on a tray full of seedlings, she wondered if she ought to think about going back to work. One of the reasons she had allowed herself to ignore the idea for so long was that she really didn't want to go back to the tedium of office work. She hated the drudgery of a nine-to-five job with the long commutes, restricting clothes, and stuffy meetings.

The bout of depression that had taken over after her dad had died had long passed, but being able to stay in his house, rent- and mortgage-free, provided her with stability enough to stay home and recover. It had been great to have this time to recuperate and regroup, but had it made her lazy and complacent? Jess trickled soft, brown peat through her fingers and eased a delicate lettuce sprout into a larger pot. As she pressed the soil firmly around the transplanted seedling, something stirred in her—a flutter of excitement. She could do something new. Something different. Perhaps she had her dad's green fingers after all. Could this be something she could do? Something she'd enjoy?

"Jess? Jess, love?"

Linda's voice filtered into her reverie. Neatly lined up in front of her sat a row of lettuce seedlings; a whole tray potted on into larger, individual pots. The rest of the group had moved away, now gathered around another long table, listening intently to the next set of instructions.

"Oh!"

"You were miles away." Linda took Jess's arm, steering her towards the others. "Penny for them?"

"I was thinking of Dad. And me. And how I should really go back to work, and then realising how much I like this. I'm surprised; I always just watched while Dad ... then Bert ... they seemed to do it all so effortlessly. I never really thought I could do it too. It always seemed like their thing, somehow, and I didn't like to interfere. But now... well, sorry, come on." She sidled between two of the other amateur gardeners and forced herself to concentrate as the tutor explained the virtues of a good composting system.

Two hours passed before they broke for a coffee break.

"Huh? Already?" Jess glanced at Linda, and the older woman smiled and nodded.

"Already. Come on." Linda looped her arm through Jess's and led her in the wake of the tutor and their fellow would-be gardeners.

Shay bustled with a noisy kettle in the corner of a cramped portacabin, foisting tea- and coffee-making instructions on a selected few, who then delivered the beverages to their classmates in an assortment of chipped mugs.

The gardeners jostled for folding chairs, scraping and shuffling until all were squished around a long table. The gardeners passed the milk from one to the next, presented modestly in its carton; the sugar followed in its paper bag. A packet of chocolate digestives travelled the table, transported by dirty hands, as the class chatted about the weather, introduced themselves a bit more, and engaged in general small talk. There were twelve of them altogether, plus teacher Shay.

"How about you?" Jess asked Linda as they drained their mugs and helped themselves to a second biscuit. "Are you enjoying yourself?"

Linda was silent for a moment, her pale eyes thoughtful. "Yes, Jess. Yes, I think I am. It feels good to be out of the house, concentrating on something else, doesn't it?" She nodded, with a sad smile. "It makes me feel closer to him somehow, to be learning how to take over his garden. He'd be right proud of us, I reckon." Linda dabbed her sleeve to her eyes. "Sorry, love, I'm not sad, not today. This is a good day."

Jess stroked her friend's hand. "I know what you mean." She stared into her empty mug. "I can almost hear them, Dad and Bert, urging me on, 'Go on, Jess, you can do it,' they would be saying." Probably winking at each other conspiratorially, too, amused at the idea of Jess getting her hands quite so mucky. She grimaced at her fingers, ingrained with the deep brown of the compost, her nails filthy and chipped. Linda wore gardening gloves, but Jess had soon realised she could work better with bare hands, and already loved the feeling of the soft warm earth beneath her fingertips. Her gloves lay abandoned somewhere amongst the lettuces, from where she would probably forget to collect them at the end of the class.

Coffee break over, the team regrouped, filtered out to the polytunnels once more, and pottered in companionable silence for the next forty-five minutes, interrupted only by the odd instruction or compliment from the instructor. The soft earth, the gritty feel of minuscule vegetable seeds in the palm of her hand, and the scent of gently warming soil engrossed Jess, until once again, a hand on her arm and a persistent voice repeating her name startled her back into the company of the others around her.

"We're just finishing up." The instructor's voice was gentle but his eyes promised barely-contained laughter. "Come on, I'll show you where to put these." He gestured first to the seed trays she'd filled and then to a shelf on the far side of the long tunnel.

As the others had completed and labelled each tray, they'd put them aside where staff from the garden centre would water and mind them until the class met again next Wednesday.

Jess had somehow missed what must have been a constant flurry of movement as her classmates carried their trays around her. Meanwhile, she'd cluttered her own bench space with an array of plastic seed trays, each filled to the brim with firmed-down compost. Each pot boasted a small yellow stick on which she had carefully inscribed the name of the seeds sown and the day's date. She'd stacked some of the trays two or three high, where she'd run out of table space to hold a single layer.

"You'll be amazed at how fast they grow," Shay said with a wide smile. "Some of them may even be just beginning to show by next week, if we're lucky." The course blurb had promised an array of self-grown vegetable plants, and enough summer flowers to arrange into hanging baskets before the participants finished the course.

All too soon, it was one o'clock, and the first class was over. "Thank you, that was really great. I loved it." Jess stretched, catlike and contented, amazed at how disappointed she felt that it was time to go home, and already impatient for the next class to come around. "See you next week, Shay."

"I'm so glad we came along," Linda told Jess, as they said their goodbyes to the other participants, brushed the soil from their hands and clothes, and crossed the car park to Jess's waiting car.

Back in Orchard Close, Jess idly Googled 'Gardening Jobs' as she waited for her toast to pop. "Well, Fletch, do you reckon I ought to think of a new career? I wonder what I would need to do to retrain properly?"

Fletch looked up but said nothing. Instead, he trotted to the door, tipped his head to one side, and whined softly.

"Fletch, mate." Jess leapt up. "I'm so sorry, I was so distracted, I didn't even let you out." She pushed open the door and the desperate dog ran out, lifting his leg in relief against the plum tree in the corner. "We'll go for a nice walk as soon as I've had lunch."

Along the road into the village, Fletcher snuffled at the verges, rooted in the hedgerows, and tried to roll in a patch of something unidentifiable.

Alerted by the tension on the lead, Jess yanked him from whatever it was, then let her mind drift again. Birdsong tinkled from the hedgerows, and early primroses added splodges of pale yellow against the new spring grass. After the busyness of the morning, Jess was happy to amble.

Fletcher stopped to investigate a gateway smell.

Jess leaned onto the same gate and mulled over something Kate had said yesterday. She had, in her usual, "I shouldn't have told you that; confidential, you know," kind of way, mentioned that Ann from Number 11 was

Slimmer of the Week. As she'd said it, something triggered in the depths of Jess's mind.

They walked on.

As they passed Marcus's cottage and drew level with the end of Angela's road, Jess remembered something else. Something Kate had said about Angela getting the same "You're the best this week" kind of accolades. And Bert. And Dave. Kate had definitely said something like that ... hadn't she?

She fired out a brief text as she walked, relying on Fletcher to guide her along the pavement without crashing while she peered at her phone: *Hey, did ya say something before about Bert, Dave + Ang getting awards in the group?* She pressed SEND, keeping the phone clutched in her hand in the hope of a quick response.

It remained silent.

At the far end of the church driveway, Father James stood on the church steps chatting to someone.

Jess waved and called a greeting, but didn't stop.

Beyond the church, cars lined the road, some parked haphazardly on the pavement. School pick-up time.

"Guess we'll turn here then, huh?" She patted Fletcher's head, and spun around, homeward bound. A car horn behind her made her jump, jerking Fletcher from the edge of the pavement. She looked up, ready to glare.

Marcus stopped beside her and wound down his window. "Hello, you two, I'm just heading home, do you fancy that cuppa?"

By the time he parked outside his cottage, got out of his car, and stood stretching beside the still-open driver's side door, Jess and Fletch had reached his gate.

Marcus reached into the back of his car, retrieved a bag, and slammed the car door.

Jess unlatched the gate, holding it for Marcus to pass through before shutting it carefully behind them and unclipping Fletcher's lead.

Marcus unlocked his front door, allowing an excited Snowflake out to greet first his master and then Fletcher.

The Westie sniffed briefly at Jess's feet but found her unexciting in comparison to his Labrador friend. He bounded towards the side of the bungalow, tongue and tail wagging. Every few seconds he glanced at Fletcher, as if saying, "Come on, follow me! Let me show you my garden; come and play!"

Summarily dismissed, Jess laughed as the dogs charged around the little garden as if they were a pair of greyhounds at the Lambskillen dog racing stadium. "Go on, Fletch. Have some fun with your friend." She turned to Marcus and shrugged. "Tea, then?"

"Come on in." Marcus gestured through the open front door towards the back of the house. "Go straight through. Kitchen's at the back. Go on into the conservatory if you like; make yourself comfortable. Give me a sec to get changed. I'll be with you in a minute."

A little table in the hall displayed a framed photo of a small child, her glossy, black hair in a neat bob, and a gap-toothed grin on her face. On a table in the conservatory stood another, more casual, picture of the same child. This time she was on a blue bicycle, giggling at the camera, her hair in her eyes and mud on her knees. Jess was still holding the photo when Marcus, changed into blue jeans and a fresh shirt, appeared in the doorway between the hall and the conservatory.

"Tea? Coffee? Something cold?" he asked, as she replaced the photo, ducking her head to conceal her embarrassment.

Chapter Thirty-Six

"Whatever you're having," Jess said, straightening the picture and moving into the kitchen doorway. "Nice plants." She nodded towards an almost dead houseplant in the corner of the conservatory, withered and brown.

Marcus gave a guilty laugh. "I think it's too hot there—besides, I forget to water them. I work too erratically to even take proper care of myself and Snowflake most days, never mind worrying about plants."

Jess remembered the promise made to Fletcher the other day. "I could mind Snowflake while you work, if it helps. Although, I have been wondering about going back to work myself, too. I've been dossing around for far too long really. It's nice, but ..." She held her hands out in a helpless gesture. "You must work pretty long hours, though?" She backtracked to his dilemma, to distract him from thinking she was a totally lazy cow who just slobbed around all day. "And nights, too, you said? Sometimes? Often?"

Marcus shrugged. "Yes. Both. There is a pattern to the shifts, but not one you'd recognize. I do a couple of long days, a couple of short days, a couple of nights ... give or take. But it depends a bit on what's happening. It's quiet right now, but when there's a big case or an emergency, schedules get messed up ... all hands on deck and suchlike. Mrs Harris from the vicarage comes in to mind Snowflake on the days I'm out all day, but it's not ideal for him, poor pup. I have thought about rehoming him, but ..." His gaze slid past Jess into the garden, where the Westie rolled on his back while Fletcher bounced over him, then towards the photo of the little girl, lingering on the image for the briefest of moments. "Still, it's not really fair on him for me to be out so often. The days in between shifts are great, but when I work long hours, he's very neglected. I do take him with me occasionally." He lifted a shoulder, dark eyes on Jess. "It's not ideal."

A lump lodged in Jess's throat at the expression of almost unbearable sadness on his face. She threw another surreptitious glance at the photo, a question forming but dying away, unspoken. The sun shone through the large conservatory windows, and the glare threw deep shadows onto Marcus's face, making him seem older, tired, and surprisingly vulnerable. Unsure how to lighten the moment, or even what had caused the shadows, Jess gestured to the kitchen and asked, "Tea? I'll do it if you like? You must be wrecked."

He began to protest, but Jess held up a hand, cutting him off. "Seriously, you sit down. Tell me where to find things—if you don't mind me rummaging around in your kitchen, that is?"

Marcus raised his hands in surrender, opened the conservatory door to let in a cooling breeze, and sank gratefully into an old-fashioned cane armchair. "I feel a bit guilty about letting you do it," he said, as she went into the kitchen, "but I won't stop you. I'm always a bit bushed after a long shift. I'm not getting any younger."

She sensed the smile in his voice, aimed at her departing back, as he accepted the help. Jess busied herself with the kettle, calling occasional questions to Marcus about finding milk, teabags, and whether he took sugar or not.

Jess placed a heavy blue Denby mug filled with steaming tea on the small table next to Marcus's chair, before settling herself companionably on the cane sofa at right angles to his chair, a matching mug in her hands.

They sat in comfortable silence as they sipped the tea. Marcus closed his eyes and leant his head against the wall behind his chair. Jess let her mind drift, replaying the day, remembering the contentment she'd felt whilst doing the course that morning. Stilled for the first time all day, she scanned the rest of the neat conservatory. A few more plants stood along the window sill—considerably healthier than the first one she'd noticed, —and a series of framed cartoon-style political prints bearing the tell-tale speckles of significant age. A similar series of prints hung in an elderly uncle's dining room, and she had a notion they were quite valuable. Another photo was visible on the kitchen wall, just inside the door, above a wall-mounted telephone and a calendar showing March depicted by an arty print, Constable, Turner? Jess could never remember which did seascapes and which did horses. The photo in the kitchen showcased the child again, her arms wrapped around a squirming, awkwardly-held puppy who must have been a much younger Snowflake. She looked from the photo to Marcus, noting their same east-Asian features and obvious similarities in eyes and jawline.

Marcus, eyes still closed, seemed unaware of her gaze. He lifted his tea to his lips without opening his eyes, and drained the cup. Now, he reached out, without looking, to place the mug back onto the table. Only then, with a sigh, he opened his eyes and smiled.

"Thanks. Sorry. Terrible host skills. I didn't realise I was so tired. There's not much happening, but it was a long enough shift. Bit of trouble in town

... the usual drunks, a minor traffic accident, but I'm finished now for a couple of days anyway. What's been happening around here?"

Jess weighed the options. Small talk about nothing much? Gather up Fletcher and leave Marcus to relax after his long shift? Quiz him about the locals? Tell him about her course? She went with the latter, animated and excited in retelling the pleasure she had felt from the course, the planting, the fun of learning something new. As she relayed the list of vegetable seeds she'd sown, the two dogs stopped playing and dashed out of sight, barking frantically.

The barking plotted the dogs' journey around the side of the little cottage, increasingly persistent.

Jess jumped up, ready to quieten her bad-mannered dog. She stepped into the garden, traced the dogs' path around the house, and found them flinging themselves at the front gate in a frenzy of four-way barking.

"Just Elizabeth and Breda and their dogs," she reported to Marcus, back in the conservatory. "That reminds me—Elizabeth has a dent in her car, and scratches of red paint. Do you think ...?" She didn't finish the sentence, leaving Marcus to draw the inference she was reluctant to voice.

He said nothing but raised one eyebrow quizzically.

Knowing she was prattling, but wanting to say the words anyway, she continued into his silence. "When we were delivering those leaflets ... me and Kate ... you know, on Saturday? Well, we were checking cars ... well ..." A warm flush crept over her.

"Jess," his voice was soft, but carried a warning, "you can't go around examining people's cars. You really can't." He pulled himself from his chair, and refilled the kettle, leaving Jess sitting in the sunlit conservatory. Kettle on, he stood framed in the doorway, arms folded. "Okay, let's pretend for a moment you are right, and there is a violent and dangerous mass murderer in the village? Yes?"

Jess nodded, feeling like a child in front of a headteacher.

"So then, do you really think going around examining their cars and interrogating them is a *good* idea?" He held his hands out, palms upturned, as if weighing something. "If they are so dangerous, I mean?" The twinkle was back in his eyes and his face creased into the smile that was becoming quite familiar.

Unwilling to join him in laughing at herself, she tried to stop the smile that tugged at her mouth, but Marcus's amusement was infectious. "All right, you've got a point," she conceded. "But even so ... and Elizabeth isn't the only one with a dented car either." She listed the other neighbours with offending vehicles, counting them off on her fingers like a preschooler. "And you did say it was quite possible Dave had been knocked off his bike, and you did say there was black paint on the bike. You did say that." She pointed an accusatory finger at him.

His eyes crinkled as he attempted to keep his face straight, but her determined arguing did nothing to quash his smile.

"Thing is," Jess continued, "Elizabeth says she was in town in Henry's car that day. You could check her alibi, though? Couldn't you? If you wanted to, I mean?"

Marcus laughed. "Jess, Elizabeth is a lovely lady, a perfect neighbour, a kind and pleasant woman who would never hurt a fly. And you? You have an overactive imagination." He looked straight at her, and a flutter rose in her chest as she met his eyes.

Embarrassed, she looked away, and her eyes fell back onto the photo she had noticed earlier. "Who's that?" She gestured towards the child, hoping her voice was casual.

Marcus didn't turn to look where she was pointing but stared out across the garden, as if the child might come around the corner on her little blue bicycle.

Jess squirmed in the silence, wishing she could recall the question.

"That's Lily. She's my daughter," he said, his voice so quiet Jess wasn't sure she had heard him properly.

Chapter Thirty-Seven

The following Wednesday brought clear blue skies and a hint of summer. Jess took Fletcher for an energetic early morning stroll before shutting him in the house and skipping over the road to bang on Linda's door.

Linda had offered to drive to the gardening class this week, determined to begin driving again. She had been reluctant to drive much since Bert's death, worried about the little things like what to do if she got a puncture, needed to change the oil, or other tasks that Bert had always taken care of. "I know it's not very modern, but it was the way we did things," she would explain in response to Jess's gentle encouragement. "Bert took care of the car and I took care of the cooking. He took care of the garden and I took care of the house. I'm a little old in the tooth to start learning these new skills."

"Ah, you'll be grand, Linda, sure, aren't we both learning new things together by coming out to this course? You're never too old to learn something." Jess smiled at her neighbour reassuringly as she slid into the passenger seat and pulled the door shut with a clunk.

Linda adjusted the seat, the mirror, and the seat again. She fussed with the radio for a moment, inhaled deeply, and started the engine. Rather than releasing the handbrake and pulling out of the drive, Linda jiggled around some more, checked both wing mirrors, wound her window down a crack and up again, and flicked the window wipers on and off. "You never know when a day like this will turn to rain, can't trust an April sky, love."

Enough was enough. "Linda, you'll be grand," Jess said. "Let's go, or we'll be late. You can do it. Clutch down, first gear, handbrake off. There you go." The car rolled forwards, and Linda flicked a sideways glance at her passenger, her head still facing the road ahead, and chuckled.

"I am being a silly," she said, switching on the wipers instead of the indicator as they approached the junction out of Orchard Close. "Oops a daisy." She paused, gave a little shake, straightened herself, and set a determined expression across her face. Taking a deep breath, she pulled out of the cul-de-sac, and they were on the way, albeit somewhat slowly.

Despite the early hour, the garden centre was busy, and all except one of the course participants had returned for week two. Shay, already propped against a workbench in the nearest polytunnel, looked toned and tanned in a grey T-shirt and mud-stained jeans.

Jess approached the plant-laden bench, a twinge of excitement creeping through her. She dug her hands into an open bag of potting compost, and crumbled handfuls of the damp, warm earth between her fingers. "What are we doing today?"

Shay looked up and threw her a welcoming smile. "Hello, Jess, good to see you. We've some young seedlings to pot on. Get stuck in."

The class got underway, with the students chatting between bouts of concentration.

As the murmur of chatter filled the polytunnel, Jess let her mind wander. One by one she studied the others, wondering why they were there and what their stories were. She recognised a couple of them. One lived at the far end of Ballyfortnum—the postmistress's husband, Mike Flannery—and she also knew Gillian who worked in the bank on Saturdays, but the rest were strangers, united only in their mutual interest of joining the course. She caught the eye of a man opposite her on the other side of the long workbench and smiled. *I'm really enjoying this.*

Shay's voice penetrated her thoughts and she tuned in to his instructions as they pricked out a tray of something-or-other she'd missed the name of while daydreaming. "... when we stop for the break in a bit," Shay said, "we won't really stop. Today we'll talk about some basic safety issues to consider when gardening, including using tools safely and a brief introduction to some common poisons you might come across ... I always like to discuss poison over tea and biscuits."

A ripple of laughter rolled around the polytunnel as the chatter resumed. They worked for the next twenty minutes or so in contented near-silence, save for the odd question and the buzzing of the few insects that flitted amongst the plants, until Shay announced it was coffee time.

Shay served a beginner's crash course in careful storage of tools, weed killer, and seeds along with the promised tea and biscuits.

Linda busied herself with making the tea; another of the participants took care of the coffee, and Jess's mind wandered again. *Weed killer ... everyone in the village has weed killer in their sheds.* Could that have killed Angela? Or might someone have slipped some poisonous plants into something she had eaten? Could you stir a drop of poison into a cup of tea without the recipient noticing? She tuned back into the conversation as Shay reeled off a list of common poisonous plants, highlighting which were the most dangerous.

The students bent diligently over notebooks, everyone scribbling furiously to keep up, punctuated by the crunching of biscuits and the occasional "Pass the milk."

"... opium, of course, is common in the garden. Poppy-seed bun, anyone?" Shay offered around a plate of black speckled cake, his voice deadpan but his eyes giving away the humour.

More laughter bounced across the table, along with plenty of feigned reluctance to accept the offering as the students weighed the consequences of opium ingestion.

"Don't worry, poppy seeds won't harm you. Nightshade, now, that's a different matter." Shay passed around a sheaf of photos, the pictures following the plate of poppy-seed cake like a faithful dog. "... also, St John's Wort, holly, foxglove."

Jess jerked her arm back from the proffered photo, spilling tea into her lap. "That's digitalis isn't it?" She glanced along the table at Shay while dabbing ineffectively at the wet patch on her jeans with a paper towel.

"Clever girl. Yes, that's the Latin name ... it's used widely in medicine, like lots of these toxic plants, but they can be dangerous. Deadly even. You would want to be careful—no self-medication."

"I saw it somewhere recently. What's it used for?"

"I dunno," Shay said, with a shrug. "Heart medicine I think, but you'd want to check—don't be taking my word for it, I just know that you don't go around eating this stuff unless you want an early grave."

"How much would kill you?" she asked.

He laughed. "Dunno. Why? Are you thinking of bumping someone off?"

Jess caught Linda's eye and raised an eyebrow, hoping to convey a mix of curiosity and sympathy. She filed away the information Shay had shared to consider later. Maybe Marcus could check Angela's medical records. She'd have to find out if anything odd had shown up in Bert's notes. Linda would have access to those, wouldn't she? And Dave. Hmm, his might be trickier to access. Marcus, again? Jess flicked back to an earlier page in her notebook and scrawled *Foxgloves* into the margin beside the notes relating to the deaths. She circled it twice for emphasis and thumbed the pages forward again, returning to the list of noxious plants Shay was still reciting.

Linda, more confident behind the wheel on the drive home, chattered about the morning's work, agreeing it really had been a good idea to sign up. "We are indeed learning new things and new skills. Bert would be proud, I reckon." Linda snuck a happy glance at Jess, before returning her focus to driving, with an over-corrective swerve. "Oops. I must keep my eyes on the road, eh love?" Despite the momentary lapse of concentration, Linda's earlier stress had lifted and she hummed to an old song on the radio, a soft smile playing on her lips.

"Linda," Jess said, the song too old for her to know, "was there anything unusual in Bert's medical records?"

Linda's eyes flickered momentarily in Jess's direction, the song fading as a slight frown crinkled Linda's face.

"I mean was it really just a straightforward heart attack, or did something else trigger it, do you think? He wasn't allergic to anything, was he?"

"No, why?" Linda kept her attention on the road.

"Or eaten anything funny that day?" Jess persisted.

Linda's hands tightened on the wheel, her knuckles paling. "I did worry about that. Especially as I had tried a new recipe, but it was nothing unusual, and the doctor said it was a heart attack—stress, exertion, anything or nothing. These things happen, love. Seems his time was up. It's hard to believe it's been six weeks already, isn't it?"

"I know." Jess blinked away the prickle that threatened to bring tears. "He was careful, wasn't he? In the garden, I mean? Had he been gardening that day?"

Linda looked at her again. The car swerved.

"Oh, I'm sorry, Linda! I'm babbling. Sorry. I … I was just thinking about all those poisons Shay was just telling us about; over imagination, you know me." She forced a light-hearted tone into her voice. "You concentrate on driving. I'll shut up."

Linda regained her composure and, still gripping the wheel and looking straight ahead, answered, "It was February, Jess. He was hardly swallowing down seeds or flowers out in the garden that day." Linda's gentle tone softened the chastising words. "He pottered in the greenhouse for half an hour maybe, tidying and straightening things, I expect, that's all. And even though the cake I'd made was a new recipe, he didn't try any of it, what with slimming and all that malarkey. Besides, Jeanie and I ate a huge slice. So did you if I remember rightly, and we were all fine."

Jess was contrite. "You know I don't think for a moment you poisoned anyone with your cooking. But … I *do* think it's fishy that Angela and Dave died so close together, and then our poor old Bert, too. I think something strange is going on."

Linda was silent as they left Ballymaglen and joined the main Lambskillen road.

After a few miles, another well-known golden oldie set her humming again and Jess knew her friend had taken no offence at her probing.

"Oh! I know this one, too! Dad used to play it ..." Jess joined in with the song, offering a loud mishmash of misheard lyrics.

Linda stopped humming to add her full voice, emphatically overriding Jess's mistakes with the correct version.

In Ballyfortnum, Linda shunted into a parking space outside the shop, her ingrained years of driving skills having finally overruled her nerves.

Jess left Linda singing to the radio while she ran in to grab a pint of milk, and it was only as they pulled off the kerb and passed Elizabeth's house that Jess remembered precisely where she had seen the foxglove-digitalis-medicine-poison.

Chapter Thirty-Eight

Incoherent sobs rendered it impossible for Jess to understand what the middle-of-the-night caller was trying to say. She held the phone away from her ear to check the caller ID. Kate. Jess wriggled up the bed to half-sit against the headboard and groped for the bedside light switch, eyes watering in protest at the sudden brightness. She closed them and flopped against the pillows, trying to process Kate's garbled speech.

"Kate, stop, I can't understand you. Take a deep breath." Jess winced and held the phone further from her ear as Kate blew her nose, sniffing loudly as she grappled for composure. "Okay, now, tell me again. Are you hurt? Are you okay? What's up?"

"Jess, shut up and let me tell you." Kate's voice came into sharper focus now. "I need a favour."

"Sure, what? Are you okay? What time is it anyway?" The clock on Jess's bedside table showed two-thirty-two. *Oh dammit, Kate! It's two-thirty in the morning. I guess you're not okay.* "Kate, what the ... where are you? What's happened?"

"I'm in the Garda Station. I got stopped ... Can you pick me up? I didn't know who else to call."

"Stopped? What do you mean? Why? Garda Station? Which station? Ballymaglen?" Jess swung her legs off the bed, feeling around for her slippers with her feet as she talked. She gripped the phone between her ear and her shoulder while she fumbled on the floor for yesterday's discarded clothes. The phone fell, and she scrabbled to reclaim it while Kate attempted an explanation.

"... swerved ... lights ... stopped ... station ..."

Jess brought the phone back to her ear.

"Lambskillen. They don't have the breathalysery machine thingy in Ballymaglen. I'm in Lambskillen. My car is still on the roadside ... we can get it on the way home."

A muffled, male voice filtered into Jess's ear. "Not unless you want to come straight back in here, you won't."

"Kate! You were over the limit? And driving?" *Again*. "Have you been arrested? Hold on, I'm getting some clothes on, it'll take me half an hour to get to you. You can tell me then. I'm on the way. See you in a bit." Jess disconnected the call and finished dressing. "You," she told a confused Fletcher, "can stay here. Be good."

Twenty-seven minutes later, Jess asked the uniformed Garda manning the reception desk of Lambskillen Garda Station where to find Kate. He gestured towards a row of orange plastic chairs, each one stained, chipped, and unwelcoming.

Above the row of chairs, a notice board boasted dog-eared posters depicting uniformed Gardai pointing accusing fingers; warnings about locking up valuables, and a picture of a lost cat.

The Garda at the desk picked up a phone and mumbled something into it. "Take a seat," he said tersely, nodding to the ugly chairs. "She'll be out soon."

Some twenty minutes later, a door opened into the waiting area, and another Garda ushered a sombre Kate through to the lobby.

Jess yawned and got to her feet, too tired to initiate a confrontation with Kate about why she had been dragged into the police station, or what she had been doing out at this time of night.

The Garda on the desk handed Kate some paperwork to sign, and her car keys. "You're free to go," he said, already turning away with the weary manner of one who had seen far too many drunk drivers in his time at the station. As he kicked open the door through which he'd emerged with Kate, he threw a parting sigh over his shoulder. "You're damn lucky we caught up with you before you killed anyone." He glared at Kate and let the door swing shut, only to reappear a moment later behind the plexiglass of the front desk.

Kate opened her mouth to reply, then shrugged and walked out of the station door into the cool night. On the station step, she stopped and lit a cigarette. Bringing it to her mouth for a long drag, she squinted through the dark to peer up and down the street, searching for something. "Where'd you park?"

Jess stepped around her and gestured across the road; the dark, cloudy night punctuated only by dim pools of orange thrown from the street-lights. She marched silently to the church car park opposite, not looking back to check whether Kate was following. Neither said a word, Jess unconvinced she'd be able to restrain her temper. Only once they were seated in Jess's car, the heater turned up high, and back on the road out of town, did Jess trust herself to speak.

"Where's your car?"

"By the lake. That's where they pulled me over. Drop me there and I'll get on home. Thank you for coming." Kate was terse and defensive.

"You're joking!" Jess snapped her head around to stare at her friend. "I will not drop you anywhere but home. I assume they locked your car? But, honestly, I don't even bloody care if it gets stolen. What the hell were you thinking? Oh, wait, let me guess—you weren't thinking at all."

Kate said nothing.

Jess fiddled with the radio, dialling up the volume to drown out the frosty silence that filled the car.

Kate turned her face away, looking out of the window into the darkness, or, at least, pointedly averting her face from Jess. For the rest of the journey to Kate's home in the tiny hamlet of Little Mason, the only sound in the car was a late-night recorded radio program playing a mix of eighties music with recurring advert breaks but no DJ interruptions.

Jess did not sing along, despite knowing all the lyrics.

"I'll call over tomorrow afternoon to bring you to get your car." Jess pulled into the gateway at the front of Kate's low bungalow, not bothering to drive up to the front door. Nor did she cut the engine, nor move to get out of her car as the engine idled outside Kate's gates.

"Jess, I— thank you. I'm sorry for calling you out like that."

"Just go on in, get some sleep. I'll see you tomorrow. I'll text to check you've sobered up enough first." Jess let the car roll forward slightly, indicating to Kate that she was leaving.

"All right ... wait a sec while I find the door key though, please." She stepped forward to the front of the car to grope in her bag by the glow of the headlights. "Okay. Got them." Kate slumped up the drive, her steps heavy despite the teetering heels.

Jess watched until she had unlocked the door and stepped over the threshold, before driving away.

It was almost five a.m. by the time she was home again. Instead of going back to bed, she made a cup of strong, black coffee and sat in the dark at her kitchen table, hands wrapped around the warm mug. Fletcher's head rested on her lap. By about twenty past five, coffee mug both drained and refilled, she had moved to the sofa, cocooned a blanket around her shoulders, and turned on the television.

Fletcher woke Jess mid-morning, licking her face in steady wet strokes. The pale sky edged in around the curtains, casting dim light across the wall. The television had faded to standby, an insistent blue light blinking from the corner of the screen.

She nudged the remote control with her foot, and over-cheerful presenters on a morning chat show immediately filled the screen, discussing some inane viewer's recipe suggestions. Jess groaned and stretched. Bloody, bloody Kate and her bloody notions that she could down a few drinks and still drive home. It was a wonder she hadn't been stopped before now. Only a couple of weeks ago she'd driven home from Jess's house after half a bottle of wine. Should Jess have tried harder to stop her? She shrugged off the thought, not willing to take responsibility or berate herself for her friend's irresponsible attitude.

"Dammit, Kate, did you actually hit something last night?" Kate's car was in the car park overlooking the lake—a glorified layby where tourists, fishers, and commuters alike stopped to enjoy the picturesque view across the water. The abandoned car sat tucked into a space right next to the entrance, where the Garda had presumably left it for her. And, what Jess was now staring at in stunned horror was the dent in the driver-side wing. "Bloody hell!"

Kate froze, colour draining from her face, eyes wild, until she saw where Jess was pointing. Relief replaced the panic. "Oh, that! Phew. No, I did that ages ago. It's been there ages. You had me really panicked there for a moment."

"I never noticed it before," Jess said. "How'd you do it?"

"I dunno." Kate shrugged. "I just noticed it one morning when I got it washed, hadn't even noticed it before then. I guess a pheasant or something. Or Dec may've done it and not said anything. I did ask him, but he said he didn't know, either."

"Wow. All that time we were looking at everyone's cars and I never even noticed you had a dent in yours." Jess couldn't hide the accusation in her voice. "Kate, would you even know if you hit something ... if you were—well, you know, like last night? If you drove home after you'd had a drink?" She paused, almost too afraid to voice the rest of her thoughts. "Or someone. Would you even know if you had hit someone?"

Chapter Thirty-Nine

M arcus's little Westie bounded around Jess's garden, Fletcher in hot pursuit. As Fletch caught up with the smaller dog, they swung around to switch places—Snowflake now the chaser and Fletch the chased.

Jess carried two mugs of tea to the patio table and plonked one in front of Marcus.

"I wanted to know," Marcus said, "did you mean it when you said you could mind Snowflake a bit? I hope you don't mind me calling in like this, but I've been thinking about whether it's fair for me to keep him, and this might be a solution. I really don't want to lose him too." He gulped a mouthful of tea and turned away from Jess to watch his dog charging around the lawn. He hadn't moved quite fast enough, and Jess had caught a brief glimpse of the sadness shadowing his face.

She wondered what he meant by "too," wrestling for a moment with finding the words to ask.

Before she could speak, Marcus continued, directing his words down the garden towards the two dogs. "It would be a real help, but I don't want to put you under pressure. I know you said you might go back to work, but even if you could have him for a few weeks, it would give me time to think of other options. He likes you, and he adores Fletcher."

Jess followed his gaze, laughing as the two dogs rolled each other over and over like a pair of choreographed wrestlers in a ring. "They do get on well, don't they?" she agreed. "Of course I will help out, when I can, and for as long as I can. What do you need? You'd better tell me your work schedule and see how it works out? I'm glad you came by anyway. I wanted to tell you something—ask you something."

At this, he drew his attention from the dogs, peering at her with curiosity.

She fiddled with the coloured glass candle holder on the patio table, twisting and turning it around to reflect shards of colourful sunlight onto the metal surface of the table. "Marcus … Kate was arrested the night before last …" she tailed off, watching the dancing rainbows spill over the edge of the table and onto the slabs below.

"I know," he said, filling the awkward pause. "I was on duty. I saw her come in. You know why she was there, I presume?"

"Yeah. I'm not even surprised, to be honest. It's not the first time she's driven after a drink or two …"

"Mmm." Professionally non-committal, he didn't disagree. Nor did he contradict Jess's generous "drink or two" understatement. Kate had admitted before that she often lost count after four or five glasses. Marcus, Jess presumed, was not allowed to discuss it. Jess smiled as Kate's own well-versed refrain echoed in her mind—"confidentiality, you know"—and chuckled as Marcus looked at her quizzically.

"I wouldn't think you'd find it funny?" he said, raising an eyebrow.

"It's not," she said, "but it is funny that you can't tell me what you know I already know because it's confidential, and Kate's always telling me she can't tell me things about her 'clients'—" Jess drew speech marks in the air with her fingers. "—because it's all so 'confidential'." She did the speech marks thing again. "And she takes it so seriously and it just made me laugh, you know? It's not funny that she thinks it's okay to down a few drinks and then get in her car though. I should've stopped her when she left here the other night after a couple of glasses ... but I didn't." She looked at her hands, tracing the outline of a pattern on the tabletop with her fingertip.

"Hmm ... that is difficult," agreed Marcus. "Especially if someone really doesn't want to listen ... but yes, I knew she was in. I did talk to her. I wanted to check on her, knowing she's your friend, but it wasn't my job to question her. I just made sure she was okay, offered to call someone for her, that's all. She was in a bit of a state, didn't know who to telephone. That's why I suggested she call you."

Jess looked up sharply. "You told her to call me? She didn't tell me she'd seen you."

"Embarrassed, by the time she'd calmed down, I should think."

"Yeah, I guess ... but, Marcus, when we picked her car up yesterday, well, it has a huge dent ... driver-side wing ... I never noticed it before. I thought she did it that night, but then she said it was ages ago, and well, and ... Marcus?" Jess's voice trembled. She pushed back her chair and stood. "What if she did it when she was drunk? Another time, I mean?" She spun on the ball of her foot, went inside the house, ripped off a sheet of kitchen roll, and blew her nose.

For a few moments, Jess stood in the kitchen with her back to the French doors, sniffing back the tears that threatened as she considered her friend may not only have a drinking problem, but she may also have knocked someone—Dave, for instance—off the road and killed him.

With another loud blow into a wodge of kitchen roll, her composure in check, she turned to go back outside to Marcus and almost swung into him. He must have followed her into the house, and now he pulled her to him in a hug.

"It's okay," he said into her hair. "You had a shock seeing her in the station. I expect it's only now catching up with you." He gave a reassuring squeeze and released her. "Go and sit down, I'll make us a fresh cup of tea, shall I?"

Unnerved by the hug, as well as her mounting horror at the thought of Kate running Dave off the road, Jess didn't argue. She padded meekly into the garden and sat tearing the crumpled piece of kitchen roll into tiny shreds as Marcus made tea in her kitchen.

"Just like a policeman." She tried to make it into a joke when he reappeared with the freshly filled mugs. "Reassuring, calm, and making tea. I bet you put in two sugars for the shock, too?" She smiled feebly at the table, unwilling to meet his eyes.

"All part of the service." He stretched his hands across the table and laid them over hers. "Or payback for you making tea in my kitchen the other day? Jess, do you want me to look into it? Do you really think it's possible that your friend was on the road the night Dave died? And drunk? Think carefully before you answer, and decide what you are telling me as your friend, and what you are telling me as a policeman." He lifted his hands from hers, giving a gentle pat as he did so, and picked up his mug.

"Yes. Yes, I do. I mean I do think she was. She was definitely on the road that night. It was a Get Slim night, so she would have been here in Ballyfortnum that evening. She would usually go home the long way, round by the main road, when it was icy, because she was nervous of driving on the back roads in bad weather. It's extremely possible she drove that way home that night. Almost certain I would think."

"Are you sure?"

"Yes. The roads were icy. She was giving out all winter about having to go the long way around, after she got a fright skidding on a nasty bend going home one night sometime last year. She definitely would've gone through the village and onto the main road. She would have driven right past where they found Dave." Jess looked at Marcus, holding his dark eyes and seeing reassurance, comfort, and friendship reflected back at her. "If she went straight home after the group, she wouldn't have had anything to drink though. But ..."

"But?"

"Well, I think sometimes a couple of them might go to the pub after the meeting, just for the one, she said once, to celebrate their achievements. But it would only be a small glass of something without any calories—sins—whatever the heck they call it. They wouldn't be drinking anything to counteract their fabulous weight loss, would they? So, she wouldn't have had more than one, not in their company anyway?"

As she spoke, the memory of the evening Kate had left Declan shoved its way forward. The night they got so drunk Kate ended up staying the night. Hadn't she wondered then whether Kate had been seeing someone? Hadn't Kate said herself Declan had accused her of it? "Oh!"

"What?" Marcus looked at her with piercing eyes. "What is it?"

"Marcus ... I think ... I think maybe she was seeing someone in the village. She said her husband thought she was having an affair. That's partly why he left her. She may have gone somewhere after the group, mayn't she?" A lump lodged in her throat, accompanied by an uncomfortable thrumming that rose from the pit of her stomach. She pressed her fists against her eyes, afraid she may cry again. Surely not? Surely not Kate?

"I'll ask her again. I can't remember if she admitted to anything; we'd both had too much to drink that night when I asked her—she stayed here, she didn't drive home," she added hastily, lest Marcus think that Jess made a habit of giving Kate alcohol and letting her drive home afterwards. "But it wouldn't be the first time. It's how we got to be friends, actually. I found her crying after breaking off an affair with someone at work … I'll ask her again, see if she'll tell me anything."

Chapter Forty

After Marcus left, with a promise from Jess to mind Snowflake for him as often she could, Jess curled up on the sofa in the bay window and stared blankly at the turned-off television screen. She cupped the remote control in her hands but didn't press any of the buttons. Instead, she tossed it idly from hand to hand, deep in thought. What had happened when Dave died? What was it Kate had said? She'd been upset, for sure—really upset—she'd phoned Jess in a panic to ask if Jess had heard anything about what had happened to him. Kate was almost hysterical during that call, going on and on about how upset the group would be and what it would do to their morale.

"Some of them will probably even binge on comfort food," she'd said, the horror evident in her tone as she paused her sobs. At the time, Jess thought Kate was being dramatic; overreacting. She had even (somewhat nastily, she recalled with a twinge of guilt) entertained the fleeting thought that Kate wanted to be a part of the drama somehow. Ever since Kate had thrown herself headlong into the midst of the Bal-lyfortnum community, Jess had the impression Kate resented anything happening in the village without her knowing about it.

"They like to confide in me," she'd said, on more than one occasion, usually followed by her customary, "Of course, I can't divulge what they tell me—client confidentiality, you know—but ..." and in this way, Jess often became party to the snippets of village gossip missed by Mrs Dunne's eagle eyes and slippery tongue. Which, to be fair, was not very much. Still, Jess usually just listened and made agreeing non-committal noises while Kate rabbited on, not letting on that the 'exciting' gossip was often old news to Jess.

Jess knew Kate had attended Dave's funeral. Jess hadn't gone. The veritable Mrs Dunne, conveyor of all gossip, had informed Kate that Jess had appeared at the funeral "dressed like a widow-lady from one of them Victorian gothicky novel things, all black hats and dabbing hankies. She's some airs on her, has that one ... and those shoes ... sobbed like a mad thing too, so she did, all delicate sniffs and waterproof mascara she was ..." Jess had laughed, agreed Kate did like to get herself noticed, paid for her milk, and left Mrs Dunne shaking her head and muttering about "those shoes."

Now, three months after Dave's death, Jess replayed Kate's upset and wondered if there was a greater reason behind it than dramatic value. Had Kate been so distraught because she had, in fact, been responsible for Dave's death? Did she know she'd killed him? Had guilt overcome her and driven her to attend his funeral, crying with the horror of what she'd done and the weight of keeping it a secret from everyone?

Jess sat on the sofa for a long time, playing out the scenario, trying to make it fit—or not fit. The more she thought about it, the more convinced she became that it must be what had happened that night; Kate, drunk after a few drinks in the Ballyfortnum pub, enjoying the company and the warmth, feeling like she belonged in the centre of village life, had one—or several—too many, got in her car and drove home. It had been late, dark, icy … possibly a patch of fog down there in the dip near the river that ran through the village a hundred yards or so further on from the site of Dave's demise … Kate would have been distracted by the fun she'd had surrounded by her group, all of them heaping accolades on to her, buying her 'just the one' to thank her for bringing the Get Slim group to the village and helping them get their weight and fitness back on track. She would have reached over to twiddle with the radio dial, or to phone Declan to say she'd be late, or skidded on a patch of ice …

"Is that what happened, Kate?" Jess murmured to her unresponsive television set. "Is that what happened that night?" She dropped the remote control on the sofa cushion and reached for her phone. Skimming through for Alice's number, she typed a text.

Do you still see much of Declan? You know, Kate's Decko?

An answer came almost immediately. *Now and then ???*

D'ya reckon you could find out something from him?

Huh?

The phone vibrated in Jess's hand, ringing loudly and flashing with Alice's name.

"Jessica O'Malley, what are you on about? Just ask me, wouldn't you? Stop with all this cryptic texting and non-questions. What do you want?"

Jess spilled her jumbled hypothesis to her sister, who listened without comment, interjecting only the occasional "mm-hm" whenever Jess paused to take a breath.

"Jess, you are completely mad. And what do you think I can do about it? Engineer a meeting with a bloke I barely know, and ask him did his ex-wife call him one random night three months ago to tell him she'd run over a bloke from her slimming group?" Alice snorted into the phone.

"Yes. Yes, Alice, that's exactly what you can do."

"Okay, I know you always thought I was the mad one in the family, but really, I was never this mad. You have completely lost it, Jessica O'Malley. Welcome to Madland."

As they talked, they agreed on an only very slightly less obvious plan. Alice would get her mate Anna to text a bloke she knew quite well who knew Declan quite well, and sound out the likelihood of getting a few of them from Declan's firm to go out for a few drinks, making sure to include Declan in the invitation.

"Honestly, she'll think I fancy him or something," Alice protested, but Jess maintained her wheedling persuasion, unashamedly playing on the new-found friendship between the sisters.

"... then you can just casually ask him about Kate, why they split up, was she in the pub after the slimming group most weeks, that kind of stuff. Do your best. Remember the questions all our fictional detectives ever asked."

Alice laughed again. "They were your and Eric's thing, remember, not mine! You two were the ones always snooping around; you haven't changed a bit." Alice's uncontained laughter embraced Jess like a warm blanket, even though she was laughing at Jess.

"Well, then it's your turn now, big sis; prove you are one of us again? Think of it as an initiation challenge?"

Alice didn't answer for a moment, then said, "You guys were always so close, you and Eric. I envied you a bit, you know? You had all your stories and your games, and I was too busy trying to be cool to join in. I wanted to, sometimes."

"Well then, aren't you lucky! It's never too late, now's your big moment to join our club. We'll make you a badge and tell you the club password if you pass this first test." The sisters laughed together at the memory of the little cardboard badges seven-year-old Jess had made for herself, Eric, the current family dog, and an assortment of teddy bears. They were supposed to be magnifying glasses but had turned out more like wobbly lollipops.

Alice had dubbed her younger siblings' club 'The Lollipop Club' and teased them about it when she could be bothered to talk to them at all. The brightness of Alice's chatter rose through Jess like sunrise on a winter morning, and she basked in the closeness as they continued reminiscing for almost an hour, until Alice screeched, "Oh my God, look at the time! I must go! I'm supposed to be working."

"Don't forget Declan," Jess said as the line went dead.

Chapter Forty-One

As it turned out, Jess didn't need Alice's sleuthing. A remorse-filled Kate arrived on Jess's doorstep the following day, clutching a bunch of limp garage-forecourt flowers like a guilty lover. Uncharacteristically, she didn't let herself in, but rapped on the front door and stood fidgeting on the doorstep until Jess answered.

"Shut up, Fletch, it's only Kate, you idiot. What's up? Are you not coming in?"

Kate shuffled, holding the flowers in front of her like an Olympic torch. "I wasn't sure you'd be happy to see me, but I came to apologise."

Jess held the door open and gestured Kate inside with a wave of her hand. Kate took her usual place at Jess's kitchen table, while Jess filled the kettle and rooted in the fridge for a carton of milk.

"So ...?" She wasn't going to make it easy for Kate. She was still angry, and the thoughts of Kate's dangerous driving having killed Dave were still jostling for space.

Kate fiddled with her cigarette packet and lighter but made no move to light one, or to step outside onto the patio.

Jess put a cup of coffee in front of her, glancing at her friend in surprise. "You're not wearing make-up?" Kate never left home without her customary layers of makeup. Jess slumped onto the chair opposite Kate and peered more closely at her friend.

Kate's eyes filled with tears. Her sharp cheekbones propped up dark bags; her lips, free of her trademark slash of red, disappeared into the pallor of her face, and her hair hung in a lank ponytail.

Jess mellowed. "C'mon," she prompted, "what's brought all this on? You didn't use to be like this?"

Kate tried to speak but wracking sobs took over, smothering the words.

Jess tipped on her chair to scoop the roll of kitchen paper from the worktop, wordlessly passed it across the table, and waited.

Eventually, Kate stopped crying, blew her nose, and wiped her face. "Sorry. I'm a mess. I did something terrible. I need to tell someone before I go crazy." She stood and extracted a cigarette from the packet. "I know you've been worried. I've been shit, haven't I? Come outside, I need to smoke." She nudged open the door and stepped into the garden.

Jess sighed but picked up her tea and followed Kate outside. Was she about to confess? "Okay, I'm listening. What's wrong?"

Through more tears and about half a packet of back-to-back cigarettes, Kate explained how things had gone downhill since the start of the year. The new slimming group had been the best thing, she was loving it, it was amazing, and she loved both the focus the group brought her and the unexpected bonus that many of her clients had also become new friends. "I hadn't expected that," she said, "I thought it would be all business-like—you know, you don't make friends with your teacher? But it wasn't like that—they seemed to really like me, and I was getting to know some of them really well. We would sometimes go for a drink after, you know. Just the one, obviously."

Jess hid a small smile behind her hand. "Obviously. Go on."

"But even before that, well, one evening, one of the farmers brought one of his lads along. He'd been down a few times—the farmer, I mean—said his wife was nagging something rotten about his pot belly and she'd been threatening to stop cooking him his Sunday dinners if he kept getting fatter—it was making him snore, she said, and anyway, he was doing great, said he was even enjoying it. And feeling much fitter, too."

"I've no idea where you are going with this, Kate. Stop rambling and get to it?"

"I'm getting there. It's hard to say it ... I haven't told anyone this ... It's been eating me up. Literally." She gestured at her skinny frame. "You've been banging on about how much weight I lost, but I'm not anorexic, I promise, it's just ... I haven't had any appetite, that's all."

Jess nodded again but Kate stared into the garden, her back to Jess.

"So, anyway, like I said, one night one of the farmers brought two of his lads along with him. Said they'd been ribbing him about how much he was talking about the group, but how they'd got more interested when he told them there was a fit young girl running it—me, he meant." She gave a self-deprecating snort. "So that's how they introduced themselves to me—'Hi, you must be the fit one Bob's always on about?'"

She paused to light another cigarette. "One of them didn't come back, but the other came along every session after that, sometimes with Bob, sometimes not till later. He was pretty fit himself, to be honest, didn't really have to do much to get in shape. He was really interested, though, after that first class. The next time, he asked me about the recipes and said he'd always loved cooking, but didn't like to admit it, what with working in such a blokey job, he said, and them thinking it wasn't something a man should get excited about. He said his mam used to cook the best dinners, and he still kind of missed them, you know? And as the weeks went by, he would hang around at the end, help me stack the chairs, tell me which recipes he'd tried that week, that kind of thing. He didn't like to talk about it in front of Bob, because he felt daft, he said."

Jess couldn't think of any farm worker she would describe as 'fit' from around here. Bob wasn't a name she recognised, either. She zoned out as Kate kept talking, running a mental list of local farmers through her head, trying to match first names to surnames and nicknames. Harry O'Dowd, Billy White, Old Higgins—what the heck was his name? Nope, she couldn't dredge it up at all. She shook her head to dislodge the frustration of not being able to get it. George Harris, Thomas Docherty, Tractor O'Sullivan ... another one whose real name evaded her—despite him living just around the corner from Orchard Close, and Kate's flirtation with him the day they were leafleting the village—so well-stuck was his nickname that she had never heard anyone refer to him as anything else but Tractor ... Kate would know ... *oh wait! James, that's it.* Old Man Geraghty, Young Harris—to differentiate him from his uncle George, perhaps?

"Jess?" Kate's sharp voice cut through Jess's trawl around the parish landowners. "Are you even listening? I'm trying to confess my biggest secret and you're not even listening."

"Sorry, I was just trying to work out who you were talking about," she said, "but, *confession*? Confession, Kate? What have you done?" Fear rose in her voice. "Kate, I don't want to know. Don't tell me any more."

Kate's eyes filled with fresh tears, but she continued with her story. "We got chatting, more and more, he was quite lonely, he said, looked forward to the group more than he'd ever expected, told me it was becoming really important to him. I made him Slimmer of the Month in November, to encourage him to keep coming. I told myself it was because I thought the group was good for him, but he didn't really need it, you know. We were stacking the chairs, as usual, one night, at the start of December, and his hand touched mine, just accidentally, but Jess, I swear to God, Jess, I felt it all the way down me."

"Oh no, Kate, not again ... please tell me you didn't—"

"You know you asked me before, was I having an affair?" Kate cut off Jess's question before she could finish asking.

"Oh Kate," Jess said softly, a mix of sadness, sympathy, and curiosity. "But who is he?"

Kate continued as if Jess had not spoken. "That was kind of the start of it, really. He would catch my eye in the group, while I'd be talking to someone else, or he'd come in late but even if I wasn't looking, I'd know it was him. I think the others began to suspect, although nothing had happened. A couple of the women were annoyed that he'd got Slimmer of November, didn't think he deserved it, what with being fit to start with. They complained a bit, said they'd lost a lot more weight than he had; it wasn't fair. He did deserve it, though, he was sticking to his plan, and was one of the best at trying new recipes and that kind of thing.

"I suggested we do some photos—he'd look good in the magazine. I was going to submit an article about how Get Slim is great for anyone, even young men and physical outdoor labourer types. I didn't want to discuss it in the pub, what with everyone else getting all green-eyed about him anyway, so we went back to his after the group one evening. Everyone else had gone home, so I followed him in my car." Kate stopped and turned away again. "We ended up having sex on his sofa," she said, so quietly Jess wasn't sure she'd heard her properly.

"Wow," Jess said after a long silence.

Kate paced to the far end of the garden, not stopping until the fence blocked her path. She rested her hands on the top rail, and for a moment Jess thought she was about to climb over and run for the distant hills.

Jess moved to stand beside her friend and they gazed out towards the bog, saying nothing.

Eventually, Kate spoke, still looking out across the fields. "Yes, wow. Really wow. It was incredible. After that, I started spending loads of time with him. I'd leave my car round the back of his house so no one passing would see it. The hours he worked, I'd spend the afternoons with him while Dec was still at work, go back to his after the group. Dec thought I'd extended the class. I told him it was going so well I'd added a second session straight after. Another two hours each time, I told him. And Thursday nights. I told Dec I had started a new group on Thursday nights, too. He found out, of course, and we had a huge fight. It was over, of course, by then."

"Of course?" Jess was confused. "Why 'of course'? You ended it then?"

Kate swung around to face her at last. "He died, didn't he?" She kicked a stone across the garden. "He bloody died."

Fletcher leapt after the stone, thinking it was a new game Kate wanted to play.

"Died?"

"Huh?" Kate swung an incredulous look towards Jess. "You know, in January, remember? It's hardly that long ago!"

Jess gasped, stumbled, and leant heavily onto the fence. She pushed herself off and took a step towards Kate, then stopped again, opened her mouth but couldn't form words. She tried again. "Dave?" she said, when she could speak coherently. "You were having a thing with Dave?"

Kate nodded, meeting Jess's eyes with a pain so raw a lump of pity lodged in Jess's throat.

Chapter Forty-Two

"With Dave," Jess said again, disbelieving.

"Yep. With Dave. We really had something special. I felt like after all this time I had finally found the one, you know? All this time I haven't really been happy with Dec; looking at other men, you know …?"

Jess nodded. She did know. That didn't mean she thought Dave could possibly have been 'the one', particularly after only a couple of months of them knowing each other. She bit her tongue to stop her from asking the question that popped into her head—had Kate also thought the guy she'd had the fling with at work a few years back was 'the one' in the beginning? A more pressing question surfaced in its place. "So, then what happened that night? How did it happen?"

"How did what happen?"

"How did he end up in the ditch? Did you just not see him, or had you had a fight, or what?"

"You what?"

Jess couldn't understand Kate's bewilderment. "Well, when you hit him with your car, how did it happen?"

Now it was Kate's turn to open her mouth, shut it, open it again, and have no words come out. "Wait—you mean … You … you think I killed him?" Kate's eyes blazed with fury, her voice rising as she paced away from Jess, crossing the lawn in a few long strides. "How dare you? How would you think such a thing? I loved him! Why ever would you think I killed him?" She smacked her hand down onto the table.

The candle holder fell, shattering onto the patio slabs in hundreds of colourful shards.

Jess followed Kate to the patio, throwing a glance towards the fence between her house and the neighbour, hoping the neighbours wouldn't hear Kate's violent outburst. "Didn't you?" she asked quietly, hoping to calm Kate down by lowering her own voice. "But—but you have that dent in your car. You said you don't know how it got there; you drive when you are drunk ..." She tailed off, sinking back onto the garden chair.

The flash of anger drained from Kate as fast as it had arrived, and she, too, sat down.

When she spoke again, her voice was barely audible.

Jess leaned closer to catch the words.

"No Jess, it wasn't me. You are right to say all those other things. I drink too much, I drive afterwards, I have a dent in my car. But I did not knock Dave off the road that night. I didn't." She said it with a firm, calm conviction, looking Jess straight in the eyes as she spoke. "I may not remember how I bashed my car, but I do know it wasn't me who hit Dave. I also don't believe he was really drunk that night. I was with him—"

"With him? When he fell in the ditch?"

She shook her head. "Don't be stupid. Of course not. I was with him earlier, we'd gone back to his after the group, had ... you know ... well, we'd gone to bed for an hour or so, but then I had to get home—Declan was wondering where I'd got to, worried about the roads. I'd already told him I was taking care, driving slowly, but he was worried I still wasn't home. I had to go. I left Dave's house at about tennish. He was still there when I drove away. We didn't even have a drink first, we went straight to bed—we just had a glass of wine after, just before I left. I only drank a mouthful of mine though." She broke off and looked at Jess.

"I was worried about the ice, and I wasn't about to drink a glassful and then drive home. It's only since then that I've been drinking so much."

Jess nodded, realising that was true.

"He said he'd go down the pub after—" Kate's voice broke, and she brushed tears away with a swipe of her sleeve. "I didn't see him again. I texted him when I got home, but he didn't reply. He often left his phone when he went to the pub, and I didn't hear from him ... and then, and then—"

Jess wrapped Kate into a hug as her friend crumpled into painful, heaving sobs. "Bloody hell, Kate. Why didn't you say anything?" Then she realised something else. "And that's why you haven't been eating? And why you look so ill all the time? It's not from excess dieting, it's from grief."

Kate nodded. "Pretty much. I just haven't been able to eat, and I feel sick all the time. I cry all the time too, when I'm at home. Decko knew something was wrong, he guessed I was seeing someone, and then he looked in my phone and saw some messages. He knew I was planning to leave, so he left first."

"Wow." Jess hugged her closer. "You should've said something. Why didn't you say something?"

"How could I? I couldn't tell anyone. It's totally unprofessional to sleep with one of my clients. I'd be struck off! And Decko ... I mean, he guessed anyway, but I didn't want anyone else to tell him. I couldn't tell you, you'd have been all judgy, and think it was just the same again, like last time, and then he died, and ... and then I hadn't told anyone, so I couldn't tell anyone, could I?"

Jess patted Kate's back. "Hmm, I s'pose. Oh, Kate." They sat in silence, Jess's arms still locked awkwardly around her friend, Kate sniffling but no longer sobbing. Jess lessened her grip, sat back on her chair, and met Kate's eyes. "But, now—now we really should tell someone. It may make a difference—they didn't know what time he'd died, and you can narrow that window. If you didn't leave him till ten, and the pub shuts at eleven—wait! Did anyone ever check whether he was even in the pub that night?" She jumped up and rushed into the kitchen to find her phone.

Kate followed, peering over Jess's arm to see what she was typing.

Did anyone ask in the pub if Dave had even been in that night?

"Jess! You can't tell anyone—"

"Kate, I have to. And he's the police; he can help. Don't you want to know who did this to him? To Dave?" She added a second message.

I know where he was until about 10pm the night he died

She lay the phone on the counter and turned back to Kate. "Do you want to stay tonight?"

"I'd better get home. I need to come to terms with what's happened. And start taking some responsibility for my health, stop drinking so much. Especially ... Oh, Jess ... especially—especially since I found out—there's something else—" Kate burst into tears all over again.

When Kate had left, Jess stumbled to the sofa, still reeling from Kate's latest bombshell. She collapsed onto the cushions and let her head fall back, closing her eyes and replaying Kate's words through her mind. Her phone

vibrated and she lifted her bum from the cushion just enough to manoeu-
vre the phone from the back pocket of her jeans. Marcus. Responding to
her text about Dave being in the pub the night he died. It didn't say much:
I'll check.

Jess nodded at the phone as if Marcus could see her acceptance of the
wait while he traced the information. She dragged herself from the sofa
and did the only thing she could think of to clear her head: she pulled on
her walking boots, grabbed Fletcher's lead, and set off down the road, the
Labrador bouncing along happily beside her as if nothing else mattered but
his walk in the afternoon sunshine.

Chapter Forty-Three

J ess approached the ringing phone with trepidation. Not many people called her landline. Her mother, or the phone company trying to sell her things she neither wanted nor needed, probably. She didn't want to talk to either.

"I've caught him! Have you got a basket thing?"

Jess couldn't recognise the voice, let alone make any sense of the words. "Erm ... er ... Who? What? Er, who is this please?"

"Jess?" Now the voice at the other end sounded unsure too. "This is Jessica, isn't it? It's me, Linda, your neighbour." Without the excitement, the voice sounded more familiar, although Jess was still bewildered as to why Linda would phone her when she would usually either text or pop over the road and knock on the door.

"Linda? What's up? Hold on, what did you say? Who have you caught? Not a burglar?"

"The cat! What did you call him, Maigret, wasn't it? He's here in the utility room, eating a piece of salmon. Have you got one of those cat basket things?"

Jess agreed to look in the shed, where she was sure there might be one lurking—a relic from all those old family cats—and hung up. Sure enough, behind the lawnmower and under a pile of sacks, she found a dusty, cob-webby cat carrier. She cleaned it out, shut Fletcher in the house, and took the crate over the road to Linda.

The front door opened before she reached it, to reveal an excited Linda hopping from one foot to the other, a wide smile wrinkling her face like a storybook grandmother.

"Where is he? However did you manage to get him into the house?"

"I've been laying a trail of treats for him, bringing him nearer and nearer every day. He's come in a few times in the last few days, but this time he came right past me." Linda's voice was high and excited, her words tumbling out in a rush. "I managed to get the door shut and trap him inside. At first, he was startled, and leapt around in a panic, trying to find a way out. I stood quietly, calmly, talking gentle nonsense to him until eventually, he went back to the large lump of salmon I'd thrown down for him."

Linda babbled on as she ushered Jess into the hall and shut the front door behind her. It had taken her another half hour to get back past the cat and through to the kitchen without him escaping into the rest of the house, she explained, but all was quiet at the moment. She had already phoned the vet, who promised to take him in and neuter him if only she could get him there. "And that," said Linda, triumphantly, "is where you come in."

"Oh," said Jess, eyebrows raised, "and how do you propose we get him into the basket then?"

Linda's eyes twinkled. "I thought you could work that out, now I've done the hard bit." She giggled, and Jess caught a glimpse of the mischie-vous, young girl Linda must once have been. "I'm joking, silly, we'll put a huge piece of fish in the back of it, he'll go in soon enough. You give me that basket now, and then go on through and make yourself a cup of tea.

Sit yourself down and stay quiet and I'll have him shut in here in no time."
She waved the cat carrier as if to emphasise how easy it was going to be.

"Hmm," said Jess, unconvinced. "I'll have a cup of tea, but if you don't
have him by the time I've drunk it, I'm going home. You can call me back
over once you have him shut in. Will I make you a cup, too, or is that
optimistic?" The older woman's enthusiasm was infectious, though, and
Jess couldn't help but smile. "I can't believe you actually got him! Dad tried
for years. Nice one!" She gave Linda a gentle shove on her arm, and Linda
tiptoed through the utility room door with all the stealth of the burglar Jess
had initially accused her of catching.

It took another forty minutes, but Jess had waited it out in Linda's
kitchen, flipping idly through a women's magazine. She had long since
exhausted all the articles about knitting, baking, and readers' true experi-
ences about '*I can't believe it happened to me*' or '*Back from death's door*'
and moved on to the puzzle page, simultaneously checking everyone's
horoscopes on another page as she pondered crossword answers.

The utility room door swung open and Linda appeared in the kitchen,
the cage held aloft. A football champion bearing a hard-won trophy would
not have looked so proud.

"Well," Jess said, "your horoscope is spot on, listen. 'A challenging time
will be rewarded. Persevere, and you'll have your prize.' Prize; feral cat,
what's the difference?"

"Go on then, love, what's yours? Read it out while I make tea. Then I'll
call the vet and tell him we got this cat caught."

"Mine? Hmm ... 'A week of surprises. Like buses, if you haven't had one
come along lately, expect several at once.' Yep. I've had that all right, wait
till I tell you about it! You'd better call that vet first, though." Jess put aside
the magazine and got up to make a fresh pot of tea while Linda made the

phone call. Jess eavesdropped Linda's half of the conversation through the open doorway, while the kettle bubbled to the boil.

"Yes, I can bring him along now ... thirty minutes?" She frowned at Jess, who nodded, guessing the unspoken question and the gist of the conversation. If Linda brought the cat along now, the vet would perform the operation later today, as well as anything else the cat might need before being released back into Orchard Close under the new guise of Linda's Pet.

"Great, and of course I'll run you down there. I've nothing else to do today. Not till later, anyway. I promised to mind Marcus's dog overnight, while he works the night shift, see how he gets on sleeping on my sofa ... the dog, not Marcus, that is." Heat flooded her face, and she looked away quickly before Linda could ask why she was blushing—not that she knew herself. *Why ever would Linda think Marcus would sleep on my sofa? Or anywhere in my house?* There was definitely something about the policeman that made Jess feel ... well, slightly odd.

They left Maigret with the vet, who promised to run a course of worming, de-flea treatment, all the necessary injections, and a general check-up, as well as doing what needed doing to what Linda sweetly referred to as 'his boy bits'.

"He'll probably settle down and make a nice house cat once that's all done," the vet told Linda, "if you can manage to keep him in for a few days, to get him used to it. He might make a nice companion. They do, sometimes, especially the older ones. He'll appreciate a warm spot and not having to hunt for his dinner."

On the way home, laden with new cat paraphernalia—a litter tray and a bag of litter, a bulk bag of cat food, and a few plastic cat toys—Jess told Linda all about Kate's revelation.

"Pregnant? Kate?" This part of the news seemed to be a greater surprise than that Kate had been seeing Dave. "She'd want to put on a bit of weight pretty sharpish then. She looks like she's barely keeping herself alive, never mind a little one. Send her over to me and I'll soon feed her up."

Jess didn't doubt it, and resolved to do exactly that. The relief she felt at Kate's explanation for not eating was immense. Her worries about Kate's waiflike figure still remained, but the mix of grief and morning sickness went a long way to explain it. Kate hadn't even realised she was pregnant until a week or so ago, she'd said. She had passed off the sickness and loss of appetite as shock and sorrow. Only when she'd noticed a nearly new box of tampons mocking her from the bathroom cabinet a month ago, and suddenly realised the same box had been there since Christmas time, had she felt the first twinge of worry.

She'd ignored the growing realisation for another couple of weeks until she decided she really should find out for certain. That, she'd admitted, was the day she'd been stopped for drunk driving. In fact, she had only barely been over the limit, but the mix of shock and the couple of drinks on a habitually empty stomach had been enough.

Distracted, she'd allowed the car to swerve erratically over the central white line, unaware of the Garda car on her tail until it manoeuvred around her, flashed its blue lights, and signalled her to stop. Even then, numb with the confirmation of Dave's legacy growing inside her, she had been so incoherent and dazed that the Garda had no choice but to bring her to the station. And, he cautioned her, she *was* over the limit, even if it wasn't by very much.

"That would be great, if you could help her," Jess said to Linda. "I don't know how she'll cope. She wanted a baby before, with Declan, when they first got married, but it never happened, and now—well, she's completely alone. Dave's gone; Dec's left her. I don't know what she'll do. She might not keep it, I suppose … she didn't want to talk about the future yet. Said she's still coming to terms with the idea of it being real before she makes any big decisions. That's good, I suppose? I think she thinks it's a part of Dave—like a parting gift, you know, to remember him by. A little part of him?"

Linda, despite being from the generation of Irish Catholics who traditionally considered no possible option other than seeing a pregnancy through to its natural result, shrugged and said, "The poor girl. Bring her over to me and we'll fatten her up a bit. She'll need her strength, whatever she decides."

Chapter Forty-Four

With Kate in the clear as Jess's chief suspect in the mystery of how Dave died, Jess flipped through her notebook in the hope that something else would leap out at her. The list of dented cars repeatedly snagged her attention, and in particular, Elizabeth's name beside one of them still niggled. The dent in her car and the foxglove poison in her fridge were incriminating, but Jess couldn't believe that mild-mannered, neighbourly Elizabeth could be responsible for anyone's death.

She traced the notes on the page with her index finger, muttering aloud to Fletcher. Curled on the rug at her feet, he obligingly lifted an ear anytime she said, "Eh, Fletch?" but flopped it down again when the word "walk" didn't follow. Snowflake, too, was peaceful, sleeping beside her on the sofa. The two dogs were temporarily exhausted from an early morning run around the garden. Very early.

They had woken Jess a little after six, fidgeting and snuffling on the end of her bed. With Marcus due to collect Snowflake straight after his night shift, Jess surrendered any notion of further sleep, stumbled downstairs, shoved the dogs outside, and plodded back upstairs to shower while they played. Snowflake had slept well enough, once Jess had given in and invited him to join her and Fletcher on her bed. She had initially tried to leave him downstairs, but the little Westie had whined sadly at the door, unimpressed at the blatant rejection of him and the favouritism shown to the larger dog. Giving in, Jess eventually grumbled her way downstairs, kicked the door open, and hissed, "Come on then, you brat, but don't you dare tell your owner I let you sleep on the bed."

Doodling ever-widening circles around Elizabeth's name while munching marmalade-slathered toast, Jess's thoughts drifted back to Kate's predicament. What *would* she do about the baby, alone and without any financial help from anyone? Should she contact Dave's family—tell them that Dave had left behind a little son or daughter, and hope they might offer to help out? Would Kate even know how to contact them anyway? Probably not. They had been so secretive, and together for such a short time, would anyone even believe her if she suddenly claimed any interest in Dave's estate? Jess weighed up Kate's options, still doodling.

As she scribbled a new pattern on the page, her eyes settled on a different name in her notes: Susan. Hadn't Susan said her daughter had been seeing Dave until not long before he'd died? Her stomach lurched. Had Dave split up with Helen because of Kate? Susan was already furious with Kate about the Get Slim group, but if she'd got wind of Kate's carry-on with her daughter's boyfriend too … Jess scrawled *Helen—Dave?* down the edge of a new page, the words jolting into a sharp line across the paper as the dogs leapt up, barking. They tumbled over one another towards the front door, each trying to outdo the other in terms of both volume and speed.

Jess hadn't even heard the car pulling up outside, but sure enough, when she yanked open the living curtains, there, on the doorstep was Marcus, arriving to collect his dog. While Jess was desperate to fill him in on her latest discovery—Kate's revelation about being with Dave the night he had died, and now her sudden realisation that Susan had a motive for both hurting Dave and for destroying Kate's slimming group—the sight of a bleary-eyed, unshaven, and exhausted Marcus standing on her doorstep told her the news could wait.

"You should've slept first. Looks like you've had a busy night. Snowflake could've stayed longer—d'ya want to leave him till later? He's been no trouble."

Marcus shook his head, stifling a yawn behind his hand. "I wasn't sure how he'd have been, didn't want him imposing if he hadn't settled. He's been all right for you then, has he?"

Jess didn't mention the early start or the whining. Instead of letting on she'd let the little Westie upstairs, she offered coffee and breakfast.

Marcus shook his head again, covering another yawn, and clearly ready only for bed.

Oh shite, I'm blushing again. What was going on with her that an innocent and obvious observation would make her feel uncomfortable? *His own bed,* she told herself firmly. *We are just friends. Nothing else.* He was too old, they'd only just met—although he was becoming a good friend—and he clearly had baggage; the mystery daughter he seldom mentioned, and the hints that something was amiss with his past. Someone else harbouring secrets ... another unbidden thought ... luckily, he was too tired to consider what Jess might be thinking about this morning. He instructed Snowflake to heel, and the little dog obediently followed him to their car.

"I'll call later, to talk properly," Marcus promised, as he slid into the driver's seat. "Thank you. I really do appreciate your help. Talk later, I must get home before I fall asleep here at the roadside." He waved and drove away, leaving Jess in the doorway juggling her thoughts. In her daze, she didn't realise the door was still wide open until Fletcher bounded past and darted across the road, tail wagging madly.

"Fletcher!"

He didn't look back, too intent on chasing one of Orchard Close's resident cats.

Jess swore, stepped back inside, and groped under the hall table for something to put on her feet. Wriggling into her boots, not bothering to stop and lace them, she jogged across the road after the Labrador, laces whipping at her ankles.

Fletcher ran across the neighbours' front gardens, squirming under hedges and bouncing over low fences, until Patricia, the veterinary assistant from Number 12, stepped out of her house and apprehended him with a no-nonsense command.

"Fletcher! Sit!"

Jess was impressed. She stopped on the pavement outside Patricia's garden to catch her breath. "Nice one. I can tell you have practice in stopping absconding animals. Thanks," she called, still huffing a little. She stepped over the low box hedge that divided the lawn from the pavement, grabbed Fletcher's collar, and scolded him sternly. "Sorry." She smiled an apology. "How's Maigret after his operation?"

Patricia looked blank for a moment, and Jess tilted her head in the direction of Linda's house, reminding Patricia about the feral tomcat she and Linda had deposited at the vet's the previous day.

"Oh, the stray! He's doing fine—well, he was when I left at eight last night anyway. I'd say he'll make a good companion for Linda actually. He was quite friendly when he woke up—a bit groggy, but subdued rather than worried, took a piece of ham from me not long after he came around. I'll check in on him when I get to work, in fact, I may as well bring him home with me this evening, save Linda the trip. Would you let her know? I'm running late, so I won't go over and tell her now."

"Sure, thanks, I know she'll appreciate it. And thank you for catching this idiot, too." Jess ruffled Fletcher's head with the hand that was not gripping his collar, restraining him from further escapade. "I'll drag him home first, grab us some breakfast, then run over and let her know."

Jess stacked her breakfast dishes in the sink, clipped on Fletcher's lead, and tugged him over the road to Linda's door, waving a greeting as her neighbour spotted their arrival from behind her kitchen window. Not waiting for an answer to her knock, Jess stepped inside and pushed the door shut behind her, calling a cheery "Hello!" as she unclipped Fletcher's lead.

"Through here, love, come on in," Linda called from the kitchen.

Delighted that someone seemed pleased to see him after his earlier disgrace, Fletcher rolled over and presented his belly to Linda, who obliged with a hearty tickle while Jess relayed Patricia's message.

"We're just off for a walk, do you want to come?" Jess asked the same question often, but Linda never accepted the offer.

"No thank you, love, I'd only slow you down." Linda smiled as she gave her standard response. "Besides, I'm baking today. Hot cross buns and a Simnel cake. There'll be some for you later if you pop back. I'll get on even better now I don't have to collect that cat. Would you mind very much if I changed his name? He's been answering to Hansel since I started laying food trails for him, you know?"

Agreeing it was a most suitable name, Jess and Fletcher left Linda to her baking and set off towards the village. She hadn't planned to go that way, but as she walked, she realised she was heading for the shop and Mrs Dunne's gossip.

As they neared the village, Jess composed a list of questions in her mind, trying to give order to the things she wanted to discover.

She was in luck. Mrs Dunne was not alone, and barely glanced at Jess as she entered the shop. Elbows planted on the counter, the shopkeeper was deep in conversation with none other than the person Jess wanted to quiz her about: Susan.

"Oh good!"

The two women broke from their chat to look quizzically at her.

She blushed, realising she'd spoken aloud. Ah well, now she'd started she may as well keep going. "Erm … well … I was actually just thinking about you, Susan." She tipped her head towards Susan in case the two women had any doubt as to which of them Jess meant.

"Me? Why ever were you thinking about me?" Susan asked with a gentle smile. She may not have been typically good-looking, but her face was kind, and Jess had a sudden flash of certainty that she would be an empathic and kind slimming consultant; undemanding and encouraging.

"How's your group going?" Jess opted for small talk, not wanting to jump straight in to ask if her daughter's boyfriend had been cheating on her before they split up.

Susan prattled for a few minutes, interspersed with Mrs Dunne's additions to the commentary. When the two finally paused for breath, Jess segued into the topic she really wanted answers to: "How's Helen? I've not seen her around for a while."

Susan and Mrs Dunne, being natural gossips, didn't need any further encouragement to chat about Helen and her problematic love life. The conversation turned towards Dave far easier than Jess had anticipated.

"Ah, sure, she's bin keeping herself right busy, she's bin right upset since that fecker went and died hasn't she, God rest his soul." The two older women hastily crossed themselves, but the moment of reflection did not last long enough to stem the flow of their chatter. "She didn't barely leave the house for a good few weeks, an' now she's bin just working all the hours there are, trying to get herself over him, an' all that."

"But they weren't still together, were they?" Surely they weren't still together then? Hadn't Susan said they'd split up long before he'd died? Was it possible Jess had got that wrong and he was, in fact, still seeing Helen while hitting on Kate?

"Ah, no, they'd bin broken up all right, but she was still sweet on him, heartbroke she were, over him dumping on her like that, and then going on an' dying on her too before they's even had a chance to work things out. She's not bin herself nor since." Susan crumpled the newspaper she was holding, and looked startled at the action. "Oops, now look, haven't I made a right pig's ear of that now, just I keep on tellin' her that he weren't no good, and she should get on over him and find herself a nice young man in town instead, none of that no-good layabout type from round here like he were, but she was having none of it, said it were just a mistake and they'd get back together …"

Mrs Dunne, unused to holding her silence for this long, chipped in, "Once a cheat always a cheat, isn't that the truth of it, eh?"

Jess and Susan swivelled their heads to look at her in astonishment.

"Was he—"

"He weren't—" Jess and Susan both spoke at once. Jess closed her mouth and gestured for Susan to continue.

"Were he then?" Susan spoke quite calmly, as if she was asking about the weather. "Well, I am surprised you never said nothing about it to me, though I did have a reckoning of it meself, but our Helen, she wouldn't hear of it, said he'd never do nothing like that, but I always said he would, sure, what man would keep himself in his own trousers around here anyway, ain't they all as bad as one another?" She stopped, turned a deep red, and picked up her crumpled paper. "Well now, hadn't I better be getting along, can't be standing around gossiping all the day now can I?" And with that, she swept out of the shop, leaving Jess and Mrs Dunne gawping after her.

Chapter Forty-Five

"What was that about?" Jess asked as she and Mrs Dunne stood staring at the shop doorway as if Susan might reappear to elaborate. "Is William... has William...?"

"Not as I've heard lately, but there was a rumour a good few years back. Of course, if he had a dalliance, she'd not forget it in a hurry, but I haven't heard anything about it around the village in a long while now." Mrs Dunne looked almost disappointed there may be some gossip she'd missed. She rallied fast enough, adding the snippet Jess had been hoping to hear, while Jess tried not to look too interested.

"Her young one, though, Helen, well, folks did say as how Dave was seeing someone. He was all cheery and, well, friendlier. Round about Christmas time, I'd say it was. But then he and that poor wee Helen broke it off, eh? He never said anything to anyone, not as I heard, but he didn't seem to be very upset about them parting ways. Not like she was; all pasty-faced and red-eyed anytime she called in for the newspaper."

"Who? Who do you think he was seeing, then?"

"Well now, you know I'm not one to gossip," Mrs Dunne lied as if she believed it, "but there was certainly something about him, he'd not been around the pub so much as he normally would be, and was all full of the joys of spring. Had a sparkle in him like I'd never known. I did see a wee car outside his cottage once or twice, and Gerry made some comment about seeing a lady visitor leaving one morning as he came along with the post. In a right hurry, he said she was. No one from round here, or he'd have recognized her, he said."

Mrs Dunne tidied the newspapers, shuffling them into neat piles and straightening the edges. She leaned closer, and whispered, "Wee car like that one your high and mighty friend drives, now that I think about it." She said it with a certainty that told Jess this was absolutely not the first time she had thought about who may or may not have been in and out of Dave's house, making him so happy.

As if reading Jess's mind, Mrs Dunne added, "Not that I've any grudge against anyone who could make a young man smile like he did in the last weeks of his life. Who'd not want to pass away knowing they were happy? It's that wee Helen I felt sorry for, though, jilted and then having him carry on right under her nose, eh?"

How had Jess not heard any of this gossip earlier? It was unlike Mrs Dunne to hold back from regaling the ins and outs of the neighbourhood. Of course, what with Bert's death, and Angela's, maybe there had just been far too much gossip in the last few months to fit it all into the few moments it took to buy a pint of milk a couple of times a week. Still … "Did everyone know? I mean, did Helen actually have any idea, or is Susan right that she was thinking they'd a chance at getting back together?"

Mrs Dunne propped her chins into her hands, elbows on the newspapers, and thought about it for a moment. "Ah, who knows? I'd say she would have known all right, the way she followed him around and threw herself after him, but denial's a fine wee thing to have when you're blinded by love."

Jess laughed. "Blimey, Mrs Dunne, you're awfully philosophical today." She tugged a copy of the local paper out from under Mrs Dunne's arms, paid for it and her milk, stashed them into a bag pulled from her pocket, and left.

Fletcher leapt at her as if she had been gone for months.

She looped the bag onto her arm and released him from the drainpipe. "So, Fletch, I am the only person who hadn't had any idea that Dave had been seeing Kate?" The Labrador loped alongside her, tail wagging and tongue lolling, as she strolled through the village, past Marcus's cottage, Elizabeth's house, and onwards. No, she'd have heard it from somewhere, if everyone else around had known. It must have just got overlooked in the drama of first Angela, then Bert, dying so soon after Dave. But all the same ... *damn you, Kate; you could have told me, aren't we supposed to be friends?* "Mind you, Fletch, I s'pose I've not been a great friend to her recently, either ..."

Fletch lifted his leg against the hedgerow and said nothing.

Being Tuesday, Kate would be in Ballyfortnum that evening for the Get Slim group. If Jess got her here a bit early, she could take Linda up on her mission to "fatten that girl up a bit". She stepped into a gateway to compose a text: *Come down for tea? Linda wants to feed you up. How're you feeling?*

Kate answered almost instantly. *Sure, and yeah, better, thanks. I think I made my decision.* She followed it a few minutes later with a second text: *It's better now I told someone. Thanks XXX*

Great, I'll tell Linda now. See you later x

Kate coming this afternoon, will bring her for that cake. x

Linda, still new to the world of emojis, answered Jess's text with no words, but a smiley face, a winky face, and a baby emoji.

Jess laughed as she walked along, causing a startled cow to poke its face over the hedge, and replied with a return emoji of a smiling cat face.

Jess left Fletcher at home, sleeping off the walk, and drove to town to stock up on proper groceries—those far beyond the remit of Bally-fortnum's tiny shop—and perhaps some new summer T-shirts, now the weather was getting warmer.

Mooching up and down the supermarket aisles an hour later, picking up things, looking at labels, and putting them either back on the shelf or into her trolley, a tall, well-toned man stopped his trolley alongside hers and greeted her by name. At first, she didn't recognise him, and only after he asked if she was looking forward to the class tomorrow did she realise it was Shay from the garden centre.

"I didn't recognise you; I didn't expect you to be anywhere other than the garden centre, covered in mud." She grimaced. "Sorry. I suppose you don't actually live there all the time, do you?"

He laughed and pushed his shopping cart to the side of the aisle to allow other customers to pass.

"Actually, it's handy you're here," Jess went on. "Would you say these seeds are worth buying, or would they not grow, being cheap supermarket ones?"

Shay held out a hand to take the packet from her. He flipped it over to study the details on the back. "They aren't too bad from here usually, as long as you follow the instructions and mind them. You getting the bug then?"

"I think I might be. I was wondering, what do you need to do to work as a gardener? Like are there qualifications and stuff? I mean, sorry, I don't mean to sound rude, but, did you have to go to college for it or can you learn on the job, like?"

As good-natured in the middle of a supermarket as he was in class, Shay laughed again before answering her string of questions, seemingly unperturbed by Jess's clumsy inquisition. "I went to college, but others might train as apprentices, or just through working as a dogsbody and learning as they go—old Jack, for instance, he started there in Ballymaglen straight from school, age fifteen. About a hundred years ago, thereabouts."

Jess chuckled. Jack reminded her of a friendly-faced garden gnome, with his long white cotton-wool beard and his face weather-beaten and crumpled. "Sprightly, for a hundred-and-fifteen," she said, enjoying the moment of banter.

"Sure, he's not a day over seventy, really. I'm not sure he's even that old. A hard worker, though. Never went to college or got any qualifications, and he'd be the one of us knows the most about everything. You could ask him the most obscure question about plants and he'd give you an answer without even thinking about it. Test him on it tomorrow, go on, I challenge you. Think up some questions you'd think he wouldn't know—long as they're about gardening, of course. Or rugby—he'd know a fair bit about that, too." Shay passed her the seed packet. "And, tell you what, don't buy those now. We'll plant up some of the same thing in the class tomorrow, get them started in pots in the greenhouses, and then they'll have a head start before you put them outside?"

"I love the course," Jess blurted. "My dad was a keen gardener, and I always left him to it—it was his thing, so I didn't want to get in the way, but now ... well, at first I wanted to just not let him down, now he's gone, and keep his garden nice, but I think I've accidentally stumbled into something I really like doing." She'd told Shay some of this before, when they all introduced themselves in the first week of the course, but she hadn't known, during that first session, how natural it would feel to be working with the soil, the plants, the seeds. "I know it's only the third week, but I think I want to pursue it further. Will you tell me more about how and where to train up?"

Shay promised to put together some information about courses and a list of websites, smiled as she put the seeds back on the rack, and walked away, his trolley laden with cider, crisps, fresh fish, and a loaf of crusty bread.

Jess turned into the wine aisle, smiling as she selected a bottle of her favourite red to celebrate the first real sense of direction she'd felt since her father died.

Chapter Forty-Six

A s Kate nibbled tentatively at a freshly baked hot cross bun, guilt burned in Jess's chest. Even under her makeup, Kate looked pale and wan. How could Jess not have noticed there was more going on than the drastic weight loss? Had Alice's history affected Jess so much that she had automatically assumed Kate was starving herself?

"I shouldn't really let you eat these before Friday, but I needed a guinea pig to test them." Linda patted Kate on the hand. "How are you feeling, love? Jess told me about your predicament." Her voice was tender, and tears sprang to Kate's eyes at the kindness.

"I suppose I just thought everyone would judge me," she said, tearing pieces off the bun, and popping each ripped-off fragment into her mouth rather than just pushing them around her plate as she would have done a week or so ago.

"I'd say you've done enough of that yourself, love," Linda said. "You've been through a terrible time, haven't you? You poor thing. What with you and this cat, I can see I'll have my work cut out."

Jess raised an eyebrow. "You're collecting up waifs and strays all over the place. You'd better not tell Sophia you've so many poor creatures depending on you to stay out here in the sticks."

Linda's face wrinkled as she laughed. "Ah now, she's stopped pestering quite so much about that, thanks to you telling her to lay off a bit. She'll be down at the weekend, for Easter Sunday, with the little ones in tow. I need to make sure this cat is well-trained before they arrive, in case they accidentally let him out. He needs to know this is his home now, so he knows to come back."

There was no sign of the cat, but Linda told them he had run straight upstairs and settled himself in the middle of the bed almost as soon as Patricia had delivered him home.

"She only left him back here about ten minutes before you two arrived," Linda said.

"Fletcher sniffing around the kitchen and hallway like an over-excited vacuum cleaner will hardly encourage him to come downstairs and socialise," Jess said with a wry smile. "I'd have left him home if I'd realised Patricia would finish work so early."

"Early shift; eight 'til four," Linda explained, before turning her attention back to Kate. Under Linda's gentle probing, Kate slowly opened up, grateful for the support and for someone to confide in after keeping things to herself for so long.

"I do want to have the baby, obviously," she said, not meeting either Linda's or Jess's eyes. "I mean, I couldn't get rid of it, anyway, but especially as me and Dec, well we'd been trying for so long, and then, well, Dave was really special." Her voice faltered a little, and tears splashed tiny pools onto her plate. "I can't not keep it, can I? I just don't exactly know how to ... well, how to do anything really. Money, and keeping working, and then who will mind it when I work? And, and ..." She stopped and looked at them both in turn. "I mean, it will be really, really hard, won't it? Especially by myself, but people manage, don't they?"

"What about your mother?" Linda asked. "Or any other family? Isn't there anyone who will help you? Someone who could move in for a while, while you get yourself sorted out? And, I would think, if you talk to your doctor, they would be able to suggest some help, tell you what's available. I'll come with you, to ask, if you would like me to?"

As Kate tried to express her gratitude through a fresh spill of tears, Jess realised that Linda had needed something like this—some project to focus on, to give her some meaning to her days and fill the gap Bert had left in her life. Not that Kate was a 'project' of course, but, well ... what with the cat and Kate, and the gardening course, Linda would have little time to dwell on how to cope without her husband after the decades they'd spent together. Kate already looked as if there was a little less weight on her shoulders now she'd shared her secret without repercussion.

Jess plucked another hot cross bun off the plate, pushed back her chair, and excused herself on the pretext of taking Fletcher home before he went ballistic trying to hunt out the cat. She let herself out, leaving Linda fussing around Kate, and crossed over the road to her own home.

She dumped her keys onto the hall table, noticing her phone lying there, forgotten. A list of missed messages lit the screen accusingly as she brought it to life.

The first was Alice; she and Eric had been talking—they were all coming down for the Easter weekend, was that okay with Jess? *Eric, Belinda, the girls, and me, can you cope with us all?*

Of course!!!!! YES YES YES, Jess answered as a warm fuzzy glow spread through her. She scrolled to the next message—an almost identical one from Eric, which she answered in a similar fashion—and on to the third message. Marcus.

Thanks so much for having S, you're a star. Are you home? He's something for you.

Just home now, Really, it was no bother, anytime. Happy to help.

He answered almost instantly: *So, you are in if we call round?*

Sure.

She was still running the hoover around the living room, trying to zap up at least some of the dog hair, when Fletcher announced the arrival of their visitors. Suddenly shy, she opened the door to let them in. Who really was this man? What was his story? Where was the little girl from the photos and why had he looked so sad when he'd told Jess the child was his daughter? Did this mean he wasn't gay? Or he was? And, mixed in with all those unanswered questions, was the ever-pressing fact that someone had killed Dave, and possibly Angela and Bert, too.

She gestured Marcus into her house. "Sorry," she said as she pushed the hoover out of the way with her foot. "I was trying to clear up, but I only just got back. Go into the kitchen, there's less dog hair in there." She ushered him through and opened the French doors to shoo the dogs outside.

"Wait—oh, too late, they've gone." Marcus waved a hand towards the dogs as they bounded into the garden. "Snowflake was supposed to give you this." He held out a potted gerbera he'd been holding behind his back. It was a vivid orange, as cheerful as the vibrant yellow they'd recently painted onto her kitchen walls. "He said he thought it would look good with the decor, and he knew you were enjoying the gardening course, so he figured you might like it. He says thank you for minding him last night and if you really think it might work, he would love to stay again." He pushed the gerbera into Jess's hands and met her eyes. "Seriously, Jess, it was a real relief to not have to worry about leaving him alone for so long. Thank you."

Jess bent to sniff the plant, not that it had much aroma. "It's gorgeous, I love gerberas. Thanks, Snow," she called into the garden in the vague direction of the white blur that charged around madly as if he hadn't seen Fletcher for weeks, instead of mere hours ago earlier that day.

"Jess," Marcus said, pulling out a chair and sitting, uninvited but welcome. "I made some inquiries about Dave. He wasn't in the pub that night. So, by your reckoning, he was unlikely to be drunk, if what Kate told you is true. If it is, he would only have had a glass or two of wine. Let's assume he may have drained her glass, if she only had the mouthful you say she did. I checked the records, there was an open bottle on the table when the officers checked his house. Not empty, but not full. They would've gone in to check a few things, to see if there was anything unusual. There wasn't, they said. I sent someone to ask in the pub, and it appears likely Dave never got there.

"So, I asked for a more thorough check on the postmortem results. He did have alcohol in him, as we knew, but not as much as everyone presumed. The side of the road he was found on suggests that if he'd been riding the bike and not pushing it, he was probably on his way to the pub, not on his way home. I should have listened to you sooner." He stopped and looked into her eyes. "Sorry about that. If what your friend says is right, it looks like we can pinpoint the time of death to between ten and ten-thirty, give or take. That changes things a little. It means the alcohol was still a fresh intake when he died, not a huge amount consumed over an evening of drinking, but dissipating while he lay dead. Not enough to make him inebriated.

"So, if he wasn't drunk, it seems very likely that someone did, in fact, knock him off his bike and into the ditch. We are going to review the files and ask some questions, but it may be too late to be conclusive. We will be asking the locals again about who was on the road that night. I thought you should know. After all, it's your persistence that made us look harder."

A mix of sorrow and excitement ignited in Jess. So, it looked like she was right; Someone really had caused Dave's death. It wasn't down to his own drunken stagger into an icy ditch on a sub-zero night. But then who? Who would have knocked a man into a ditch and not stopped? "So, do you think it was an accident? Or deliberate?"

"We really can't tell. But we will ask questions. We'll try to establish exactly who was driving home at that time, or out of the village—but it will be harder to track down anyone who was just passing through. We'll start with some door-to-door questions. Jess," he added, stern and official-voiced, "you mustn't say anything. Don't give anyone any chance to think about what they will say if they are questioned. That's important, okay?" He held her gaze until she nodded.

Now Marcus believed her, things seemed more serious, more real—a lot less like the detective stories lining the bookshelves on her landing and stacked in haphazard piles around the house.

"Now let me tell you about Susan," she said, putting on the kettle.

Chapter Forty-Seven

A t the kitchen table, hands clasped around cooling mugs almost drained of tea, Jess told Marcus her suspicions of Susan, who had every motive for wanting to harm Dave. Add to that Susan's self-confessed jealousy and annoyance about Kate having stolen her business and hijacked her clients, and Jess was certain she was a likely suspect.

"She already told me she wanted to kill Kate, remember? I told you that before? And Dave had spurned her daughter, and she's been bad-mouthing Kate all over the place. You did question her about being on the road that night, didn't you? Of course she'd want revenge, wouldn't she?" Jess got up to refill the kettle, thought better of it, and offered wine instead. Daylight was fading. "Do you want something to eat? I can throw some pasta together, or something? I can rustle up a passable bowl of pasta or stick a pizza in the oven?"

"Mm, pasta, if you're sure?" Marcus didn't need much persuading. He opened the bottle of wine Jess passed him, while she rummaged in the fridge for ingredients to make a pasta sauce.

"Here, grate this, won't you?" Jess set a cheese grater and wedge of parmesan in front of him, and for the next few minutes, they worked quietly in easy companionship.

Once the sauce was simmering, Jess called the dogs inside, closed the door against the cooling evening air, sank onto a chair with her wine in hand, and continued with her theories about the potential killer.

"Trouble is," she said, sipping wine, "it's also indisputable that Elizabeth has a whacking great dent in her car, and poison in her fridge—I told you about that, didn't I? The digitalis I found in her fridge?"

"Jess—" Marcus shook his head and started to speak, but Jess dismissed his interruption with a flap of her hand and spoke over him.

"Well, I did. Find some. When I was there making tea. Anyway, Dave got hit by a car, and Angela got poisoned. I like Elizabeth, I really do, she's a lovely woman, and I can't think why she'd want to kill anyone, but ... She's a nurse, too, so she'd know about things like poison and what would be detrimental to a man with diabetes, and all that stuff, too. I really don't want it to be her, but why would she have poison in her fridge? And Harriet did say one of the women from the slimming group had given Angela the dodgy seafood, too. What if she'd mixed in the foxglove to be sure it would be bad, even if the seafood wasn't enough by itself? Or to disguise the poison with the pretence of seafood poisoning ... or ... or something?"

Glass in one hand, the other propped under his chin, Marcus shot her a sceptical look, accompanied by a sparkle of amusement in his eyes. "Okay, so you may have been right about what happened to Dave, and, I promise you, the police are looking into some of what you say. If it turns out Dave was killed deliberately, or even a hit and run—"

"But—" Jess interrupted, but he held up a hand to stop her.

"And it does seem probable that was in fact the case. So, one step at a time, yes? Now, are you going to serve up that pasta before I expire from hunger? It smells divine. No more sleuthing tonight?" His eyes widened, holding her gaze firmly and reminding Jess of Fletcher's endearing 'I want something from you' looks. "I'm off duty now. We've got a bit to work on, down at the station, all right? I will keep you posted."

Jess scooped pasta into shallow bowls and topped it with a generous scoop of the sauce.

"Within reason, anyway," he added with a smile that crinkled the outer corners of his eyes into well-worn laughter lines.

"Okay," she conceded, and set a bowl of pasta in front of him.

He sighed in appreciation and reached for the pepper.

Jess brought her own bowl to the table and sat facing him across their dinner. "So, can I ask you something else then? Unconnected. A bit personal?"

Marcus looked wary, a shadow crossing his face, but he nodded slowly.

"You said you have a daughter? The girl in the photos? Where is she?"

Marcus closed his eyes and leaned back in the chair. "She was five in that photo, the one on the bike. It was the last time I saw her ..." He opened his eyes and stabbed at his pasta, securing a twist of fusilli on the fork that he didn't lift to his mouth. He let the pasta slide back into the bowl and looked at Jess.

Jess recoiled at the pain emanating from those twin pools of almost-blackness. Her heart skipped with a sudden thump of dread. Shite. "I'm so sorry, I shouldn't have asked. Is she ...? Is she ...?" She couldn't say the words.

He fiddled with the pepper pot. "No," he said eventually. "No, she's fine. I think. Her mother took her away. They live in America now. I haven't seen her in over a year. Not long before I moved out here. I sold the house in Lambskillen—that's where I lived, before. I wanted to get away; somewhere new. They couldn't take Snowflake, of course. Lily adored him. They were babies together." A smile flickered and died as he remembered.

"I didn't even see it coming. She—Lily's mother, I mean—she left with a friend of mine, someone I worked with. They only told me once they had booked the flights." His eyes were wells of infinite sadness.

Jess gazed wordlessly across the table; her fork held halfway to her mouth. Silence stretched between them. "I'm sorry," she said eventually. "I'm so sorry."

"Me too," he said. "Me too." He shrugged and scraped the last mouthfuls of pasta from his bowl. "That was great. It was good to share a meal with another human for a change. Thank you for feeding me. I'd better be off, before we are tempted to have another glass of that wine. It certainly wouldn't do for the local Garda to be drinking and driving, would it?"

A hint of the earlier sparkle flickered into his eyes, but his face was tired and sad. "I should go," he said again, getting up. He took a couple of steps across to where Jess sat, still speechless at his story, and stooped to place a quick kiss on her cheek. He straightened, called Snowflake, and was letting himself out of the front door almost before Jess had got to the hall after him. "We'll talk tomorrow?" He turned on the doorstep and gave her a sad smile. "Thanks for listening."

Not five minutes after he had gone, Kate pulled up. Their friendship back on solid ground, she rapped lightly on the living room window to announce her presence, then let herself in. "Was that a certain local copper I saw leaving as I drove up?" She leered at Jess.

"It's not like that."

Kate ignored Jess's protests and continued to quiz her on why Marcus had been at her house so late in the day.

"Actually," Jess said, when Kate ran out of teasing, "he wants to talk to you. About that night. Anyway, how was the group tonight?"

"Ah, not so bad." Kate's smile was wan. "I felt more up for it, after eating something. I'd been feeling quite faint doing the group the last few weeks. Linda's great, isn't she? A real sweetheart. What's that smell?" Kate sauntered into the kitchen, heels clicking on the tiled floor. She cast a smirk at the remnants of the meal on the table. "Ooh, two places? Nice one!" She nudged Jess in the ribs, and Jess caught a glimpse of Kate's old self shining through as she teased Jess. "And wine, too? Did I interrupt?"

"No." Jess was adamant. "Now, tell me about you. What did Linda say? Are you going to take her with you to the doctor, to ask for some help?"

Ignoring the mess in the kitchen and eschewing the debris of dinner for the comfort of the sofas, she grabbed the wine bottle and her glass and pushed Kate into the living room. "You can't have one, not in your condition. Grab yourself something else, I'm beat." With that, she plonked herself down on the smaller sofa and tucked her feet under her.

Kate slouched into the other.

Fletcher, traitorously, jumped up to snuggle beside Kate.

One hand resting on Fletcher's head, absently caressing his fur, Kate talked more freely than she had in months. Jess only half-listened, churning Marcus's news around in her mind while Kate's words drifted in and out.

"... Appointment on Monday ... new woman ... fresh spring greens, ask tomorrow, would you?"

Jess threw in the odd encouraging, "Mm-hm" at random intervals, but the thoughts swirling in her mind were of Marcus, his child, his wife—was she his wife? He hadn't said. And the news that they were going to reopen an investigation about Dave ...

Kate's voice faded in again, "... Elizabeth ... Slimmer of the month for April ... Easter ... chocolate. Get Slim Easter Eggs, can't even taste the difference, I'll give you a few of them. Remind me."

Jess forced herself back to the current conversation. "Mm, yes, sounds nice," she lied. "Hey! Alice and Eric and his lot are all coming on Saturday, for Easter, haven't had them all together since—since forever really. I wonder if Alice would eat one of your Easter Eggs? I'll ask her. Why'd Elizabeth get Slimmer of the Year?"

"Month," Kate corrected. "It's only April, you daft cow. You really aren't listening, are you? Thinking of Mr Sexy Garda are you?"

Jess opened her mouth to protest, but stopped. If she insisted it wasn't Marcus, she'd have to admit she was thinking of the Gardai questioning the villagers about Dave, and she'd sworn not to say that to anyone. Instead, she gave another non-committal "mm-hm," resigned to letting Kate think what she wanted to if it kept the secret of the investigation.

Chapter Forty-Eight

Over the interlude of the Easter weekend, Jess forgot everything but her family. Alice arrived by train after she finished work on Good Friday, and on Sunday, their brother, Eric, and his wife and daughters arrived to join them. Amid much chocolate, wine, and laughter, the siblings enjoyed Easter in a way they could not recall in all their adult years.

Jess laid an egg hunt in the garden for Bryony and Clara, whose shrieks of laughter and hilarious attempts at bunny hops did nothing to abate Fletcher's excitement as he charged about helping them to sniff out the hidden chocolate.

Eric pretended to help prepare lunch, but mostly lounged against the kitchen counter picking at food while he critiqued Jess's cooking.

Belinda, being 'you're still a guest, you don't have to help', threw endless tennis balls for Fletch in futile attempts to distract him from the egg hunt.

Alice willingly sampled one of Kate's 'no sins, can't even tell the difference' Easter eggs, but tipped most of it into the kitchen bin after even Bryony and Clara turned it down, the horror on their faces accompanied by over-dramatic exclamations of, "Yuk. Really yuk. So yuk it's yukkier than yuk."

"Must be bad," Belinda said. "These two eat anything that looks like chocolate. She patted Clara's cloud of black curls and was rewarded with a foot-stamp from her younger daughter.

"Disgusting muck," Alice said, pulling a face, and breaking off a large chunk of Jess's standard calorie-laden chocolate egg instead.

All too soon, Monday came around, and after an early lunch, Jess stood on her doorstep waving off Eric's packed car, as the girls and Alice waved frantic goodbyes from the back seat. Once the car was out of sight, she closed the door, flopped onto the sofa, and allowed the village mystery to consume her thoughts once more.

By Tuesday morning, a growing sense of unease fizzed through the village, as word got out that the Gardai were asking questions about the January night when Dave had died.

"Why now, after all this time?" asked Jess's neighbour, Ann, jogging on the spot as she stopped to chat for a moment.

"How's anyone supposed to remember what they were doing that day? It was ages ago!" Jess's joined-on neighbour complained over their mutual fence, as he took advantage of the spring sunshine to hang a load of laundry on his line.

As it turned out, most people could remember exactly where they had been when they heard the news of Dave's death, the morning after, but were less certain of where they had been the night he died.

Marcus, collecting Snowflake early Tuesday morning, had relayed the barest of information as to how the investigation was proceeding—a balance between stopping her nagging for news and not breaking protocol, probably—and emphasised the problem by asking Jess where she had been on that particular evening.

"I was out walking Fletch when the women told me he was missing ... and in the shop with Mrs Dunne—and Susan—when they said he'd been found." She thought for a moment. "But, yeah, I really couldn't say for sure what I was doing at ten o'clock the night before. I imagine I was home, in my pyjamas, because, you know, it's not likely I would be anywhere else at that time of night." She laughed. "I don't get out much."

"Exactly. Everyone's the same—they know where they were when they *heard* about Kennedy, or Princess Di, or whoever, but no one can recall where they were at the moment any of those people actually died, can they?"

"Well, unless they did know exactly where they were, because they killed them ... and then they wouldn't tell you, would they? Hmm ... so you need to look for someone who says they don't know, but is lying, instead of someone who says they don't know because they don't know!"

"Something like that. That's the fun of being a detective, I suppose. We talked to Kate. You'll be happy to hear they believe her. The secrecy of their relationship makes it hard to corroborate, of course, but my man said she was very genuine, and her phone data confirms she texted Dave at around half past ten that night."

"What about the others?" Jess asked. "Bert and Angela? Did you go back through their medical records?"

"There's not much of use. Bert had a heart attack, attributed to natural causes. Angela's records state only that she died of heart failure due to food poisoning—also not suspicious. Trouble is, if no one informs the medics a death might be suspicious, they won't look beyond the obvious. All overworked; no time for extra work or initiative."

"Did your people ask Kate if she could come up with anything more than simply attending her group to link them? I'm sure there must be something ... You know, I'm sure she said they had all won awards, recognition things—Best Ever Slimmer, Slimmest Loser, that kind of crap ... might make someone jealous? Biscuit? Keep you going until breakfast?" She pushed a packet of chocolate digestives across the table towards him.

"People have killed for less. I'd better be off, thanks, come on, Snowflake, say goodbye to Fletcher." Marcus bent to pat the Labrador's head, extracted a biscuit from the packet, and let himself out.

Since that first night, Snowflake had settled well into the routine of spending Marcus's working hours at Jess's house, and Fletcher seemed to enjoy his company.

Closing the door behind Marcus, Jess murmured a confession to Fletcher: "It's not just you who enjoys a bit of company, to be honest." The conversations she shared with Marcus as he dropped off or collected his dog were easy and relaxed, and she relished the company of someone far nearer her age than most of her neighbours in the close. Sometimes, in the evenings, when he had finished a day shift, he'd stay to chat for a while, dragging out a bottle of wine or a shared meal over a couple of hours. Mornings were a hurried drop-and-go most of the time, or a bleary-eyed collect-and-stagger back to his car, depending on whether he was starting his day's work or finishing a night shift.

A week later, another Tuesday rolled around, bringing Kate with it. She called around to Orchard Close after the Get Slim meeting, catching Jess already in her pyjamas and curled up with a mug of hot chocolate and a Miss Marple.

"I kind of expected you earlier, on the way to the group, not after it." Jess groaned and moved to push herself up from the sofa. "Want some hot chocolate?"

"Stay there." Kate waved her down. "I'll make myself a coffee. Just popping in. Not stopping, honest—I've been so busy since I saw you—thought I should fill you in on how I'm doing."

Jess knew already that Linda had accompanied Kate to the doctor, and they had come away with a much clearer idea of what help was available, including some grief counselling to help Kate come to terms with what had happened. Although it was not even a fortnight since Jess had seen Kate, her friend looked so much better. Of course, she was slathered in make-up, as usual, but even under the make-up, Kate had a soft glow, her face less gaunt.

"Yeah, I feel better, too. A mix of having told a few people, and not throwing up every morning anymore," Kate called from the kitchen over the rumble of the kettle. "I mean, it's still all really shit, but at least I can talk about it now. At least with you. And Linda's been great. I really do need to try to contact Dave's mam, I think. She might like to know ... but I don't know how to find her."

"I'll have a think about it. Someone round here must know how to get hold of her ... I mean, someone must've called her when he died, right? I can ask around." Maybe Susan or Helen would know—she'd have to think of an excuse to bring it up subtly.

"Be discreet, Jess, yeah? I don't want the group to know. It was so unprofessional to be seeing a client... At the moment, the group is all I have going for me. I can't afford to lose it." Kate glanced at her still-flat stomach and rubbed it gently. "Well, the group and this one, of course."

Two cups of coffee and a piece of toast later, Kate was on her way home, and Jess was already snuggled under her duvet, reading, with Fletcher at her feet. She'd climbed into bed almost before Kate had driven away and was just finishing a chapter of her book when her phone rang on the table beside her.

At the sudden noise, she jerked upright, giving Fletcher an accidental kick. He cast her a sorrowful look, stood up, turned around a few times, and laid heavily on her feet as she grappled to answer the phone. Kate.

"Huh, what's up? Did you forget something?"

"There's an ambulance at Elizabeth's house. I thought you'd want to know. Its lights are flashing, no siren, but the house door is shut. I couldn't see anything."

Chapter Forty-Nine

Marcus's phone went straight to voicemail.

"Marcus? Are you home? Kate says there's an ambulance? What's going on? Do you know? Is everyone all right?" Jess stared at the phone for a moment, sure he would be able to hear the rising panic in her voice, willing him to pick up.

He didn't.

She hung up. Not another one, please, not another one. All chance of sleep vanquished, Jess pulled on her dressing gown and slippers and went downstairs, where she paced, checking her phone every few minutes, and wondering who else she could call. She didn't have a number for Breda and didn't really know Elizabeth's other neighbours. Marcus was her best bet to discover anything.

She tried his number again. "Marcus? Is Elizabeth all right? And Henry? Do you know what's happening? Please call me."

There was no way he would have slept through an ambulance arriving almost opposite his cottage. In his line of work, he must be finely tuned to respond to disturbances. Perhaps he was at Elizabeth's, helping, or at least making sure everything was okay.

Her phone remained stubbornly silent.

After an hour or so, Jess went back to bed. She slept badly, and when she woke, it was with a headache reminiscent of a hangover but without the alcoholic precedent. She grabbed her phone, hoping for reassurance; fearing the worst. Nothing. She pulled her legs from under Fletcher's bulk and dragged herself out of bed, already scrolling for Marcus's number. She shook her head and dropped the phone onto the bed without calling him. He'd let her know as soon as he could. Hassling him would help nothing. She'd walk Fletch to the village, see if anyone knew what was going on.

While she scrabbled in a drawer for clean underwear, the phone vibrated, its abrupt, high-pitched bleep sending a ripple of fear through her.

It was Linda: *Are you driving today or will I?*

Jess stared at the phone blankly for a moment. Of course—Wednesday. The gardening course. Shite. No time to walk to the village. She pulled a pile of clothes from the heap on her bedroom chair, shuffled into yesterday's jeans and a black, slim-fit T-shirt, and grabbed a tattered hoodie she probably wouldn't need from the bottom of the now-scattered pile.

The sun was already well up, and the day promised warmth and blue sky. She ran downstairs, shooed Fletcher out to mooch around the garden while she poured cereal into a bowl, slopping milk over the counter in her hurry. Swearing at the mess, she swallowed a huge swig of black coffee in the hope of it waking her a bit, and texted Linda: *Be there in 5.*

Linda, as Jess had already realised, knew nothing of the ambulance in the village last night. As they drove through the village, there were no signs of activity at Elizabeth's house, or anywhere else. It wasn't until they were halfway to Ballymaglen that Jess's phone beeped to announce the news she had been waiting for. One hand on the wheel, she scooped the phone from the door pocket and pressed at random buttons, trying to open the message.

Linda snatched the phone from her hand. "You're not reading that while you're driving," she snapped in a tone Jess had not heard from her before.

"Sorry. You're right. Can you see who it is?" she asked. "I hope it will be Marcus to let me know everything is okay. That's the only reason I was going to look." Her face was warm, and her hands trembled on the wheel.

"Not much point in him telling you Elizabeth and Henry are all right if you drive us off the road, is there?" Linda peered at the screen. "It is Marcus. Shall I read it?" She pressed a couple of buttons and drew a sharp intake of breath, causing Jess to swerve despite Linda's precautions.

"What? What does it say?"

"Elizabeth is in hospital. He says, 'E in hosp. Quite sick. Talk later.'" She glanced at Jess. "That's all."

Shock hit Jess like a punch in the gut, followed by a wave of tentative relief. If Elizabeth was sick, she wasn't dead. "Quite sick isn't *really* sick, is it?" She turned to Linda, and the car veered onto the central line again. An angry beep from an oncoming car jerked her attention back to the wheel. "So, it sounds like she just got taken ill, would you think? Hope she's okay. We'll call in on the way home; see if Henry needs anything?"

Linda patted Jess's leg. "We'll do that. I'm sure it's nothing to worry about, love."

For the rest of the morning, Jess tried to push her worries about Elizabeth to the back of her mind as she potted on and planted up and pinched out various seedlings. She patted soil and whispered endearments at each tiny seedling with the same kind of maternal pride she had seen flash into Kate's eyes last night when she had rubbed her belly and talked about the baby. She was proud of her thriving seedlings and impatient to bring them home to transfer into the garden. The air around her shifted, prickling her neck. She looked up from the potting table into Shay's amused eyes and he winked at her as their eyes met.

"You were talking to them," he told her. "You have got it bad, haven't you?"

"Oops." She gave him a wry smile but was too happy with her achievements for her embarrassment to linger. She held her palms out to him, shrugged, and laughed. "Ah, I'm sure you understand. I bet you talk to them, too?"

"True, that." He laughed with her, nodding. "You're a natural, you know."

"I'm going to apply for that course, the one you were telling me about? To start in September."

"You are? Wow, that's fantastic! I'll see if they'll pay me commission for recommending you." During the few weeks the Ballymaglen gardening classes had been running, she and Shay had developed an easy, banter-filled camaraderie, and the information he'd sourced about training courses had spurred her into making some decisions about her future.

"Yeah, I realised I really, really don't want to go back to office work," she said, "but I need to do something. My siblings will chuck me out of the house if they think I'm never going to work again because I can live there rent-free, while they both have mortgages to pay." Neither Alice nor Eric had ever raised the issue, but she worried resentment might surface if it looked like she was taking advantage.

"Tell you what," Shay said, across the trays of mixed lettuces, "why don't you come down and help out here a bit over the next few months—we get really busy at this time of year—I could use an extra pair of hands. What do you think?" He held her gaze for a little longer than necessary, one side of his mouth turned up in a questioning smile. "It would be fun to have you around."

During the break, Linda passed Jess a chipped mug of hot tea, and pushed the plate of biscuits along the table towards her friend. "He's definitely sweet on you." Linda's eyes twinkled with mischief.

The old-fashioned phrase made Jess smile. "Nah, he's just friendly; he's like that with everyone."

Linda chuckled. "If you say so, but I've seen the way he looks at you. It would do you good to date, get yourself a nice young man. You haven't had much fun in the last few years, since you came to Ballyfortnum. It's about time you got out a bit."

Jess didn't answer, not wanting to acknowledge the ring of truth in her friend's words. She hadn't been out with anyone since finishing with Whatsisname—Owen—way back when. She had barely even been out with her girlfriends since she'd moved to Ballyfortnum. She may have told Marcus she couldn't be certain where she'd been the night Dave had died, but, unless she had run out to the little town to the east of Ballyfortnum to pick up a takeaway for one, or been drinking cocoa in Linda's kitchen, she would have been nowhere but home, alone with her dog. Linda was right. Perhaps it was time to get out more.

"That's why I'm applying to college," she said. "A change of direction."

Chapter Fifty

Henry opened his car door and slid into the driving seat just as Jess bumped up the kerb onto the pavement outside his gate.

Leaving the engine running, Jess jumped out. "Henry! Wait!"

He pushed open the door he was about to close, and looked up as Jess jogged along his drive towards him.

"Henry, what's happened? I heard Elizabeth is sick? Is there anything I can do? What do you need?"

Henry's face was grey and drawn, smudged with the dark shadows of a man who had been up all night. He stifled a yawn behind a liver-spotted hand as he greeted her from his driving seat, but didn't move to get out of the car.

"Are you going back to the hospital now? Would you like me to drive you?"

"I'll be grand. Don't you worry yourself." Henry smothered another yawn and rubbed his hand across his face.

"I'll take Linda home, pop in and let Fletcher out for a pee, then be straight back," she assured him. "Twenty minutes, give or take, and then I'll run you to the hospital. No argument. You'd do the same for any of the neighbours."

Henry dragged himself wearily from his car, agreeing to make himself a cup of tea and a sandwich while Jess dropped Linda home.

Exactly eighteen minutes later, having left Fletcher with Linda instead of taking the time to stand around waiting for him to pee, she was back outside Henry's house. She rapped on the door. There was no answer, so she let herself in. The house hummed with silence.

"Henry?" Jess quelled the worry rising in her chest and walked down the hall towards the sunny kitchen at the back of the house. "Henry?" A pile of dishes stood stacked by the sink, awaiting washing. The fridge thrummed in the corner, but all else was silent. She put a hand to the kettle; warm. She traced her steps back along the hall and peered around the living room door. From a sumptuous blue velvet armchair beside the fireplace, Henry snored gently; a cup of tea cooling beside him.

Jess left him undisturbed and went into the kitchen to forage until she found bread, butter, ham and salad. She plucked a couple of plates from the draining board, rooted in a drawer for a knife, and set about making a pile of sandwiches and a fresh pot of tea. Only when it was brewed and ready to pour did she tiptoe back to the sleeping Henry and gently wake him. "Henry … Henry, I made you some lunch, and a fresh cup of tea. Will you eat it in the kitchen, or shall I bring it to you here?"

At the kitchen table, they each selected a sandwich before Henry rummaged in a cupboard for a plastic tub for the rest. "I'll bring them with me," he said, washing down a last mouthful with a swig of tea. He also took a pair of lidded, insulated cups from a different cupboard, into which Jess poured their half-drunk tea, also to bring in the car. Henry retrieved the overnight bag he had already put in the back of his own car, and with Jess juggling the tea and sandwiches and Henry carrying the bag and his house keys, they walked down the drive to Jess's waiting car.

On the way, Henry filled in some of the gaps. Elizabeth had complained of a headache not long after coming home from the Get Slim session. He ran her a bubble bath and helped her into it, leaving her alone to relax. Almost an hour later, wondering why he hadn't heard her either getting out or topping up the cooling water with more hot, he went to check on her. At first, he said, he thought she was asleep, but when he couldn't rouse her, he realised she was unconscious and in danger of slipping underwater.

"I have never been so relieved that our bath is quite short. She'd have gone under in a longer one." He shuddered, and Jess threw him a sideways glance before nosing her car out of their side road to join the flow of traffic on the busy dual carriageway that led to Lambskillen.

"So, I pulled out the plug, and tried to wake her—gently at first but then shaking and shouting," Henry continued. Still unresponsive, he then tried to lift her out, but was unable to manage her weight. He'd put a couple of towels over her to keep her warm and dialled 999. Assured they had immediately dispatched an ambulance, he went back to sit with Elizabeth, wrapping her in blankets, just as the emergency operator had advised. While he sat holding her hand, willing her to wake up, he phoned Breda, whose number he knew, to ask her to call Marcus, whose number he didn't. Marcus arrived within minutes and helped Henry lift Elizabeth gently out of the bath.

"And then I got some clothes on her, and that wasn't an easy task, I tell you, but I couldn't have her going undressed into an ambulance, she would hate that." Henry's voice tremored and he wiped his forehead with a shaking hand.

Jess, dawdling behind a slow-moving truck, nodded in sympathy. "She would. You poor thing." She checked her mirrors, signalled, and pulled across the central reservation to overtake the lorry.

"I could only manage her elasticated trousers and a cardi, but at least she was covered, can you imagine what she'd think if …?" Henry's words tailed off as he imagined the horrors of it. "Marcus, God bless him, had placed her in the recovery position while I was finding the clothes and a pillow. She was breathing, but it was so shallow. I thought she was gone." He broke off and gulped, rubbing at his eyes with his leathered hand. "He was great, Marcus. Kept checking all her—what do you call it—vital signs? He stayed until the ambulance came. I was in a right state by then … thankfully he was able to let them in and show them upstairs." Henry's voice trembled again.

Jess rested her hand on his arm for a second, before returning it to the steering wheel. "Goodness," she said, stunned that Elizabeth could have easily drowned in her own bathtub. "You poor things. That must have been such a fright for you. How is she now?"

"She came round, eventually. It took a while. They think she must have taken something. I said she'd complained of a headache, taken a couple of paracetamols, nothing else, I didn't think. They seemed certain she must have taken something else, but when she did come round she couldn't remember. She was quite confused by it all, to tell the truth. I'd just come home to get her some things when you arrived. They insisted that she was out of the woods—that I could leave her for an hour—so they could run a few more tests. They said I should come and get her some things … that's when you arrived …" He broke off with a feeble, aborted laugh. "Listen to me, repeating myself like an old fool."

In Lambskillen Hospital, Jess walked with Henry to the lifts, ensured he had her number, and promised to come back to collect him when he needed. "I'll text you later for an update." The lift doors slid closed, ready to whisk Henry up to the fourth floor.

On the quiet drive home, Jess's mind once again switched to overdrive. Had Elizabeth taken something more than paracetamol? Deliberately, or accidentally? Or had someone else given her something, which would explain why Henry didn't think anything was missing from their medicine cabinet? Henry'd said she'd felt unwell straight after arriving home from the slimming group, hadn't he?

Jess braked sharply and swerved into the layby at the lake, indicating only after the event.

The car behind veered into the opposite lane to avoid ploughing into the back of her car. Its irate driver blared his horn and waved an angry fist as he passed.

Jess raised an apologetic hand he wouldn't see, and picked up her phone to call Kate. "Hey, it's me. What did Elizabeth have to eat or drink at your group last night?"

"Huh? Wait a minute … Just the usual, I expect—a cup of tea and maybe a biscuit, I should think. I don't know. Why? How is she?"

"Just wondering if someone could've given her anything without her knowing. I dunno … It's just, they think she must have taken something, but Henry thinks she hadn't. Only paracetamol."

Kate was silent for a moment, considering the question. "You know, I already had the Gardai come by and ask me the same questions … That's weird, isn't it? Do they think it's suspicious then, do you think? I guess they do. I told them to ask Breda. They usually come together, and they sit together to drink their tea. Elizabeth doesn't always have a biscuit, she's much more disciplined than Breda. Breda has two, sometimes—she tries to laugh it off, or pretend she only had one, but I've seen her … it's no wonder she struggles to meet her target."

Unlike Kate to divulge her members' eating habits or success rate, Jess took advantage. "Who else struggles, Kate? Is there anyone who could be jealous of the others' successes, do you think?"

"Hmm ... I'll give it some thought," Kate said. "But I won't be able to say anything, what with confidentiality—"

As Kate reverted to her business-like persona, Jess cut her off. "Kate, if one of your lot is poisoning the rest of them, you had better bloody say something. If not to me, then to the Gardai, don't you think? Before your whole damn group drops dead."

"Mm. Suppose you've a point," Kate conceded after a pause. "All right, I'll call you back later."

Jess started to pull out from the layby, but changed her mind, manoeuvring instead into a proper parking space further into the car park, with a better vantage point of the water. She cut the engine and gazed over the rippling lake. The sleepless night and the busyness of the day were catching up with her, and she tipped her head against the headrest and closed her eyes.

Chapter Fifty-One

M arcus arrived early to drop off Snowflake that evening.

"You must be tired before you even start, after being up half the night? Come for dinner first if you like?" Jess had urged, mindful of how busy his last twenty-four hours had been. He'd accepted gratefully, and she'd rustled up a quiche, salad, and new potatoes.

"First pickings of the lettuce we've been growing." She felt quite smug, knowing she had grown and nurtured the food she was putting on her table. This vegetable-growing lark certainly had a feel-good factor about it, and she was already planning to clear out the garden shed to turn it into a potting shed, and get herself a little greenhouse.

Marcus was usually easy company, but that evening he forked salad and quiche with robotic rhythm, punctuating Jess's chatter with only the odd, badly-placed, "Mm-hm." He barely blinked when Snowflake chased Fletcher in ever-increasing circles in the garden, or when Fletcher swung around suddenly to become the chaser.

Jess made them both a fresh cup of tea, cleared away the plates, and ushered him to the comfort of the living room sofas. After a little probing, he admitted his melancholy was due to a disastrous conversation with his daughter earlier.

"What happened?"

"Having finally persuaded Sal—that's her mother—to set up a Skype chat, Lily couldn't focus on it at all and I could see she was bored. She hardly knows me now," he said sadly, "and I doubt Sal will let us try Skype again—she wasn't exactly keen to start with. I'm losing her ..."

He looked so heartbroken Jess wanted to jump up and put her arms around him. "I'm sorry. I don't understand how any mother could take a child away from their other parent. That's awful." On the other hand, at least Lily's mother hadn't disappeared off with her new man and fled the country leaving her child behind. Jess had missed a call from her own mother that afternoon, but hadn't bothered to return it.

Doreen had been typically chirpy on the voicemail she left for Jess, talking about her tan; her yoga class, and the new British couple who had moved into the complex recently: "Visit soon, sweetheart. Got to go, Al has just come back from the bar with my G and T." Jess didn't care. She had no desire whatsoever to visit *Costa del* Whatsit and lie around on a sunbed while her leathery mother talked about how great Alan was in bed.

"Eugh." She gave an involuntary shudder as she recalled the voice message.

Marcus looked at her in surprise.

"Sorry," she said, blushing at her lack of concentration. "I was just thinking of my own mother and her running off like that ... sorry ... It must be really hard for you." She forced the image of her mother in a bikini firmly out of her mind, and cut Marcus a large slice of Linda's latest offering.

"Yeah, I'm sorry too." In his habitual kind manner, he acknowledged her own mother's rejection before changing the subject. "I hate to say it, Jess, but I think you may be onto something. Elizabeth does seem to have ingested a drug she claims she has never heard of. We've had Henry check through the contents of their medicine cupboard, and there certainly isn't anything there containing the ingredient found in the tests. It does seem possible she was given something by someone else, whether in deliberate malice or inadvertent kindness, we don't know. Your friend Kate can't remember if Elizabeth poured her own tea that evening, or who made the pot, but we'll ask around. She's to give us a list of who else attended, so we can see if anyone else got sick."

Once Marcus had left for his night shift, Jess called Kate, to repeat the same questions. "C'mon, Kate, you must know who was there, and which of them went into the kitchen? Can't you ring around, pretend it's something else, find out if anyone else got ill? Go on, it'll take your mind off things."

Kate, either bored or having succumbed to Jess's curiosity and insistence, agreed to make the calls.

"How're you feeling anyway?" Jess added. "Sorry, I should've asked that first."

Kate, it transpired, had been talking to Declan. "I thought I owed it to him to tell him. Dunno why, but it seemed like the right thing to do. I was a bit crap to him." Declan, she told Jess, had been more understanding than anyone would have expected, after an initial bout of anger. "He went on a bit about how the bastard got what he deserved anyway, serves him right, but then, weirdly, he calmed right down. Said I'd got what I'd always wanted; to get pregnant." She paused, and Jess heard a hint of something wistful.

"He got a bit sad after that," Kate went on. "Apologised that he'd never been able to give me that, said maybe I wouldn't have felt the need to look elsewhere if he had been any kind of a man. I ended up having to comfort him, in the end. It was okay talking to him, weirdly."

"That's a turn-up," Jess said. "You don't think he had any idea before, though? I mean, you said he thought you were seeing someone, but did he know who? Might he have run Dave off the road out of jealousy and rage?"

"Don't be stupid," said Kate. "He was at home waiting for me, wasn't he? He was pacing up and down like a mad thing when I got home, yelling about how worried he'd been that I was out so long when it was so icy ... said he thought I was dead in a ditch—oh my God! They weren't his exact words, I don't suppose, but it was something to that effect. He was raging. Raging, I tell you. But, no, he hadn't been out. His car was iced up and there were a couple of empty beer cans in the sink."

"Besides," Jess said, dismissing the idea as she remembered that they were looking for someone with reason to kill not just Dave, but Bert and Angela too, "he'd have no grudge against Angela or Bert, would he?"

Or Elizabeth, she added silently.

"Well, unless he just wanted to get at me, stop me doing the group, but no, he wouldn't do something like that; he'd have to get off his arse and find out who was in the group, and he wouldn't make the effort. And," she added as an afterthought, "he may shout a bit, but he's soft under it. He wouldn't actually hurt anyone—he doesn't even kill wasps."

They fell quiet, each thinking; the shared silence causing the line to echo. Kate was probably mulling over Declan's good points. Jess hadn't known he had any, but to be fair, Kate must have had *some* good reason to have married him.

Kate spoke again first. "He was devastated when he hit a rabbit on the road one night. Came in almost in tears, poured a huge whiskey, and sat staring into his glass muttering 'poor little thing' for ages. I almost felt sorry for him, except it was funny seeing him like that—oh! I bet that's why my car is dented, come to think of it! It was my bloody car he'd been in!"

One more mystery solved. Jess wandered barefoot to the kitchen counter and flipped open her notebook. She tucked the phone under her chin and rifled through the pages until she found her list of suspects, where she scratched a line through Declan's name. It really didn't seem likely it was him.

"So," she said, winding up the phone call, "have a ring round, yeah? See if anyone else is ill, and find out who made the tea? Tell me how you get on?"

Chapter Fifty-Two

E lizabeth remained in hospital the next day, so Henry had asked Breda to mind Stanley, their spaniel, while he traipsed back and forth to the hospital.

Jess, knowing Breda would struggle to walk the two dogs by herself, had offered to call in. She assured Henry she'd water his greenhouse too—one less thing for him to think about with all the coming and going. She left Fletcher at home, sulking with his head on his paws and a mournful expression on his furry black face, and zipped into the village in her car.

The two women walked Stanley and Daisy a short way down the farm track opposite the church, strolling along in companionable silence, punctuated only now and then by the odd comment about nothing important, neither wanting to voice how close poor Elizabeth had come to death.

When they returned to Breda's house, Jess stepped inside so they could close the door before letting the dogs loose. "We don't want Stanley running off home, best be sure it's shut first," she said, as the dogs scurried towards the back of the house.

"Will you have a cup of tea?" Breda's voice was apathetic and Jess guessed the invitation was insincere.

Nonetheless, never one to turn down a cup of tea and a sit-down, Jess hung her coat on the newel post and followed Breda to her cluttered kitchen at the back of the house, eager now to quiz Breda on the events leading to Elizabeth being taken ill. "How was she earlier in the evening?"

"Same as always," Breda answered. "Not a bother on her."

"She didn't seem ill?"

"Not really—she mentioned a slight headache as we were leaving, that's all."

"Did she drive?"

"No, for once my car started, so I said I'd drive. I wanted to—" Breda stopped and glanced away.

"To what?"

The older woman gave her head a little shake and turned her focus back to Jess. "Nothing. I just wanted to repay all the times Elizabeth has driven me around." She waved a hand airily. "She's always helping me out, what with them having two cars and both of them reliable at that." A frown creased Breda's forehead and she turned to look out the window again.

Jess followed her gaze. "The gardens are looking lovely, aren't they?" In truth, Elizabeth's garden was a picture of immaculate early summer colour, but Breda's, while neat and tidy, was much less colourful. Henry's constant dedication to his and Elizabeth's garden was evident. Breda's face darkened again as she looked first at her own bare lawn and green shrubbery, and then over towards the fence, where a riot of clematis and well-trained roses adorned the top of the wooden panelling.

"I haven't time enough for it, really." Breda shrugged. "What with working all hours and keeping the house and everything ..." She tailed off, picking an unruly pile of papers from one end of the table, and shuffling them into a slightly neater stack before dumping them down again.

Jess rinsed her mug under the kitchen tap and placed it beside a cluster of other dirty dishes awaiting the dishwasher. "I'll be off. I'll come again tomorrow, about the same time?"

Breda smiled, the clouds gone from her face. "Thanks, pet, yes, that would be grand." She shut the kitchen door to restrain the dogs, and followed Jess down the hall to see her out. "Bye now."

Jess stepped into bright sunshine and blinked. Remembering another question, she swung to face Breda on the threshold. "Did she have anything to eat or drink? Elizabeth, I mean, at the group?"

Breda thought for a moment. "We always have a cup of tea, don't we? And there would be biscuits and Get Slim bars—taste like muck, they do—never eat them myself. I had a biscuit ... maybe two ..." She grimaced. "No wonder I don't lose weight, is it? But Elizabeth is very good, she wouldn't have had a biscuit, that's for sure ... she may've had a bar, I don't rightly remember."

"Who made the tea that night?"

Breda shifted her gaze towards the driveway, as if the answer may be written somewhere in the gravel. She shrugged and emitted a short laugh. "How would I remember a thing like that? Could've been any one of us! Sometimes the caretaker does it. Not your one Kate, though; she wouldn't lift a finger to make us tea, too busy weighing and taking notes and trying to persuade us to buy those awful bar yokes."

Jess laughed. "They are truly disgusting, aren't they? Kate's forever giving them to me—I have tons of them hidden in cupboards." They exchanged a conspiratorial smile. Jess walked down the drive to where she'd left her car parked on the roadside with two wheels on the pavement, waving as she latched the gate securely behind her.

As she indicated to turn into Orchard Close, Breda's words reverberating in her mind, a cat sauntered across the road in front of the car. *Bloody Maigret.* She jammed on the brakes, heart pounding in her chest. *Hansel. Whatever his name is.* Swinging around the final bend, she shunted into her driveway and cut the engine, allowing Breda's comments to surface once more.

Those bloody disgusting bars.

Taste like muck.

Bert used to eat them too, much to Linda's annoyance. "Why would he want to eat that processed muck when I've made him a lovely cake, eh, love?"

Angela must have bought them, too, because Harriet had happily eaten a stack of them when she'd been helping Jess with the painting.

"I quite like them actually," the girl had admitted, "but I doubt they're much good for losing weight if you eat four in one go." They had both laughed, and Jess remembered encouraging her to eat as many as she could and take a good supply home with her.

"Go on, take them. Please! I'm running out of places to hide them." She'd pushed a box into Harriet's hands as she'd left, after the teenager said sadly they didn't have any left at home, and wouldn't be likely to get any more, obviously.

Jess had returned the sad smile, wryly telling Harriet that at least now she knew what to do with her own stash.

And, she yanked her thoughts back to the present, *Dave would have probably had loads of them, too*, what with him and Kate having their fling and all that. Surely Kate would've foisted boxes of them on him, too …

Still sitting in her car, the car engine twanging as it cooled, she grabbed her phone off the dashboard. *Kate, did Dave eat those bar yokes?*

Fletcher barked from inside the house, his front legs on the back of the sofa, and his nose pressed against the glass of the bay window. "Come on," his bark urged. "What's keeping you?"

"All right, all right, I'm coming!" Jess hit SEND and clambered from the car. Inside the house, phone still in hand, she kicked off her shoes and padded through the house to the kitchen, where she threw open the French doors to let Fletcher into the garden. She followed him out, pulled a garden chair from under the patio table, its metal legs scraping on the slabs in a spine-jarring shriek, and sat, one leg tucked under her on the chair. As Fletcher meandered across the flower beds, Jess wriggled her phone from her pocket and composed a text to Marcus.

Can you check the Get Slim bars? They taste gross and everyone who is dead or sick ate them.

She shuddered and fired off a second text, this time to Harriet, just in case: *Hey, how're you? Just a thought ... don't eat any more of those Get Slim bars, in case there's something wrong with them. I'll get back to you!*

She didn't want to worry the girl, but equally didn't want to risk her eating them if they were responsible for poisoning people. She couldn't bear it if they turned out to be the problem, and she had given Harriet such a huge quantity to devour.

Jess sat there for a while, until pins and needles crawled into her leg, forcing her to move. She uncurled, rubbing her calf as it tingled into painful life, and her phone buzzed on the table. She stood, shaking her tingling leg, and checked the message. Kate.

Yes, Dave loved those bars, sad face emoji.

She was about to hit the call button to talk to Kate properly when the phone buzzed in her hand—Marcus. She sank back onto the chair, swung her feet up onto its partner, and hit the answer button.

"Hi, what's up?" Stupid question. He'd be calling to answer the text she sent him only a few minutes ago, of course.

Chapter Fifty-Three

Once Marcus had both mocked her over-active imagination and promised to investigate what he referred to as "your latest mad notion," Jess realised her latest theory was probably mad indeed. After all, surely loads of people ate those hideous bars, Kate included. Not to mention all the other slimmers from all the other groups all over the country.

"So, probably not exactly the bars themselves," she suggested to Marcus. "But would it be possible for someone to tamper with them, do you think?"

"I suppose it's possible ..." His voice was laden with doubt.

"Marcus, please. Indulge me. In case I'm right."

"Okay, okay, I'll look into it. Leave it with me. Are you around tomorrow evening? It's my turn to cook for you; return all those endless favours. Come for dinner? About seven? Nothing fancy, mind. Bring Fletcher, of course."

Jess disconnected the call, and dialled Kate's number, still smiling. It was so nice to have someone to share dinner with sometimes. The evenings did get a little lonely, just now and then, out here in the quiet of the countryside.

"Hello?"

"Huh?" said Jess, wondering who was calling her, neither having glanced at the display nor heard the phone ring.

"Jess?" Kate didn't bother to disguise her irritation. "Are you there? You called me—do you plan to talk to me or not? What's up?"

"Oh. Sorry, I was miles away. Oops! How are you?" She forced her mind back to the purpose of the call, fanning her hot face with her other hand as she spoke, grateful Kate couldn't see the blush. "I didn't mean to upset you earlier, asking about Dave. Sorry."

"It's okay," Kate reassured. "I want to know what happened to him, too, now you've convinced me it wasn't an accident. I've been thinking about it too. I rang around a bit after you asked yesterday—"

"Did you get—" Jess cut in, but Kate kept talking.

"—about who made the teas and coffees. I think a few of them went in and out of the kitchen actually. The caretaker was around, but she was busy with some bloke who came in about renting the hall, so I'm pretty sure she didn't organise our refreshments that night. Ann definitely went into the kitchen, because her hay fever was bad and she went to get a glass of water.

"Elizabeth, Patricia, Louise, Sheelagh, Breda … it's always the ladies. Bloody sexist if you ask me, but the men always leave it to the women. Mind you, the blokes don't usually bother with tea anyway—they mostly just weigh in and then leave pretty fast. Except Father James; he does make tea now and then, come to think of it, but not if he can avoid it."

"Was he there on Tuesday?" Jess asked.

"No, he didn't come this week; some meeting or something, so it was definitely only the women who went into the kitchen. I don't know who made the tea or who washed up or anything though, I don't really pay attention until the end when I check it's all been left tidy. I was chatting to the caretaker a bit then, but she said it was all done before she got finished with her other jobs."

"Was anyone else sick? Did you ask them that? You were okay, weren't you?"

"I talked to a good few of them. I couldn't get everyone, but the ones I did get said they were fine, and to pass on condolences and get-well messages to Elizabeth. She's well-liked, you know? She's always so nice to everyone, like a mother hen."

"I know what you mean. It's mad to say it, but in a way, I'm glad she got sick because I couldn't bear to consider she might be the culprit—you know, the one making the others ... well, you know."

Kate was quiet at the other end of the phone. "Yeah," she said after a long pause, "except she's not actually dead, is she, so it could be to throw us off."

Jess considered this, shaking her head slowly as she thought it through. "No," she concluded. "Marcus and Henry both said she could have died. She's still very sick. She wouldn't have planned to nearly drown in her bath, would she? She'd have gone to bed to sleep it off, maybe, but not risked getting in the bath? Kate, I know you don't like to disclose confidential information or anything, but ..."

Kate sighed, rolling her eyes, no doubt. "Go on. What do you want to know, Jessica? Spit it out."

"Just, well, I don't know ... How were they all doing in the group? I mean, like, were any of them doing really well, or not so well, or anything?"

"Right." Another brief silence. "Jess, look, you mustn't gossip, yeah? Promise? I'll lose clients if they think I'm talking about them. Promise?"

Jess promised, and Kate kept talking.

Nonetheless, she didn't tell Jess much she didn't already know—Elizabeth was doing well, meeting targets, achieving her goals, had received several accolades during the months she'd been attending the group. Kate had recently announced her as Slimmer of the Month, but Elizabeth remained modest about her achievements and, as they had already mentioned, she was well-liked by everyone. Breda, as Jess knew, showed less dedication to the cause. Her weight fluctuated. Some weeks, Breda not only fell far short of her weight-loss goals, but added several pounds to her progress chart. Kate knew, as did Jess, that Breda was partial to a biscuit with a cup of tea.

Kate sighed into the phone. "There's nothing wrong with *one*, if they count those sins accurately," she said, "but I have a feeling that with Breda, it's one biscuit with *every* cup of tea, probably two, sometimes. That's a lot of sins in a day, overall. She's not got the willpower of some of the others, that's for sure. Patricia, now ..."

Once Kate had told Jess about the first few members, it was as if a floodgate had been released. For the next half hour, Kate regaled the ups and downs of the group's weight loss, weight gain, and eating and exercise habits. Patricia—again no surprise to Jess—had an active enough job to keep her weight under control regardless of what she ate, what with assisting farmers with livestock problems as well as helping with small animal ailments in her role as a veterinary nurse. She must also spend a fair bit of time cleaning out cages and heaving around heavy boxes of medical supplies.

Patricia's next-door neighbour, Ann, apparently had a great exercise regime to balance out her fondness for fried food. "She sticks to a well-planned routine. She's got one of those exercise bikes; spends hours on it in front of the telly, catching up on the soaps and reality programmes, so she tells us."

Jess, despite being a close neighbour, never had cause to go inside Ann's house, but chuckled at the image of her pedalling up a storm in her living room, the *EastEnders* cast bickering on the screen in time to the squeak of the pedals.

Kate went on.

Mrs Harris, the vicarage housekeeper, while partial to the many scones and cream cakes that passed through the vicarage every week, had upped her fruit and veg intake and was trying to take more exercise to compensate.

"Pilates," Kate said, and Jess could almost hear the pride in her voice, as if were down to her that Mrs Harris was so health-conscious.

"No!" said Jess, laughing. "I wouldn't have guessed that! She must be almost a hundred by now!" Father James's elderly housekeeper was almost the last person Jess would have equated with Pilates.

As Kate divulged the information about the rest of her clients, with increasing abandonment of decorum or secretiveness, Jess doodled notes, adding question marks, underlining, or crossing through, nodding every now and then even though Kate couldn't see her.

"You may as well tell me about the blokes, too," Jess said, once Kate had exhausted the list of women, "although I reckon we're looking for a woman, don't you?" She paused, scribbling and thinking into the silence. "You know, I had been getting quite suspicious about Elizabeth, what with her dented car, the digitalis in her fridge, but I couldn't find a motive anyway—" She broke off as another thought occurred to her. "Kate? That's everyone who was there this week you've told me about, so have you got a list of who was at the meeting the night Dave died? And the week Bert died? And Angela? Let's see if there's anything there—any connections or patterns? Do you still have the records?"

"Of course I bloody do! I keep a register. How else would I keep track of progress?" Kate's voice rose in indignation.

A ripple of excitement fluttered through Jess. It was just like being a real detective!

"Can you check through? Let me know asap? Go do it now! Talk in a bit." Ending the call to Kate, Jess texted her brother.

Hey, Eric, how're ya all? Got me a real-life mystery here! Miss Marple eat your heart out! I think I'm getting close! Okay, so maybe the last sentence was not exactly true, but hopefully Kate's register would help her to make fast progress. She tossed her phone onto the counter, grabbed Fletcher's lead from the hall table and called him to her with a promise of a walk.

Chapter Fifty-Four

What with helping Breda walk Elizabeth's dog; walking her own dog, and bumping once again into the cycling sensation that was Father James, Jess's Friday morning had raced away. On the plus side, she felt no guilt whatsoever as she tucked into a cream-filled scone in the vicarage kitchen, having now walked around the village with Breda and then all the way back into the village with Fletcher. She still had to walk home again, and drive into town to visit Elizabeth, then home again to catch up with Kate, who would hopefully have printed out lists of meeting attendees. And, after all that, she would still have to find time to get ready before going to Marcus's for dinner that evening. A scone with lashings of cream was certainly no hardship.

In typical fashion, Father James had almost sent her flying half an hour earlier, as he rounded a bend a little too fast, swerved at the very last moment, and narrowly avoided tipping them both into the hedge.

"If you weren't a man of the cloth, I'd be convinced you were trying to kill me," Jess had said, laughing as she wound in Fletcher's lead to stop him becoming entangled around the bicycle. As she said the words, her laughter died away, replaced by a sudden shiver. Could Father James be the mystery killer? Surely not. The fleeting moment of panic must have shown on her face, as Father James jammed his feet on the ground, steadying the bike, and reached out to touch her arm. She flinched.

"Jess! I am sorry, of course I'm not—but I have given you an awful shock, haven't I? You've gone awfully pale—you're not going to faint, are you? Here, take my arm." He jumped off his bike and stuck out an elbow for her to lean on.

Instead of taking his proffered support, she stepped backwards in alarm, almost falling into the hedge after all.

"Jess?" The priest peered at her in concern. "Come on, let me get you up to the vicarage for a cup of tea?"

Okay. Of course it's not him. He's the local priest and he's my friend and he would never be the local murderer. I am being stupid. Jess laughed nervously. "I'm fine; you just gave me a fright. I don't know why I should be surprised really; it's becoming quite a habit. You're lethal on that bike, you know?"

He hung his head, looking up at her through lowered lashes like an errant child. "There are scones," he said, with a glint in his eye that told her he knew she wouldn't resist. "And Mrs Harris will have the kettle on. I'll text ahead now." He extracted his phone from a pocket in his too-snug cycling shorts.

A wave of relief washed over Jess. Knowing that the housekeeper would be there in the kitchen with them, she would be quite safe in Father James's company, and could graciously enjoy a plate of scones without worrying Father James would stab her to death with a butter knife.

Despite her advanced years, Mrs Harris could be quite intimidating when armed with a rolling pin or carving knife, and would not hesitate to use either if anyone tried to attack another in the homely vicarage kitchen. Jess gave herself another little shake to clear the remnants of sinister thoughts, and instead allowed the smile to return with the observation that those form-fitting Lycra shorts were really most un-clerical.

"Okay, I concede." She spread her hands in a 'you win' gesture, and they walked companionably onwards to the vicarage.

Father James wheeled the bike between them, and on the other side of Jess, Fletcher sniffed along the verge all the way into the village, tail wagging incessantly.

"I'm sorry," Jess said, as they passed the village sign, "I'm a bit jumpy—there's too much going on around here, and I suddenly thought I was about to become the next victim."

"I'm the one who should be sorry," Father James said, his pale freckled face flushing a deep red. "I seem to be making an awful habit of running into you, quite literally, and I must have frightened the life out of you."

A sense of *déjà vu* settled over Jess as she sat at the large vicarage table, pouring tea into two china cups as Father James disappeared to "make myself more presentable." She was spreading a generous helping of jam across her scone when he reappeared, in his more usual attire of blue jeans, black shirt, and clerical collar.

Fletcher sat hopefully by the oven, staring up at Mrs Harris with soulful eyes as she deftly skinned a large white fish. For a few minutes, Fletcher's tail swishing back and forth across the tiled floor, and the steady ticking of a large, old-fashioned wall clock were the only sounds in the quiet vicarage kitchen.

"You like fish on Fridays too, do you?" The housekeeper rewarded Fletcher's patience by dropping a sliver of haddock surreptitiously into his waiting mouth. Don't tell your mistress," she whispered conspiratorially as Jess smiled into her teacup.

"You spoil him—" She feigned crossness. "—and he adores you for it!"

"That dog gets better treatment than I do," Father James grumbled as he reached for his tea.

"He doesn't try to kill me every time I walk to the village!"

Father James blushed again, his red-head Irish colouring clashing with his scarlet face.

Mrs Harris waved the lethal-looking fish knife in his direction. "I keep telling him it's not seemly for him to be out on that bicycle contraption," she said, "never mind running people down left, right, and centre; it's not seemly for a man of his position to be out in those—those unsavoury clothes." She glared at the priest and winked at Jess, who spluttered her amusement into her cup.

"I was just thinking the same thing when he knocked me into the ditch; I don't know what's scarier, being knocked flying, or the sight of a priest in skimpy Lycra."

Father James held up his hands in surrender. "Okay, okay, perhaps I should get a nice dog of my own to walk instead. Perhaps cycling is not my ..." He looked around the room as he floundered for words to describe what cycling was not. "... not my cup of tea!"

Jess and the housekeeper groaned in unison.

Father James leaned back in his chair and took a large swig of said tea, draining the little cup in one mouthful.

Refreshed and replenished by the vicarage hospitality, Jess said her goodbyes and started on her way home, conscious that time was slipping away. She would need to hurry if she was to see Elizabeth before visiting hours were over. She tied Fletcher outside the shop and shoved open the door. The bell tinkled to announce her entrance.

"Hello, Jess, love, what can I do for you today?" Mrs Dunne flashed a welcoming smile over a dog-eared romance novel propped open on the pile of newspapers.

"Chocolates for Elizabeth. What have you got?" Jess sauntered to the small display and selected a box of Milk Tray. "I'm going to visit her this afternoon. Any messages?"

"How is she?" Mrs Dunne asked, not waiting for an answer. "Tell her I'll call in myself tomorrow if she's still in, eh?"

"Will do." Jess handed over the money and waved aside the offer of a bag.

Elizabeth, now quite stable, had been moved to a regular ward. Cocooned by a cloud of pillows, she sat in bed thumbing through a magazine and looking pale but cheerful. Her eyes lit up as her visitor approached, and she pushed the magazine aside.

Jess handed her the chocolates. "Hello, I brought you these—who wants grapes when they are ill, anyway?" She stooped to kiss Elizabeth's cheek. "How are you feeling? You look much brighter."

Elizabeth gave a weak smile. "I gave everyone quite a scare, didn't I? I'm glad I was unconscious for most of it, or I would have given myself quite the fright too. I don't remember much, to tell the truth. Poor Henry has been filling me in. And the police have been in and out. They think I was poisoned. Fancy! Someone trying to poison me! I'm sure it's all just a mix-up." She fussed with the sheets, straightening and smoothing them over her nightgown.

"Do you really not remember? Not any of that evening?"

"I remember going to the group; Breda driving home. It's all quite a blur after that, I'm afraid." She shivered. "Poor darling Henry, he got an awful fright. Good thing Marcus was home. I'd still be lying in the bath with all my glory on show if Henry hadn't called him for help. God bless Breda for running to get him. How's my little Stanley? Behaving himself for her, I hope?"

Elizabeth seemed more far concerned with who was minding the dog than being a victim of an attempted murder. Then again, maybe everyone had played that part of the events down, so as not to worry her.

Jess poured Elizabeth a glass of juice from the jug on the locker beside the bed, and tidied a pile of books and magazines before she spoke again. "Elizabeth," she said, perching on the side of the bed, "can you remember, way back to the night Dave died, and you said you'd been at that wake in town? And you said you'd been home in time to go to the slimming group? Only, are you quite sure about that? I heard that Susan is quite sure she saw your car, in front of her at the level crossing, when she came home from her own group in town, much later that evening ..."

Marcus had told Jess when the police had questioned the villagers, Susan had readily admitted to being out and about that night, on her way home from her town-based Get Slim group. She'd also mentioned she had followed a car the same make and colour as Elizabeth's for part of the way, but as Elizabeth had a ready alibi, they'd concluded it must have been another, similar, car.

Elizabeth can't have killed the others; not now she's lying in hospital herself. She can't have done... Jess shook her head to dispel the doubt.

"I may not remember what happened to me this week, but I am quite certain that I was home early enough. I went along to the group not long after I got home, drove on down in Henry's car—it was still warm—Oh!" Elizabeth broke off, jerking her face towards Jess, her mouth falling open and her eyes wide. "My car wasn't there, was it? I'd lent it to—" Elizabeth gasped and put a hand to her mouth, her eyes widening further as she remembered.

"Go on," Jess encouraged, leaning closer, a flicker of excitement rising. "Who had you lent it to?"

"Breda. I'd lent it to Breda. Her car wouldn't start that morning, and she needed to get to work. She asked for a lift to the station. She was in a right old fret. Something about covering late night opening in a pharmacy out on the edge of town after her normal shift, and having to get from Lambskillen to there, and the last train being too early for her to get home, and she supposed she'd have to get a taxi home after ... Anyway, I didn't need my car that day. Henry was home early and we were off to the wake in town together, so I gave her the keys and told her to take my car."

Jess recalled her conversation with Breda the day she gave her a lift home from Ballymaglen station—hadn't she told Jess she'd been on the train the day Dave had died? Or had she only said her car wouldn't start, and she had to work? Had Jess jumped to the conclusion Breda had taken the train that day? And hadn't both women gone to the group together? She was sure they'd said that; way back when she'd first begun questioning everyone. She sat rigid on the bed, mouth opening and closing as she tried to formulate a coherent sentence to answer Elizabeth. "But you ... she ... I mean ... you went to group together that evening, I thought?"

"No, we were supposed to, but Breda got asked to work overtime, and I only remembered once we pulled into the drive and my car wasn't there, and I just ran inside to get changed and straight out again. I got back into Henry's car. I was pleased not to need to defrost mine. Of course, I would have probably taken Henry's car anyway by that point, seeing as it was already warm. Breda wouldn't have been home till later—the late-night pharmacy stays open until ten. They work on a rota system; different pharmacies open late on different days. Breda doesn't often work at that time, but with it being near Christmas the rotas were all messed up. She was covering for someone else that night."

Jess gawped at Elizabeth, her mind racing. Breda had been on the road that night after all, and hadn't admitted it to anyone. Why would she not have said? Also, Breda would have access to all kinds of drugs and medicines, in her line of work. She would know exactly what doses of what drug would cause illness or death. If only Jess hadn't been so quick to conclude Breda had been on the train that night and not in a car.

She shuffled to retrieve her phone from her pocket, texted Marcus, then stood and kissed Elizabeth's papery cheek. "I must go, Elizabeth. I think I've worked it out!" Without explaining, she swept from the ward, leaving a bewildered Elizabeth sinking tiredly against her pillows.

In the car park, Jess had just started her car when her phone beeped in her pocket, announcing a text from Kate.

I have those lists, you home?

Jess typed out a rapid reply. *I think I know who it is. Just leaving the hospital. Home in 30, meet me there?*

Chapter Fifty-Five

F eet tucked comfortably beneath them, Jess and Kate sat at opposite ends of the sofa in the bay window, papers and notebooks spread on their laps and over the cushions.

Fletcher was sulking on the rug, shoved away when he'd tried to jump into the gap between them, crumpling 'January' under his front paws.

Kate had been initially cagey about allowing Jess to see her paperwork, but as time passed, she became increasingly embroiled in the excitement of solving the mystery. Over the first cup of coffee, she'd been reluctant to do more than read out names and tell Jess who had attended each week's meetings. By the time they'd drained a second cup each and eaten half a packet of Custard Cream biscuits between them, she had opened several other folders and was intently flipping through much more than the registers of attendance. Head bent low, she spread papers across the sofa, mumbling to herself. She dropped a sheaf of thin cardboard folders to the floor with a dull *thwuck* and pulled a bulky lever-arch file onto her lap.

"Here!" Kate unfolded her legs, kicking over her empty cup and spilling biscuits from the packet and across the floor. She leaned towards Jess and waved a highlighted piece of paper under her nose. "Would you look at that!"

"What?" Jess pushed it away so she could read the print. "Oh! I knew there was a connection! I knew it!" There, in front of her, was Kate's record of achievement, and in black and white Comic Sans with lime green and pink highlighting was a short list of names, including Bert, Angela, and Dave. Below them all, penultimate on the list: *Elizabeth*. "What do the colours mean?"

"Green is Slimmer of the Week; pink, Slimmer of the Month. Blue for the whole year, but there hasn't been one yet this year. Hold on, though ... there's more ..." Kate rustled papers in a different folder, this one labelled for the previous year, and extracted a similar list. "Look." Kate's manicured fingernail was jabbing at the last name on the list: *November, Slimmer of the Month, Dave.*

"And here, look, Slimmer of the Year, nominee shortlist—"

"Not just Angela!" Jess also swung her legs out from under her and grabbed at Kate's arm. "Motive. We've found a motive! I'm going to call Marcus. This puts everything together!" Ignoring the upturned coffee cup and the sprawl of biscuits Fletcher was inching towards, she leapt up and went to the kitchen to get her phone. "Dammit," she called to Kate. "Voicemail. Marcus; Jess. Call me! It's urgent."

But it was almost an hour later when Marcus texted back to say simply, *Caught up with work, talk later? Dinner at 7 still ok with you?*

By then, Kate had tidied away the papers into her orderly folders, and Jess had added many lines and annotations to her notebook. Kate stood half-in, half-out of the French doors with a lit, but unsmoked, cigarette dangling from her hand, while Jess paced the kitchen. Outside, the sky had darkened.

Fletcher sat at Kate's feet, watching the rain fall.

"If you're not going to smoke it, put it out and shut the door?"

"I'm trying to give up—you, know, for the baby." Kate gestured to her belly and tossed the cigarette onto the patio. "But it's such a habit ... I've realised that if I light them, I mind less about not smoking them; I know, mad, right?" She laughed and closed the door. Now her pregnancy was no longer a secret, and she had Jess and Linda supporting her, Kate was more accepting of her situation. She was eating more now, and the initial stages of sickness had passed as she settled into her fifth month.

Jess stopped pacing for a moment and looked her friend up and down. "You know, you're beginning to look quite ... well—"

"Pregnant?" Kate twisted her mouth into a wry smile.

"Glowing, I was going to say. You're much happier about it now."

Kate's face clouded for a moment. "It's a piece of him—a reminder, I suppose. It feels a bit like a blessing, somehow. I've been talking to Dec a bit about it too. It's funny how we suddenly seem to have something to talk about again, even if it is—" She broke off and shrugged. "Well, you know—this." She cupped both hands across her gently rounding belly. "I mean, it's not even his, and I was cheating, and I was so damn happy, and Dave was ... he was so special ..." She blotted away tears with her sleeve. "But, you know ... Dec's being really ... supportive, I suppose. It's weird. But nice."

Jess passed the roll of kitchen paper. "That is a bit weird," she agreed, and resumed her pacing. "Should I call the police station, do you think?"

Kate blew her nose. "I'm not sure they'd listen. Or take you seriously. It's only a few hours till you'll see Marcus anyway. It's not like anything can happen between now and then, is it? Anyway, I'd better be going, I guess. Leave you to get ready for your date."

"It's not a date!"

Kate held out her hands, snorted in a most unKatelike way, and shook her head. "Of course it's not. Of course it's not. Anyway, you'll be far too busy solving murders to get romantic tonight."

Jess snatched a towel off the worktop and swiped at Kate, who laughed again, and made a hasty exit towards the front door. "See you later; let me know what happens, won't you?"

The smell of spice wafted through Marcus's cottage as he opened the door to Jess.

"Mmm, smells fab."

Fletcher, manners forgotten, barged past Marcus to greet an equally excited Snowflake. The two dogs scrabbled on the wooden floor of the tiny hallway until Marcus shooed them through the conservatory and out into the garden.

"Go on you two, out!" He shooed them out, shutting the door behind them. "Never mind the rain, they'll drive us mad charging around in here. Sorry I couldn't talk earlier. Something wrong?"

"Me and Kate ..." Jess spilled out their discovery, tripping over words and garbling incoherently.

Marcus gestured to a chair in the conservatory. "Sit," he commanded. "Wait a second. Let me turn off the food and get us a drink, then start again."

Five minutes later, glass of white wine in hand, Jess unravelled her theory, coherently this time. She flipped through pages of her notebook for emphasis, and as she presented her well-reasoned arguments, Marcus listened.

As she neared her conclusion, Marcus held up a hand. "Hold on," he said, and picked up his phone. He dialled a number and listed instructions to the person at the other end, wandering into his kitchen as he did so, so Jess could only catch disconnected snippets of the conversation. Marcus hung up, stirred the pot on the stovetop, and re-joined her in the conservatory. "Right," he said, in a tone that left no room for argument, "we will eat first. Dinner is about ready, and they won't get here for thirty minutes or so. There is nothing I can do without backup, so we'll eat while we wait. Okay?"

Jess opened her mouth to protest, but fell quiet under his stern gaze.

"I must wait for backup. I can't just go over there all guns blazing. There's protocol to follow. It will be a long night now, and we'll be hungry if we don't eat. Besides," he said, with a smirk that made Jess's stomach somersault, "I've been slaving over this for hours, and you can jolly well appreciate it and pretend to enjoy it."

A delicious but somewhat hurried curry and forty minutes later, Fletcher and Snowflake announced the arrival of a car outside the gate.

A door slammed.

Marcus opened his front door just as the two wet dogs threw themselves onto the approaching uniformed Garda as if he were their dearest friend. Before he reached Marcus's front door an irregular design of soggy pawprints adorned his trousers.

Jess shoved her feet into her boots and stepped out to restrain Fletcher, leaving Marcus to tell Snowflake to "*Sit down*!" in the same 'don't argue' voice he had used on Jess earlier.

Snowflake promptly sat, his head cocked to one side and a remorseful look on his face.

Fletcher, still straining at his collar, showed no such decorum and was unable to refrain from emitting a few more small barks as Jess glared at him.

Marcus beckoned the policeman to step inside, then shut the dogs outside again. He instructed Jess and the uniformed Garda to go through to the conservatory, where they sank onto the cane furniture, and Jess apologised again for Fletcher's over-enthusiastic welcome, before she repeated her theory to the young officer.

"So," Marcus said, once she had finished, "let's go. Will you be okay here by yourself, or do you want to head home and I'll fill you in later?"

Jess's mouth fell open. "You what? I'm coming with you!"

Marcus and the uniformed policeman exchanged glances.

"What?" Jess could hear the irritation in her own voice as she leapt to her feet and glared from one to the other. "You aren't really going to keep me from this, are you? Not when I'm the one who's done all the work to solve the crime? You must be joking!" And with that, she stomped towards the door, determined to go with them, whether they agreed or not.

Marcus was there before she stepped over the threshold. He put a restraining hand on her arm. For a moment, their eyes met as hers blazed towards his. His own dark eyes were as gentle as ever, and she softened as she looked at him. Under his calming stare, she averted her gaze, embarrassed by her outburst.

Forcing composure, she appealed to him once more. "Marcus, she is my neighbour. I've been in and out of that house most days this week. I have put this together where the police couldn't—or wouldn't—even try to solve it because they didn't believe there was anything to solve. These people—these *victims*—were my friends and my neighbours, and I think I have earned the right to see what she has to say for herself. I am going over there whether you like it or not." She held his gaze, fighting the tiny flutter in her belly as their eyes met. "Unless you are actually going to arrest me and stop me, that is?"

Palms upwards, arms outstretched, he folded. "Okay, but let us handle the talking. We'll leave the dogs here. Come on." He nodded to the younger policeman and together, they left the little cottage.

The uniformed officer got back into the police car, and moved it a few yards up the road, while Jess and Marcus crossed over and unlatched the gate to Breda's driveway. The officer parked across the gateway as Jess herself had done only that morning when she had called in to help walk Elizabeth's dog.

The three of them approached the door.

Marcus stretched ahead of them to ring the bell.

Inside the house the jingling echo of the bell brought Daisy racing to the door, yapping in high-pitched welcome. Beyond the frosted glass, a shadowy figure approached but bent to scoop up the dog before swinging open the door.

"Jess? Marcus?" Breda looked first surprised to see them there together, then worried. "Is something wrong?" Her hand went to her mouth, panic replacing the concern. "What is it?"

"Can we come in?" Marcus asked.

As Breda stepped aside to let them pass into her hallway, she noticed the uniformed policeman and paled. Her hands moved abruptly to her throat, where they clawed at the neck of her sweater. "Has something happened?"

"I hope you can tell us that," Marcus said. "Shall we sit down?" He gestured towards the living room, and without waiting for her consent, he ushered everyone in, taking a seat next to Jess on a velour sofa.

The uniformed policeman did not sit; instead, he remained standing just inside the living room doorway—blocking the exit, Jess realised with a start.

Breda moved a crumpled newspaper off a shabby armchair, and sank into it, visibly deflating.

"Breda," Marcus began, "I need to ask you a few questions."

Chapter Fifty-Six

Breda fiddled with an ugly brown cushion, twisting it in her hands, turning it over, picking it up and putting it down again. "Jess? Why are you here? What is it?"

Jess didn't know where to look. Maybe she was wrong.

Daisy nuzzled her head onto Jess's lap, seeking the attention she'd become used to receiving from Jess over the past few days.

Stanley wandered in from the kitchen, nudging his way past the Garda in the doorway, and sniffed at the doggy smells around Marcus's legs, tail wagging.

Marcus dropped his hand to pet the silky fur, but didn't take his eyes off Breda.

Jess fondled the whippet's ears absent-mindedly, took a deep breath and looked at Breda. "You led me to think you were on the train the night Dave died, but you weren't, were you? You were driving Elizabeth's car home from a late-night shift at work. And you put the dent in Elizabeth's car that night, didn't you?"

She couldn't voice the words to outright accuse the woman of killing Dave, but even so, Breda froze; a deer in headlights. Then her face crumpled, and the last shreds of energy dissipated. She slumped into the chair, head in her hands.

"Yes," she said at last, so quietly Jess almost thought it was just the newspaper rustling in the breeze from the open windows. "Yes," she said again, a little stronger. "But I didn't realise. Not until later. You're right, it was the night I borrowed Elizabeth's car. Mine wouldn't start; I was late for work. Elizabeth lent me hers."

Jess nodded. "Go on," she said, avoiding Marcus's gaze, unwilling to let him stop her inquisition.

"My phone rang," Breda said. "I reached down to answer it, in case it was important, and the car swerved a little. There was a bit of a thud, a small jolt, but I thought I'd just hit the verge." She pressed her hands against her face. "Oh Jess, I really didn't know."

She swept her gaze around the room to encompass Marcus and the Garda, before settling it on Daisy, who whimpered and rested a paw on her mistress's lap. "Even after—the next day, when I heard he was missing, it never crossed my mind that *I* had knocked him down. It was only much later, when I realised exactly where they found him, and then it was too late."

"So, you said nothing?" Jess asked, although she knew the answer.

Marcus shifted beside her, as if to speak, then changed his mind, remaining quiet.

Breda seemed to have forgotten Marcus and the uniformed Garda were even there. Her voice and her gaze were distant, as she recalled the events of that cold January morning.

"It wouldn't have changed anything. It was far too late by then, and everyone thought it was a tragic accident—and it was an accident, it really was—so, I didn't ... I couldn't ... What would be the point? I'd lose my licence. Dave would still be dead. I'd be driven out of the village—people would talk—I had to live with it. Wasn't that enough?"

Jess almost felt sorry for her, but, remembering how much more was yet to come, immediately quashed the stirrings of sympathy. "But it wasn't enough, was it? What about when the police started to question everyone? When I noticed the marks on Elizabeth's car? I thought it was her! She had an alibi, and I still thought it might be her! And I thought it might be Susan—she had good reason to dislike Dave. I thought it was her for ages! You could've said something then?"

"Everyone thought it was an accident; it was best to let it lie." Breda was less confident now, her voice quiet in the still room.

Even the dogs had settled and now lay sedately at the foot of the sofa in an entwined heap.

"Except, then, you got an idea, didn't you?" Jess persisted. "Once Dave was out of the way, you realised you had one less person to compete with in the weight loss stakes, didn't you? One less person to be up against as Slimmer of the Year? Kate hadn't announced the list for the previous year yet, just given a few hints. But you thought Dave was on that list, didn't you? Something Kate said made you think you had a chance, what with Dave no longer in the running, and then ..." Unbidden tears prickled her eyes. She wiped them away with a furious sweep of her arm. She was not going to cry about Bert, not now, not until she had said her piece. She sniffed. "Bert." She spat the word into the room, her voice wavering. "You found out Bert was put up for it instead. Lovely, kind, generous Bert who never did wrong to anyone ... Bert had taken the place on the shortlist instead, so you killed him too." She let out a gulp as her voice wobbled, dangerously near to tears. "How could you?" The words rose into a shrill warble.

Marcus laid his hand on Jess's leg, offering both comfort and the suggestion that she had said enough. "So," he said, "what happened to Bert, Breda? And Angela, and Elizabeth?" All the names on the shortlist, alongside Dave's name, nominated for the Slimmer of the Year accolade.

Some hint of colour had returned to Breda's face, but she remained shrunken and fragile as she shuffled forwards onto the edge of her seat, her hands in her hair. "Bert had a heart attack. You know that. He was sick—he had diabetes, and he lost too much weight." Her voice turned bitter with the last sentence, turning almost inaudible as she muttered, "Another one who was able to lose weight, not keep gaining it."

Marcus shrugged and pressed on with another string of questions. "And Angela? Her daughter says it was you who gave her the seafood? The bag of prawns she cooked up the night she died?"

Breda's head jerked up. She shot a vicious glance at Jess, who recoiled. "You gave me that idea," the older woman snapped. "I'd seen you in the supermarket, remember? At the seafood freezer? We had been talking for so long that you put yours back. The recipes in the Get Slim magazine that month were all about ways with seafood, and I'd told a couple of the other women I'd pick some up for them while I was in town. I realised once I got home that maybe they had got warm while we were talking, and that gave me an idea.

"I'd told Angela I'd get her some, and she was doing so well, and I thought about coating them with butter or something to add some calories, but I knew she'd taste it, so then I thought … I thought they might just cause a small stomach upset. Not enough to kill anyone! I never meant to kill anyone! I just thought if she was sick, she wouldn't be your Kate's little pet for a while." Again, she shot daggers at Jess, who shifted away.

Jess let her body tilt towards Marcus, solid and reassuring beside her.

"I didn't know they'd bloody kill her, did I?"

The uniformed Garda spoke from the doorway. "But we think you did know, actually. We think a bag of dodgy prawns alone wouldn't have killed her. She was fit and strong, and prawns rarely cause fatal poisoning. We believe now that there was an added drug. A drug you would easily be able to get your hands on, in your line of work. The only blessing is that the rest of the family didn't eat them too."

Breda was trembling now, and again, Jess almost felt sorry for her. Then an image of Harriet, bereaved and motherless, came into her mind, replaced swiftly with a vision of another coffin beside Angela's—and another, and another: Harriet, her father, her brother. What if they had *all* eaten the prawn dish that night? She shuddered and a surge of nausea rose in her throat.

Breda plucked at a loose thread on the cushion she hugged to her chest, as if it might defend her against the policeman's words. "She told us no one else in her family was keen on prawns. She said it in the group when we were talking about the recipes. I knew they wouldn't touch them." Breda didn't deny the policeman's accusation about adding another ingredient to the prawns.

Jess glanced at Marcus. How had they known she'd added another poison? How did they discover it? Or were they just guessing?

The young Garda continued, providing the answers to Jess's unasked questions. "There were some drugs missing from the pharmacy. We asked your boss for a list of all stock, and to check for discrepancies. We found what you had given Elizabeth—the drug we were looking for—but we hadn't expected the bonus of learning something else was missing too—something that the pathologist agrees would have enhanced, and been disguised by, the symptoms that killed Angela. A lucky find on our part."

Tears ran down Breda's cheeks. "I'm sorry. I didn't mean anyone to die, really I didn't. But once Dave had died, I should've been in line to get nominated for that award—haven't I been going along to the group since the very first meeting? And then ... and then ... well, Elizabeth is always so much *better*, isn't she?"

Her tears stopped abruptly as she encompassed her audience with renewed fury. "Her bloody perfect life and her lovely house and her beautiful garden and her perfect bloody dog." She broke off long enough to glare at Stanley, who cocked an ear and whimpered.

Jess bent to pat his head in reassurance, murmuring almost under her breath, "It's okay, Stanley, you're a great little dog." An image of the whippet, running happily amongst the cows the other week while Breda called her helplessly popped into Jess's head, followed by the image of Elizabeth's dog, lovely Stanley, sitting obediently at his mistress's feet while they tried to entice Daisy away from the cows.

Breda's tirade continued. "... and her bloody marvellous husband, and her always going on about how wonderful everything is and how easily she can say no to bloody biscuits and cakes and how the weight just falls off her and I can't keep the pounds off at all ... and then I saw Kate's list, and I still wasn't bloody on it was I?" She stopped to take a shuddering breath.

Jess's mouth opened and shut again as she struggled to put her thoughts into words. How could anyone feel such intense jealousy?

Marcus got there first. "So, you were jealous of other people's ability to lose weight and your own lack of willpower, and inability to say no to an extra biscuit, and that's a good enough reason to kill, is it? I think we've heard enough. Let's formalise this." He nodded to the young Garda, who produced a pair of handcuffs and stepped forward.

"Sure thing, boss. I've heard some motives over my time in the force, but this one definitely takes the biscuit." His mouth twitched almost imperceptibly at the joke, already turning serious again as he crossed the room in two strides.

Breda rose from the armchair to meet him.

"Breda O'Reilly, I arrest you on suspicion of the murder of Angela Murphy, on the tenth of February ..." He continued with the rest of the spiel, that until now, Jess had only known from her beloved mystery programmes or between the pages of her books.

Breda, sobbing as the policeman led her from the room, turned appealingly to Jess. "The dogs," she spluttered, but the rest was lost to the sound of her crying.

Jess understood and nodded. "I'll mind them. I'll take them home for the night and ..." She didn't know what the 'and' would be, so she let the sentence tail off unfinished. She nodded again. "I'll mind them."

The policeman ushered Breda to the waiting police car, leaving Marcus and Jess alone in the cluttered living room.

The dogs, disturbed by the movements, had followed the policeman and his prisoner to the door, where they stood whining expectantly, wanting to go out too.

"I'll need to go with them to the station," Marcus told Jess. "Will you really be able to take these two dogs tonight?"

Jess nodded again, dazed by the events. She had suspected Breda must be the culprit as soon as Elizabeth had told her Breda had driven her car that night. Kate's paperwork backed up her suspicions, both with its records of attendance and the list of achievements and nominations that included all the victims' names. Despite her certainty that she and Kate had identified the Get Slim killer; she hadn't wanted them to be right. It was hard to accept someone she had only that morning drunk tea with could have killed three of the villagers, and almost killed Elizabeth. How could this happen in a community like Ballyfortnum? A village where everyone knew each other and looked out for their neighbours? She shivered, suddenly cold despite the warmth of Breda's stuffy living room.

Marcus reached for her hands, taking one in each of his own and holding them for a moment. "Jess, I know it's a bit of a shock. I must go to the station, sort things out, you know that? Why don't you leave Fletch over at mine? I'll pop in now and shut them in the house. You take these two—" He gestured to Daisy and Stanley. "—back to yours now. Shut them in your garden. They will be fine there for an hour or two. Then go and have a nice cup of tea with that lovely neighbour of yours—Linda—and I will be back as soon as possible. Then, I'll bring Fletcher home to you and fill you in?" He let go of one of her hands and lifted her chin with his finger to make her look at him. "Yes? Can you do that? Jess?"

Jess nodded, unable to speak.

"I'll call Linda and tell her to expect you." Even as he spoke, he was pulling out his phone. "Linda, Marcus Woo, I have Jess here, she's had a bit of a shock, can you pop your kettle on and mind her for a couple of hours? She'll be with you in about ten minutes." He looked at Jess for confirmation.

She nodded dumbly, again.

"Yes, about ten, fifteen minutes. I must go to the station. I'll come and check on her as soon as I'm finished ... Yes, a couple of hours, I should think. Thanks." He disconnected the call and disappeared into Breda's hallway.

"Jess," he called back through the doorway to the living room where Jess still stood, unmoving. "Where might I find leads for these two?"

It was enough to shake her from her stupor and she went to the back door to retrieve the two leads from the hook beside the door, where she'd seen Breda hang them only that morning. She called the dogs, clipped on the leads, and led them out of the house.

Marcus, behind her, shut the door after them and turned Breda's key in the lock.

At the end of the drive, Marcus stopped to speak to the policeman in the patrol car, then leaned into the back to address Breda, now subdued and compliant. She wouldn't cause any more trouble, not tonight.

"Right, Jess, come on." He took her arm to guide her across the road to her car. "You go on home, leave those dogs somewhere they can't escape or cause mischief, go over to Linda, and I will be back to you with Fletcher later, yes?"

She nodded yet again. *I have become a nodding dog,* she thought, incongruously.

"My keys are on your table," she finally managed to say.

It was his turn to nod. "Okay, you hold onto these two, I'll get the keys and shut our two in. Wait there." He was back within a few minutes, her keys in one hand, his own in the other. He opened the car door for her, coaxed the dogs onto the back seat, and waved her off as he walked back to where the patrol car was waiting opposite.

Chapter Fifty-Seven

Hours later, Jess dozed on Linda's sofa, exhausted. She had already spoken to Henry, to reassure him Stanley was with her for the night. "Breda has been called away unexpectedly," she'd said. Marcus had warned her not to give details to anyone—except Linda—until he got back to her.

Linda had popped over to Jess's a couple of times to check on her canine houseguests, but they, too, were tired out and had been dozing in Jess's kitchen on both occasions.

Jess texted Kate to say it looked like their hunch had been correct, but she would know more by the morning and couldn't talk now.

Linda cut a generous slab of fruit cake, and made copious cups of tea, then poured two generous glasses of red wine.

Maigret, aka Hansel, while not exactly friendly, sleepily observed Jess from his perch on the back of Linda's armchair.

Jess had not said much to Linda. Mindful of Marcus's request to not divulge any more than necessary, she'd said only that Breda had to go to Lambskillen Garda station about something, waving away the vagueness and disguising it with a yawn. She couldn't bring herself to worry Linda over what might have really happened to Bert until Marcus was there to help.

Marcus arrived in Orchard Close a little after eleven, with an excitable Fletcher bouncing up Linda's garden path ahead of the weary-looking Marcus.

Linda shooed them away to Jess's house and took herself to bed. Before they had even got to the kerbside to cross the street, Linda's downstairs rooms plunged into darkness and her bedroom light flashed on.

"I think I kept her up," Jess said, a stab of guilt in her chest for having tired the elderly widow.

"She's a tough lady, and you needed her tonight. She won't be minding about it." Marcus, as always, was reassuring and gentle as he pushed open the door to admit Jess into her own house. "You should lock your door, you know," he admonished, but she waved his concerns aside with a tired flap of her hand.

"Not here in Orchard Close." She yawned. "Sure, aren't we all neighbours who look out for each other around here?" Jess clasped a hand to her mouth. "Oh! I suppose you just don't really know people after all, do you?" She sank onto the sofa and kicked off her shoes.

Daisy and Stanley, still confined to the kitchen, whined in protest at being ignored.

Jess sighed and pushed herself up from the cushions.

"Stay there. I'll do it. Fletcher, stay." Marcus crossed the room and opened the kitchen door, squeezed through the gap without allowing them to escape, and shut the door behind him. He pushed open the French doors, and hustled the dogs outside. Next, he filled the kettle, a rattle of cups and spoons and cupboard doors marking his progress through the kitchen.

Jess leant her head against the sofa and closed her eyes. *I could get used to this part*, she thought.

"Jess? Jess?" The voice was soft and distant. A faint clink of a cup on the table; the jangle of keys.

With some effort, she opened her eyes. "Oh," she said as Marcus came into focus. She struggled to open her eyes and sit up, pinned down by a blanket she hadn't put over herself. "What time is it?"

"It's only midnight," he told her. "I was just going. I would have gone as soon as I realised you were asleep, but I wanted to give the dogs time outside before shutting them back in, and besides, I had two cups of tea to drink, since you didn't look like you wanted one after all. I'll tell you the rest tomorrow, shall I? After we've slept?"

She wriggled a little more upright, pulling the blanket back around herself, and smiled through a yawn. "No, I'm sorry, I guess I was exhausted, but tell me now? Unless you're too tired yourself? I'm awake again now, honest." She tried without success to stifle another yawn and Marcus laughed.

"It can wait. Breda will stay in cells overnight, so nothing will change tonight now. It can wait till tomorrow; you should go to bed."

Jess yawned again. "Tell me some? How did she kill Bert? That's what I really can't work out. I think I got the rest ... but Bert ..." The relentless pressure of grief threatened to engulf her. She gulped back tears, smudging at her face with the corner of the blanket.

Marcus sat on the other sofa, at right angles to her own, in the seat he had just risen from, judging by the two mugs beside it, and turned to face her.

He rested his elbows on his knees, and his head on his hands, and tried to hide a yawn of his own. "I don't think she killed Bert, Jess. She has admitted to the rest, but denies having anything to do with Bert's death. I believe that she wasn't responsible for his death at all, it was just a coincidence. It seems most likely that his time really was simply up."

He reached across the gap and took her hand. "I hope that helps?" He squeezed her hand and let it go. "Now, you must get some sleep. And so must I." They both yawned again, smiling feeble smiles as each tried to suppress their tiredness. "I must get back to Snowflake, anyway. You need a good night's sleep. I'm sorry dinner was interrupted—shall we try again tomorrow night?"

Jess didn't answer.

Marcus stood and gathered the empty cups. From the kitchen, he called the dogs in and issued them with a firm warning to stay quiet and go to sleep. Back in the living room, he tucked the blanket back over the almost-sleeping Jess. For a long moment, he gazed down at her.

Exhausted, she didn't move, her eyes too heavy to open.

He stooped to brush her hair from her face and placed a gentle kiss on her forehead. "Stay," he whispered to Fletcher, as he turned out the living room lights. In the dark hallway, he shrugged his feet into his shoes and opened the front door. "See you tomorrow," he murmured into the darkness of Jess's house as he let himself out, shutting the door behind him.

Acknowledgements

As always, my first thanks are to you, the reader, who *chose* to read my book rather than being forced to. If you got this far, I hope that means you enjoyed it!

A huge thank you goes to my husband, who supports me through the thick and the thin, and doesn't complain when I work through long nights to hit deadlines, or drag him off to potential murder spots 'for research'. His light shines brightly.

Thank you to my children, although honestly, since they have both left home and haven't had any part to play here, their mention is only to stop them saying I didn't include them and to see if they read this. To add insult to injury, I thank my dogs in this same paragraph, as they are the ones who provide me with endless country walks to dream up stories.

Thank you to the village I live in for providing the basis for Ballyfortnum and the foundations from which many of the Ballyfortnum villagers grew. Sometimes, when I am out walking, I am taken by surprise to realise that Orchard Close is not really there, and the two villages are not the same at all! A special thank goes to my friend and neighbour, whose own experience as a slimming consultant gave me the idea for this story. She's not Kate, but without her, Kate would not have emerged.

My parents, like Jess's dad, provided me with a vast library of books to grow up with. My dad has the entire collection of Agatha Christies, bar one elusive something-or-other, and my love of reading is certainly inherited from him. Thank you, Mum and Dad, for always giving me books.

Thank you to my tutors and peers on the 2017-18 Open University Advanced Creative Writing module, especially Nessa, who cheered me on as I developed the first chapters of this story for my final assignment, and to the Dublin bookshop in which Nessa arranged for me to read Chapter 1 as part of Culture Night a few years ago. That was a large factor in ensuring I finished the book.

Thank you too, to my beta readers, in particular the ones who checked that I'd done okay with my portrayal of Alice's long-term eating disorder and Jess's response to it.

Your help got me here, every one of you, and I am truly grateful to you all.

About the Author

For up-to-date news and exclusive content including your own map of Ballyfortnum and extra stories about the characters in this series, please sign up for Jinny's newsletter by popping over to her website:

www.jinnyalexander.com

Say hello at facebook.com/JinnyAlexanderAuthor

or

instagram.com/jinnyalexanderauthor/

If you enjoyed the book, please take a moment to leave a review on Amazon and Goodreads. Thank you.

Jinny was first published in Horse and Pony magazine at the age of ten. She's striving to achieve equal accolades now she's (allegedly) a grown-up. Jinny has had some publishing success with short story and flash competitions and has been long-listed for the prestigious Bath Flash Fiction Award, placed second in Flash 500, and has been published in MsLexia Magazine and Writing Magazine, among other publishing credits. Jinny has recently completed an MA in Creative Writing with the University of Hull, for which she was awarded a Distinction.

In December 2020, Jinny secured a publishing deal for her first three novels, of which *A Diet of Death* was her second. These novels were briefly published in 2022, but following problems with the publishing house, Jinny reclaimed the rights to her work, and is excited by the new possibilities ahead!

Jinny also teaches English as a foreign language to people all over the world and finds her students a constant source of inspiration, for both life and stories. Her home, for now, is in rural Ireland, which she shares with her husband and far too many animals. Her two children have grown and flown, but return across the Irish Sea when they can. She quite likes to shut the door on them all and write.

Also by Jinny Alexander

The second Jess O'Malley mystery, ***A Hover of Trout***, will be published in late 2023.

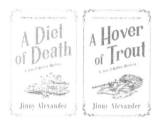

The third Jess O'Malley mystery, ***A Wake of Buzzards***, will be released in 2024.

Jinny is currently working on more sequels in the Jess O'Malley series, and plotting a new series: Mrs Smith's Suspects.

Jinny also has stories and flash fiction in anthologies and magazines.

A more comprehensive list can be found on her website at www.Jinny Alexander.com

Dear Isobel (March 2022, Creative James Media) is currently out of print following Jinny's reversion of rights.

Printed in Great Britain
by Amazon